# PALACE OF TEARS

I0611392

## Eamonn Vincent

ARBUTHNOT BOOKS

This edition published by Arbuthnot Books

Second edition 2025

https://www.arbuthnot-books.com

ISBN: 978-1-0687038-2-9

Cover illustration: Eamonn Vincent

Also by Eamonn Vincent

**Non-Fiction**

Me Neither - A Memoir

**Fiction**

Who Was Nightshade?
Foul Papers

**The Thieves of Time**

Book 1: Event/Horizon
Book 2: Palace of Tears
Book 3: The Parallax View

**Poetry**

Only More So
Even More So

In memoriam Patrick Coyne 1946-2024

And this is even truer in youth, for a young man who is always sensible is to be suspected and is of little worth – that's my opinion!

*The Brothers Karamazov, Fyodor Dostoevsky*

# CONTENTS

# Tenison Road

## Monday, 16 December 1974

GINNY STERN STARED INTO the test-tube in disbelief. The 'dough-nut-like ring', reflected in the little mirror at the bottom of the test-tube, was all too apparent. *But how could she be pregnant?* She had heard that episodes of vomiting, diarrhoea or not taking the combined pill at the same time each day could affect its reliability. In the five or six years that she had been taking it, she had not had a single pregnancy scare, despite a somewhat chaotic personal life. Until now.

It was true that the events surrounding the Frankfurt Book Fair, when her affair with Peter Newman had become public, had resulted in her drinking more than she was wont to, and, yes, throwing up on a couple of occasions. It was also true that she and Peter had spent a lot of time in bed during that period, but, even so, what the pregnancy testing kit was now telling her was damned inconvenient. From the very start of their relationship, the one thing she and Peter had agreed upon was an antipathy to having children. There was therefore little reason not to seek a termination forthwith. Indeed, might it not be better not to bother Peter with the news and simply attend to the matter herself? Yet, was this not also an opportunity?

For understandable reasons, mainly those relating to the chaotic way she had conducted her life in recent years, her father had been keeping her on a tight financial leash. She had, however, cleaned up her act considerably in the previous six months, a period that had coincided with her brief relationship with Steve Percival. It would be an exaggeration to suppose that Steve had been the cause of that improvement; she had already been on the road to recovery. But it would also be wrong to imagine that he had not had some kind of beneficial effect on her.

Unfortunately, her father, who was a very sick man, had not yet caught up with the progress she had made in stabilising her life. Under other circumstances she might have wished for his demise, but she was only too well aware of the arrangements he had made for extending that control beyond his death: unless she was married to a man of whom he approved, access to his considerable wealth post-mortem would be governed by a trust.

In those months that she and Steve had been together, she had seriously contemplated asking him to marry her in the hope of meeting her father's conditions. She was pretty certain Steve wouldn't have taken much persuading. Yes, he was younger than her, but not by much. He had good manners and was well-educated. The difficulty lay in his being something of a dreamer, with little to show for himself so far. While her father would have found it difficult to openly disapprove of him, she was fairly certain he wouldn't have gone so far as to approve of him either.

So she had jumped ship and thrown in her lot with Peter. He might be a curmudgeonly fellow, but everything else about him – his more mature years; the fact that he was the boss of a successful publishing company; his Jewish heritage; even his curmudgeonliness, for goodness' sake – was likely to find favour with her father and recommend him as a suitable spouse. In point of fact, the two men had bonded almost immediately. Relations had cooled a little when it became clear that Peter was already married. Still, weren't there such things as quickie divorces?

Well, yes, and no. Grace, Peter's wife, seemed in no hurry to grant him a divorce, and as the self-declared adulterer, Peter could not be the petitioner.

So here they were, in touching distance of Godfrey's millions, but unable to fulfil the formal requirements. Unless …

Ginny put the bits and pieces of the test kit in the bin, washed her hands, and went back into the bedroom.

Peter was lying in bed reading a typed document. 'You were a long time in there. Are you feeling okay?'

'Can't give my little secrets away. Women need to preserve a bit of mystery.'

'Is that what you call plucking your eyebrows?'

Ginny attempted a light-hearted laugh. 'You wouldn't want me with beetling brows, would you?'

'I want you just as you are.'

'Be careful what you wish for.'

'Ginny, you are the sexiest woman on the planet.'

'Well, that's very nice to hear, but I bet you'll soon be missing Grace's curves.'

'Nonsense, she doesn't have a fraction of your raw sexual power.'

'I'm sure Grace has her own magic.'

Ginny slipped into the bed and turned to embrace Peter, running her hand across his broad chest. Peter allowed her to hold him for a moment and then said, laughingly, 'Not tonight, Josephine! I've got a very early start. I need to get my head around this document for tomorrow's meeting.'

Ginny pouted theatrically, but secretly she was glad he didn't want to make love. She needed some time to think what to do if she really were pregnant. Even so, it was not like Peter to work in bed, at least not in the short time that they had been living together. 'What's the meeting about?'

'It's with the bank. They're being difficult.'

'I thought the firm was doing well.'

'We are, but we've also got cash flow problems.'

'And they won't extend your credit?'

'Correct.'

'So what can you do?'

'We could raise some more capital, but I wouldn't be able to participate in the funding round, which means my shareholding would be diluted and I would then control less than fifty per cent of the shares.'

'What's the problem with that?'

'I wouldn't have absolute control of the company.'

'Would that matter?'

'Only when it matters.'

'So what are you going to do?'

'I don't know. Do you think your father would lend me the money?'

'I doubt it. You know how he keeps me on a shoestring.'

'But that's absurd. He's not going to be around much longer and you're his only heir.'

'I know, but he's not going to dissolve the trust unless we get married.'

'I thought he liked me.'

'He does, but he's a stickler for formalities, and that means you need to speed up the divorce from Grace.'

'We've been through this. The law has changed. It now takes two years unless I admit to adultery, which I'm happy to do. But, in that case, I can't be the petitioner.'

'Why doesn't Grace want to proceed with the divorce?'

'You tell me.'

'Surely she doesn't still entertain hopes of you two getting back together.'

'No, I think she's just being bloody-minded.'

'Actually, in her position, I think I'd be the same.'

Peter sighed and put his document away. 'Women!'

Ginny sniggered. 'Where would you be without us?'

Peter had no intention of replying to a rhetorical question. 'Wouldn't your father accept some kind of sworn affidavit from me?'

'You know he won't. We've had that discussion with him. You know what his terms are.'

'It's so Dickensian. Surely there's something we can do, short of marriage, that would convince him to dissolve the trust.'

'Well, it does occur to me that if I were to become pregnant by you, he might soften his stance.'

'Ginny, even if we both wanted children – which neither of us does – it's not going to speed the process up by much if we have to wait for the birth of a child.'

'Pete, I think you're missing something here. The fact of pregnancy might be enough to convince him.'

'Okay, although it seems unlikely to me. But I'm not sure where you're going with this.'

On an impulse, ignoring her earlier determination to keep the matter to herself until she had done another test, she said, 'Supposing I were to tell you I was pregnant.'

'Why would you do that?'

'Because I was doing a pregnancy test in the bathroom and I got a positive result.'

'How is that possible? You're on the pill, aren't you?'

'Yes, but it is possible to conceive if you vomit or suffer from diarrhoea.'

'Okay, but why did you think to test now?'

'Because I seem to be having morning sickness and my breasts have been sore.'

Peter was thoughtful. 'Well, I can tell you one thing. If you are pregnant, I am not the father.'

Ginny wrinkled her brow. 'How can you be so sure of that?'

'Because I had a vasectomy a couple of years ago.'

'You never told me.'

'No, there was no need to. We both agreed that we didn't want children.'

'Why did you get a vasectomy? Did Grace twist your arm? Wanted to come off the pill, but didn't want a child to get in the way of her career?'

'No, quite the opposite. She wanted children and I didn't. It was a bone of contention between us.'

'So she must have been pissed off when you had the snip.'

'I didn't tell her about it.'

'As you weren't going to tell me.'

'Well, that aside, whose baby is it?'

'I think you probably know the answer to that.'

'Not Steve bloody Percival's?'

'I haven't had sex in the last six months with anyone else except you and him.'

'Well, I am not going to be the cuckoo that brings up Percival's child. You'll have to get rid of it.'

'Hang on a minute, Pete. This is all a bit unfortunate, but perhaps there is a silver lining.'

'Like what?'

'Early access to my father's millions. He won't know it's not your baby.'

'But then I'll be saddled with it for the rest of my life.'

'If we can persuade him that my pregnancy is a down-payment on our getting married, as it were, then he might agree to loosen the financial straitjacket. Which will mean that we'll have enough money for nurses, nannies and boarding school fees. It's the way the upper classes have always dealt with children.'

Peter pondered Ginny's words. 'Do you seriously think your being pregnant will unlock your father's coffers?'

'I think there's a good chance. It depends how persuasive we can be.'

'Surely he's not just going to accept our say-so.'

'No, but he might accept an ultrasound carried out by one of his own clinics.'

'When can you get it done?'

'In the next few days. Then we can talk to him.'

'Ginny, this isn't something you've been brewing up for some time, is it?'

'You must be off your chump if you think I'm delighted to be pregnant.'

Peter threw the document that he had been studying on the floor. 'In that case, the bank can go and get fucked. Is sex in pregnancy allowed?'

'Oh, I think it's highly recommended.'

Grace Mitchell had slept badly. She had tossed and turned all night, only falling asleep a little after six a.m. But when she woke a couple of hours later, her thoughts, after several weeks of turmoil, had clarified. By some miracle of the sleeping brain, she had now resolved to have a child, even though Peter Newman, her husband of ten years, had walked out on her several weeks earlier and, so far as she knew, she was not yet pregnant.

Grace drew the curtain back and looked out at the grey, dismal day. It was only eight days until Christmas, but she was finding it difficult to get into the festive spirit. She put on her dressing gown and went down to the kitchen to make herself a cup of coffee. Thank God, term was over, which meant, for a change, nothing in the diary. So it was an ideal day not only for making momentous decisions, but also for getting back to running. Her ankle had healed for some weeks now, and a run would do her good. But life itself was far from being back to normal.

During the years of their marriage, she and Peter had spent much time apart: he on the international publishing circuit; she buried in libraries in Paris, Berlin or Cambridge. But there had always been the comforting sense that it was only a matter of time until they were together again. Being on her own in the house in Glisson Road had not been a hardship. She had got on with her research, her writing and her teaching. But now, even though she resisted the implication that she might be missing Peter, she felt bereft.

It was as well, then, that they had not met since the breakup, and had confined themselves to a couple of brief telephone calls, during the last of which Peter had asked if he could come and get the rest of his stuff, mainly clothes and the contents of his filing cabinet. He had made it clear that he had no interest in the fixtures and fittings of the house. Grace saw no reason to object to the proposal and readily agreed to the date he suggested. But nor did she have any desire to be on the premises while he was dismantling the last outward signs of their relationship. So she'd asked Branwen, her neighbour, to let him in and to lock up when he'd gone.

What hadn't been discussed in that telephone conversation was who was to arbitrate about those items where ownership was moot. If Grace had given the matter any thought, it was only to assume that it would be fairly obvious. Even at this late stage in the disintegration of their relationship, she had still not learned that Peter's approach to life was to abide by the letter but not by the spirit of agreements. It had not occurred to her that his definition of which items belonged to him would be considerably more expansive than her own. On the appointed day, when Branwen in her role as invigilator saw how full-blooded Peter's approach was to filleting the shelves and cupboards of the former marital home, she had felt more than a little uncomfortable but also, rightly, felt that it was not part of her remit to intervene. In any case, she had always had a bit of a soft spot for Peter, a fact of which he was keenly aware. So he gave himself *carte blanche* in deciding what was his.

When Grace arrived home later that evening, having dined at High Table, a perk of being a fellow of which she rarely availed herself, she was profoundly shocked at the sight which presented itself; empty shelves, cleared cupboards, and walls denuded of the paintings and prints that had adorned them, all the more noticeable because of the darker patches on the walls where the artworks had previously hung. It felt like an assault, a smash and grab. Feeling faint, she sat down on the chesterfield. How could she have been so stupid? She should have realised that Peter was not to be trusted and would not play fair. Why hadn't she asked her solicitor to make an inventory and act as an intermediary?

She went over to the drinks cabinet and poured herself a Scotch. At least he hadn't taken the whisky, or not all of it. As she sipped her drink, she looked around the room. She was surprised that Peter on his own had been able to extract so much so quickly. But then it occurred to her that perhaps Ginny had given him a hand. Grace already knew from Steve Percival's account of the transformation that Ginny had wrought on the little house in Ainsworth Street, which he had rented for the summer, about her almost magical powers in this regard. It somehow made it even more of a violation that not only had Ginny stolen her husband, but she had also contributed to the desecration of her living space.

Grace had no objection to a fair division. It was clear to her now, however, that Peter's definition of those things that were undoubtedly his was considerably wider than her own. At that moment, while it was not immediately possible to identify the books and LPs that had been spirited away, it was much easier to identify the pictures that had been taken. But here, the annoyance was not so much with what had been taken, as with what had been left behind, namely, several large nudes, for which Grace had been the model. Presumably, Ginny had put her foot down. She would not have wanted a constant reminder of Grace's rather more generous curves in pride of place in the Barbican flat which she and Peter now called home. But nor conversely did Grace want a daily reminder of the abjection that Peter had required of her, and not only when she was posing for him. Furious with herself, she strode across to Peter's homage to the Rokeby Venus, in which she flaunted her rump to the world, lifted it off its hooks and propped it with its face turned to the wall behind the small table next to the chesterfield.

Since then, Grace had come to feel that Peter had done her a favour. As long as his clothes and papers remained in the house, she would be unable to feel free of him. If the price of him clearing his personal effects from the house was the loss of books and LPs she really considered hers, it was worth it. In the end, it had not taken her as long as she had originally feared to reorganise shelves and cupboards, and to find new pictures to cover the darker patches on the wall. Soon the house no longer looked as if it had just been ransacked.

But as the effect of Peter's powerful glamour began to fade, other grievances rose to the surface. About this time the previous year, they had resumed the conversation that they had been having on and off for the previous ten years about whether to have a child. Peter had at least been consistent in his reluctance to become a parent. For many years that had also been Grace's view although she hadn't expressed it in such forthright terms. At the back of her mind, she had kept open the possibility that their views might change once they were both securely established in their respective professions. But in her case it was not so much professional advancement that had triggered a more positive attitude towards the idea of being a mother as a mounting realisation that she was now more than halfway through the normal period of fertility. Pregnancies in a woman's later thirties and early forties were not unknown, of course, but could by no means be guaranteed.

She wondered now whether that last conversation on the subject, in which she said that she had changed her mind and would like them to try for a baby, had had some influence on Peter's subsequent behaviour. He had certainly been less attentive to her sexually and had asked her on more than one occasion whether she was still taking the contraceptive pill. If so, it was ironic that he had gone off with Ginny, a woman ten years younger than Grace. On reflection, however, Grace would have to acknowledge that Ginny was probably the least maternal woman on the planet.

But now that Peter had actually left her, it made Grace all the more determined to have a child, on her own if necessary. It helped that she had just been appointed as a university lecturer and would probably also be confirmed as her college's director of studies in modern languages in the new year, all of which would boost her income. So, if it was too late to reliably find a permanent partner keen to become a father, perhaps one of her male friends would be prepared to supply the seminal material.

Her oldest and dearest male friend, and the one to whom she would feel most comfortable putting this kind of proposition, was Gary Lewis. They had met when they were both undergraduates, and had briefly been lovers. Gary had soon realised that while Grace might be his best friend, when it came to sex he preferred men. Grace had been dismayed at first. Had she actually put him off women? It had been a stupid thought. Gary had made it clear that he'd always supposed that was the way he was made, but had not had the courage to reveal this aspect of his sexuality until he left the family home. Thereafter, the relationship with Grace was all the stronger for the brief period during which they had been lovers. They both felt able to discuss the joys and tribulations of their subsequent relationships, and could count on getting a sympathetic and sexually disinterested hearing from the other. When, eventually, Gary had settled down with Matt, she had been delighted for him. In contrast, Gary had had reservations about Peter from the start, reservations which were borne out long before the recent final rupture. He was unlikely to say *I told you so*, of course, but only because he'd said it on at least two previous occasions.

However, despite the fact that she and Gary had had a sexual relationship when younger, he might now, for all sorts of reasons, be reluctant to grapple with the female sex organs regularly and intimately enough to ensure a successful pregnancy. He had not been the most enthusiastic lover when they were undergraduates. Even then, before she had had much to compare it with, she had felt that he had been more than a little squeamish. Of course, there were other ways of transferring the seminal fluid into her vaginal tract, but the use of yoghurt pot and syringe might be even more embarrassing than the more conventional penetrative act. There were also the feelings of Gary's boyfriend, Matt, to be taken into account. Matt was a total sweetheart, but he would be entirely within his rights to find the arrangement not to his liking.

As she sipped her coffee in the big kitchen-dining room at the back of the house, mulling these thoughts, she realised that she had not seen Gary for many weeks, which was unusual. Had she upset him in some way? There was only one way to find out. She would invite them over for a pre-Christmas supper on Friday evening and decide then whether the conditions were right and whether she had the courage to put the idea to them. She went out to the hall and dialled Gary and Matt's number. A sleepy voice, that Grace recognised as Matt's, answered the phone.

'Hello?'

'Matt, Grace here. I'm sorry, I realise it's a bit early.'

After a beat, Matt said, more brightly, 'Oh, hello, love. Are you alright?'

'I'm sorry. Have I disturbed you?'

'If only! Lover boy is far too busy at the moment.'

Grace laughed. 'Too busy for you to come round here for some supper on Friday evening?'

Grace could hear a muffled conversation through the receiver. A moment later, Matt removed his hand from the mouthpiece and said, 'No, we'd love to. Gary has been promising me that he'd take an evening off soon, and he could hardly refuse one of his oldest friends.'

'Great. See you at seven-thirty on Friday then.'

Grace put the phone down. She was slightly terrified. She hadn't really sorted out yet what she was going to say to them, but she had a few days to focus her thoughts and work out whether this was a serious plan or simply loss of self-esteem consequent upon Peter's infidelity. In an attempt to clear her head, she now decided to go for the run she had been contemplating earlier.

She went upstairs and dug out her running kit from the wardrobe, making sure to put on several layers to protect her from the bite of the fenland air. As she was preparing to step out into the chilly morning, the postman pushed several letters through the letterbox. She flipped through them and saw that one of the letters was from her publisher. She tore it open and glanced over it, immediately wishing she hadn't. It wasn't a rejection as such, but neither was it a green light. They thought her analysis of the existentialist movement couldn't be bettered. Nor did they object to the portraits of the personalities involved in the movement. In fact, they loved that aspect so much that they wanted it expanded.

Grace sighed and put the letter on the hall table. What her editor was asking for would involve a lot more work. He was intent on a substantial rewrite with extended biographical sections. It didn't sound as if he wanted just a few more details to be slipped into the existing manuscript. She would have to think the matter over carefully before she responded.

She let herself out of the house, locked the door and tucked the keys under one of the flower pots in the porch. She set off on her usual route which would take her across Parker's Piece and down towards the river. Once she had got into her stride and had reassured herself that the ankle she had twisted in the Cambridge 10K was holding up, her thoughts returned to the letter from her publisher. The trouble was that since submitting the manuscript and in the turbulence surrounding Peter's decampment, she had agreed to give the Lent term lectures on twentieth-century French poetry, following the recent and sudden death of Frida Jedburgh. At the same time, she had been asked by her college to increase the number of students she supervised. She had been happy to oblige on both counts; the lectures because it was a mark of her standing in the faculty, and the increased student workload because it had seemed like a good idea to fill her diary for the foreseeable future. The result was that she would have little time in which to do the extra reading and organise the bibliography, which the expansion of the book would need.

But she had to hand it to Steve Percival, one of her former students. His intuition had been spot on. It had been his idea to look at the existentialist movement as a cultural phenomenon as well as a philosophical one. He had encouraged her to incorporate biographical material because, as he'd said, these philosophers were fucking each other and fucking each other up and documenting the whole *scene*, as he put it, in an avalanche of writing. When she had mentioned Steve's suggestion to Peter, he had said that it chimed with his own view of Steve as a talented generalist rather than a scholar or writer. Grace, who had been Steve's supervisor and was a published poet herself, didn't concur with this view of Steve's talents, but Peter, who was a successful publisher, had meant it as a compliment. He had even said that he was considering offering Steve a job. But that had been before a chance encounter at the Frankfurt Book Fair had revealed Peter's affair with Ginny, a development which had not only ended Peter and Grace's marriage and Steve and Ginny's relationship, but had made it impossible for Peter and Steve to work together thereafter.

She was glad now that she had not passed on Peter's observations to Steve. He was unlikely to have been delighted by the knowledge that a leading publisher didn't consider him much of a writer. Poor Steve! She should never have taken him into her bed, not because it hadn't been enjoyable; quite the contrary. But neither of them had been in the right emotional state to enter a new relationship, even leaving aside the fact that not only was Grace considerably older than Steve, but she had also been his teacher.

With luck he'd got over her by now. The young were resilient. But it grieved her to think that he now probably considered her cold and calculating, especially as she had asked him not to contact her. It was sad, really, because until those terrible few days she had enjoyed his company. She'd particularly enjoyed their early morning conversations when they went running together. She wondered if he'd kept up his running. He had put in a good time for the Cambridge 10K and had the makings of a good runner. But if her assessment of Steve was correct, he had probably stopped running as soon as she was no longer on hand to chivy him. Lost in these thoughts, she suddenly realised that she'd reached Midsummer Common and was still feeling comfortable. No tweaks or twinges. She stopped to take a breather and re-tie one of her shoes.

As she set off on the return leg, she was unable to shake the image of Steve from her thoughts. Wouldn't it be odd if he had actually kept up the running and she were now to bump into him? Did that mean she would like to bump into him? Well, yes, if she were honest with herself, she would, though she doubted that he, for his part, would have any time for her now. Slightly perturbed by the direction her thoughts had taken, she raised her pace, and the consequent effort required soon drove such speculations from her mind.

Later that evening, as she sat down to her solitary supper, her thoughts returned to Steve. She owed him an apology. After the way that Ginny had treated him, the last thing he'd needed in that terrible week was to be abandoned by the only other person who knew exactly how much he was hurting and how thoughtlessly cruel Peter and Ginny had been. Yet Grace, more concerned with her own hurt and her work, had simply cut off from him. Hardly the behaviour of the supposedly more mature partner in the relationship.

Thinking of Steve, it also now occurred to her that if she were looking for a source of copious and motile sperm from someone who had no reservations about frequent copulation, then Steve might be a better bet than Gary. It was a completely crazy idea, yet somehow she felt more comfortable asking him than asking Gary, or anyone else for that matter. But if she wanted Steve to impregnate her, she was going to have to find him first. Unfortunately, she had no idea of his current address or even if he was still in Cambridge. Their social circles didn't overlap. Nor could she approach Ginny, who might anyway be as much in the dark about his whereabouts as she was. Otherwise, the only solid piece of reasonably current information relating to Steve was that he had lived in Ainsworth Street. Well, that was something. Maybe his former landlady would have a forwarding address for him. It wouldn't harm to ask. Grace would go around the following day.

## Wednesday, 18 December 1974

SHORTLY AFTER ELEVEN O'CLOCK the next morning, Grace set off along Glisson Road in the direction of Mill Road. Little more than ten minutes later, she found herself at the top of Ainsworth Street. Even though she had heard a lot about the house in which Steve had lived and the way Ginny had transformed it, she had never been there. So, which house was it? She glanced at the address in her notebook and realised it was one of those opposite the little shop.

She stepped up to the front door and was just about to knock, but paused for a moment. Was this a good idea? Perhaps Steve had done a moonlight flit, leaving no forwarding address, and she would encounter someone who was not well disposed towards the errant lad. How, then, was she going to establish her bona fides? As she stood there, thinking through the possibilities, she was surprised by the front door opening and seeing a familiar face smiling at her across the threshold.

'Grace, how nice. I saw you through the window, standing on the doorstep. To what do I owe the pleasure of this visit?'

It took a moment for Grace to compose her thoughts. 'Beth, so this is where you live!'

Beth Wilkinson creased her brow in puzzlement. 'You weren't expecting me to be here?'

'No, I wasn't expecting the person who answered the door to be you.'

Beth laughed. 'That doesn't make it much clearer. But please come in.'

Beth showed her into the little living room and invited Grace to take a seat on the sofa while she settled herself into an armchair. 'So what can I do for you?'

Grace had anticipated a brief encounter with Steve's former landlady. But now that the landlady had turned out to be one of her college colleagues, she realised that she was going to have to give a rather fuller account of her reason for wanting to find out Steve's new address. She could hardly say she was hoping that he might be her sperm donor. But what was she to say?

Playing for time, she said, 'I didn't realise we lived so close to each other.'

Beth shrugged. 'Clearly.'

Grace shifted uncomfortably in her seat. 'I should have invited you round to dinner.'

'Grace, I don't think senior members of the college have an obligation to socialise with graduate students for whom they have no pastoral or academic responsibilities, even if you and I have sat next to each other at High Table once or twice.'

'I know, but I always felt we got on rather well.'

'Me too.'

Having got that out of the way, Grace cleared her throat in an attempt to drain the nervousness from her voice. 'So I was hoping that you'd be able to give me Steve Percival's address.'

'You know Steve?'

'Yes, he was one of my students.'

'Okay.' Clearly, Beth didn't find this to be a compelling explanation.

But suddenly Grace had an idea that also had the merit of containing more than a grain of truth. 'During the Long Vacation, he did some work for me as a research assistant. I've got some more work for him, but he didn't give me his new address. I was hoping that his former landlady, which turns out to be you, would have an address for him.'

This now satisfied Beth. 'Of course, I'll just go and get it.' As she headed out to the kitchen, Beth said over her shoulder, 'Could I offer you some coffee?'

'That would be lovely. Black, no sugar, please.'

In Beth's absence, Grace looked around the room and noticed the french doors. She stood up and peered through them at the neat little garden beyond, attractive even in its winter state. Beth re-entered shortly, with two mugs of coffee and handed Grace a slip of paper with Steve's Tenison Road address scrawled on it.

Grace glanced at the address. 'Oh, that's only five minutes from me.'

Misinterpreting Grace's surprise, Beth said, 'Has he been avoiding you then? Should I not have given you his address?'

'No, no, I don't think so.'

In an attempt to steer away from another awkward question, Grace said, 'This is a nice place you've got here.'

'Very much thanks to Steve and his girlfriend.'

'Ginny?'

Beth looked at Grace quizzically. 'Ah yes, Ginny. What a stunner! I was rather shocked when I met her. She wasn't what I was expecting. But then I suppose Steve is quite cute. Maybe he brings out the maternal side of some women.'

Grace realised that Beth was ostensibly referring to Ginny, but it could also apply to Grace herself. Did Beth suspect something? 'Why do you say thanks to Steve and Ginny?'

'They transformed the place. I'm afraid that Sandra, my former co-tenant, and I were not very good homemakers. We left it in a pretty bad state. I assumed that there was not much point in tidying things up for a male student wanting somewhere to crash for a few months after finals. How was I to know that my tenant would be one of the fastidious ones?'

'The fastidious one was Ginny. I don't mean to disparage Steve, but I don't think that's one of his core qualities.'

Beth smiled. 'And Ginny seems to have been a considerable artist too.'

'You've seen some of her work, then?'

'Yes, a rather lovely nude of Steve. Sandra and I came around halfway through the tenancy to move Sandra's things out. I noticed an easel standing in the corner over there with a fine study of a male nude, which was recognisably Steve.'

Grace nodded slowly. 'She used to come to my life classes. She was way better than the rest of us. Not that I ever saw the work she made when Steve sat to her. We were hoping to get him to model for my life class, but sadly, for a variety of reasons, it never happened.'

With a glint in her eye, Beth said, 'He's clearly one of those people who looks better unclothed.'

Grace nodded more enthusiastically this time. 'Yes, you're right.'

Beth, reflecting on the fact that Grace had only just said that she'd never seen Ginny's studies of Steve, nor succeeded in getting him to model for her life class, and wondering how Grace could be so certain of Steve's unclothed state, did not reply.

Grace, realising that she had been unguarded, attempted to cover her sudden embarrassment. 'What a pair we are, sitting here mentally visualising a young man with his clothes off.'

Beth laughed. 'Guys do it all the time vis-à-vis women.'

Grace, grateful for the quip, said, 'So much for Julia Kristeva's theorizing of the male gaze.'

'Quite. So are you planning to see Steve soon?'

'Yes.'

Beth went across to the mantelpiece and picked up a batch of letters that had been propped there. 'Oh, good. There's some mail here for him. Would you mind acting as postwoman? I should have forwarded it really, but the notes he left suggested that he would drop by from time to time.'

Grace took the letters from Beth's outstretched hand. 'Of course. So now that we have established that we are reasonably close neighbours, you must come around to supper.'

'That would be lovely, not only neighbours, but also linked by the enigmatic figure of Steve Percival.'

Grace, uncomfortable with the rejoinder, did not reply. She got to her feet, put the small pile of letters in the pocket of her coat, and said, 'Thanks for the coffee.'

Beth accompanied her to the door. As Grace stepped into the frigid fenland air, Beth said, 'Was Steve's poem ever published?'

'No. Sadly, Martin Lockwood died and *Outwrite* folded.'

'What a pity. I cast my eye over a page or two when I came round before I went off to the USA. It looked interesting.'

'It is.'

'You've read it?'

'An early draft. It was the main reason he blew his finals.'

'Is it going to be published elsewhere?'

'Not that I know of. I think his confidence took a bit of a knock.'

'Poor guy. Send him my best. Oh, and could you ask him to drop by soon? I've received the electricity bill and he needs to pay his share of it.'

Grace said she would and set off towards Mill Road, muttering under her breath: *Hands off, Miss Wilkinson. He's mine.*

Spurred on now by the thought that Beth might herself have designs on Steve Percival, Grace decided to go straight to his new address. It was only a further five minutes' walk down Tenison Road, and the letters that Beth had given her provided the perfect excuse. She would say that she understood one of them to be urgent, not that there was any good reason to assume such a thing. In fact, as far as she could tell, they were all personal letters. Indeed, not only did one bear an Edinburgh postmark, but Grace could tell from the handwriting – which she had come to recognise when she was acting as a dead letterbox for Steve – that it was probably from Angie, his former girlfriend. She had never met Angie, but felt she knew her from Steve's frequent references to her. It had been clear, even when he was with Ginny, that he had never really got over Angie and had at one stage hoped to get back together with her. It probably didn't make the current situation easier for Steve that Angie had taken up with Rob, his best friend and amanuensis. No doubt, Angie was just staying in touch as an old friend, but perhaps she too hadn't entirely given up on the relationship either, and still cared about him.

Not many minutes later, she reached a house she had passed many times, even in recent weeks, on her way to the railway station. There were five doorbells affixed to the side wall of the shallow porch, all of which were labelled with names, apart from the bottom bell, which was unlabelled. Not surprisingly, the name of Steve Percival was nowhere to be seen. It would have been very much his style to remain incognito. Without allowing herself to think about whether she had made the correct inference, she rang the bottom bell. A few moments later the front door opened.

'Grace!'

'Steve.'

'What are you doing here?'

'I came to see you, you idiot.'

Steve seemed nonplussed. 'Oh!'

'Well, are you going to ask me in or are you going to make me stand on the doorstep?'

'No, no. Come in. I'm just surprised to see you.'

Steve stood back to let her into the entrance hall and then closed the front door. He looked uncomfortable. 'Welcome to the world of multiple occupation. The public spaces are a bit squalid, but my room isn't too bad.'

He pushed open the first door on the left-hand side of the hall and ushered Grace inside. She looked around the bedsitter with its meagre furnishings; a single bed, a wood-framed armchair, a small kitchen table, two wooden kitchen chairs, a gas geyser over a little sink in the corner of the room, and a gas fire fitted into what had been the fireplace. It was not immediately apparent that it was any less squalid than the entrance hall. Steve invited her to take the armchair and he perched on one of the kitchen chairs. 'So what brings you to this end of Tenison Road?'

'I've got some letters for you.' She pulled the letters that Beth had given her from her coat pocket.

Steve was puzzled. 'Letters for me have been coming to Glisson Road?'

'No, I picked them up at the house in Ainsworth Street.'

'You went to Ainsworth Street?'

'Yes, I went to get your address from Beth.'

'You know Beth?'

Grace felt there was nothing to be gained by explaining the encounter in detail. 'Yes, she's a graduate student at Newnham.'

'Oh yes, of course she is.'

'She asked me if I'd mind dropping off these letters.'

Grace placed them on the table. Steve glanced at them but made no attempt to open them. 'Thank you.'

They stared at each other in silence for a few moments. Steve was holding himself stiffly, unsmiling. Grace was already coming to the view that it had been a mistake to ring the doorbell. She should just have stuffed the letters through the letterbox. But now that she was here, she wasn't going to let Steve freeze her out. 'Well, you could at least offer me a cup of coffee.'

Steve jumped up. 'Yes, of course, but I'm afraid I haven't got any milk.'

'Steve, I take it black. I thought you might remember.'

'Oh yes.'

He put a pan of water on the gas ring and spooned instant coffee into two mugs. Clearly there was no kettle. Grace watched him. If there was going to be a conversation, it would be down to her to make the running. 'So, how have you been? How are you keeping?'

'Okay. What about you?'

'I've been incredibly busy. Jedburgh died.'

Steve was visibly shocked. 'That's terrible. What happened?'

'An aneurysm. Did you go to any of her lectures?'

'Some.'

'I'm not sure I believe you.'

'Well, I read her book on twentieth-century French poetry.'

'At least that's something. Her death means I've been standing in as director of studies in modern and mediaeval languages at Newn-ham. With luck, I'll be confirmed in the role permanently after Christmas.'

'Congratulations.'

'Thank you. But I'm not counting my chickens yet. More importantly, I've been asked by the Faculty to cover her Lent term lecture series on twentieth-century French poetry.'

'Wow! Maybe I'll sneak into a few of those and hear what you've got to say.'

'Steve, you're no longer an undergraduate.'

'But no one checks. I went to plenty of lectures outside my subject. Not the lectures I should have gone to, of course. I realised early on that I wasn't a scholar. I'm more of a bricoleur.'

Grace laughed. 'That's what Peter said about you.'

She noticed the frown on Steve's face. Why on earth had she brought Peter into it? 'I'm sorry, Steve. That was tactless.'

'It's alright. Have you heard from him?'

'A couple of times. He's moved all his stuff out now, so that involved some negotiations. We didn't meet. I arranged for my neighbour to let him in.'

'Was Ginny with him?'

'Yes, apparently. Have you heard from her?'

'No. Nor am I expecting to. But I did notice that one of the letters you've brought round is from Angie.'

Grace refrained from mentioning that she too had recognised Angie's distinctive handwriting on one of the envelopes. Maybe she should leave Steve to catch up on his correspondence from his former lover. He was, after all, being distinctly taciturn. Grace stood up and took a step towards the door. 'You should have said. I'll leave you to read her letter. It's been nice to see you.'

Steve shook his head. 'No, it can wait. Finish your coffee.'

'If you're sure.'

Grace sat down again and sipped her coffee. Steve stared at her moodily. She wondered what he was thinking. It was hard to tell whether he was pleased to see her or just being polite. He certainly wasn't making conversation easy. In a moment of inspiration, she said, 'Are you still running?'

Steve's demeanour brightened. 'Yeah, quite a lot, actually. Most days. If I didn't do that, I wouldn't get out much.'

'You're not working then?'

'No, not for gain, anyway.'

'How are you surviving?'

'I'd saved some from the Arts Theatre box office job, and Ginny gave me something to help towards a deposit on a new place.'

'That was decent of her.'

'Yeah, but it's nearly all gone.'

'Have you looked for a new job?'

'I've applied to loads, but you know what the economic situation's like.'

'Why don't you sign on? Lots of people do. There's no shame in it.'

'Yeah, I'll probably have to. I was putting it off until after Christmas.'

'What are you doing for Christmas?'

'No plans at the moment.'

'Oh, Steve.' Grace was unable to prevent a note of concern creeping into her voice.

Steve shrugged. 'I don't mind. I'm not big on Christmas.'

'So how do you occupy your time, day to day?'

'Well, apart from the running and playing the guitar, mainly reading and some writing.'

'A new poem?'

'Not really. I've done a few bits and pieces, but I seem to have lost interest in poetry. So I've been working on a play.'

If he were being honest, he would have told her that he was actually in mourning, not just for his relationship with Ginny, but for the long poem he had been working on, which, in a moment of petulance, he had destroyed on his first day in Tenison Road. At first, it had felt like a burden had been lifted from his shoulders. But, almost immediately, he had regretted this act of vandalism, and the following day had gone down to the bins to retrieve it. Unsurprisingly, it was no longer there; the bins had already been emptied earlier that morning.

He'd gone back to his room in a mood of black despair. He had not made a copy of the final draft, nor did he have any of the early drafts. There were one or two extracts in existence. His friend Rob had one, and Angie's former boyfriend Declan had a slightly later but revised version. The fourth section, a portrait of Ginny, which he'd been writing in the dying days of his relationship with her, had only ever existed in draft form. He'd briefly considered trying to rewrite the poem but had quickly dismissed the idea. You might be able to do that with prose, whether fiction or non-fiction. But the lyric was a form with its roots in the lived (and loved) moment. Anything he wrote now would be a reflection of the squalid bedsitter land he was condemned to, not of the glorious but terrible days he had spent with Ginny.

Grace could see the sadness in his expression but was unable to guess the cause. Treading carefully, she said, 'A stage play? I can imagine you have a good ear for dialogue.'

Steve didn't really want to talk about his writing. 'Yeah, for the stage. What else?'

'Well, there's TV and radio.'

'I suppose so, but I want to work in the classic form.'

'Of course. How's it going?'

'Slow. I'm having the devil of a job getting characters on and off stage.'

Grace laughed. 'It probably helps that you've had a bit of theatre experience.'

Steve looked glum. 'Yeah, but probably not in a box office.'

She immediately regretted the quip. 'Quite.'

Grace studied him closely. Physically, he looked fine, but he seemed to have lost his zest; or maybe he was still angry with her.

'Steve, I'm sorry I cut things off between us and haven't been in touch. It's been difficult for me, too. But now that Peter has collected his stuff, I feel a lot better. And, as I was saying, I've been very busy.'

'Grace, there's no need to apologise. I understand. I wasn't expecting to become a live-in lover. I'm sorry if I went further than I should have after the 10K.'

'Are you talking about the race or the subsequent wantonness? If the latter, let me assure you the impulse was mutual. Or maybe we were both seeking solace.'

'Well, that's a way of looking at it. But I would prefer to see what happened between us in a more positive light. As far as I'm concerned, it was an amazing experience. You are a beautiful woman with a first-class mind. Not that someone with a middling degree is really in a position to judge on the latter point.'

'Oh, come on, Steve. You know that the class of your degree doesn't reflect your intellectual ability. But let's not argue about it. As a woman, I am happy to accept your judgement on the former point because I can assure you, it doesn't feel like that when one has been in close proximity to Ginny, even with her clothes on.'

'I'd rather not talk about her.'

This was not going well. Steve was angry, as well he might be. He was certainly not in a state of mind conducive to the discussions she had planned. In fact, his sullen demeanour suggested that he would rather she didn't prolong the interview. Perhaps she had let her thoughts run ahead of the practicalities. The first thing to do was to establish whether there was still any spark between them, and the simplest way for her to do that would be to attempt to embrace him. But right at that moment, Steve seemed very buttoned up, arms crossed, a distant look on his face. The risk was that her gesture might come across as one of maternal consolation rather than a re-establishment of libidinal dynamics. But perhaps he no longer desired her. Perhaps he never really had. Their coupling might have been a reaction to the situation they'd found themselves in. For what she had in mind though, he didn't need to be in love with her in the way that he'd been in love with Ginny; he just needed to desire her enough to consider fathering her child.

Ah, Ginny. What would she do in this situation? What a ridiculous thought. How was that going to help? Anyway, she really knew very little about Ginny other than her propensity to reveal the physical beauty of her naked body at crucial moments, stunning whichever poor male she had set her sights on, while somehow managing to do this without abasing herself. It helped that, having been both a professional life model and a catwalk model, Ginny had supreme confidence in her unclothed body. That was obviously not the case for most women. Grace kept herself in good shape, but she was at least ten years older than Ginny and even ten or fifteen years ago would never have been considered catwalk potential. Nor was she in the habit of removing her clothes in pursuance of her goals.

She glanced nervously at Steve, conscious that neither of them had said anything during what was now becoming an uncomfortable period of silence. He seemed to be watching her intently, clearly leaving it to her to either come to the point of her visit or finish her coffee and go. Grace took another sip of her coffee. Using Ginny as a guide to affairs of the heart was probably not the best way for her to proceed. The rules for moving from a clothed to an unclothed state were tightly circumscribed. She couldn't simply undress in front of Steve as he sat there and watched her. He would probably laugh or be disgusted. Even if she had the courage, it was beneath her dignity. But if she was going to have a child on her own, she had better forget standing on her dignity. To hell with dignity, then. She would adopt the Ginny approach and see how things developed. Trembling and with her heart beating fast, she stood up, took her cardigan off, then folded it over the back of the chair.

Steve looked at her quizzically. 'Is it too hot in here?'

Unable to speak but aware that the room was actually very chilly, Grace nodded and undid the top button of her blouse. She paused and looked despairingly at Steve, willing him to intervene. But he remained silent, frowning slightly. Her mouth was dry. There was nothing for it. She must press on. She undid another button and hesitated again. Did she detect a smile of derision forming on his lips? She felt for the next button. Undoing a third button would surely indicate something more significant than just being too warm. But now her courage deserted her. She picked up her cardigan and said, 'Sorry, Steve, I'd better go. It was wrong of me to come here.'

Steve leapt to his feet. He was stern. 'Don't go. Carry on with what you were doing.'

'What do you mean?'

'You were starting to take your blouse off.'

Grace blushed. 'Steve, I realise you've probably been sex-starved for a few weeks, but taking off a cardigan is not the preamble to a striptease.'

'Not normally, I agree, but you seemed to be putting a lot of thought into undoing each button of your blouse. You had my full attention. Anyway, even if that wasn't what you had in mind, I'd still like you to carry on. It's the least you could do.'

'I don't know how you get to that.'

'I'll tell you how. I think you see me as cute, as I suppose did Ginny. Over these last few weeks, I've been thinking about how I'm perceived and I'm not comfortable with it. If you knew what was going on in my head, you wouldn't think I was cute. By accident, when I moved in here, I discovered that I could be someone else. It was the first time that I'd entered a social network without the baggage of others' presuppositions. All I needed to do was assert myself, and I'm afraid that's the approach I'm committing myself to from now on. So, what I'd like you to do is take your clothes off. If you don't want to, that's fine. You're free to go.'

Grace could find no words. She replaced her cardigan on the back of the chair and resumed unbuttoning her blouse. As she artlessly removed the rest of her clothes, making no attempt to titillate her audience, she was aware that where she was standing was in view of anyone approaching or passing the house who might glance in at the front downstairs window. She just hoped that no one would be inquisitive enough to peer through Steve's grimy window. Her first impulse when she finally stepped out of her knickers was to cover her pudenda with one hand and her breasts with the other arm and hand. But this was no time to show fear. She spread her hands wide, with palms out.

Steve was studying her carefully. 'Very nice. What happens now?'

'I hope you might see your way to fucking me.'

Steve ostentatiously looked at his watch. 'Well, I suppose I do have a bit of time on my hands.'

Grace was starting to shiver, only partly from the chill of the room. 'Steve, would you mind if I got into your bed?'

'Be my guest.'

Grace stepped towards him and started to unbutton his shirt.

Some time later, as they were lying together in Steve's narrow bed, Grace said, 'I think I'm going to like the new Steve. How did you find him?'

'He appeared when I was moving in. There's a young woman called Jude who lives in one of the rooms upstairs. She was being a bit superior so I thought I'd fight back.'

'How did you do that?'

'I just pretended I was self-confident and asked her out that same night. She agreed to go out with me, but said that I shouldn't think that meant she was going to sleep with me on our first date. It seemed to me that what she really meant was that she didn't discount sleeping with me at some point in the future. And if then, why not now? So we went for a drink that evening, and then we ended up in bed. I was surprised by how easy it was. If I'd been the old Steve, sensitive to what everyone else wants, it would never have happened. The risk was that she would never speak to me again, or she might have slapped me in the face, but in fact she was very obliging.'

'Should you be telling me this?'

'I think it's better if I do.'

'Because it's what new Steve would do – does.'

'Yes, and it makes things clearer between us.'

'I suppose so. Are you still seeing her?'

'We have slept together twice more, but as far as I'm concerned we're not in a relationship.'

'If you and I were to take this further, would you expect to go on sleeping with her from time to time?'

'I don't know what you mean by *taking this further*, but I don't see why not.'

'Oh dear, maybe I'm not going to like new Steve, after all.'

'Grace, I'm not going to beg you to like me, whichever version of Steve I am. You're the one who told me not to contact you. Then suddenly you appear out of the blue, initiate sex, and wonder whether I'd be prepared to dump the girl I'm currently seeing. I feel old Steve was always having his agenda set for him. More fool, old Steve, you may say. So, you'd need to talk a bit more about what *taking this further* means.'

Grace was a little irritated by this callow display of *new-Steve* strength, but felt it would advance her purposes better, were she to act as if she had been chastised.

'You are quite right. I owe you an apology – several apologies. I'd like us to get back together on some basis. Until we've worked out what that is, I can't expect to have exclusive access to you.'

Steve replied, with a note of pomposity in his voice that did not become him, 'Well, I'm glad we've established that.'

Grace was minded to reproach him, but she couldn't help noticing with some amusement – which she disguised as best she could – that her small display of submission had resulted in a change not only in his tone of voice but in his physical state at the point where their lower torsos were pressed together. Steve seemed to be taking her apology as an invitation to initiate a second bout of lovemaking, but Grace was not about to indulge him further until she had regained the initiative and moved things on.

When she had set off for Ainsworth Street earlier in the day, her only aim had been to get Steve's new address with a view, in the first place, to re-establishing contact with him. Discussions about his providing her with a child were to be deferred to an unspecified date in the future, once other matters had been worked out. She had certainly not planned to go to bed with him in the middle of the day in his horrible little bedsitter on the ground floor with the curtains undrawn and the daylight flooding in. But here she was lying in his arms with his sperm already inside her, somewhat pointlessly, as it happened, since the contraceptive pill she took for three weeks in every month would protect her from pregnancy for a while yet.

Anyway, she had no intention of getting pregnant by Steve until she had thought the whole thing through in greater detail and until she had his consent. Besides, in view of the somewhat desultory nature of their lovemaking in which he had remained silent and aloof – although acquitting himself admirably in the production of those materials intrinsic to insemination – it was far from certain that they would be seeing each other again, let alone creating new life. Somehow they needed to get to next base.

It occurred to her that the cover story she had improvised for Beth's benefit to explain why she wanted Steve's new address might do the trick. The poor chap clearly needed a job. She wasn't rich enough to pay him to work on her book, especially now that she had to shoulder the mortgage on the house by herself. But she could let him live at her place rent-free. If, from time to time, meetings to review progress with the research ended up in bed or indeed took place there, so what?

She cleared her throat. 'In terms of taking things further, do you think you could forgive me enough to work for me?'

Steve hesitated. Was new Steve's bluff being called? Querulously, he said, 'Work for you?'

Grace explained how her publisher wanted her to expand the existentialism book, but the work involved would conflict with her increased academic workload. So she was looking for a research assistant. Steve listened to her pitch without interrupting. When she'd finished, he rolled out of bed and, playing for time, walked across to the sink and filled the pan with water. 'Cup of coffee?'

'Yes, please.'

She watched Steve make the coffees and bring them back to the bed. 'Steve, you've been strolling around starkers in full view of passers-by.'

Steve shrugged. 'New Steve. Anyway, you were pretty much in the same part of the room when you took your clothes off for me.'

Grace laughed. 'New Grace. I took my clothes off for *me*, as you will discover in due course.'

Steve handed her the mug of coffee. 'Okay, I could get to like *new Grace*. But, returning to your proposal, what would be in it for me? Sorry to be mercenary about it. Surely all you need to do is find a graduate student whose thesis is on the same subject, and both parties benefit. Whereas I have no good reason to get to know Jean-Paul, Albert and Simone any better than I do already.'

'No, of course not. So there'd be a quid pro quo.'

'Which would be what?'

'You'd live at Glisson Road, rent-free.'

'Do you mean as a lodger?'

'Well, that might be the best way of presenting the arrangement until we've worked things out properly. You could have the guest room.'

She'd nearly said *Peter's old room*, but had caught herself in time.

31

'It has a decent bed and a good desk, although I hope you'd consider joining me in my bed from time to time. But maybe new Steve would find that a bit restrictive and not just in terms of access to Jude upstairs.'

Steve laughed. 'I'm not sure if this is new Grace or old Grace speaking.'

'Nor am I.'

Steve got back into bed and let Grace wrap her arms around him to warm him up. 'Steve, this place is freezing.'

'Yeah, that's how I knew that all that business of taking off your cardigan and unbuttoning your blouse had another meaning.'

'I'm glad to see that you are putting your reading of Barthes' *Système de la mode* to good use. But somebody had to break the ice, as it were, and new Steve hadn't put in an appearance at that point.'

'Sometimes it's important to let a situation develop. Non-action can be very powerful.'

'I'll take your word for it although that sounds very much like old Steve. Anyway, I'm cold, starving and I could do with a shower.'

'Welcome to bedsit land.'

'And I'm busting for a pee. Could you tell me what the procedure is here? I hope it doesn't involve a chamber pot.'

Steve laughed. 'It's two doors along. There's a dressing gown on the back of the door.'

Grace got out of bed, put the dressing gown on and let herself out of the room. She returned a few minutes later. The visit to the lavatory had enabled her to order her thoughts. She started to get dressed.

Worried that she had had enough of his sordid quarters and was now once again abandoning him, Steve said with a note of alarm in his voice, 'What are you doing?'

'Surely it's obvious. I'm communicating with you through the medium of clothes again. Only this time I'm signalling that back at my place there's a cupboard full of wine, a fridge full of food, a luxurious bathroom and a large comfortable bed with room for all four of us, old and new Grace and old and new Steve.'

Steve jumped out of bed. 'Message received loud and clear.'

Later that night, as Grace slept peacefully beside him, Steve lay wide awake, trying to get his thoughts straight. The day had ended in an unexpectedly pleasurable manner, but it had not started well. He had received a note from the landlord chiding him for being late with his rent and pointing out that the terms of the lease allowed him to evict Steve without further notice, should the rent remain unpaid for a further seven days.

Steve was not, in fact, completely broke, but financially things were parlous. In the weeks since he and Ginny had separated, he had applied for more than a dozen jobs. The one thing he had not done, but should have, was sign on at the Unemployment Benefit Office. Stupidly, he had imagined that it would still be as easy to get another job as it had been in the summer, but despite the narrow Labour victory in the autumn, the economy remained in the doldrums.

So Grace's proposal, surprising as it was, had much to commend it, particularly as she had made it clear that she was happy for the arrangement to start immediately. The problem was that although Grace was not expecting him to pay any rent, he would feel uncomfortable about not contributing to the household expenses. The best way of making a financial contribution in the absence of formal paid employment would be for him to sign on at the DHSS as a lodger in Grace's house. But he would then have to have some document from her confirming the amount of rent he was paying a week, something she might, for all sorts of reasons, be reluctant to do, even if he were to remit to her the rent element from his benefit. She might, for instance, feel uncomfortable about getting the state to fund her live-in lover as her research assistant.

The other thing that worried him was how much time she would expect him to devote to the additional research for her book. She had been tolerant of his dilatory ways as an undergraduate, but she might be a harder taskmistress when it came to matters relating to her own work. She hadn't reached her position in the university at the age of thirty-six without a capacity for sustained hard work. It sounded like her own workload had increased considerably, so there were unlikely to be many days when they spent the entire day in bed, making love. Wasn't there a risk that he would become a harmless drudge, beavering away in the guest room and the University Library, and occasionally being required to attend to her pleasure circuitry?

The Glisson Road house was spacious and comfortable, but he and Grace had spent very little time together, indeed less than he'd spent with Ginny before they'd become a couple. Even though their earlier lovemaking had been delightful, mightn't they get on each other's nerves when it came to everyday life? Steve was a tidy sort, but he might not be tidy enough for Grace. Or she might be one of those people who was a delegator and liked to have others run errands for her. It was one thing to be a research assistant, but he didn't want to be a housekeeper too, the one rustling up a quick supper while she prepared her modern French poetry lectures.

The more he thought about the mechanics of the arrangement, the more he saw problems. He was a bit of a loner, but even so, there might be the odd occasion when he'd like to bring a friend back. Would she be relaxed about that? Would she mind if he went out for a drink? Would his guitar playing irritate her? The uncertainties seemed to be proliferating exponentially.

Unable to escape the loop in which his thoughts were now trapped, he decided to get up and go into another room to read. He slipped quietly out of the bed, took a dressing gown from the back of the door and stepped out onto the landing. He walked past the bathroom towards the back of the house, pushed open the first door he came to and peered inside. It looked like Grace's study. He stepped inside, closed the door and switched the light on. The walls were lined with book-filled shelves. There was bound to be something here to distract him. He found a volume of poems by Paul Valéry and sat down at Grace's desk, the surface of which was empty, apart from an open notebook and a small wooden rack of books. Steve glanced at the page at which the notebook lay open and noticed his own name. Immediately, he was seized by an urge to read what she had written about him. He knew it was an invasion of Grace's privacy to read her journal without her permission, but her private thoughts about him might help him decide whether to accept her proposal. He leafed back to the start of the most recent entry and began reading.

> What a terrible period this has been! I never really had any illusions about Peter's tendencies, but after the last time, I thought he'd finally settled down. How did I not see that Ginny was exactly the kind of woman that excited him? In which case, whatever did he see in me all those years ago? Well, I suppose he was impressed by the access I was able to give him to High Table discussions and hot new academics. Of course, it was very early days for Inflexion Books, so I suppose it was useful for him to have a backstop in the shape of somewhere to live and a wife with an income of her own. I was younger then too, and slimmer. But the sedentary life of an academic is not good for the figure. Not that he minded so much when he asked me to pose for him. Curves was what he wanted in that context.
>
> Oh well, but I'm sorry that Steve suffered collateral damage too. But with Ginny, he would have suffered sooner or later. By

going to bed with Steve, I probably thought I was consoling him, but it would be truer to say I was consoling myself. Even so, it was certainly something of a shock to be reminded, in such a pleasurably physical way, of what I had been missing with Peter. It was naïve of me, however, to suppose that I wasn't adding to Steve's troubles. Neither of us was in the right frame of mind to start a new relationship, but perhaps it was a bit callous of me to ask him not to get in touch. What I meant was that I'd let him know when I was ready to see him again. It wasn't meant to be a kiss-off. I imagined that we'd eventually bump into each other and work out whether we should take things further. I didn't expect him to vanish completely.

So tomorrow I'll go around to Ainsworth Street. The people there might have an address for him. He probably won't want to see me, even assuming he is still in Cambridge. But if he does, it might be interesting to find out if there is still a spark between us. After all, where is the harm in my taking an enthusiastic young lover? Plenty of male academics of my standing have done so. The relationship might not last. Steve is a free spirit, but there would, at least, be compensations in the meantime.

Steve finished reading and pushed his chair back. There was no mention of his working for her as a research assistant. That didn't necessarily mean that at the time of the journal entry it hadn't yet occurred to her, but it did suggest that she had only come up with the idea after she had set out to resume a relationship with him. So maybe the research assistant idea was simply a way of allowing him a modicum of self-respect by disguising the fact that he would, in effect, be a kept man. Even if that hadn't been the case, the fact that Grace had also come to the conclusion that the relationship was unlikely to last, in some measure reassured him.

But he still did not feel sleepy. His brain was teeming. Steve glanced at a few pages of the Valéry, but found his mind resistant to the beauty of Valéry's stately alexandrines. He needed something more personal to read. He then remembered that the letters Grace had brought around to Tenison Road remained unread in the pocket of his jacket. He padded downstairs and, having retrieved the letters from the jacket, went into the kitchen. He put the kettle on for a cup of tea and then spread the letters on the table. He thought he recognised the majority of correspondents from the handwriting. There were two letters from his mother, two from Angie, one from Alan (an unexpected pleasure), and one from Rob. He put all those to one side and placed the two unidentified letters side by side. The handwriting of the letter on the left was an untidy scrawl, almost certainly from a man; that on the right stylish, enigmatic and feminine. He ran through the small number of women who might want to write to him and who also knew his Ainsworth Street address. Apart from Beth, who had no need to write to him at her own address, the only name he could come up with was Ginny's. But surely she wouldn't have the temerity to write to him? Even as he thought this, he knew that temerity was Ginny's home turf. Well, there was only one way to find out. He slit the envelope with his thumbnail and unfolded the letter. His deduction had been correct. It was a short note from his former lover.

> Dear Steve, you are perhaps a little surprised to be receiving a letter from me. I must admit I'm a little surprised to find myself writing one. But don't worry, I'm not about to apologise for my behaviour or to suggest we meet. I'm not even sure you will get to see this letter, as perhaps you will rip it up without even reading it. However, I'm inclined to think this unlikely. You are not so impulsive. If you do not read it, it is more likely to be because Beth does not have a forwarding address for you. Though I have my spies everywhere, no one seems to know where you are now living. That worries me a little. I still care about you and had hoped I'd left you more than capable of looking after yourself. My graduates normally go on to do quite well.
>
> But enough of this twaddle. I hope you found the sketchbook, which I left you, entertaining. I made it for you in gratitude for encouraging me to get back to art. But I realised recently that there was one character missing from the book, namely me. When I was making the book, I thought it would be more considerate to you if I did not figure in it, in view of the hurt I was about to cause you. But I have since come to think that without me it is not a true record of those months. I have therefore made some studies of myself in the same vein (or should that be vain?). If you would be kind enough to supply me with your new address, I will send you the images.
>
> I can imagine some of the thoughts going through your head as you read these lines. I can only assure you, the offer is made in a positive spirit. So, the ball is in your court, my lovely. Let me have your new address and I promise I will send you the images. With love, Ginny.

Steve put the letter down and took a deep breath. His immediate reaction was one of anger. How dare she trifle with him like this? She was just trying to hold on to him, keep him spinning in the wind. If he did send her his new address, she would know at once that she still held sway over him. But she had also correctly surmised that he had sensed the vacancy at the heart of the book and would welcome images of her. Now she was offering him access to that dark central place. He looked at the date at the head of the letter. It had been written several weeks previously, so she must have assumed by now that he had declined her offer. This realisation by no means lessened the sense of anxiety her letter had induced in him.

Steve opened the other envelope, which had unfamiliar handwriting. It turned out to be from Jon. Steve was spooked by the coincidence that the two letters he had chosen to open first were from the former king and queen of Cambridge hipsterdom, who, while no longer a couple, still seemed able to coordinate their actions and could, in some respects, be considered the joint authors of Steve's predicament.

Steve read the letter.

> Steve, you crazy poet, how are you, mate? But more importantly, where are you? I'll be back in Cambridge at Christmas. Let's get together. I don't suppose you've still got the camper van? I wouldn't blame you if you'd got rid of it. But if you do still have it, I'd like to pick it up. Be in touch, you motherfucker. Don't make me have to flush you out. Cool vibes, man. Jon.

Steve laughed. Jon was as shamelessly outrageous as ever. Steve had indeed been working on the assumption that Jon had given him the VW, not lent it. Furthermore, he had been considering selling it as a way of drumming up some money. But he had taken no tangible steps to put it up for sale. In an attempt to conserve his finances, he had not driven it since he'd moved into Tenison Road. Truth be told, he'd felt uncomfortable being responsible for it.

He checked the date on this letter. It had only been sent a week ago. Still time to give that one some thought.

Which one next? The least contentious or upsetting one was probably that from Alan. He opened it, noting that it had a British stamp, not a French one.

> What ho, *mon cher*! Where are you, you bugger? Not where I've sent this letter, I'll be bound. And where am I? Not where you might have thought before you noticed the stamp affixed hereto. As a matter of fact, Nice was no longer so nice. So we have returned to Blighty, and I am currently doing a law course which will enable me to sit (and pass) the Law Society exams next sum-

mer. My father said he'd pay the fees and give me an allowance until I get a traineeship with a decent firm. I know, I know. How the mighty have fallen! It doesn't mean I will actually become a solicitor, but it buys me time.

Oh yeah. Me and Di have split up. She didn't fancy life with a trainee lawyer. Let me know how you are. And where you are. And when we can catch up. I could come up to Cambridge, if you can accommodate a guest in your current gaff. Or you could come down and spend the weekend with me. I've got a spacious room in a house share in Islington. Don't keep me waiting, old chap. Reply pronto. Al.

Steve chuckled to himself. It was all so predictable, but good all the same. He would write back first thing the following day.

Now it was a toss-up between Rob's letter and Angie's two letters. He wondered whether the letters might be connected. Obviously, they were, in the sense that Angie and Rob were now living together. But might not the sequence of letters reflect the unfolding of some event in their lives together? He looked at the postmarks. The earliest one was from Angie, then Rob's, followed shortly thereafter by Angie's second letter. Was it too much to hope that Angie had now realised that she had made a terrible mistake with Rob (letter 1) and was sharing her concerns with Steve? In the scenario that rapidly unfolded in Steve's imagination, she and Rob had had a terrible row and she had given him his marching orders. Meanwhile, Rob had written to Steve to tell him the terrible news (letter 2), acknowledging that Angie had never really got over Steve. Finally, Angie had written again to say that there was no encumbrance to their getting back together and why didn't Steve think about coming up to Edinburgh to see her? Indeed, consider moving there. Steve noted that the last two letters had been sent within a day or two of each other, which somehow lent more weight to these ludicrous speculations.

He opened Angie's first letter and glanced over it. It was a long, chatty letter about graduate student life in Edinburgh. There was nothing about any problems in her relationship with Rob. In fact, it was rather full of encomia upon Rob: what a fine scholar he was, what a brilliant poet, what a nice guy, what a great time they were having together. There was only the briefest enquiry as to how Steve's life was going. She clearly didn't know that he and Ginny had split up and that he was no longer living in Ainsworth Street. It was hardly surprising really, given that he had not been in touch with her since Martin Lockwood's funeral, after which he and Rob had nearly come to blows?

He threw her letter down in disgust and picked up Rob's.

Dear Steve, how are you, *cher maître*?

I'm sorry I haven't been in touch. It's been a busy first term, not so much on the academic front, as on the bardic. The poetry scene here is very active, most stimulating. I have given several readings, which have been well received, and have had one or two pieces published in little magazines. But the main reason for being so busy is that a local publishing house, Grassmarket Books, is going to publish my first collection. So I have been working hard with my editor Fiona Stewart to perfect my meagre store of poems. It has been a bracing process. She is not one for sloppy writing. Every word has to earn its keep. We have had some mighty rows, but I think the book will be better for it, and will present my work in the best possible light.

I wish you could meet her. I have spoken to her about your poetry and shown her one or two of your pieces. I have also mentioned the *Event/Horizon* poem, but decided not to show her the early fragment I have because I'm sure it is now a much more substantial piece. Why not aim to come up here sometime? I know you probably find it hard to tear yourself out of Ginny's embrace. Who wouldn't? Please send her my regards, but do not relay to her my comments about her embrace. Write back and let me know your news, especially what you're working on now.

All the best, mate. Rob.

As usual, Steve felt guilty about how mean he was towards Rob, who seemed only ever to want to help him. What had he ever done for Rob? Not much; but attribute base motives to him. Yet once again, Rob was continuing to promote Steve's work. Also, once again, Rob's career was going from strength to strength. Perhaps that was the reward for being so positive and open-hearted. How could Steve expect any sympathy from either Angie or Rob when neither of them had any idea that he and Ginny had split up? He had been wallowing in his own misery and had communicated with no one.

Feeling very low now, he thought he'd better read Angie's second letter.

Dear Steve, I hope you are okay. I was slightly worried not to have received a reply to my earlier letter. Perhaps you are very busy. I'm sorry if that is the case, but I hope it means that you are doing lots of writing and that you and Ginny are doing lots of exciting things. But please do try and reply. Otherwise, I really will start to worry. My other reason for writing is to let you know that Rob and I are coming down to Cambridge after Christmas. I know it is an impertinence, but I was wondering if we might stay with you and Ginny in Ainsworth Street. Now that we are both in stable relationships with other people, that should pose no problem.

Of course, if either of you is uncomfortable with the idea, I will not pursue the matter. I have not mentioned this to Rob. His idea is that we stay in a hotel, but I am a little short of funds. There have been problems with my grant; some glitch between the English and Scottish education departments. I'm sure it will all sort itself out. But it means I'm a bit stretched at the moment. I'm sorry to ask you this, and I completely understand if you think it inappropriate. Regardless of your response to my approach, I would love to hear your news and what you and Ginny have been up to. As a quid pro quo, we would love you and Ginny to come and stay with us here in Edinburgh. We have a lovely flat in New Town. The ceiling heights are ridiculous. I hope you're not too irritated with my approach.

Steve, I miss you. I would love to see you. I know that things have changed. But I'd like us to stay friends. Anyway, that's enough from me for now. Do please get in touch. With love, Angie.

Steve finished reading, with tears in his eyes. He was upset and remorseful, but mostly he was just angry. Not with Angie but with himself. If you wanted things fucking up, just get Steve Percival on the job.

Oh, well. He might as well overdose now on self-reproach and read the letters from his mother. He opened the first one. His mother was worried about him. He could at least phone her and let her know that he was okay. Why didn't he come and see her? She would still like to meet Ginny. The longer she went without meeting her, the more likely she was to worry that the relationship was unsuitable. What were his plans for Christmas?

He put the letter down. Why did he treat his mother so badly? He was her only child. She had no one else. She didn't demand much from him.

He opened the second letter.

Dear Steve, Either you are ignoring my last letter, or for some reason you did not get it. And so might not get this one either. But if you do, please phone me. I'm very worried about you. I do not know why you are treating me like this. I just need to hear that you are okay. Please, Steve. I have something important to tell you. Love, Ma.

Steve felt terrible. Was she ill? Why did she need to write to him? Why didn't he automatically write to her from time to time? Because he was ashamed of the situation he was in? Or because there was nothing good he could say? He had let himself down. He had let everyone down. But most of all, he had let his mother down. Tears welled in his eyes and spilled down his cheeks.

At that moment, the door opened and Grace appeared in her nightdress. 'Steve, are you okay? Can't you sleep?'

Then she saw the tears. She went over and put her arms around him. 'Oh, you poor thing! What's happened?'

He buried his head in her breast and sobbed uncontrollably for some moments. Grace stroked his hair and pulled him close to her. She saw the letters spread out on the table. 'Oh, dear. You've had bad news? Let me put the kettle on.'

She released him and went over to the hob. Steve watched her listlessly. When she'd made the drinks, she said, 'Steve, I've only got this nightdress on and I'm freezing. Can we go up and talk in bed?'

Steve nodded and gathered up the letters. They went upstairs and got under the blankets. Grace took him in her arms. 'Do you want to talk about it now? Or would it be better in the morning?'

Steve sobbed again and said through his tears, 'Just hold me. We'll talk tomorrow.'

Soon he fell asleep, more miserable than he'd ever been but safe in Grace's embrace.

It was now Grace's turn not to be able to sleep. Wasn't the idea of Steve moving in with her – being her research assistant by day and her sperm donor by night – completely impractical? Wasn't she just adding to Steve's burdens? Wouldn't it be better to keep him at arm's length? He could stay over from time to time, and they would sleep together. If she had to share him with Jude or even Beth, so what? One way or another, he would eventually move on. In the meantime, she could help him stabilise himself while she would have a companion who was an attentive lover and who might also give her a child.

Nor would either of them have to go public about the relationship, which was probably more difficult for her than for him. Sooner or later, if he actually moved in and they became a couple, she would have to let friends and colleagues know, and, more worryingly, her parents. Steve might not feel so apprehensive about letting his friends know; indeed, he might be quite proud of himself. But he might also have some reservations about letting his own family know. Steve's mother, for instance, might not entirely welcome her son taking up with a woman fifteen years his senior who apparently only wanted him so that he could give her a child. Grace seemed to recall that his mother had not entirely approved of Ginny, who was much closer to Steve in age, although her disapproval may have been for other reasons.

When she had shared the research assistant idea with Steve in his room in Tenison Road, she had been thinking that he could move in immediately and certainly before Christmas. But seeing how distraught he had been after reading the letters she had brought him, perhaps it would be better to defer any move – or indeed any decision – until after Christmas. Especially since she had agreed to spend Christmas in Somerset with her own parents, and it would be premature for her to ask Steve to accompany her. In any case, he was probably going back to his mother's for the festive period. They could think things through during the Christmas break and, if they both felt confident about the plan, they could see the New Year in as a couple, however temporary.

As she finally drifted off to sleep, having come to no conclusion, she wondered whose letter it was which had upset Steve, or whether it had simply been an overload of news from afar.

# Thursday, 19 December 1974

AFTER A LATE START the next morning, while they were having coffee and toast, Grace said, 'You seemed very upset last night after reading your mail. I hope it wasn't bad news.'

'Not bad news as such. At least I hope not.'

'I couldn't help but notice that one of the envelopes had an Edinburgh postmark. I got to recognise Angie's handwriting when I was acting as your dead letter box and her letters to you were arriving here.'

'There were two from Angie actually, one from Rob, Angie's boyfriend, one from Ginny, one from Jon, Ginny's partner before me, and two from my mother. Why don't you read them?'

'I wasn't prying...'

'No, I didn't think that. But it will give you a better idea of what a thoughtless person I am.'

He went up to the bedroom to get the letters and, on returning, handed them to Grace.

She was hesitant. 'Are you sure?'

'Yes. Perhaps you can help me sort this mess out. I'll make a pot of fresh coffee while you're reading them.'

Grace picked up the pile of letters and started to read. Having made the coffee, Steve sat and watched Grace reading, fearful that by the time she had finished, she would have a very low opinion of him.

Grace finished the last letter with a sigh and tucked it back into its envelope. 'Oh, dear, Steve. Thank you for letting me read your letters. That was very brave.'

'Or foolhardy.'

'I don't think so. Some tangles are clearer to a third party than to the person caught in the tangle. So I'm going to tell you what I

43

think you should do, which is not necessarily what you might feel inclined to do.'

Steve shrugged. 'Okay.'

Grace took a sip of her coffee. 'Firstly, you must contact your mother. I want you to phone her when we've finished this conversation; she says she's got something important to tell you. She might be ill. I will go out while you're making that call, so you don't need to worry about being overheard. I also want you to tell her that you will spend Christmas with her.'

'Grace, I'd rather spend Christmas with you.'

'You are not going to spend Christmas with me. I am going back to my own family. What's more, if you don't go and see your mother, you can forget living here with me. It's up to you, but you might as well know that I am not going to be swayed on this.'

Steve stared glumly out of the window. Grace tapped the table sharply with her forefinger. 'She's your mother. She's on her own.'

It was the most severe ticking-off that he had ever had from Grace. He hung his head in shame. 'Okay.'

'Good. Let's now dispense with the minor actors. I presume Al was a contemporary at St Rad's. What you do *vis-à-vis* him is up to you. I suggest you see him when you are in London over Christmas. As for Jon, who I presume is Ginny's ex, you don't have to make any decision there until he arrives in Cambridge to pick up his camper van, which you should definitely get rid of.

'Which brings us to Rob. What a very nice man he is! You should be very pleased that Angie has found someone so reliable. I know it must hurt because he is your best friend. But as I understand it, the fact that he is in a relationship with Angie is a consequence of your own actions. Clearly, Angie is still fond of you but she is also enjoying being with Rob. So you must put out of your mind any thoughts of reuniting with her. It will only torment you. As for her request to stay at Ainsworth Street, I am happy for her and Rob to stay here at Tenison Road, but they must come together and it must be for no more than two nights. That is, of course, assuming we have jointly decided that you are going to be living here.

'And finally, *La Belle Dame sans Merci*. Well, what a one she is! Regardless of my earlier strictures, I think you should reply to her, giving this as your address. I am possibly letting my own feelings get in the way here, but I would be very happy for her and, by extension, Peter to know that you are living with me. I would also be interested to see the sketchbook she made for you and the new images she promises to send. But, of course, that is entirely up to you. So there we are; I think that about covers it.'

Steve got up from his chair, went over to Grace and put his arms around her. 'Thank you, Grace. You are so clear-sighted. I will do everything you say.'

Grace allowed herself to be embraced for a few moments, then pushed him away. 'Right, no more hanky-panky until you've made that call.'

She stood up. 'I'm going to put my coat on and walk up to Mill Road to get a few supplies. I will be gone for at least half an hour. Let's hope your mum is in.'

When Grace got back from doing the shopping, before she had even taken her coat off, she said to Steve, 'If you haven't spoken to your mother yet, I'm going out again.'

Steve assured her that he had had a long conversation with her and that he was now going up to London on the twenty-third of December and would return to Cambridge on the twenty-seventh of December.

Grace took her coat off and hung it up. She was relieved. 'What was the important news?'

'She didn't say. She said it could keep until I was with her. But she promised me that she wasn't ill.'

'Well, that's a relief. I'm sorry about this, Steve, but I've been thinking things through while I've been out and I'm afraid we need to have a serious talk.'

'Oh dear. That sounds bad. I thought we had already had a serious talk.'

'You make a cup of tea while I'm putting this shopping away and then I'll tell you what's on my mind. There's nothing to fear.'

Steve did as requested and then seated himself at the table, curious as to what Grace wanted to talk about.

Grace sat opposite him and slid a packet of digestive biscuits towards him. 'I couldn't resist them.'

Steve opened the packet, took two and then handed the packet back to Grace, who limited herself to just one. As she nibbled it, she said, 'First of all, I thought I'd let you know that we're both running tomorrow, so you'd better go back to Tenison and get your kit later.'

'Is that it? What you had on your mind?'

Grace laughed. 'If only. No, that's the penance for eating biscuits.'

'Well, that's one form of motivation, I suppose, but a strange one.'

'You can't believe the tricks I have to play on myself. Anyway, that's not what I wanted to talk about. What's really worrying me is we're contemplating something quite similar to what you had with Ginny.'

Steve nodded, 'Yes, that's been worrying me too.'

During her brief shopping trip to the Mill Road shops while Steve was making the call to his mother, Grace had dismissed her misgivings of the small hours and come to the conclusion that it was time to be bold. She took a deep breath.

'So I think we've got to manage it completely differently.'

Suddenly nervous, Steve said, 'Okay.'

'Although you and Ginny were a couple, this was only known to a very small group of people. In many ways you were a clandestine couple. You never met Ginny's father; she never met your mother. I doubt that you introduced her to your colleagues and Ginny had no colleagues, as far as we know.'

Steve bridled. 'I introduced her to Martin Lockwood.'

'I know you were in discussions with him, but I seem to recall it was largely thanks to Rob.'

Steve, slightly crestfallen, acknowledged that was so.

'So I don't want us to be hugger-mugger about our relationship. Believe it or not, this is probably going to be harder for me than for you.'

'Yes, okay. What would that involve?'

'I want to meet your mother. I want her to come and stay here with us and when you're with her at Christmas, I want you to fix a date at some point in the next few weeks.'

Steve was silent. Grace looked at him. 'Well?'

'Isn't this a bit back to front? I mean we haven't yet decided whether we're having a relationship or not. You only came around to see me yesterday. I haven't agreed to be your research assistant yet.'

'I'm afraid I haven't got time to indulge you in your penchant for prevarication. In case you hadn't noticed, we *are* in a relationship. The question is, what are the parameters? Since you haven't immediately agreed to my first requirement, let me set out the others. I also want you to meet my parents. We will go down to Somerset early in the New Year and spend a weekend with them. And finally, I want you to meet some of my colleagues and come and dine at College as my partner.'

Steve was searching for a response, but Grace held her hand up. There was no point holding back. She might as well unpack the whole thing for him. 'I haven't finished yet. You need to hear the whole deal before you respond. If you decide to live with me as my lover, whether you work as my research assistant or not, I want you to understand that I will do my best to become pregnant by you. In other words, I would like you to be the father of my child. I am not asking you to be in love with me, simply to love me while we are together. I am not asking you to be with me forever or even until the child grows up. I am not asking you to take any financial responsibility for the child, but I am asking you to acknowledge to the rest of the world that you are the father. I want your name to be on the birth certificate and even if we break up I would like you to maintain an independent relationship with our son or daughter. I know it's a lot to take in and I don't expect you to reply immediately.'

It was as well that she did not expect an immediate response because Steve was at that moment struggling to comprehend the ramifications of what she was asking. How had the game changed so much in such a short space of time? When Grace had called on him at Tenison Road, he had, in a fit of curmudgeonly pique, unleashed his new Steve persona. It had been gratifying in the crudest possible way when she had submitted to his desire for her to remove her clothes and he had felt that he had been imperious when they were making love. He was beginning to suspect though, that she had contrived the situation. Not least because in the afterglow of their lovemaking, she had put a very businesslike proposition to him. She must have calculated that his financial resources were dwindling, that he was lonely and miserable in his grotty bedsitter and would therefore be susceptible to her offer. Now even that offer was being revealed as a proxy for something much more extraordinary.

So here he was less than twenty-four hours later back in her lovely Glisson Road house being asked to present himself to the world as her partner and subsequently, should the fates bless their union, as the father of her child. Not six months had passed since he had graduated and he was already being asked to settle down. Wasn't that precisely what he had been trying to wriggle out of in his dealings with Angie? Buying himself some time in which to sow his oats? Had the era of free love already ended?

On the other hand, there was something about the proposal that excited him. Grace was not asking him to profess undying love; she was only asking him to love her. It was not a conventional arrangement, but then Steve did not consider himself a conventional person. The relationship with Ginny had also been purely physical or, at least, it had been missing an intellectual component. Grace might compare herself unfavourably to Ginny when it came to physical beauty, but to Steve's eye, where Ginny tended towards the androgynous, Grace was distinctly feminine, which had undoubted compensations. She was also the possessor of a powerful intellect. He would learn much from her in their day-to-day interactions.

But how would he feel on those occasions when Grace had a lecture to give or faculty meeting to attend and he was left holding the baby, literally? Would he be able to cope with a wailing baby, the sleepless nights, the changing of nappies and, looking further ahead, the tantrums and accidents and health scares? But oddly, he thought the answer was yes. In the radiance of what he was feeling for Grace at that moment, it all suddenly seemed like it would be the most marvellous adventure. How was it that the mind could range so far and so wide in just a few moments and then resolve itself with such dizzying finality?

Careful not to sound too unthinkingly flippant, he said, 'Grace, I'm overwhelmed and amazed. I don't know what to say. I'm humbled by the trust you're prepared to put in me, but frightened that I'm not grown-up enough for such a serious responsibility.'

'That is an entirely sensible answer. Let me say something more about having a child. It was an issue between Peter and me and may have led to the breakup. At the start of our marriage neither of us was ready to have a child. But in the last couple of years I started to change my mind. I wanted a child before it was too late. For a woman, age is a crucial factor. No one is much surprised by a man becoming a father at fifty, but there are few if any women giving birth at fifty, and not that many at forty. Peter and I had a number of rows about it and he withdrew from me and finally left me.

'In those weeks since you and I first went to bed together I had been coming to the view that I would have the child my own. I was planning to ask Gary to be the donor because he and I were lovers when we were undergraduates before he came out. But it occurred to me that he and perhaps Matt, his partner, might not take kindly to the idea.

'While I was casting around for suitable donors, I realised that the only other man whom I had had sex with, apart from Gary and Pete, and a couple of unfortunate liaisons when I was a research student in Berlin and Paris, was you. Not only was the sex good, but you are a vigorous young man with, one imagines, top-notch semen.

'That was why I set out to track you down. Not because I am in love with you, but because I wanted to ask you to be the father of my child. But when I got to Tenison Road I was too cowardly to ask you outright. I felt I needed to seduce you first and then have a cover story. So I took my clothes off and, after the consequences of that, asked you to be my research assistant. But that is not a necessary part of the conditions I am asking you to accept. While it is true that I am going to have to add some material to the existentialism book, I could, as you surmised, get one of my graduate students to do the work. It was just that it was the reason I gave Beth for trying to get in touch with you.'

'Was she convinced?'

'Curiously, I don't think she was. But we're getting away from the subject. Do you think you'd be prepared to help me have a baby? It would involve a lot of sex, especially at certain times of the month, and a nice place to live, rent free.'

Still trying to keep the tone light, Steve said, 'How can I refuse when you put it like that? Actually, the idea terrifies me. But it thrills me as well. What terrifies me most, though, is telling my mother what we have in mind.'

'I must admit that I feel much the same about my parents. Maybe I'm making us rush our fences. Perhaps it would be better to establish that we are a couple first, age gap and all, and let them get used to that fact. Then, if and when I become pregnant, we can tell the relevant people. Pregnancy is, after all, a common consequence of a couple living together.'

'I'd prefer that. It's not that I don't want to be the father of your child, our child. It's that I'd rather deal first with meeting your parents, meeting your colleagues as your partner, and your meeting my mother. All that stuff is daunting enough.'

'I agree. I'm sorry about my full-on approach; I just didn't want to chicken out of discussing the most important point with you. My dad says that I often seem to put the cart before the horse.'

Steve laughed. 'I don't even know where the horse is.'

'I'm sorry if this is too much too fast. If you want to back out, now is the time to do it. I would completely understand. But I think we can have a lovely relationship. The thing is, this is real life. If we're going to do this, let's be bold and open about it. It still might go wrong, but it won't be because we've been half-hearted. It's mad, I know. We both have other people to whom we have been attached and who can still exert some pull on us. Perhaps at the back of our minds there's this thought that we might be able to revive one of those attachments, but that's not the way to live a life. This is where we are. Let's take the opportunity before us with both hands. There will be difficulties, even embarrassments, but we can overcome them if we do our best to be honest with each other.'

She banged the table with her hand. Steve, still dizzy at the magnitude of what he was agreeing to, covered her hand with his. 'Yes, I agree to your conditions. How could I not?'

'Thank you, Steve. I'm so pleased. So, when you go back to your mother's for Christmas, I want you to tell her about me. I will do the same and tell my parents about you. Neither of us need say anything at this stage about babies.'

Ignoring the fact that the single child of earlier was now in the plural, Steve said, 'Okay. But I have to say that even so it will be with a certain amount of trepidation.'

'Of course. I will be feeling much the same. My father is a vicar. Both families might consider our attachment unsuitable, but at least they'll know. We won't have to pretend.'

'But I don't want to be dependent on you.'

'If you're saying that you don't want to be my research assistant, I completely get that. It was just a way of giving you some independence, but I can also see that it makes things more difficult for you in terms of the power dynamic between us. Anyway, I am sure that you will soon be able to make a contribution to our joint finances. In the meantime, I'm happy to take the strain.'

They both fell silent. Grace looked at Steve. 'How are you feeling?'

'Weird.'

'Me too.'

They sat in silence for a few moments until Grace said, 'Good. So now you've got some letters to write, starting with one to your landlord, giving notice on Tenison Road. You can use my study. There's notepaper and envelopes in the top right drawer. I'll let you get on with it.'

Steve went up to Grace's study, and noticed that her journal had been put away. He still felt guilty about reading her private writings, but it now occurred to him that perhaps she had left it there on purpose in the hope that he would read it. Steve sat down at Grace's desk and penned notes to the letting agent, Alan, and Jon, all relatively easy to deal with, since the news about him and

Grace was either irrelevant to the purposes of the letters or could wait until another time to be divulged. In each case he forbore to give the Glisson Road address. For the agent he wrote as from Tenison Road. For the letters to Al and Jon he simply put Cambridge at the top of the letter and the telephone number of the Glisson Road house. He told Al that unless he heard to the contrary on the telephone number at the head of the page, he'd drop by his address in Islington on Monday afternoon and suggested to Jon that he ring him on the same number when he was back in Cambridge.

Dealing with Angie and Rob was a bit more awkward. He didn't really want to have to write two separate letters, but nor did he want to betray Angie's confidence about her financial position and her reluctance to put up at a hotel. So he addressed his missive to both of them. Nor was he inclined to give a blow-by-blow account of what had happened since they had last had news from him. Best to come straight to the point. He had been delighted to receive their letters. He apologised for the delay in replying. He and Ginny had split up and he was now living with Grace Mitchell, but the letters, of course, had gone to Ainsworth Street and had only just reached him at Glisson Road.

For a moment, as his mind's eye lingered on a mental image of Angie, he considered changing the phrase *living with Grace* to *living at Grace's*. Who knew what the true state of affairs was between Angie and Rob? Why slam shut the door to the possibility of his getting back together with Angie? But in his heart he knew this was crass pusillanimity. He shook his head. He must jettison these old Steve ways. It was not fair to Grace or Angie and it was not conducive to his getting his life sorted out. He should stop behaving as if Angie was, in some deep sense, his girl.

He resumed writing. He was glad to hear that Angie and Rob were coming to Cambridge. They would be welcome to stay at Glisson Road for a night or two. He was sorry not to be able to ask them to stay for longer. He and Grace were very busy. (He knew it was a distortion of the facts to imply that he too was busy, but it seemed ungallant to single out Grace's reservation.) He signed off affectionately, saying he was looking forward to coming up to Edinburgh to visit them.

That only left the letter to Ginny. When he had sat down to deal with his correspondence, it was replying to Ginny that had filled him with the most dread. But now he saw that it was in many ways the easiest to pen. He could let Ginny draw whatever inference she wanted from the fact that his address was now Glisson Road. He thanked her for the sketchbook and said he would be grateful for the new images. He wished her well and signed off without any kind of endearment, feeling curiously relieved. He then addressed the envelopes, remembering not to seal the one to the letting agent, to which he would need to add a cheque when he was back at Tenison Road. He put Grace's writing pad back in the drawer, then went downstairs and found Grace reading in the sitting room.

She smiled at him. 'There's a set of keys on the kitchen table. They're yours. Don't forget your running kit.'

Steve promised he wouldn't. It was odd to think that this was now his home. Not much more than twenty-four hours earlier, he had been sunk in despair. Now, suddenly, a door had opened to a way of life full of new terrors and delights.

Ten minutes later, he let himself into his room in the Tenison Road house. He wrote the cheque to the letting agent and sealed the envelope. He then set about packing a bag with his running kit, a change of clothes, his toilet bag and a couple of books. He would get the rest of the stuff in a day or two. As he was zipping up the bag, there was a knock at the door. He opened the door. It was Jude.

She eyed him severely. 'Where have you been? We were supposed to be going out last night.'

'Were we?'

'Yes, you could have let me know you couldn't make it.'

'Sorry, something came up.'

Jude laughed derisively. 'So I understand. Garth said you had a woman in here.'

Garth was the tenant with the room directly above Steve's. He'd probably heard the sounds of passion. Grace had not restrained her cries.

Steve pondered his response for a moment. 'Yeah, my former supervisor was here.'

'I see.'

'She was offering me a job as a research assistant.'

'For which she had to take her clothes off?'

'Er, I think Garth assumes everyone is as much of a naturist as he is.'

'No, that detail is not from Garth. You forgot to draw your curtains.'

Jude walked to the middle of the room. 'I saw her standing just about here, slowly taking her clothes off. I couldn't see you, so I imagine you were sitting or lying on the bed getting yourself ready to defend your essay. As if.'

Steve didn't know quite what to say and could only manage a somewhat strangled, 'Ah!'

'Ah, indeed, Steve Percival! Is that what it takes to retain your interest? I mean if you'd told me, I'd have been happy to strip for you on a daily basis, even with the curtains back.'

She started to unbutton her blouse.

Steve was aghast. He'd better put new Steve back in his box, and pronto. But just for a moment he thought: *She's calling my bluff. Why don't I just let her get on with it?*

She undid another button. Did she really intend to take all her clothes off? Now her blouse was open. She was not wearing a bra. She had come prepared.

She looked at him steadily. 'Do you want me to go on?'

'It's up to you.'

Jude started to unzip her skirt. 'I've never met anyone with as much of a brass neck as you.'

She let her skirt fall and stepped out of it. She was not wearing knickers. Then she threw off her blouse. 'Is that how it's done?'

Steve was having difficulty in getting new Steve back in his box. 'You definitely get extra points for the lack of underwear.'

She stepped towards him. She really was rather hot and was clearly determined to reassert her rights over him. Where was the harm in one last roll in the hay with Jude? Grace knew that he'd slept with Jude several times and had even acknowledged the fact that she didn't have exclusive access to Steve until they'd worked out the nature of their relationship.

Jude pressed herself against him. The animal scent of her body was intoxicating. She reached her hand down and ran it over his groin. Satisfied that she had aroused him, she started unbuttoning his shirt and nuzzling his neck. 'Is there something else I have to do? Or can we go to bed now?'

Steve's heart was pounding hard. He wanted to take her hard and fast up against the wall and then, without withdrawing, slowly and lingeringly. But at that moment he heard the front door bang. The noise and the implication that someone was in the passage outside his room brought him to his senses.

He gently removed Jude's hands from his shirt and stepped away from her. He went over to where she had dropped her clothes, picked them up and then tossed them over to her. 'Jude, I can't tell you how much I want to fuck you, but I just can't do it.'

Jude put her skirt back on. 'I'm no expert, but I'd say you were just about ready to blow your top.'

'I don't mean I couldn't do it physically. I mean ethically. I'm in a relationship with another person.'

'I thought you were in a relationship with me.'

She started to put her blouse back on. Steve took a last, lingering look at her breasts, suddenly back in old Steve mode.

'It wasn't really a relationship, was it?'

'Well, until yesterday we were sleeping with each other. Then your *supervisor* comes along, does a strip and that's it. End of Jude.'

'Yeah, you and I were sleeping with each other, but we weren't living with each other.'

'But you're not living with – what's her name?'

'Grace.'

'Thank you. You're not living with Grace.'

'Well, I am now.'

'You might have stayed with her last night, but I don't think that counts as living with someone.'

Jude had finished buttoning her blouse and was looking dejected and bedraggled. 'Do you think we could have a cup of coffee?'

Steve felt sorry for her now. 'Yes, of course. I'm afraid it'll have to be black.'

She nodded and sat down on his bed. 'You could at least give me an explanation.'

Steve put a pan of water on to boil. 'It's complicated. I've known Grace for a long time.'

'So she really was your supervisor? Were you having a relationship with her when she was teaching you?'

'No, but we were before I moved in here.'

He brought the coffees over and sat on one of the chairs. 'It's a long story. I was living with someone else and Grace was married, still is married as a matter of fact. But my girlfriend went off with her husband and so Grace and I fell into each other's arms. But we thought that probably wasn't the best way to start a relationship and so we took a break from each other. In fact, Grace didn't even know where I was living until she tracked me down yesterday. We realised then that there really was a spark between us despite all the difficulties that might be involved and so we've got back together. I've compressed the story a bit, but that's the nub of it. So you see I couldn't cheat on her, not on the very first day we got back together.'

Jude looked at him searchingly. 'So is the woman in your poem Grace or is it your girlfriend who went off with her husband?'

Steve was taken off guard. 'I don't know what you mean. What poem?'

'The one you threw in the bin out the back, *Event/Horizon*.'

'You know about that?'

'I rescued it. Read the whole thing, several times. It's brilliant.'

Steve put his head in his hands. 'Oh, Jude, I don't know what to say. That's very lovely of you. I'm a bit overwhelmed.'

'Okay, you have to give me a bit more. Why are you overwhelmed? I assume you have a more up-to-date draft.'

'Well, no. It was the only copy I had.'

'Why were you trying to destroy it?'

'Basically, I screwed up my finals because I was writing it for most of my last year. I also screwed up the relationship I was in at the time and probably disappointed a lot of people.'

'But you didn't disappoint Grace?'

'I certainly disappointed her academically. But she believes in me as a poet. I owe her so much.'

'So much so that you decided to destroy the poem.'

'No, it's more than that, but I can't go into all the details now.'

'Okay, but I still don't get why you're overwhelmed. I can't be the only person who thinks it's a great poem.'

'No, there are some others, not many, though. The reason I'm overwhelmed is because I was in such a dark place when Ginny left me that I never wanted to see the poem again.'

'Is Ginny the woman who went off with Grace's husband?'

'Yes.'

'She's the figure in the last long section of the poem?'

'Yes, I wanted to get rid of anything that reminded me of her. So I destroyed my fair copy of the poem. Since then I've been trying to convince myself that it was a good thing to do and that I had given up poetry. But I kept thinking that I'd made a terrible mistake. So I can't tell you how grateful I am to you for getting it back to me.'

'Well, I haven't actually got it back to you yet.'

'True.'

'Maybe there are a few other steps to be taken first.'

'Like what? Can't you just go upstairs and get it?'

'To begin with, it's not upstairs.'

'Where is it then?'

'At my office.'

'Okay, presumably your office is not far away.'

'Not very far. Unfortunately, I'm off now until after Christmas. But that's not really what I mean. To have saved something so precious from oblivion is surely worth something.'

'You want some money?'

'No, of course not. There are more personal ways of showing your appreciation.'

Steve suddenly realised what Jude was driving at. 'That's ridiculous, Jude. You can't seriously want me to sleep with you to get my manuscript back.'

'I admit that it's a slightly unusual situation, but I don't see why not.'

Steve desperately needed an intervention from new Steve here. But he was pretty sure that new Steve would say: *Oh, for Heaven's sake, just fuck her. Don't make a meal of it.*

Steve's mind was racing. Something didn't quite hang together here. 'Wait a moment. I put the manuscript in the bin the day I moved in. The bins get emptied once a week. So you've probably had the manuscript for nearly three weeks. During that time we've slept with each other three times.'

'Four, actually.'

'Okay, four. Why are you raising the matter only now? Why don't those previous four times count as payment or reward for saving my manuscript?'

'Because you can't be grateful for something you don't know about.'

'Okay, I accept that you probably hadn't found the manuscript that very first day, which was also the first time we slept together. But why didn't you tell me about it thereafter?'

'Because it took me some time to reassemble the torn sheets and get the pages in the right order. Nor is it a quick read. But the main reason is that your name was not on any of the pages. It might have been by someone else in the house.'

'Well, if it wasn't by me or you, that only left Garth and Kelly, and Jason and Susan. And Garth is off his trolley.'

'It would be quite easy to come to the view that the author of *Event/Horizon* is off his or her trolley.'

'Okay, so what persuaded you that it was me?'

'I've been in everyone's room in this house. You're the only person who has volumes of poetry and books by Nietzsche. You are the one arrogant enough to do something so crazy.'

'Hang on. Are you saying I'm arrogant?'

'Well, aren't you?'

'I really don't think so. What you've been experiencing is new Steve.'

'What?'

'I invented a new persona for myself when I moved in here. I don't normally sleep with a woman on the first day I meet her.'

'Or refuse to make love to her when she subsequently offers you her body.'

'That's old Steve.'

'A kind of Jekyll and Hyde?'

'Yes, I suppose so.'

'So who am I with at the moment? The cruel one or the nice one?'

'The nice one.'

Jude laughed scornfully. 'It doesn't feel like it.'

'Jude, I had no objection to sleeping with you. I really enjoyed it. You are a beautiful sexy woman. But I don't want to fuck things up with Grace.'

'Does she need to know?'

'No, but that's not how it works. It's a matter of honesty.'

'But she's not going to say to you when you get back to her house, you were gone a long time. Did you have one last fuck with Jude when you were out?'

'She might.'

'Did you tell her about me?'

'I did.'

'Okay, I give you credit for that.'

'Anyway, it's also a matter of ethics and self-respect.'

'One of the Steves, let's say old Steve, is ethical?'

'Yes.'

'Okay, shall we leave it like this? Your manuscript is safe. I'm going back to my parents in Manchester and I won't be back until the twenty-eighth of December. Why don't we meet up then and discuss further how we're going to work this out?'

Jude stood up, put her scarcely drunk coffee mug on the table, and walked out of the room.

Steve felt faint. Why hadn't he just fucked her? They had already done so several times in the three or so weeks he'd been in the house. It would hardly have been an unpleasant experience. Grace need never know about it. In the ledger of his sexual exploits, it could easily be reclassified as an entry, as it were, in the preceding accounting period. Then Jude would have given him the manuscript back.'

Well, maybe not immediately if her story about it being in the office was true. That troubled him. Why had she taken it to her office? For safety? To keep it out of his hands? To give her leverage over him? If the latter, at least he had withstood the moves that she'd been trying to put on him. Which meant that if questioned further by Grace about Jude, he would be able to answer with a clear conscience.

Steve picked up his bag, put the letters for posting in his jacket pocket and stepped out onto Tenison Road deep in thought. The recent propensity for women to take off their clothes in front of him, while very pleasurable, was disquieting. He was nothing to write home about, neither film star, rock star nor fêted writer. So why was it happening?

Looking back over the previous six months, it seemed to have started with Ginny, when she had walked naked into his room in the shared house in Ainsworth Street. Of course, Ginny, having been both a life model and a mannequin, was very much at home without her clothes on. But now within a short space of time, both Grace and Jude had undressed in front of him. Was this simply a further stage in the development of the sexual revolution? If it was, it was a curious form of female assertiveness. On the other hand, each time it had happened, it had certainly thrown Steve off course. The fact that he had been able to withstand Jude's adoption of the technique was a matter for some kind of satisfaction, if not the kind he would have preferred.

So far as he knew the three women had not previously known each other or even *of* each other. But there did seem to be some kind of cryptic linkage between them. Ginny in particular seemed to know things and be able to do things that were on the face of it not easily explicable by the normal laws of nature. It was almost as if they were competing with each other. But what were they competing for? Given their tendency to remove their clothes in front of him, one might imagine that he was being required to judge their physical beauty.

Yet it was more than that. In some arcane way his poem seemed to be involved. Ginny, Grace and now Jude had all taken an active interest in the poem. This was in contrast to the huge indifference the poem had provoked generally. It was true that Angie and Rob had been supportive of his writing, but at some point after he had moved into Ainsworth Street, the poem had become something much more powerful and mysterious, a receptacle for otherworldly forces. Hadn't Angie said the poem was an illusion when they'd had their clandestine meeting in the Eagle? Declan, her boyfriend at the time, had asked him whether he was doing the Robert Graves thing, to which he had replied flippantly that, yes, he probably was. Had he not only taken too many drugs, but also taken Graves's *The White Goddess* too seriously?

At that moment, he saw a pillar box on the other side of the road and crossed over to post his letters, conscious, as he did so, that even though he had used first-class stamps, his belated correspondence was quite likely to get caught up in the Christmas backlog. He just hoped that the letters to his mother and to Al arrived before Christmas.

When Steve got back to Glisson Road, Grace was still buried in her book. He glanced at the cover. It was an anthology of modern French poetry. A notebook and pen lay beside her on the sofa. Clearly, she had already started making notes for her lecture series.

She looked up and smiled. 'All done?'

'Yes, letters all posted. Running kit and some clothes for the next few days in my rucksack, and a handful of books in a carrier bag.'

'We'll sort things out properly when we get back after Christmas. But for now, you can store your stuff in the room at the end of the landing upstairs.'

'Was that Peter's room?'

'Yes, you don't mind, do you? All his stuff has gone, apart from the furniture, which wasn't really his anyway. There is a single bed in there, but you'll be sleeping with me, I hope. If you'd rather not use his old room, there are two rooms and a small bathroom on the attic floor. But I use one of them as a guest room and the other for storage. Anyway, the room at the back of the house has a nice view over the garden.'

'No, that's fine.'

Steve went upstairs and dumped his stuff. When he came back down, Grace was in the kitchen making a cup of tea. She said, 'I'm afraid we've got one hurdle to negotiate as a couple before Christmas. Matt and Gary are coming to supper on Friday evening. It will give us an opportunity to practise how we present ourselves.'

'What are we going to say?'

'We're just going to tell it how it is. We're in a relationship. You are moving in. The age gap is not an issue, not for us, anyway. We don't care what other people think. We won't say anything about a pregnancy.'

'Will they be sympathetic?'

'Yes, I think so. Not only is Gary my oldest friend, but he also had a low opinion of Peter, mainly because I used to confide in him about Peter's serial indiscretions.'

'He might have reservations about me too.'

'Oh, I don't think so. I know him pretty well. We were lovers briefly before he found the courage to admit that he preferred sex with men. But please keep that to yourself, the fact that we were lovers, not that he is gay.'

'Of course.'

'You get on well with Matt, don't you?'

'We both like jazz guitar.'

'Did you bring your guitar?'

'No, but I'll get it and a few more books tomorrow. I promise not to play it too loudly.'

'I look forward to hearing you play.'

'I'm not much of a performer.'

'Tsk, tsk. A bit more new Steve, please.'

'I'll try.'

'Steve, I know this isn't going to be easy, but if we do our best to be kind and forgiving to each other, we've got a chance of making it work.'

'I expect you'll have to do more forgiving than me.'

'Why do you say that?'

'Well, I'm not sure how much control I'll have over new Steve.'

'Maybe we have different views of what being new Steve involves.'

'There was a guy at the theatre called Butch…'

'Ah yes, he's a friend of Gary's.'

'Yeah, he is. When I was upset about Ginny, he took me out for a drink and said that Ginny shouldn't be trying to change me. That's not what partners should do in a relationship.'

'Well, I agree with him. I hope you don't think that's what I'm trying to do. But I do think that ideally the partners should be prepared to adapt to each other and help each other. Even if you decide you don't want to be my research assistant, I hope you'll contribute to my thinking not only on the existentialism book, but on my lecture series too.'

'Grace, I don't know a fraction of what you know about either of those subjects.'

'But you know other things. I trust your intuition. You are a poet.'

'I'm not, Grace. Whereas you are an actual published poet.'

'I'm using poet in a deeper sense. And I'm looking forward to seeing the latest iteration of *Event/Horizon.*'

Steve realised he was on thin ice. 'I've abandoned it. I don't want to look at it for several months.'

'So, are you saying I can't see it?'

'Well, for now. Do you mind? You've got so much on your plate anyway.'

'I do mind a bit, but if that's what you want, then okay.'

Steve was anxious to change the subject as quickly as possible. 'What can I do to help prepare for Friday evening?'

'I'd like to give the house a bit of a clean-up. Do you have skills in that department?'

Steve laughed. 'I do. I think I got quite high marks from Ginny on that count.'

'Excellent and I doubt that my standards are as high as hers. But we'll leave that for tomorrow. Let's just have a bit of a lazy day today.'

'You're talking my language.'

## Friday 20 December 1974

GRACE HAD A TOWEL wrapped around her and was drying her hair. Steve was lying on the bed, watching her. He was already dressed for the evening, simply because he had nothing smart to change into.

'I'm sorry to interrupt your contemplation of *la femme à sa toilette*, but would you mind laying the table and putting a bottle of champagne in the fridge? I lost track of the time, but I'll be down in a moment to help.'

Steve went down to the kitchen. It took him a while to find the champagne. He still didn't know where things were kept. Before he'd finished laying the table, Grace appeared – now fully dressed, burnished and glowing. He was not used to seeing her in sophisticated evening wear. She suddenly seemed like a different person. 'You look amazing.'

'Thank you, Steve.'

'I'm sorry I haven't got any smarter clothes.'

'You look fine.'

Fifteen minutes later, the doorbell rang. Grace was dressing a salad. 'Would you mind letting them in?'

'Do they know I'm here?'

'No, but they won't be surprised.'

Steve went out into the hall and opened the door. In fact, Gary and Matt were momentarily taken aback. Gary said, 'Steve, you've resurfaced. Good to see you.'

'You too. Come in. Grace is doing something to some salad.'

The couple divested themselves of their coats and hung them on the hat stand to one side of the front door. Steve was pleased to see that neither of them had made an effort to dress up. He ushered them into the kitchen. Grace dried her hands, removed her striped apron and came across to greet them both with kisses and hugs.

Gary held her at arm's length. 'Ooh, someone looks glamorous. Is a new special friend joining us?'

Grace freed herself from his grasp and put her arm around Steve. 'No, he's already here.'

Gary looked blankly at the pair of them for a moment until the penny dropped. Smiling broadly, he said, 'Congratulations. This calls for a toast.'

Grace said, 'Steve, would you open the champagne?'

A few moments later, glass in hand, Grace said, 'You two are the first to know.'

Matt said, 'We are honoured. Here's to you both.'

Glasses clinked and champagne quaffed, Grace said, 'We are both terrified. It seems mad for all the obvious reasons, but we decided to go ahead anyway.'

Gary put his glass down, took Grace in his arms and kissed her. 'Where would any of us be without a bit of madness?'

Then releasing her, he turned to Steve and hugged and kissed him too. 'You're a lucky man. She's one in a million and she needs a loving companion. I know you'll look after her.'

Retrieving his glass, Gary said, addressing Steve, 'I wondered where you were hiding. I've had Butch trying to track you down.'

Steve looked worried. 'Me?'

'Yeah, I'll explain later.'

In the meantime, Matt was offering his own hugs to the couple.

Grace handed around some nibbles and invited everyone to take a seat around the big farmhouse table. Steve took the chair beside Grace and she squeezed his hand under the table. Then she said to Gary, 'Matt said you'd been very busy. Are you pulling a new show together?'

'Several new shows actually.'

'Several?'

'Yeah, I'm re-opening a theatre that's been dark for many years.'

'Where?'

'Here, in Cambridge.'

'Where in Cambridge?'

'Newmarket Road.'

'Really?'

'Yes, I've got a short-term lease on the old Festival Theatre.'

'The *what* theatre?'

'The Festival.'

'Which is in Newmarket Road?'

'Yes. Just beyond the Zebra pub.'

'I don't think I've ever noticed a theatre in Newmarket Road and I've been up and down that road many times. I used to be in digs in Auckland Road.'

'Well, it's definitely there. In fact, it's the oldest theatre in Cambridge, indeed one of the oldest in the country.'

'How is it that no one knows about it?'

'I suppose it's just another example of the great forgetting. The theatre was built in 1816. It operated until the 1870s when it became a nonconformist chapel. Over the next fifty years it fell into disrepair until in 1926 a local millionaire called Terence Gray acquired it. Gray was many things but in particular he was a follower of Gordon Craig, the theatre theorist and director, who also happened to be the son of Ellen Terry.

'Gray poured a huge amount of money into the building, remodelling it along modernist lines, so no proscenium, and promoting it as a crucible for the new drama. He ran the theatre for a number of years, but eventually became discouraged and gave up the project in the mid-nineteen-thirties. Once again the theatre went dark and was eventually acquired by the Arts Theatre and used as a wardrobe store and workshop.'

Steve said, 'But that's terrible. Why hasn't the Arts run it as a theatre?'

'They have enough trouble keeping the Arts itself financially viable without taking on another loss-making theatre space.'

Grace looked concerned. 'So why have they granted you the lease?'

'Because I'm paying them a considerable amount of money.'

'That's what I was afraid of. Are you putting yourself at financial risk?'

'To an extent, but I've got other backers, one or two of them with deep pockets. They all know they're not likely to see their money back.'

Grace could not hide her concern. 'So why are you doing it?'

'It's just something I've always wanted to do, put on a season of work of my own choosing. Not at the Festival specifically, but when I realised that the Arts were open to the proposal, that just made it seem all the more appealing. It is a truly beautiful building and it deserves to be wakened from its long slumber.'

Grace was now excited. 'When can we see it?'

'Soon. After Christmas.'

'And when do you hope to open?'

'At the moment the first night is scheduled for the beginning of March.'

'Ooh, that's not far off.'

'Quite. There's a huge amount of work that needs to be done just to ensure that the building complies with modern fire regulations and licensing conditions.'

'You've kept this all under your hat.'

'Yes, and you've had a lot on your plate too. I didn't want you putting on your dungarees and spending the evening whitewashing the cyclorama.'

'I couldn't think of anything nicer. But have you actually got people working on it at the moment?'

'Well, not at this precise moment. I've given them the weekend off.'

Matt said, 'He's only half-joking. He's had builders and decorators in round the clock for the last couple of weeks.'

Later on the short walk back to their own place, Matt said to Gary, 'Do you think that's a positive development, Grace and Steve?'

'Well, I'm glad she's not on her own. Steve is a nice guy and I'm sure it does her self-esteem no harm. But he's just a kid. He's not going to want to settle down with someone who's got her sights firmly fixed on becoming a professor. He'll have itchy feet before long.'

'Gaz, you can't protect her like that. There's no one who's going to be good enough for her as far as you're concerned.'

'But he'll break her heart.'

'More than Peter?'

'She had no illusions about Peter. She should have kicked him out years ago.'

'What did she see in him?'

'It's no good asking me. I have no idea why she persisted with him. Maybe she was just trying to prove that she hadn't made a terrible mistake right at the start. There was something distinctly unhealthy about the relationship. Peter, as you may have noticed, was domineering and lecherous, whereas I *get* Steve's appeal for her.'

'We all *get* Steve, Gary. Poor boy, he always seems completely bemused by the reaction he produces.'

'You can get a long way with a tight little arse like that.'

'He's not a tart, Gaz.'

'If you say so. You guitar players have to stick together, I suppose. I wonder if that girl Ginny knows what she's got herself into with Peter?'

'Oh, I think she knows what she's up to. She'll have Peter neatly trussed up in no time at all.'

'Well, it didn't take her long to suck all the vitality out of Steve and spit out the leavings.'

'I'm not sure that's actually the case. I'm not saying she didn't knock him off course a bit, but I think she discovered that he was curiously immune to her particular magic and turned her attention to a more rewarding victim.'

'Hmm, we will see. Anyway, it gave me pause for thought about asking Steve to be my assistant at the Festival. If he were to hurt Grace, I'd find it hard to work with him.'

'I wondered why you didn't tell him why you'd asked Butch to try and track him down. But honestly, Gaz, he's not going to hurt her and I think you'll get good value out of him. You know how highly Grace rates his intelligence.'

'Yeah. Even so, I think I'll sleep on it for a bit.'

At much the same time that Gary and Matt were discussing the new romance between Grace and Steve, Peter and Ginny were in a cab rattling back to the Barbican from the Inflexion Books Christmas party. Peter was in good spirits. The party had gone well. The staff had been pleased with their bonuses. It had also been the first public unveiling of Ginny to the rank and file of the firm. Of course, his business partners had already met her at a series of stylish dinners and had been suitably impressed, but this evening's event had been an opportunity for more junior colleagues to behold the thousand watt glamour of Virginia Stern.

Indeed it was as Virginia rather than as Ginny that she now wished to be known, at least to the wider world. Virginia Stern was how she had been known when she was a catwalk model. In the intervening years as she had lost her way in a grubbier milieu, she had been careful not to draw attention to her starry past. But that period was now over and she was ready to rejoin the glitterati. As a concession she was prepared to let Peter call her Ginny in the privacy of their own home, but as a matter of fact he was not at all against letting it be known that he was in a relationship with a former glamour model. It had already done wonders for the firm's public profile. He was looking forward to spending even more time in the gossip columns.

In the tumultuous days following the Frankfurt Book Fair, Peter had given little thought to Ginny's financial standing. It was her looks and her evident sexiness that attracted him. He was a reasonably wealthy man and was happy to subsidise her up to a point. What he hadn't expected was that her prospects might dwarf his. It was only after she had been living with him in his flat in the Barbican for some weeks that he came to understand that she was rather more than a beautiful, hippy chick.

The first time that Ginny had taken him to visit her ailing father, the opening exchanges with Godfrey had been chilly. But once it had been established that Peter had been brought up in Frankfurt, Godfrey's own birthplace, and was a member of the Jewish diaspora, Godfrey visibly warmed to him, especially after Peter let slip the fact that his father had been a judge in the Weimar Republic and that he himself was the chief executive of a successful publishing business. But Godfrey couldn't pretend that the fact that Peter was currently married to another woman wasn't unfortunate. He felt certain, however, that Peter would sort that out as soon as possible.

The encounter with Godfrey and a true appreciation of Ginny's background had also subtly, or perhaps not so subtly, altered the balance of power in the relationship with Ginny, a recalibration which had not escaped Ginny's notice either. In the early stages of their relationship Peter had been assertive, which one might say was his default mode. But now that he saw Ginny as the gateway to becoming a serious member of the bourgeoisie, he had begun treating her with more deference. This was a mode of behaviour that did not come naturally to him and indeed was not what Ginny found attractive in him. She, as befitted someone born to wealth, was prepared to do without money. Peter, as someone who had had a hard time establishing himself in the world, was unable to comprehend such flippancy.

But the real reason that he was feeling pleased with life and why he had felt confident enough to pay the staff bonuses was that Ginny's father had accepted, as confirmed by an ultrasound scan in one of his own clinics, that Ginny was pregnant and that Peter was the father of the child. He was still anxious that Peter should regularise his relationship with Ginny by marrying her as soon as his divorce from Grace could be arranged, but he was happy in the meantime to relax the conditions governing Ginny's, and by extension Peter's, access to his wealth. However, he was not prepared to dissolve the trust completely until Ginny and Peter had actually tied the knot. Even so, the substantial sum that had recently appeared in Ginny and Peter's joint account had temporarily solved Inflexion's cash flow problems.

In any case, Godfrey saw in Peter a man who would look after both the pennies and the pounds and who was also equipped to deal with Ginny's wayward tendencies. Peter certainly shared Godfrey's assessment of his own financial acumen, but was not so confident about being able to deal with Ginny's wayward tendencies. After all, he had already allowed Ginny to talk him into accepting her pregnancy by another man, a boy in effect. Had the firm not been so strapped for cash, he would certainly have urged her to seek a termination forthwith. It was ironic that having spent the best part of ten years countering Grace's maternal tendencies, here he was effectively committing himself to bringing up another man's child. Admittedly, access to the Stern millions softened the blow somewhat, but he was unable to resist the thought that Ginny had worked a number on him. Had he not had a vasectomy, would she have been quite so ready to declare the baby Steve's?

Ginny could see that Peter had something on his mind. 'What are you thinking about?'

Peter snapped out of his reverie. 'How beautiful you looked this evening. How deft you were with the hoi polloi. I hope you didn't find it too tedious.'

'No, it was good to see you in your natural environment. And to identify potential threats.'

'Threats? I'm the chief executive.'

'I mean threats to me, to us. That little Felicity couldn't keep her eyes off you.'

'Really. I didn't notice.'

'Pete, I don't know who does the hiring at your place, but you seem to have a job lot of dolly birds.'

'That's publishing, my darling. The galley slaves are mostly young women. I can assure you, though, that none of them interest me as much as you do.'

'Well, let's keep it like that.'

'Ginny, I've got my hands full with you in a pleasurable way and with Grace in not such a pleasurable way at the moment. I am not about to begin manoeuvres on another front.'

Ginny laughed. 'Speaking of Grace, I had a letter from Steve today.'

'That sounds like a *non sequitur* to me. Anyway, how did he get our address?'

'I gave it to him.'

'What?'

'In the sense that I put it at the top of my letter to him.'

'You wrote to Steve?'

'Yes. I want to send him a couple of drawings I did in Ainsworth Street, but I didn't know his current address.'

'Ginny, I'm not sure I like the idea of your being in touch with him. Especially not in view of recent developments. Does he know about the little alien?'

'Of course not. Nor is he going to. Anyway, I thought you might like to know that Steve is now living with Grace.'

Peter was silent for a few moments. Was Ginny winding him up? 'Really?'

'Well, he wasn't explicit about it, but the address he was writing from was your former address in Glisson Road.'

'That's absurd. It's outrageous.'

'I thought it was quite sweet actually.'

'It's ridiculous. She's fifteen years older than him for a start.'

'That's not as big an age gap as there is between us.'

'But it's different when the woman is older by that much.'

'I don't see anything wrong with it. Benefits on both sides, I would say.'

'I do not want to hear about Steve's ability to keep going all night.'

'That's not the direction my thoughts were taking.'

'Well, what direction were they taking?'

'It occurred to me that if we were dealing with a sexually fulfilled and financially secure woman, Grace might be persuaded to agree to a quickie divorce.'

'Well, yes, there is something in what you say, but there's not much we can do to ensure Grace's financial security.'

'On the contrary, we could sign over the whole of your interest in the Glisson Road property, if she agrees to expedite the filing of the divorce petition.'

'Ginny I have poured every last bean I have into that house. I don't mind splitting it fifty-fifty. But to hand over the lot would stick in the craw.'

'Pete, look at the big picture. I have no idea what your share is worth, but it is probably a fraction of what the Hampstead house is worth, not to mention the shares I will inherit in the clinics.'

'I want my own stake. I don't want to be beholden to the Stern millions.'

'You won't be. Now that we've managed to plug the cash flow hole, Inflexion under your dynamic leadership will be on the takeover trail. Growth by acquisition, I believe they call it.'

'They do. How do you know about that kind of thing?'

'Learned at my father's knee. The only thing he really liked to talk about was business strategy.'

'So what are you suggesting?'

'Pop up to Cambridge. Put your cards on the table. If she agrees to a quick divorce, she gets the house. If she doesn't agree within a fortnight, you'll fight her all the way.'

'Really?'

'No, it's a bluff.'

'Well, I'm not sure. In any case, the only free day I've got before I fly to New York is Saturday the twenty-eighth.'

'That's perfect.'

'Well, alright. I doubt she'll play ball, but it's worth a shot.'

'I'm so pleased we see eye to eye on this. I might even try and stop worrying so much about the girls in the office.'

Peter sniggered. 'Virginia Stern, you are quite an operator.'

'Don't you forget it, Peter Newman.'


It was a bitter Saturday morning in Edinburgh's New Town. Angie and Rob had been to a gig in Broughton Street the night before and had not got to bed until late, but it was nearly Christmas, so there was no imperative to get up betimes and trudge down to the university library. When they eventually woke, Rob volunteered to go and make the tea. He also wanted to check if there was a package from his publisher containing the page proofs of his first collection of poems. He let himself out of the flat and padded down the communal stairs in his dressing gown, painfully aware of how cold the flagstones were to his bare feet. He was looking forward to bringing back with him in the new year the slippers he had requested from his parents for Christmas. At the foot of the stairs he opened the mailbox for their flat, disappointed to see that there was no package. There were, however, several letters for him and for Angie, and one addressed to both of them in what he recognised as Steve Percival's illegible scrawl. He tucked the letters into the pocket of his dressing gown and went back up to the flat. A little while later, having made the tea, he climbed back into bed with Angie, who winced as his freezing feet came into contact with her warm leg. 'Don't touch me until you've warmed up.'

'I thought you might help me in that respect.'

'I think you've had enough warming up for one night.'

'It's a new day.'

'Not as far as I'm concerned.'

Rob, who was still wearing his dressing gown under the bed-clothes, pulled the small bundle of letters out of its pocket and leafed through them, passing over to Angie those that were addressed to her. 'There's one addressed to both of us, from Steve, if I'm not mistaken. Do you want to open it?'

Angie would have preferred to be the one to see it first. But it was still a matter of some sensitivity with Rob. She had tried to reassure him that she was no longer interested in Steve in that way, but he wasn't totally convinced. 'No, you read it and tell me what mess he's got himself into now.'

Rob opened the envelope. A few moments later, he said, 'Well, I'll be blowed!'

Angie was intrigued and now slightly worried. She hadn't really meant her comment about Steve getting himself into a mess. 'What's he say?'

Rob tossed the letter towards her. 'He and Ginny have split up. He's living with Grace now. Reading between the few lines of a very typically opaque Percival letter, *living with* does not seem to mean he is a lodger. But on the plus side, he and Grace, presumably, have invited us to stay with them when we go to Cambridge in January for the Flynn fest. You must have told him we were coming down because I didn't mention it in my letter.'

Glancing at Steve's letter, Angie said, 'Yeah, I did, but I didn't know that he and Ginny had split up and I certainly wasn't expecting him to invite us to Grace's place.' Which, strictly speaking, was true.

Rob, oblivious to the fact that Angie might have had some hand in the invitation, said, 'Well, that's very decent of them. I'm quite keen to meet Grace.'

'Me too. He used to talk about her a lot. Grace this and Grace that. I suppose he was very lucky to have such a supportive teacher. Many other supervisors would have washed their hands of him very early on.'

'But she's Grace Mitchell, isn't she? She's a published poet and she probably recognised Steve's gift.'

'I didn't know she was a poet. Steve never mentioned it.'

'Well, that's Steve for you. He probably didn't know either. He's not particularly plugged into the scene.'

'Yeah, solipsism, thy name is Percival.'

Rob laughed. 'Quite. Clearly he didn't waste much time brooding about Ginny. Do you know, when I met him after Martin's funeral, he said that he didn't consider himself successful with women?'

'He's monumentally naïve and I'm afraid many women find that attractive in a man, including me at one stage.'

'Really? I mean, really is that what women find attractive?'

'Rob, I don't want you trying to emulate Steve Percival. I much prefer you as the competent, hard-working, kind person you are.'

'But… a little boring?'

'Stop it. You are no such thing. Now that your extremities have warmed up, I will show you how false that idea is.'

She rolled over and drew Rob towards her. He did not resist, but he was aware that she was the one doing the showing, not him.

## Monday, 23 December 1974

As Grace and Steve were sitting opposite each other across a table on the train down to Liverpool Street on the Monday before Christmas, Grace said, 'So, Steve, if you're not certain about what we're doing, this is the time to back out because later today or perhaps tomorrow I will have told my parents about us. It will confuse them terribly, if I then have to tell them in a week or two that I was mistaken about you.'

Steve had certainly been upset that Ginny had never introduced him to her father or even allowed him to have the telephone number at her parental home. But Grace, by bringing her own parents' feelings into their fledgling relationship so early on, did seem to be putting unwarranted pressure on him. She had also said that she would ring him on Christmas Day to wish him a Happy Christmas, and she had asked whether she might introduce herself telephonically to Mavis at that point. He knew that he could rely on his mother to deal with the situation politely. But what would she make of it all?

Steve would have preferred to keep things under wraps and not involve others until they were really sure about what they were doing, but he didn't have the courage to raise his concerns. In truth, old Steve was once again in the ascendancy. 'No backing out for me. Not that I'm not terrified. You must know by now that I'm a terrible coward.'

'You'll be okay. I'm not saying that everything will work out between us or that it's going to be plain sailing. But I think we need to be bold and give ourselves a chance.'

When she spoke like this, he felt everything was possible and he would do his best to live up to her expectations. But he was afraid that once he was out of her orbit, he would find his confidence

73

wavering. He had also sensed that Gary and Matt, well, Gary in particular, had been less than enthusiastic about their liaison. But knowing now that Gary and Grace had once been lovers, he felt there was possibly an element of jealousy there, even though Gary had come out long ago and was happily living with Matt. They had been young lovers, so no one was ever going to know Grace the way he'd known her. For the same reason perhaps, Steve had been finding it hard to accept Rob as a suitable partner for Angie, even though Rob was unfailingly kind and helpful to Steve himself.

Just before they got to Liverpool Street, Grace slid a small package across the table. 'It's a little Christmas present. It's nothing much. There's not been much time for either of us to organise anything and I don't yet know the things you like.'

Steve was horrified, but mainly because it hadn't occurred to him to get her anything. 'Grace, I'm sorry I haven't got a present to give you in return. I was planning to give you something after Christmas.'

She waved away his paltry and untruthful excuse. 'It's just a token. I know things are tight for you financially, but we'll sort that out soon.'

He put the neatly wrapped gift in his bag, feeling miserable and hating himself.

Grace could see the emotion clouding his face. 'Steve, I'm not disappointed. I wasn't expecting you to give me anything and I'm sorry I've put you on the spot. You are my Christmas present. We'll celebrate properly at New Year.'

Steve offered her a sickly smile of thanks.

They went their separate ways at Liverpool Street, Grace descending to the District and Circle line to travel on to Paddington, and Steve exiting the concourse to hop a 43 bus to Islington. He sat on the top deck so that he had a good view of the city streets, despite the unpleasantness of the smoke that filled the cabin. It was good to be back in dirty old London.

Half an hour later, he stepped off the bus and made his way to the address in Duncan Terrace Alan had given him. It was a tall Georgian house which had seen better days, but convenient for the Angel tube and the pubs of Upper Street and Islington Green. He rang the bell and almost immediately the front door opened and Alan's smiling face appeared. 'Thank goodness you're here. I thought we were going to miss the lunchtime session. Let's get going. The York is only a couple of minutes away.'

Soon they were seated in front of their pints. Alan wiped the slight froth from his lips with the back of his hand and said, 'How've you been? Sorry I haven't been in touch.'

'That's okay. I didn't expect you to be. I imagine you were having too much of a good time. I'm sorry to hear about you and Di, though.'

'Yeah, I was a complete idiot.'

'Couldn't keep your hands off the demoiselles?'

'That kind of thing.'

'Di doesn't take prisoners.'

'No.'

'One of your students?'

'*Naturellement.*'

'So why aren't you still there?'

'It's fine in the summer, but not quite the same in the winter. Even Nice has bad weather and the language students fly south, or something.'

'But law, Al…'

'I know, I know. I keep telling myself that I'm just buying time. Anyway, London's a gas. You should move down here.'

'Perhaps you're forgetting I come from London. I'm just on my way to spend Christmas with my mum. Admittedly, our part of London is on the other side of the river.'

'You could move into my place. There's a room coming free at the beginning of January.'

'I'd love to, but I'm a bit tied up at the moment.'

'Angie won't let you?'

'Angie and I are no longer together. Haven't been for ages.'

'I don't believe it. So who replaced Angie? Can I guess?'

'I doubt it. It's complicated. I seem to remember your saying look, but do not touch.'

'You didn't have a go at Ginny?'

Steve nodded.

'So how come you're still alive? Didn't Jon try to rearrange important bits of your anatomy?'

'No, he kind of welcomed it. He's been touring with Alien Hand Syndrome.'

'Cool. So he asked you to look after her and you took the offer seriously.'

'You could put it like that. I'll give you chapter and verse another time, but it all got very weird.'

'That I can imagine.'

'Basically, Ginny and I transformed the Ainsworth Street house and garden. Made it into a des res.'

'That doesn't sound like you.'

'I just did what I was told.'

'Ooh, nice!'

Steve chuckled. 'Yeah, it was.'

'So how come you're going home to your mum's?'

'Ginny went off with someone else.'

'Bummer!'

'Yup.'

'Jon didn't come back and reclaim her?'

'Nope.'

'Anyone I know?'

'I doubt it. His name is Peter Newman and he's the boss of Inflexion Books.'

'Blimey, I've seen his name in the papers. That was a bit of a change of gear. So you're in Ainsworth Street on your own now?'

'No, the lease came to an end and I've been in a bedsitter in Tenison Road.'

'Present perfect tense rather than present.'

'Well spotted. You must have done languages at Cambridge.'

'Teaching English in Nice, actually.'

'Quite. Well, I am, as it were, betwixt and between.'

'Your tale gets no clearer.'

'I'm moving in with someone else.'

'Another hot chick?'

'Yes, although she probably doesn't think of herself like that.'

'Do I know her?'

'You do. Grace Mitchell.'

Al scratched his head. 'The only Grace Mitchell I know is the woman who was your twentieth-century French literature supervisor.'

'Yes, her.'

Al scrutinised Steve's face, looking for the giveaway that this was all some elaborate joke, but Steve continued staring at him impassively, even somewhat lugubriously.

'Steve, I really don't know what to say, but how the fuck did that happen?'

'When we've got more time, I'll give you the nitty-gritty, but suffice it to say that Grace and Peter were – actually still are – married.'

'Okay, so I'm getting a sense of full-on shenanigans.'

'That would be a way of putting it.'

'You've clearly got yourself involved in a three dimensional game of chess.'

'Except I feel that I'm one of the pieces rather than a player.'

'All the more reason to come down here and share with me.'

'When I say I'm moving in with Grace, I mean we're living together, sharing a bed.'

'Really? I mean, really? She's a fair bit older than you.'

'So what? I've fancied her from the first day I saw her.'

'Gazing dreamily at her cleavage during a supervision on Flaubert?'

'Exactly. She's a published poet as well.'

'Of course, she is. What's her stuff like?'

'Actually, I haven't read any of it yet.'

'Isn't that a bit of an oversight?'

'You're absolutely right. Thanks for the tip.'

'What does your mum think about it?'

'She doesn't know yet.'

'So saving it up for a little chat over the mince pies?'

'Trying not to think about that aspect of things at the moment.'

'You'll be alright. Your mum's cool.'

'She is, but I don't like to upset her.'

'Will I be able to meet Grace?'

'I don't see why not. I haven't officially moved in yet. We're talking to our respective families over the Christmas period to get them used to the idea.'

'Bloody hell. It sounds serious.'

'It is. I'm sure you could come and stay for a weekend once we've settled down.'

'You settle down, Percival? Do me a favour.'

The barman called time. Alan emptied his glass. 'Just before they chuck us out, have you got any theory about how all this happened?'

'It was that sodding poem I was writing.'

'That's another *non sequitur*, Steve. If you'd said you overdid it with Jon's homegrown, I would be nodding sagely, or maybe even thymely. But poems don't distort reality.'

'That's where you're wrong, Al. Anyway, to give you some credit, the outward sign of the inward manifestation was a tiny tab of lysergic acid.'

'So you've tripped?'

'Just the once. I'll tell you about it another time, but I need to get a move on now. I need to buy my mum a Christmas present.'

'How do I get in touch with you?'

Steve scribbled his new address and telephone number on a scrap of paper. Alan glanced at it and then stuffed it in his top pocket. 'I'll be up there soon, just to make sure Miss Mitchell knows what she's dealing with.'

Steve laughed uncomfortably.

As the Paddington to Penzance train pulled into Castle Cary, Grace could see her father's battered old Morris Traveller in the station car park. It was high time he got a new car, she thought. But Gideon was always saying that it had another 10,000 miles under the bonnet at the very least. Being a bit of a mechanic, he could fix virtually anything that went wrong with the car himself. Not so long ago, he had even fitted a new head gasket. Grace wasn't sure what kind of thing a gasket was. But Gideon assured her that the car was running better than it had for many a year.

Grace normally looked forward to seeing her parents, but this time she was apprehensive. They knew about the breakup with Peter, of course, but they had only spoken on the phone and Grace had kept details to a minimum. The fact was that neither of them had ever warmed to Peter. June, in particular, had considered him bumptious and self-opinionated. But he had been their son-in-law for nearly ten years, and June and Gideon had been unaware of the difficulties in the marriage. In addition, Gideon, who was a recently retired vicar, took the rather old-fashioned view that marriage was a sacrament, perhaps not in the way baptism or the Eucharist were, but it did mean that he was very much opposed to divorce. Despite these views he was a kindly and, in other respects, liberal man.

Even as a little girl, Grace had felt able to confide in her father and had relied on him countless times to intercede for her with her mother, who was a very different kettle of parental fish. Of course, June was proud of Grace's academic achievement, but she felt that Gideon had given in to their daughter far too often when she was younger. In June's view, Grace was now a headstrong and impetuous young woman. Gideon, on the other hand, was of the opinion that Grace was simply taking after her mother and would not have done so well at Cambridge without an element of feistiness about her. He seldom dared advance this view, however. When, on one occasion, he had misguidedly done so, it had taken some time for the air to clear.

Although June was the more formidable opponent, she was not without her weak spots, one of which was that she longed to be a grandmother and was aware of Peter's reluctance to oblige in that regard. Of course, it was too early for Grace to go into the idea of Steve being the father of her child. But, although an exaggeration of the facts, it might influence her mother's perception of Grace's position to suggest that the reason that she and Peter had now separated was over the issue of having a child. So while the arrival of Steve on the scene might be seen as troubling, the fact of Peter's departure might be seen in a positive light. The other aspect of her mother's character Grace was relying on was that she was a contrarian. She was instinctively against the opinions of others, and in particular her husband's. Although the wife of a vicar and a conspicuous figure in parish life, her faith was only skin deep and in the confines of the family she took delight in opposing, indeed mocking, his piety.

Thus Grace was hoping to arrange things so that it was Gideon who would be the one to inform June of Grace's situation and with luck add some mild critical commentary about how disappointed he was from a Christian point of view. This might be sufficient to prompt June to automatically dismiss his concerns and instead advocate supporting their daughter in what must be a difficult time for her. If that required them to accept her new young man, then so be it, even if there was an unfortunate age gap. The relationship probably wouldn't last long and Grace would soon find a new partner worthy of her. Grace was far from confident this ploy would work. She might well find she had misread her parents and was facing a united front of disapproval. But what the hell!

She stepped onto the platform. She could now see Gideon standing beside the car, scanning the coaches of the arriving train. If he'd come on his own, it would give her the twenty minutes or so alone with him that she needed. A few minutes later she was freeing herself from her father's embrace and climbing into the front passenger seat of the Morris. Gideon, who was a tall man with a bad back, folded himself gingerly into the driver's seat. Soon they were proceeding at a stately pace along the Somerset lanes. It reminded Grace of times when her father used to drive her to school or to a friend's house. Those had often been their best conversations. There was something about sitting side by side on the way somewhere that made conversation easier than if they had been sitting face to face for that sole purpose.

Gideon leaned his head towards her slightly, indicating that he had something to say. 'I know it's probably the last thing you want to talk about, so perhaps it's best if we get it out of the way before we get home. I'm afraid I have no control over anything your mother might say or want to ask. No doubt she'll do that woman to woman, when I'm out of the way.'

'No, Daddy. I'm happy to talk.'

'Thank you. So it's final, this breakdown between you and Peter?'

'It is, I'm afraid.'

'Do you mind me asking if there was a definable cause?'

'I thought it was the right moment for me to have a child.'

'But he didn't?'

'It wasn't a matter of timing. He simply didn't want to have a child with me.'

'So it wasn't that there was someone else involved?'

'I'm afraid there was, a mutual friend unfortunately.'

'Oh, that is hurtful. The silly man.'

'No, I'm the silly one. I should have seen that things had not been good for some time.'

'Is there a chance he might see the error of his ways?'

'I doubt it, but even if he did, it is too late.'

'*Friendship cannot exist without Forgiveness of Sins continually*. There's something to be said for companionship even if other things are missing.'

'I'm not knocking companionship and Blake's point is a fair one. But there has been precious little of that commodity recently. I doubt that Mother was continually absolving you of your sins.'

'You'd be surprised. Good works in the public realm may well be sins when viewed from within the marriage.'

'Are you saying that mother saw your parish work as a sin within the marriage?'

'That is a rather stark way of putting it, but not so far off the mark.'

'Oh, Daddy, I'm sure that's not the case.'

'Well, let's not make a big deal about it. I don't want to pry into matters between you and Peter. I just don't like to see you on your own.'

'Well, to turn your formulation around, it is also possible to be lonely in a relationship.'

'I don't doubt it.'

'Look, Daddy, I've been dreading this moment and I'm glad we have a few moments to ourselves. The fact of the matter is that I do have a friend.'

'By friend do you mean a gentleman admirer?'

Grace was amused by the idea of Steve as a gentleman admirer. But now that she came to think about it, he was rather gentlemanly.

'Does he predate Peter's indiscretion?'

'Not as an admirer, to use your terminology, but I have known him for more than two years.'

'Well, that's encouraging. Is he a colleague?'

'In a sense, yes. He was one of my students.'

'So a little younger than you.'

'Quite a lot younger, actually.'

'I see. So it's not necessarily a long term relationship.'

'To be honest, that would probably be the case whatever age my gentleman admirer was.'

'But I take it that you are living together.'

'Not at the moment, but we're planning to do so.'

Gideon seemed momentarily relieved. 'Is he a good man?'

'Yes, I think he is.'

'Are we going to meet him?'

'I hope so. Do you think Mummy will be upset?'

'Perhaps upset is the wrong word. Perplexed maybe.'

'I don't want to perplex or upset her or you. But I wanted you both to know that I'm approaching my life in a positive spirit. I'm as happy as I've been for a long time.'

'Does your gentleman have a name?'

'Steve.'

'And Steven is the source of this happiness?'

'Yes. Although the fact that I will be a university lecturer next term is also contributing.'

'Goodness, you kept that under your hat. Congratulations.'

'The only sadness is that it is as a consequence of the unexpected death of my own dear teacher and mentor, Hilda Jedburgh.'

'Oh dear, what happened?'

'An aneurysm.'

'God rest her soul.'

'Yes, I miss her and owe her a lot. But the main reason I'm happy is that Steve has been a great support.'

Gideon was silent for a moment. Grace wasn't sure if he'd heard what she'd said. Eventually he said, 'Isn't it a bit soon to be forming a new relationship? There's no need to rush things.'

'It's not something I was planning to do. It just happened.'

'Because you're in a vulnerable state. Peter may realise he has made a terrible mistake and ask you to take him back.'

'I don't trust him any more, and I'm running out of time to have a child.'

'You can't very well have a child with this young man.'

Gideon, whether by chance or cunning, had asked her the very question she didn't want to have to respond to. 'Physically, there's no reason why I can't have a child with Steve, but that is not what we are thinking about at the moment.'

But Gideon was not about to be taken in by a blatant piece of sophistry. 'So from the perspective of fertility, isn't your dalliance with this young man also eating into your time to have a child?'

'Okay, it's true. I do think Steve is a suitable person to be the father of my child. But we are not at that stage yet. I didn't intend to take the discussion that far forward. I just wanted you and Mummy to understand how things were in my life and for you to get to know Steve. You know how it is, even with the best will in the world, we might not succeed in having a child.'

'Maybe there are times when we have to put our trust in the Lord to save us from ourselves.'

'You know I don't believe that. Why should God worry about whether I can have a baby or not?'

'God worries about every single one of us.'

'Daddy, I don't want to have a theological debate with you. What I am saying is that I am not with Peter anymore because he left me. I didn't throw him out. One of the reasons he left me is because I wanted to have a baby. When he did so, Steve was around to comfort me. Steve was not the cause of him leaving me. He has always been very proper. We are not living together yet, but we plan to start doing so in the new year, and we wanted to tell our families what we are planning to do. Whether I have a baby with Steve or not is a matter for further discussion. At this stage, it is just hypothetical.'

Despite that proviso, Grace realised that in response to her father's gentle probing she had already gone further in revelations than she had agreed with Steve.

'So you have had some discussion with him on the subject.'

'We have discussed lots of things as you do when you fall in love with somebody.'

'So you are in love with him?'

'You know love comes in many different guises.'

'Grace, there is only one love.'

'Daddy, that is too reductionist.'

'Well, does he love you?'

'I think he does in his own way. More importantly, I trust him. He is an intelligent, decent young man. He was one of my best students. We have a lot in common. He is knowledgeable about French culture, he is a poet and he is a runner. He is many other things besides.'

'Even so, I find it hard to believe you have fallen in love with someone so much younger than you.'

'It is relatively common when it is the man who is older. Is there any logic to that? Is it that women are still not the equals of men?'

'No, of course not.'

'Look, Daddy, I don't expect you to be delighted. This is a lot to take in. But I wanted to have a talk with you first because I'm afraid Mummy will be very upset. So if you don't mind, I won't say anything when we get back until you have had a chance to manage her expectations. I did think of leaving it until I was about to go back to Cambridge, but it seemed that that was even more cowardly than asking you to intercede for me.'

'My lovely girl, I am happy to do what you ask and I will support you in whatever you decide to do. I just wanted to understand your thinking better.'

'Thank you, Daddy. Let's do try and have a lovely Christmas. I may not be a believer, but I love midnight Mass and the carols.'

Later that evening, when the supper things had been cleared away and they were having a postprandial drink in the snug sitting room around a blazing log fire, June settled herself in her favourite armchair, took a sip of her Bristol Cream and said, 'Your father explained to me, when you were having a rest after your journey, about your plan to have a child with this young man you have taken up with. I must say I am rather disappointed that you did not have the courage to confide in me.'

'I knew you'd be upset.'

'I think the person most upset here is your father. You must know that what you are planning flies in the face of all his values. I know you think you can persuade him of nearly anything, but you're wrong. He is obdurate when it comes to certain fundamental matters. I think you would have done better to confide in me first and I would have brought him around gently to see that what you are proposing, while unusual, is not entirely out of the question for a person in your situation.'

Gideon spluttered at this travesty of the way the earlier conversation between him and his wife had gone. Grace strove to prevent any sign of a smile showing on her face. She kept her head bowed in a posture of repentance.

June continued. 'Of course you are an adult, entitled to and capable of making your own decisions, but I think it would be only fair to us if we were allowed to meet this young man quite soon. In the end, you can do whatever you want, but I am sure you would not want to fill our declining years with feelings of bitterness. So, now that we no longer have to fear an encounter with Mr Newman, perhaps you would consider inviting us to Glisson Road one weekend soon and introducing us to Steve or perhaps bringing him here to meet us.'

'Mummy, I'd be delighted to. I am grateful to both of you for being so understanding.'

June took another sip of her sherry. 'Does Steve have a second name?'

'Yes, Percival.'

'Oh, how dashing!'


Earlier that same day, leaving the pub after his drink with Al, Steve had remembered that there was a good bookshop in Camden Passage. Grateful for the unplanned opportunity to buy his mother a Christmas present and thus to prove that he wasn't a completely neglectful person, he'd stepped into the shop and surveyed the books that were being pushed for the Christmas season.

His mother was keen on thrillers and he noticed that John Le Carré had a new book out, *Tinker, Tailor, Soldier, Spy*. With luck, she hadn't got it yet. He also noted that both Muriel Spark and Iris Murdoch had new novels out. He flipped through Murdoch's *The Sacred and Profane Love Machine*, wondering if it might be a bit too much for his mother. The only book he had read by Murdoch was *The Black Prince* which was distinctly weird and unsettling, yet undoubtedly brilliant. He picked up the Spark. He hadn't read any of her books, but he had seen, as almost everyone had, the film of *The Prime of Miss Jean Brodie* with the wonderful pairing of Maggie Smith and Robert Stephens. He leafed through this new addition to her extensive catalogue, *The Abbess of Crewe*, a novel set in a

Benedictine convent. Mightn't that be a bit too pious for his mother? He glanced at the first few pages. Despite the setting, the text wasted no time in generating a mood of cognitive dissonance in which a very worldly abbess appeared to have bugged the precincts of the convent. This seemed much more his mother's thing. He picked up the Le Carré and the Spark for his mother and, on a whim, the Murdoch for himself. He carried them across to the sales counter and paid, realising as he did so, that the purchases had seriously depleted the cash he was carrying.

At the Angel station he bought his ticket and descended in the rickety lift to the platform. Soon, Steve was boarding the southbound train for Morden. He got off at Borough and made his way to the flat in Trinity Church Square where he had grown up. Unfortunately he had mislaid his own key to the flat in his various moves around Cambridge, and had also omitted to tell his mother what time he was likely to arrive. So it was possible she was not home yet and he would have to wait in the vicinity until she got back. But a few moments after ringing the bell, the house door swung open and his mother greeted him, a look of delight on her face. 'Steve. Come in, come in.'

They walked up the stairs to the upper flat and, once inside, Steve gave his mother a big hug. 'Ma, it's so lovely to see you. I'm sorry that I haven't been in touch.'

She waved a hand to hush him. 'Let's have a nice cup of tea first.'

He followed her into the kitchen, sat down at the little kitchen table and watched her fondly as she put the kettle on. A few minutes later, there were tea cups and saucers in front of them and a plate of biscuits between them, as they faced each other across the table. Mavis said, 'I'm sorry if it feels like I've been hounding you, but I really did need to talk to you.'

'You're not ill, are you?'

'No, not as far as I know.'

'You said you had something important to tell me.'

'I do. I'm going abroad for some time, maybe as much as a year.'

'Where? How?'

'I'm going to West Berlin. I've had to make several trips there in the last few months. My department now needs someone there more permanently and have asked me if I'd be prepared to spend a year there.'

'I didn't realise that your work involved foreign travel.'

'But you knew I worked for the Foreign Office.'

'Yes, but I thought you must do an administrative or a clerical job. Why else would we live in a flat?'

'Apart from the fact that I have been a single parent for nearly all your life, not everyone who works for a department of state is a high earner.'

'So what is your job then?'

'I can't go into the details, but this is a great opportunity for me. When you were growing up, I was unable to put myself forward for this kind of work, but now that you've completed your education, there's no problem.'

'When are you going?'

'Soon after Christmas.'

'Will you have time to visit me in Cambridge before you go?'

'I'm not sure. Do you want me to visit you? You seem to have been trying to avoid letting me know what's going on in your life.'

'Maybe I just learned from you.'

Mavis laughed. 'Fair point. So, how is Ginny and how are things in Ainsworth Street?'

Steve looked glum. 'It's a long story.'

'We've got plenty of time.'

Steve drained his tea cup and then launched into a long account of the breakdown in his relationship with Ginny and the subsequent move to Tenison Road, at which point he stopped, not quite sure how to introduce developments between him and Grace. Mavis stood up. 'I think we need a fresh pot of tea.'

Steve nodded. As Mavis washed up the cups and saucers, she said over her shoulder, 'Since then you haven't heard from Miss Stern?'

'I've had one letter. She wants to send me some of her artwork.'

'Why does she want to do that?'

'She's a talented artist and she made a sketch book for me of our time together, but there were no images of her in the book. So she's sending me some now.'

'Is she trying to keep communications open with you?'

'I suppose so, but she hasn't suggested meeting.'

'Would you meet her if she did?'

Steve didn't answer immediately. Mavis put the fresh pot of tea and the clean cups and saucers on the table. She sat down again. 'Your silence suggests you might.'

Steve pulled himself together. 'No, I wouldn't.'

'But isn't the idea of her sending you pictures or photos of herself just a way of keeping you on a string?'

'Yes, perhaps it is. But if that's the effect she's hoping for, she's got it all wrong because I'm with someone else now.'

'Who is this new person?'

'Her name's Grace Mitchell.'

'Who used to be one of your teachers.'

'Yes, how did you know?'

'You told me.'

'Did I also tell you she was married to Peter Newman?'

'No, but I knew that too. And remains married to him until they divorce.'

'How did you know that?'

'Your ex-girlfriend, Ginny, or as she is better known, Virginia Stern, has been much in the gossip columns of late with her new partner, Peter Newman, the chief executive of Inflexion Books and the estranged husband of Grace Mitchell, a don at Cambridge University. The one person who is not named at all in this *scandale* is Steve Percival.'

Steve shuddered. 'That's a relief.'

'Steve, why are you getting yourself mixed up in all this nonsense?'

'I'm not mixed up in it.'

'But you just said that you were with Grace Mitchell.'

'Well, I'm not actually with her. I live in a bedsitter in Tenison Road and she lives in a house about ten minutes' walk away. We've fallen in love and I'm going to move in with her.'

'Isn't the truth that you have both been hurt by the people you were with and you are taking refuge with each other? I assume she's somewhat older than you.'

'So was Ginny.'

'Well, of course you never let me meet Ginny.'

'I'm sorry, Ma. It all got a bit frantic, but I would like you to meet Grace.'

'Does she know about this idea of yours?'

'Yes, she wants to meet you.' Steve nearly said that it had been Grace's suggestion, but that sounded as if Steve was not quite so enthusiastic.

'When is this meeting to be?'

'I didn't know you were going away, so as soon as possible.'

'I am flying to Berlin on the seventeenth of January, so it will have to be before that, preferably the weekend of the eleventh and twelfth.'

'I am sure that will be fine. I will be speaking to Grace later. I hope you don't mind I gave her this telephone number.'

'So where is Grace?'

'She's spending Christmas with her parents. They live in Somerset. Her father's a vicar.'

'What do her parents think of their daughter taking up with someone who used to be her student?'

'I don't know, but Grace says she wants me to meet them, so that we are not hiding anything from anyone.'

'Well, that's a welcome change from your previous situation.'

'Ma, I think you'll like her. She's an amazing person.'

'I'm sure she is, but I think I've heard you say that about other young women.'

'No, this is different.'

'And what are you doing to keep body and soul together? Are you still at the theatre?'

'No, that came to an end.'

'So, you're signing on?'

'No, I'd saved some money.' He thought it better not to mention the money that Ginny had given him.

'That's going to run out at some point, isn't it?'

'Yes, but I won't have to pay rent at Grace's until I get a job.'

'Have you tried getting one?'

'Yes, but it's difficult right now. I'll have another bash at it after Christmas.'

'Steve, you are my only child and I love you dearly, but you do seem to be doing things the hard way, and I fear for you.'

'Ma, I'm okay. I've never been happier.'

'I seem to recall that your excuse earlier in the year was that you were writing a poem and it was going to be published.'

'The guy who was going to publish it died. Anyway, the poem wasn't any good. I destroyed it.'

'After all that work and everything you sacrificed.'

Steve wished he hadn't said that. Doing his best to sound positive, he said, 'I will write something better.'

Mavis shook her head sadly, 'Steve, Steve, when are you going to grow up?'

Steve got up from the table, knelt down and took her hand. 'Ma, don't be angry with me. I love you. I'm okay. When you've met Grace, I'm sure you'll realise what I'm saying is true.'

He rested his head on her lap and she stroked his head. 'I hope so. Anyway, thank you for coming home for Christmas. It would have been odd not having you here. I've got everything in. Let's just have a lovely time together, like we used to. There's no need to go out, unless the weather is nice enough for a walk.'

Later that evening, Steve and his mother were sitting in the living room, listening to LPs of classical music and leafing through the family photo albums. They were both drinking glasses of red wine. Steve had just turned over the LP when the telephone in the hall rang. Mavis said, 'I wonder who that could be ringing at this time of night.'

Steve, with some trepidation, thought he knew who it might be. Mavis went out to the hall. He heard her say, 'Oh, hello. Steve said you might ring. I'm very pleased to speak to you and I look forward to meeting you soon.'

He was unable to hear what Grace was saying. She had probably hoped that he would be the one to answer the phone. But even though his mother did not really approve of developments, she was a good-natured person and would not treat Grace discourteously. He then heard his mother say, 'I would love to come and stay with you for the weekend, but I am afraid the only free weekend I have before I fly to Berlin is the weekend of the eleventh and twelfth of January.'

There was another contribution from Grace, and then Mavis said, 'No, it's a work posting for a year in the first place. That's why I wanted to see Steve so urgently.'

Finally, Mavis said, 'I'm so glad we've had this conversation. I will go and get Steve.'

Hearing this, Steve stepped out into the hall, took the receiver from his mother and said, 'Hello, how are you?'

'Hi, darling. Much better now. I was dreading making this call. I knew your mother would answer, but she sounds absolutely delightful and I'm so pleased she can come and stay with us.'

Steve wasn't sure he'd ever been called darling by anyone before, not even his mother. She didn't use that kind of endearment. But it was lovely hearing Grace's voice. 'How has it been with your parents?'

'Tricky, but everything is out in the open now.'

'Were they angry or upset?'

'No, perplexed is the term we're using. I can't go into details now, but we can exchange notes after Christmas. But well done for keeping to your side of the bargain. I know it can't have been easy for you either.'

'My mother seemed to have worked out quite a lot of it. There's been stuff in the papers about Ginny and Peter. Your name was mentioned as well.'

Grace expostulated. 'Oh, for goodness' sake! Anyway we'd best not make this a long call. I'll ring again on Christmas Day, unless you'd like to ring me.'

'Grace, I don't think I have the courage to do that.'

Grace laughed. 'Only teasing. I'll ring in the late afternoon. So pleased to have spoken to your mum. Night, night.'

Steve wished her a slightly more formal goodnight and hung up. He went back into the living room and retrieved his glass of wine. He looked imploringly at his mother. 'What did you think?'

'She sounds very nice. She was well-mannered and sensitive. I am almost won over. But let us wait until she and I have met face to face. I heard you ask her how things had been with her parents. What did she say?'

'She said they were perplexed. But she didn't want to go into any details.'

'Oh, dear. Poor Steve. It looks like it's going to be trickier for you than for her. In the way of these things, I would say that it's her father who is the one who is more upset.'

'Why do you say that?'

'A father is never completely comfortable about entrusting his daughter to another man. A vicar probably has all sorts of other reservations as well.'

'Stop it, Ma. You're worrying me.'

'Only teasing.'

Steve wasn't amused. 'That's what Grace said too.'

Mavis smiled. 'Maybe Miss Mitchell and I have more in common than I first thought.'

## Christmas Day, 1974

AFTER LUNCH ON CHRISTMAS Day, Mavis said to Steve, 'This has been lovely. I do miss you, you know.'

'I miss you too, Ma. I'm sorry I've been so tied up in my own life.'

'It's your age. You're trying to find the right person to share it with.'

'I've found her.'

'Maybe you have.'

'I wish you'd find a friend too.'

'Do you? Then you'd no longer have my undivided attention?'

'But you must get lonely sometimes.'

'Oh, I'm too old to go through all that nonsense.'

'You're not too old. You *are* a beautiful, interesting woman.'

'Be careful what you wish for, Steve.'

Changing the subject, she said, 'There are some presents on the tree. I think it's time we opened them. Would you mind being master of ceremonies?'

Steve gathered the parcels from under the little artificial Christmas tree. He handed Mavis the two books that he'd bought for her and wrapped the previous night. There were three parcels for him, two from his mother and the present that Grace had given him on the train. Mavis opened her presents and laughed. 'Thank you, Steve. I love Le Carré. He gives the impression of knowing what he's writing about.'

'I hope you haven't read either of these. They only came out this year.'

'Oh, no. I'm never that up to date.'

It was impossible to tell if she was lying or not. She folded the wrapping paper carefully. 'Your turn.'

Steve opened the two presents from his mother, a jumper in one and socks and handkerchiefs in the other. 'Thank you, Ma. Very handy, especially the jumper. Cambridge gets very chilly in the winter.'

He then opened the present from Grace. It was a copy of her book of poems, *The Abyss Looks Back*. He leafed through it, immediately getting a sense of a body of work far beyond his capabilities. He was simultaneously delighted and downcast.

Mavis said, 'May I look?'

Steve nodded. Mavis read the author biography on the back cover carefully and then opened the slim volume and read the handwritten inscription: *For Steve, Looking forward to being together. With heartfelt love and gratitude, Grace*. Mavis blinked away a tear, turned to a page at random and tried to make sense of one of the poems. After a few moments, she handed the book back to Steve. 'So you and Grace do have something in common.'

'We have a lot in common.'

'Is this the kind of thing you write too?'

'This is the first time I've actually seen her poetry. I haven't had the time to take it in yet. But we've talked a lot about poetry and I know the kind of thing she likes. I should have looked at her own stuff a long time ago. She says that the problem with my work…' He was about to say that she considered his work too phallocentric but thought better of it. 'She says that I need to read more poetry by women and so she's started me off with her own work.'

Mavis was rapidly adjusting her view of Grace Mitchell, but was still amazed that the person she still thought of as her little boy could affect a mature and intelligent woman so profoundly. Maybe Mavis was the one who needed to update her ideas. Steve closed the book, saving the first intense read for later.

Mavis said, 'I've got two other things for you. Not Christmas presents exactly.'

She handed him an envelope. 'Go on, open it.'

Steve opened it and withdrew a cheque made payable to him for £500. He stared at it as if he'd never seen a cheque before. 'What's this for?'

'For you. I should have thought it was obvious.'

'But why?'

'Because you're my son and I want to help you through this difficult time.'

'But Ma, you can't afford this.'

'Steve, as I've said to you before, you don't know what I can and can't afford. I am sure you will use it wisely.'

She then handed him a slim leather key wallet. 'I presume you've lost your keys to the flat. So here are a new set of keys. You are welcome to use the flat whenever you like. Sheena, a friend at work, will be looking in from time to time to pick up mail and make sure the flat is secure. She will also organise a cleaner to come in. Sheena's number is in the wallet. If you do come to stay, please let Sheena know. We don't want her calling the police. You can leave a message on her answering machine.'

'Thank you, Ma, for the money and for the keys. I will treat the flat properly.'

'You'd better. Sheena is not one to be trifled with.'

As an afterthought, Steve said, 'Will I be able to visit you in Berlin?'

'I don't see why not.'

'With Grace?'

'Of course.'

In the evening the phone rang. Mavis said, 'That's probably for you. I'm not expecting any calls.'

Steve went through to the hall and answered the phone. It was, as Mavis had surmised, Grace. After an exchange of notes about the respective Christmas lunches and, in Grace's case, a brief account of the Christmas service at Wells Cathedral, Steve said, 'Thank you for *The Abyss Looks Back* and for the lovely dedication. It brought tears to my mother's eyes.'

'Not yours?'

'I made a heroic effort to retain my composure.'

'What did you think of the work?'

'I haven't taken it in fully yet. I'm waiting until after my mother has gone to bed. I want to give the book my full attention. But I am very touched by the gift. Thank you. I'm sorry I didn't get you anything.'

'You didn't have the time. But I do expect a belated Christmas present.'

'Of course. What would you like?'

'A copy of the final version of *Event/Horizon*.'

'Grace, it's not any good. I can tell without even having properly read your stuff yet that it's light years better than anything I've done.'

'Are you saying that I can't read it?'

'No, I'm not saying that. It's just…'

93

'Enough of this diffidence, Percival. If you don't provide me with my own copy of *Event/Horizon*, our relationship might be over before it's even begun.'

'You can't be serious?'

'What makes you say that?'

'It just seems such a worthless thing to argue about.'

'It's symbolic. I want to see it. Even if it's not published, I want my own copy. I don't know why you're being so difficult.'

'Grace, I'm sorry. Of course you can have it.'

Steve was cast into gloom. Why hadn't he just told her he'd destroyed it, instead of letting it become an issue? He would just have to beg Jude for the manuscript back and agree to her conditions if necessary. The problem was that he and Grace were getting back to Cambridge on the day after Boxing Day and Jude said she wasn't getting back until the following day. If only he had her telephone number. He suddenly realised that Grace had been speaking, but he hadn't taken in what she had been saying. 'Steve, are you still there? Can you hear me?'

'Yes, sorry, Grace. I think the connection must be a bit iffy. What was that last bit?'

'I said I'll phone about this time tomorrow if that's a good time for you.'

Still distracted by how to deal with Grace's demand to have a copy of *Event/Horizon*, Steve's reply was despondently monosyllabic. 'Yes.'

Grace was concerned. 'Steve, are you okay?'

'Yes, I just wish I could see you.'

'It's not long now. We'll be together again the day after tomorrow.'

Which, to Steve, looked as if it might now be a day of reckoning. He tried to pull himself together. 'Looking forward to speaking again tomorrow. Enjoy the rest of the day.'

'Thank you, darling. You too.'

Steve went back into the living room. His mother noticed that he was distracted. 'Is everything alright?'

Improvising, Steve said, 'I just miss her.'

Mavis put her arm around his shoulders. 'My goodness, you have got it bad.'

'Sorry, Ma. I'm just being ridiculous. Do you fancy a cuppa?'

For the rest of the evening, Steve managed to put out of his mind the ultimatum that Grace had issued, along with the impossibility of fulfilling it. But once his mother had gone to bed, he

returned to his brooding. He wished he'd had the courage to tell
Grace what he'd done with the poem when she had asked to see it
before the dinner party with Gary and Matt. He wouldn't even
have needed to mention Jude and her own rather bizarre demands
in connection with the poem. Sitting there in his mother's flat at
the tail end of Christmas Day 1974, he felt very distant from new
Steve. It was not the sort of thing that could easily be explained
over the telephone, especially not with his mother sitting within
earshot of his call.

So that meant that he wouldn't be able to come clean until he
and Grace were back together the day after Boxing Day. But then
she was bound to ask why he hadn't simply told the truth when
they had talked about it before. Why had he prevaricated? She was
bound to be suspicious and Steve, well, old Steve at any rate, was
not an accomplished liar. Should he just tell her about Jude and her
ultimatum? But Grace would probably immediately march down
to Tenison Road and have it out with Jude and might even retrieve
the errant poem. But it would be rather like one's mum chasing off
the rough boys, or in this case the rough girl. Not good for one's
self-esteem. No, this was something he needed to sort out for
himself and accept whatever karma might be involved. This was
the time to think the unthinkable, a time to stare the abyss out, to
misuse Grace's borrowing of Nietzsche. He was sure that's what
new Steve would advise.

He went back in his mind to the conversation with Jude. In the
state of shock he had been in, he had simply accepted her assertion
that the manuscript was in her office. But supposing it wasn't.
Supposing it actually was in her room. Then all he had to do was
gain access to her room and make a thorough search. It helped that
he already had a good idea of the layout of the room, having spent
several nights with her. Leaving aside the small problem of getting
into a locked first-floor room, there was one thing that commended
this mad plan, namely that he would be back in Cambridge the
day before Jude and that he was still an official tenant of the building and therefore had a right to be there.

He also remembered that it was a matter of general unhappiness
among the other tenants of the house that the internal doors were
not particularly secure. They had petitioned the landlord to improve the security of the building, but he had been unmoved by
their arguments and unconvinced that the expense of upgrading
the internal locks was worth it. Indeed, Garth, who occupied the
room above Steve's and spent as much time as possible naked, had

asserted that he could get into any of the rooms in less than two minutes with nothing but a couple of pieces of wire or a pair of hairpins.

But now that Steve knew Garth better, he had come around to the view that, while eccentric, he was not completely bonkers. One way of testing Garth's claim was to acquire some wire or a pair of hairpins and practice picking the lock to his own room. If anyone caught him at it, he could say that he was hoping to demonstrate to the landlord how flimsy the locks were. Anyway, there was nothing intrinsically wrong with breaking into one's own room. With luck most of the other tenants would still be away for Christmas. Then, having mastered the technique, he could transfer his skills to Jude's room.

The only problem was that he and Grace were getting back to Cambridge on the same day. She would probably not be delighted that he needed to spend an unspecified amount of time at his bedsitter and any attempt to pretend that it was because he was cleaning the place up would only result in an offer to help. The best he could hope for was that, because her journey was somewhat longer than his, she would get back to Glisson Road an hour or two later. To ensure that, he would have to make sure to leave the Borough flat as early as possible without upsetting his mother too much.

Having now devised a plan, such as it was, he didn't feel quite so powerless any more and went to bed in a better frame of mind.

When Grace rang the next day, almost as soon as they had completed somewhat routine protestations of reciprocal yearning, Steve said, 'What time do you think you'll be back tomorrow?'

There was a pause and then Grace said, 'Steve, I'm sorry about this, but I've had to change my plans and I won't actually be getting back to Cambridge until the evening of the twenty-ninth. I'm sorry. You've got your key to Glisson Road with you, haven't you?'

'Yes.'

'Good, just make yourself at home.'

'What happened?'

'I can't go into it now. I'll tell you when I see you. You could stay for a little longer with your mother if you wanted to.'

'No, I've arranged to hand over the VW to Jon.'

'Okay. Do that then. How's your mum?'

'She's fine. She said we can use the London flat and we can visit her in Berlin.'

'That would be great. What does she do?'

'She works for the Foreign Office.'

'How is she reacting to us?'

'I think she's coming around to it. What about your folks?'

'Hard to say. I think they need to meet you. Do you think you could bear to come down here?'

'When?'

'Soon.'

'Yes, as long as you're there too.'

'I'm not going to send you down here on your own.'

The call finished with whispered words of love on both sides. Steve felt awkward, aware that even if his mother couldn't hear precisely what he was saying, she could hear the tone of voice. It would not have made him feel any less uncomfortable had he realised that Grace was not only feeling something very similar, but surprised that she seemed to have reverted to being a teenager. It must have been the effect of being in the parental home.

When he had put the receiver down, Steve stood for a moment in the little entrance hall of the flat, deep in thought. He wondered what it was that was delaying Grace in Somerset. Whatever it was, he was grateful for the extra time in which to try and retrieve his manuscript.

## Friday, 27 December 1974

STEVE'S MOTHER WEPT WHEN he left the flat early on the morning of the day after Boxing Day. He'd not known her to be so emotional before. He pointed out that they would be seeing each other again in a fortnight. However, as he made his way to the Tube station, he wondered whether it had something to do with her work abroad.

The journey back to Cambridge was straightforward. He'd decided there was no point going to Grace's first. The Tenison Road house was only a stone's throw from the station. He let himself into his room, which was cold and forlorn. He put the gas fire on to warm it up and then, with the door to his room ajar, started to try and work out how to pick the lock. It wasn't as easy as Garth had led him to suppose. Half an hour later, he was no further forward. He took a break, made himself a cup of black instant coffee and strummed his guitar while the coffee cooled. Ten minutes later, having pondered his approach, he resumed his experimentation. Within ten minutes, he had succeeded in opening his locked door with the two pieces of wire. Reluctant to count his chickens, he locked the door and tried again. After another ten-minute struggle the door opened. So it was not impossible. The trouble was he felt that his success on both occasions had been more by chance than design.

He went back into his room to focus his thoughts on the operation proper. He'd been back in the house for about an hour and during that time had not been aware of anyone else in the building. There had been no sounds of movement or of music and no one had used the lavatories, bathroom or kitchen. With luck, he was the only person there.

He let himself out into the entrance hall and quietly shut the door to his room. He then climbed the stairs to the first floor and knocked gently on Jude's door, just to make sure she hadn't come back earlier than she had originally planned. There was no response to his knock. Relieved he took the pieces of wire and inserted them into the lock twisting them as he had for his own door. But the mechanism of Jude's lock felt different. Fifteen minutes later, he had got no further forward. He was starting to get anxious. If he couldn't get into Jude's room, he would have to rethink his whole approach.

He resumed his efforts and was soon absorbed in trying to feel the pins or tumblers with the piece of wire in his right hand. Suddenly he heard a man's voice behind him saying, 'What do you think you're up to, mate?' Steve jumped and dropped one of the pieces of wire. He turned around. It was Garth, naked as usual.

Garth's manner changed. 'Oh, Steve, it's you. What are you up to?'

Steve wasn't sure how to answer, so just said, 'Hi, Garth. Yeah, I just got back. How was your Crimbo?'

'Yeah, cool! Nut roast and some red Leb. What about you?'

'I went back to my mum's.'

Something occurred to Garth, scratching a buttock, he said, 'I thought you'd moved out.'

'I'm doing it today. I thought Jude was going to be here. She's got something of mine. Unfortunately, I left the key she gave me at my mum's.'

Garth sniggered. 'You two have really been getting it on. I hear everything. That girl's really got the hots for you.'

'I'm sorry, Garth. The walls of these rooms aren't very substantial.'

'No problem, man. Me and Kelly find it a turn-on. We're in the sack most of the time anyway. So, don't you know the old hairpin trick?'

Steve shook his head.

Garth said, 'I'll show you. Hang on, I'll just get a couple of Kelly's hairpins.'

He disappeared back into his room. Steve heard him talking to Kelly. A few moments later, he re-emerged, bending two hairpins into shape. He held out the palm of his hand to show Steve how he had bent them, one bent upwards at the curved end, the other straightened out with a hook at the end. He slotted the one with the bent-up curved end in first and then inserted the long straight one above it. He worked the upper one a little. 'Just got to push the pins in,' he said.

A moment later the lock clicked and the door opened. 'There you are, man, a cinch.'

'Wow! Garth. Thanks, I owe you one.'

'No problem. Hope you find what you're looking for.'

Steve stepped into the room and closed the door gently. Jude was not a tidy person. There were clothes, books and LPs everywhere. Steve was going to have to be systematic. Her room was furnished similarly to his, but it also had a desk. He sat down at the desk and looked through the drawers. In one of the drawers, he found a folder lying on top of an opened ream of typing paper. He looked inside the folder and pulled out a sheaf of A4 sheets. It was a manuscript alright, but not his poem. He looked more closely at it and realised it was the draft of a novel. He started reading and, forgetting for a few moments his real goal, entered the world of the narrative.

After a few minutes, he allowed himself to surface from the narrative. It was a competent piece of writing, more than competent and Jude's he assumed. But he needed to get on. He had not broken into her room to peruse her manuscript, but to retrieve his own. It was, of course, possible that she had been telling the truth when she'd said that it was in the office. He resumed his search, looking under the bed, in the cabinet under the little sink, on the shelves of the bookcase, in the small closet, all without success. That only left the small three drawer chest of drawers. He worked his way up from the bottom drawer, looking carefully under the pairs of jeans, the jumpers and tee shirts. Nothing.

He opened the top drawer which, as with the girls in Ainsworth Street, was the underwear drawer. With a familiar feeling of embarrassment and pleasure, he felt under the collection of slips, bras and knickers. Nothing there either. He realised that he had disordered the pile of clothes and did his best to return the contents of the drawer to its original state.

He sat down on the chair and reviewed the situation. Somehow, he had convinced himself that Jude had been lying and that the manuscript would be somewhere in her room. He had searched the room thoroughly and unless Jude had devised some ingenious hiding place for it, it was quite clear that it was not there. He would have to leave empty-handed. Or maybe not. He might not be able to carry off his own manuscript, but he could take Jude's instead. It would give him the kind of leverage that simply sleeping with her would not. He didn't feel comfortable purloining Jude's manuscript, but he'd feel even less comfortable sleeping with her now that he'd committed himself to Grace. Trying not to think too deeply about what he was doing, he extracted the typed pages from the folder and laid them on the top of the desk. He then slid a roughly similar number of blank pages out of the ream of typing paper, slipped them into the folder and closed the drawer. Picking up the manuscript of Jude's novel, he let himself out of her room.

Back in Glisson Road, Steve set the washing machine running and while it was cycling through the load, went out to get some supplies from the local shops. He thought he'd make a beef casserole for Grace's return on Sunday and bought the necessary ingredients. On impulse, he also picked up a bottle of champagne. It seemed pointless to get an ordinary claret, when Grace had so many bottles already laid in. He had never bought a bottle of champagne before and was shocked at the price. Still, thanks to his mother's Christmas gift, he now had a comfortable buffer of money, even if it was not actually in his account yet.

Back at the house he unpacked his possessions, such as they were. But where to put his clothes, at least those that were not in the wash? If Grace truly intended him to share her room, it would be inconvenient to have to keep his clothes elsewhere. Perhaps there was some space in her closet or chest of drawers. A brief inspection of the closet, however, soon confirmed that while Grace's dresses, blouses and jeans might not be as up to date, or as informal as Ginny's had been, they were every bit as numerous, leaving little room for Steve's clothes. Nor was there any space in the chest of drawers. Defeated in this particular, he carried his clothes back to his new room and divided them between what he assumed had been Peter's closet and chest of drawers.

He then decided to explore the rooms in the house that he had not yet looked into. He climbed the staircase to the second floor, emerging onto a small landing off which were four doors. He opened the first door on the right to reveal a small bathroom set into the eaves of the hipped roof, illuminated by a roof light. The room was clean and functional, equipped with a shower cubicle, washbasin and lavatory at those points in the room where there was a full ceiling height.

Working in an anti-clockwise direction, he tried the next room, which looked as if it was the guest room to which Grace referred and where his mother would sleep when she came to stay with them. A double bed was set into a large Victorian dormer, overlooking the garden. He rotated the space in his mind and concluded that this room was directly above Grace's study. The room was also equipped with a small desk, a chair, a chest of drawers and, in the alcove, a narrow closet. He also noticed a tiny cast iron fireplace let into what must be the party wall between the two houses. The room had probably been the skivvy's in former times. But in its current livery of magnolia emulsion, gloss white woodwork and orange Roman blind and bed throw, it would be a nice refuge for his mother, especially with what amounted to a private bathroom immediately next door.

He returned to the landing and looked into the next room. This was a similarly sized room to the guest room, but remained unfurnished, housing only packing crates and cardboard boxes. Clearly the room had yet to find a role in the Mitchell household. The final door opened into another room carved out of the eaves, offering further storage options, but without a roof light.

Steve stood on the landing for a moment. The house was lovely, but it seemed to him that there was something empty or provisional about it, especially on this floor. The house was bigger than was strictly necessary for a couple, even those with lots of books, records and paintings, unless this floor had always been intended as the children's floor. Would this then be where his and Grace's child would sleep and play?

For some reason, he found this thought vaguely troubling. The truth was that he knew very little about Grace, even though he had now slept with her several times. Delightful though that had been, the thought that their lovemaking was to some extent transactional, had in a curious way anonymised her. He was very aware that he was in a relationship with his former teacher, a 36-year-old rising academic, the estranged wife of a successful publisher. But who was the real person beneath that mask? He had little idea. No doubt the dreaded encounter with her family would in due course give him an idea of the environment that had shaped her, but before that moment arrived he would like to try and understand her better. Might the things in her study provide a clue?

He went back down to the first floor and pushed the door to her room open. He paused for a moment on the threshold, feeling that this was slightly transgressive. Glancing across at the desk, he saw that her journal was no longer there. Disappointed, but also relieved by its absence, he stepped into the room. Either she had taken it with her or put it out of harm's way. He was initially tempted to check the drawers of the desk. But it was one thing to read a journal left open on a desk, quite another to root through a person's desk. It was not lost on him, though, that this was exactly what he had done in Jude's room. Was he really the kind of person this implied? His purpose in coming into Grace's study had been to discover more about her, to help him find his way in the new world he was on the point of entering, not for more nefarious purposes. But in the process, he seemed to be discovering things about himself that he'd rather not know.

Momentarily becalmed, he scanned the bookshelves. There were hundreds of books arranged along the sturdily built shelves, many of them French paperbacks from the 50s and 60s with white covers and badly-cut pages, and dozens of *livre de poche* paperbacks with their, to the British eye, idiosyncratic covers and typography. Impressive though the library was, this told him nothing that he didn't already know about Grace, the scope of her reading, the breadth of her knowledge. What he was hoping for was something more personal that didn't involve his ransacking her desk and filing cabinets.

He turned his attention to those parts of the room not devoted to books and noticed several photographs propped on the mantelpiece. He picked up one of the photographs and studied it. It was a black and white photo of a girl in what he guessed was a Parisian café or bistro. The girl was holding a cigarette between her fingers, a cloud of smoke pluming her head, and smiling at the camera. She had short hair and was wearing a short jacket with a shawl collar. How effortlessly sexy French girls were! It took a moment for Steve to realise with something of a shock that it was a snap of Grace. He studied the photo for some moments, drinking in this image of a young Grace, regretting, *per impossibile*, that he'd not known her when she was younger. He replaced the photo on the mantel shelf and picked up another. This one showed an even younger and, one inferred, less sophisticated Grace as an undergraduate, with her arms around a fresh faced youth, whom Steve now identified as Gary.

The final photo was of Grace at a similar age, standing with an older couple. Steve guessed from the man's clerical collar, that these were Grace's parents. She had said her father was an easygoing man, but that was not the impression Steve got from this particular image. As he put the photo back, he noticed a passport lying on the mantel shelf. He opened the dark blue booklet and found he was looking at a much more recent photo of Grace. He glanced at the date of her birth and was shocked to see that she had been born just before the start of the war in the summer of 1939. That meant Grace was closer in age to his own mother than she was to him. That was not going to make it easier for his mother or perhaps for her own parents to accept their relationship. As Steve went down to the kitchen to make himself a cup of tea, he brooded on this documentary proof of what he already knew, but had dismissed as irrelevant.

Sitting in the kitchen, sipping his tea, Steve heard the phone ring. Was Grace now able to speak more freely? Or was it, more likely, a call *for* Grace? He went out to the hall and picked up the receiver. Cautiously, he said, 'Hello?'

'Steve, you old bugger, how are you doing?'

Steve was momentarily taken aback. 'Jon?'

'Yeah, man, sorry it's such short notice. I'm back in Cambridge. Can I come around and get the keys to the VW from you?'

'Of course.'

'And the tape recorder, if you've still got it.'

Steve hadn't been expecting to have to give up the tape recorder. But in truth, he had not made much progress with Jon's bootleg tapes of Grateful Dead performances. 'Yes, I've still got the tape recorder and your tapes.'

'Good man. So, where is this number I'm ringing?'

Steve gave him the address. Jon said he'd be there by 6 p.m. and then he'd buy Steve a drink and some supper.

Shortly after 6 p.m. that evening, there was a sharp rap on the front door. Steve opened the door to see a grinning Jon Chapman standing on the doorstep.

Jon said, 'I can see you've gone up in the world.'

'The jury's still out on that particular point. But it's good to see you. Come in.'

Steve took Jon through to the kitchen and offered him tea. Jon shook his head. 'I thought we'd get a couple of pints in the Loco.'

It'd been a while since Steve had been to the Loco. In fact, the last time he had been there was when Jon had introduced Steve to Tamsin, his new girlfriend.

'Okay, but let's get the tape recorder and your tapes into the VW.'

Twenty minutes later, they were sitting over their pints in the pub.

Steve took a mouthful of beer and said, 'So has the gig with the Syndrome finally come to an end?'

'Yeah, they managed to clean Rusty up and get him back in the saddle. Personally, I doubt that he'll stay clean for long once they're back on the road. So I'm on a retainer in case he implodes again.'

'What are you doing in the meantime?'

'Me and Tamsin, you remember Tamsin, the blonde with the big chest.'

Steve laughed. 'Ah, yes, the antithesis of Ginny.'

Jon chortled. 'And how!'

'Jon, no details, please.'

'If you insist. Anyway we've got a place up in the De Freville area.'

'Sounds to me as if you're the one who's gone up in the world.'

'Yeah, I was on a good crack with the Syndrome. And Tamsin's loaded. In another way.'

'Really?'

'I can't help it if I'm lucky. But likewise, I assume the house in Glisson Road is your new chick's.'

Steve laughed. Grace was many things, including being a property owner, but a chick she was not. 'Yeah, Grace is married to the guy who went off with Ginny.'

'Ah, Grace, I see. The main part of that story is all over the newspapers. Virginia Stern, as we now have to call her, and Peter Newman. Nice move on your part, though.'

'It's only just happened and I haven't completely disentangled myself from a girl I was seeing when I was living in Tenison Road.'

'Love 'em and leave 'em, Steve.'

'Jon, you're a rock and roller. You know how to manage these things.'

'C'mon, Steve. Just walk away.'

'The problem is she's got something I need.'

'They all have.'

'I don't mean like that. She's got the only copy of my poem.'

'How did that happen?'

'Long story. I was stupid. I don't blame her.'

'Is she hot?'

'Yeah.'

'I see. But she doesn't want to let you go. So if you don't play ball, she'll shred your poem.'

'Yes.'

'Hmm. Whereas Glisson Road is the superior gaff with all the comforts of home.'

'In a nutshell. Though there are some other issues which I won't go into now.'

'There always are. The other issues are often the clincher. Is Grace hot as well?'

'Yeah, but I'd rather not compare them like that. They're hot in different ways.'

Jon shook his head. 'Uh-uh. Hot is hot. I'm guessing the girl with your poem is the hot one.'

'How do you figure that out?'

'Because a gaff the size of the one you're living in now is a lot to set against a poem, even one you've spent six months writing. So the difference has to be the degree of hotness on either side.'

Steve laughed. 'Jon, you're a complete bastard, but you're right.'

Jon stood up. 'I think we need some more drinks.'

A few minutes later, Jon returned from the bar with two new pints. 'So what are the other issues?'

'I can't really talk about that yet.'

'Steve, this is Uncle Jon you're talking to.'

Steve drew in a breath, uncertain for a moment. *Oh, what the hell!* 'She wants me to get her pregnant.'

Jon shook his head. 'Grace presumably?'

'Yeah, how did you know?'

'What's the Tenison Road chick's name?'

'Jude'

'Well, Jude's not going to want you to put her up the duff.'

'What makes you say that?'

'I know the kind of chick who lives in those houses. They're not looking to drop a sprog for a while yet. So that means that Grace is, let us say, a little more mature than you.'

Steve couldn't fault Jon's powers of deduction. 'How did you work this all out? You seem to see it all more clearly than me.'

'Of course I do. It's not bleedin' quantum mechanics. You've read Jekyll and Hyde, haven't you?'

'Yeah.'

'Sometimes you have to let the bad geezer run the show.'

Steve wasn't sure Jon was doing justice to Stevenson's classic, but then Jon probably hadn't actually read the book. Even so, he saw what he was driving at. 'New Steve,' Steve muttered.

It was now Jon's turn to be puzzled. 'What?'

'I've been trying to do what you're saying. I thought I'd fake being a bit of an operator when I moved into Tenison Road and the result was I got to shag the hot chick on the first night there. That was my new-Steve act.'

'Of course.'

'Which would never have happened to old Steve.'

'So how did you get together with Grace?'

'She was my supervisor. Then I did a reader's report for her when you, Ginny and I were living in Ainsworth Street.'

'Ah, yes. I remember something of the sort.'

'Grace and I had a bit of a roll in the hay when Ginny went off with Peter, but didn't pursue things thereafter. Well, she wasn't ready to take things further.'

'So this is old Steve, because she's calling the shots.'

'Yes. Then out of the blue, she appeared at my new place a few days ago and offered me a job.'

'Making her pregnant?'

'That came later, when we realised that there was still a spark between us. To begin with, she was just looking for a research assistant with French reading skills and some knowledge of the existentialists. It'll be an informal arrangement. The quid pro quo being that I'd get to live rent free in Glisson Road.'

'Steve, what looks like an afterthought is often the nub of the matter. Asking a guy with whom you've had only limited sexual congress to have your baby doesn't simply pop into your mind after a particularly good session. The job was just the bait.'

Steve was horrified at the idea that Grace had been, still was, manipulating him.

Jon screwed up his face as he calculated the dynamics. 'So let me see. On one side you've got a hot chick threatening to destroy your poem unless you give her a good seeing to, and on the other you've got a broodmare with a nice pad who wants you to cover her.'

'Yes, for the sake of argument, if I understand your equine terminology.'

'But here's the difference. They both want Steve, but one wants new Steve and the other wants old Steve. The one who wants new Steve has got your poem; the one who wants old Steve wants you to give her a baby. The one who wants new Steve is not only hot but great in the sack (I'm guessing); the one who wants old Steve can offer you superior accommodation while you pump her full of premium spunk. Sounds familiar?'

'Jon, you're reducing it to basics and not taking into account other things like ethics and feelings.'

'Steve, my man. You can be new Steve or you can be old Steve, but you can't be both. Otherwise, it gets messy. Old Steve lets things happen. New Steve takes control. Old Steve lets bad Jon take him away from his beautiful blonde chick – Angie, wasn't it? – and make him a slave of beautiful dark Ginny. New Steve, on his first outing, pulls a hot chick, but now she's trying to turn the tables. Old Steve is relying on his schoolmarm to sort things out; new Steve can sort his own shit out.'

Steve looked glum. 'Yeah, I see what you mean.'

'Okay, let's look at the other side of the two equations. Jude is really into you and she's resorting to a bit of skulduggery to keep hold of you. For Grace, you are a means to an end.'

Steve was beginning to regret having confided in Jon, but only because his analysis seemed so cogent. 'What would you do then?'

'Well, clearly I'm a new Steve type. So I'd run them in tandem, but on my own terms, at least, until I'd rescued my poem. I'd also make sure there were agreed exit conditions in my baby-giver role.'

'But that sounds so cynical.'

'Maybe, but it doesn't sound like either lady's motivations are totally pure. An old Steve solution means you leave it to one of them to decide your future. In a new Steve solution, you make the moves. You can then take the credit for the wins, but you also have to take responsibility for the fails. There are never any easy calls, Steve. Any time you find yourself taking the easy way out, you're probably in old Steve mode.'

'I guess.'

'The new Steve mode doesn't come naturally to you. That's what makes you the nice guy you are. But if you want to run your own life you've got to be new Steve and that means daily practice until it becomes second nature. It's just like learning new stuff on the guitar.'

Back at home a couple of hours later, Steve reflected on what Jon had been saying in the Locomotive. No one would ever accuse Jon of being sensible, and yet there was a lot of sense in what he'd said. Waiting for the right moment to be new Steve was exactly what old Steve would do. Clearly, in Jude's eyes he was already new Steve. With Grace, it was not so certain. She had made a good show of welcoming the appearance of new Steve when he had asked her to undress, but she had also bridled, he thought, when he had refused to cut ties with Jude immediately, even though she had eventually acceded to his refusal. So he must take every opportunity to prove his new Steve credentials.

In the midst of these thoughts, the phone rang. Maybe Grace had decided to ring after all. Just before picking up the receiver, he composed himself, saying several times under his breath like an incantation: *New Steve, new Steve, new Steve. Don't take the easy way out.* 'Hello?'

But it was not Grace. A man's voice said, 'Steve. Grace said I might catch you.'

The voice was familiar, but Steve was unable to attach a name. 'Hello, who is this?'

'Steve, it's Gary.'

'Gary! Hi. I'm afraid Grace isn't here.'

'I know I spoke to her earlier at her parents. It's you I want to talk to.'

Steve was surprised. 'Oh, what can I do for you?'

'I was wondering whether you'd like to work for me at the Festival Theatre, as my assistant.'

Steve could hardly believe what he was hearing. 'I'd love to, but I've already agreed to be Grace's research assistant.'

Gary sounded a bit nonplussed. 'Oh, she didn't mention that.'

Steve wasn't really hearing what Gary was saying. He was repeating to himself the new-Steve mantra of earlier. Gary was still talking. 'Oh well, I knew it was an outside chance. Anyway, hope to see you…'

Steve suddenly realised that Gary was about to hang up. 'Gary, I'd love to work for you at the Festival. I'll sort things out with Grace. Nothing's set in stone yet.'

Gary sounded relieved. 'Are you sure?'

'Positive. What would the job involve?'

'As you know, I'm artistic director of the Festival Theatre Company, but I will also be directing two or three of the shows. I need somebody to take notes when I'm auditioning and directing, and generally back me up. It will be stressful. I lose my cool sometimes. Do you think you could do it?'

'Gary, I'll do whatever you throw at me. It's just the break I've been looking for. I can learn so much from you.'

'Okay. We're also running a short festival of new writing and we've invited young playwrights to submit scripts. I've already got a pile of them here and I'd like you to read through them and pick out the ones you think have potential. Can you come round here and pick up a batch on Monday?'

'Sure thing.'

'Right, I'll see you at ten-thirty on Monday then.'

'Gary, I can't tell you how pleased I am. You won't be sorry you asked me.'

'Great, Steve. I'll leave it to you to break the bad news to Grace.'

'I'll phone her now.'

'Okay, see you Monday.'

It was only after he'd hung up that he realised that he'd just volunteered to phone Grace at her parents'. That could be awkward. She might not be the person to answer the phone and he would have to have a conversation with her mother or father. He wasn't sure if he was ready for that encounter. No one would know if he didn't phone her and kept the news until her return.

But, *new Steve…* With a knot in his stomach, Steve dialled the number that Grace had given him before they had parted company on the train down to London.

A few moments later a female voice, not Grace's, answered.

*New Steve, new Steve.* 'Hello, is that Mrs Mitchell? This is Steven Percival, Grace's friend.'

'Ah, Steven, or Steve, as I believe Grace calls you, how nice to speak to you.'

Steve was perturbed by the warmth of the greeting. He had been expecting something frostier. Rebalancing himself, he said, 'It's lovely to speak to you too, Mrs Mitchell. I am so looking forward to meeting you and your husband.'

'Oh, please call me June. We are not that stuffy here. Did you have a good Christmas?'

'It was lovely, thank you. I spent it with my mother.'

'I believe that you lost your father when you were a small child.'

'Yes, I never really knew him, but my mother has been wonderful.'

'Grace tells me she's now off to Berlin with her work.'

'Yes, she's very excited by the opportunity.'

'For the Foreign Office, I believe. How splendid!'

'Yes, you could say she's married to her work.'

'But surely she will retire soon?'

'Oh, I think she's got a few more years to go.'

'Well, Steve, I don't suppose you phoned to have a long chat with me, but it is very nice to speak with you and I too look forward to our meeting. I will go and get Grace. Goodbye for now.'

'Goodbye, June.' He had to force himself to use her christian name. Curiously, he would have felt more comfortable calling her Mrs Mitchell. That must be old Steve trying to creep back in.

A few moments later Grace came on the phone and in a low voice said, 'Steve, how wonderful to hear from you! That was very bold of you to phone.'

'I was terrified, but, you know, new Steve. Anyway, your mother was delightful.'

'Steve, I know you well enough to know that you can turn on the charm when you want to.'

'I wasn't trying to charm your mother. I was just responding to her friendliness.'

'There's a reason for that. I will tell you all tomorrow. But for now, tell me how your day has been.'

'I've sorted my things out, done a batch of washing and then I met the guy who owns the VW and gave it back to him. But the main thing to report is that Gary phoned and offered me a job as his assistant. I'm afraid I accepted on the spot. I know I should have discussed it with you first, but for all sorts of reasons I think it's better if I work for him rather than for you. Not that I'm not grateful for your offer. So I hope you're not too annoyed with me. I know you have a lot on.'

'Steve, that's wonderful news. And exactly what new Steve should do. I'm not annoyed with you at all. It will give you some independence.'

'Thank you, Grace, for being so understanding. I was dreading telling you.'

'Steve, you mustn't dread telling me anything. If we're going to make this work, we have got to try and be open with one another.'

Steve needed a drink. He went through to the front room and poured himself a large Aberlour whisky. He then leafed through the LPs until he came across Miles's *In a Silent Way*. He put it on and settled back to think things through. She'd said that he shouldn't dread telling her anything. Easier said than done. He was hardly sure anymore whether the poem existed or not, indeed whether it had ever existed.

Having consigned it to the dustbin shortly after he first en-countered Jude, during his initial attempt at being new Steve, he had not expected it to continue playing such a prominent role in his life. In a world inaugurated by the birth of new Steve, the poem no longer existed, but it was also a world in which Jude had a legitimate reason, both because he'd slept with her and because she had rescued his poem, to feel that she had a claim on him. She was also, in Jon's terminology, hot, which, Steve was ashamed to admit, was a factor. But if the essence of a new Steve world was the absence in it of the poem, then it meant that he must consign the poem once again to oblivion. So, he was going to have to make it abundantly clear to Jude that he did not want the poem back. In fact, he would like her to destroy it. This would simultaneously free him from her grip and also enable him to assert to Grace with a clear conscience that the poem no longer existed.

But would that really be the case? The whisky was not helping him to see the situation any more clearly. Nor would telling Jude to destroy it be an easy thing to do. He would have to be resolutely in new Steve mode. He would also in all fairness have to return the manuscript of Jude's novel. Holding onto her manuscript only made sense in a scenario in which he was trading it for his own. Since he had now made a firm decision not to ask for his poem back, he must return her novel. Of course, it would involve confessing that he had broken into her room, but so would using it as leverage for the return of his poem. Either way, he would not come out of it well.

Even as he assembled this tottering logical structure, he was dimly aware that the more he placated Grace, the more he was in old Steve territory, while the more he insisted on the poem's destruction to Jude, the more he tightened the bonds of attraction between her and new Steve.

## Saturday, 28 December 1974

STEVE ROSE LATE THE next morning and had a leisurely breakfast, which he ate in the sitting room, listening to a recording of a sinfonia concertante by Johann Christian Bach, Johann Sebastian's youngest son. He was looking forward to working his way through Grace's LPs. He was aware, as he crunched his granola, that having breakfast on one's lap in the front room would probably not meet with Grace's approval. But might not new Steve want to insist on his right to do so? He wasn't sure. Of more concern was how and when he was going to handle the encounter with Jude. He knew she was travelling back from Manchester that day. So she was probably not going to get back to Tenison Road until lunchtime at the earliest. Fortunately, he still had access to his own room until Tuesday, by which time he would have to return the keys to the letting agent. So he could sit in his room reading and monitor the comings and goings in the house.

It did cross his mind that he could use Garth's hairpin trick to break into Jude's room again and silently replace her manuscript. He would then be able to communicate his decision not to want his poem back in writing, thus avoiding wrangles and having to witness displays of emotion. But he immediately recognised that the motive for this approach was very old Steve. No, he was going to have to admit to having broken into her room and tell her face to face that their relationship was over and he did not care what happened to his manuscript. It did briefly occur to him that she might report him to the police, but he thought it unlikely.

Having listened to both sides of the J. C. Bach record, he tidied up his breakfast things, put Jude's manuscript and the book he was currently reading in his shoulder bag and stepped out into an overcast day, already threatening snow. Ten minutes later, he arrived at the Tenison Road house and let himself into his room, having first tapped on Jude's door just to make sure she hadn't got back earlier than expected.

When he'd purloined Jude's manuscript the previous day, he had only glanced at a few pages and had not been able to make a proper judgement of the text. But the little he had registered had intrigued him. Since he now had an unknown amount of time on his hands, he decided to start reading it from the beginning. It would stop him from going over and over in his mind exactly what he was going to say to her. He took the sheaf of paper out of his shoulder bag and sat down in the armchair in his cold and forlorn room.

He was soon immersed in Jude's novel. She had a supple and easy-going style. The narrative concerned a love triangle between three graduate students in a lightly fictionalised version of Cambridge. The male protagonist was married to one of the female protagonists, who was secretly in love with the other female protagonist, who, in the classic triangular set up, was secretly in love with her friend's husband. After establishing the characters in the opening pages, several chapters were then devoted to fairly energetic bed-hopping. The sex scenes in the novel, which were remarkably explicit, were constructed as a kind of fugue for oral sex. Jude was clearly an organised writer. Each page of her typescript was numbered and dated, the dates incrementing from section to section, sometimes from page to page, presumably recording the date of composition or transcription. Steve doubted he could ever be so workmanlike, were he ever to try his hand at a novel. Not that he had any ambitions in that direction.

He had soon read his way through the draft and was not surprised to find that it was incomplete. At the point at which the narrative broke off, it was far from clear how Jude intended to resolve things. The date on the last page was 11 October. Perhaps she had lost heart or just got stuck. The narrative she had set up was certainly a complicated one. Steve took a blank sheet of paper and started to sketch in diagram form the narrative set-up. He then made a list of possible resolutions. He also tried mapping Jude's characters onto the people in his own complicated set of relationships, without much success. The only triangular dynamic that made any sense was Grace, Ginny and Peter, which was a constellation he preferred not to think too deeply about. Nevertheless, he was rather enjoying the exercise. It was so much easier working on someone else's material.

Pleased with his morning's work, he put the manuscript down and got himself a glass of water. As he did so, he heard the front door opening and the sound of footsteps going up to the first floor. He opened the door to his room slightly and peered out, to see Jude turning towards the door of her own room at the top of the stairs. He put the pages of her manuscript back in order and dropped the sheaf of paper into his bag. He took a sip of the water and walked around the room trying to psych himself into new Steve mode. But he wasn't feeling it. For some ludicrous reason, he tried, without success, to visualise himself as Steve McQueen. The only model he really had was Jon, and he already knew that Jon's version of new Steve was *love 'em and leave 'em*.

Taking a deep breath, he stepped out of his room, closing the door quietly behind him, walked slowly up the stairs as if to the gallows and tapped on Jude's door. A few moments later, the door opened to reveal Jude in her dressing gown, a detail which Steve found puzzling. How long had he been trying to screw up his courage?

Jude smiled at him. 'You took your time. Lost in your reading?'

Steve was mystified. 'What?'

'I saw you through your window, sitting in your chair reading something with great intent. I was going to knock on your door, but I thought I'd get out of my travel clothes. Come in. How was your Christmas?'

Steve stepped into her room, as if he were a zombie. This was not how he had imagined the opening salvos of their encounter. 'Christmas was good, thanks. It was nice to see my mother. What about yours?'

'A bit of a bore, but at least it's all over for another year.'

Steve laughed nervously. Jude closed the door. 'Drink?'

'Yeah, thanks. Coffee, please.'

'No, I meant a real drink.'

'Jude, it's the middle of the day.'

'But it's still Christmas.'

She had unscrewed a half bottle of Grouse and was now pouring large measures into a dirty tumbler and a cracked mug. 'Glass or mug?'

As Steve hesitated, she sniggered. 'Don't worry, I'll be the mug.'

Handing him the tumbler, she said, 'Cheers. Happy Christmas,' then took what looked like a large swig of the whisky.

'Cheers.' Steve raised his glass and took a sip of the whisky.

Jude put her mug on the desk. 'Before we get down to business, I just need to go to the loo. Back in a jiffy.'

Steve was disconcerted by how light-hearted Jude was. He had expected her to be tense and suspicious. Did she think she'd won him round? Nor had he been expecting her to vacate the room during what he had imagined would be a short conversation. But it now occurred to him that her absence gave him the chance to put her manuscript back in the drawer without her being aware that he had purloined it or had broken into her room. He quickly pulled the manuscript out of his bag, opened the drawer and slipped the sheaf of paper into the folder. By the time Jude returned, he was sitting on one of the chairs, staring nonchalantly out of the window.

'Sorry, that time of the month.'

Steve could only manage an embarrassed *Oh!* in response.

Jude sat down on the edge of the bed, her dressing gown gaping and displaying a considerable amount of cleavage. 'So, where were we?'

Steve cleared his throat. 'We were discussing the conditions for the return of my manuscript.'

'Ah, yes. Having been a bit of a Jack the Lad for the first three weeks of our relationship, you suddenly revealed a pious side to your personality I hadn't discerned before, precipitated, it would seem, by your former supervisor nabbing you as her toy boy. You didn't even have the decency to sleep with me one last time before we went our separate ways, even when I effectively threw myself at your feet.'

'What can I say? I'm sorry.'

'Is this where I'm supposed to say, *you will be*.'

'Believe it or not, I've had a terrible Christmas. I've spent the whole time just thinking about how to solve this problem without anyone getting hurt.'

'Did you come up with a solution?'

'I did. I decided that my poem which you rescued from the bin was the thing that was distorting my reaction to the situation. I was grateful to you. I *am* grateful to you. I would have liked to show you my appreciation, but the method being proposed seemed to de-value the previous times we'd made love.'

'So let me get this straight. You didn't want to go to bed with me because the fact that it would have been as a reward for having saved your manuscript made the sex transactional, as if I were a hooker. Which means that if I hadn't told you about the poem, you would have made love to me? I mean that seems like a very back to front argument.'

'No, I don't think I was saying that. Let me make this clear. I don't want the poem back. I am happy for you to destroy it. I threw it away because I didn't like the associations it had for me. Yes, I put a lot of work into it. I sacrificed people and things to get it done. I think there's some good stuff in there. But ultimately I think it's malign. What's happened between you and me just seems to confirm that.'

'In other words, you don't want the poem back. You have given me *carte blanche* to destroy it. In which case, there should be no problem in your fucking me because the poem will no longer be the quid pro quo. So let's go to bed now.'

Steve saw instantly that her logic was flawless. Weakly, he said, 'But you're menstruating.'

'So what? You're not worried by a bit of blood, are you?'

Steve shook his head, even though he thought he probably was.

'Don't worry, I'm not going to ask you to go down on me.'

Steve laughed uncomfortably, while Jude took her dressing gown off and climbed into bed, shivering theatrically.

'Come on, Steve. Just get it over and done with and then we can both get on with our lives.'

Steve started to unlace his shoes. He had been totally outman-oeuvred. Oh, well, there was nothing for it. He would just have to accept the consequences. He seemed to have overshot new Steve territory and landed smack in the middle of Jon's *love 'em and leave 'em* territory. He slowly removed his clothes and walked grimly over to Jude's bed.

Jude watched him with an amused smile on her lips. 'Your old chap doesn't look ready to go, but don't worry, I've got a solution for that.'

Later, when they were recovering, Jude said, 'Steve, I'm sorry about the blood. There's not normally that much. I'm impressed that it didn't deter you from going down on me, even though I'd said you didn't need to.'

Steve was now feeling more robust. He'd crossed the Rubicon and the sky hadn't fallen in – at least not yet. 'It was the least I could do after the amazing blowjob you gave me. Anyway, you tasted lovely, just a bit more metallic than normal. I guess that's the blood. It does seem to have made a mess of your sheets, though.'

'Nothing the launderette on Mill Road can't handle.'

Jude sipped her coffee. 'So that wasn't too bad, was it?'

'No, far from it.'

'It seems a pity to be bringing things to an end.'

'I know, but I'd rather not go over that again. The good thing is it's made me certain that I don't want that poem in my life. You have my full permission to destroy it.'

'Are you sure? There'll be no going back this time. I'm moving down to London soon.'

As usual with Steve, he was having difficulty keeping up. So when she'd said that they should just get it over and done with and get on with their lives, she'd meant it. 'When are you going?'

'In a week's time.'

Steve was visibly shocked. Even though he'd been trying, unsuccessfully as it had turned out, to fend off Jude's attentions, he'd imagined that they might bump into each other from time to time. 'Have you got a new job?'

'Not yet. It's a bit of a gamble. I'll be staying with a friend until I've sorted something out.'

Steve felt unexpectedly disconsolate. However awkward it had been, the poem had been a link between them. Now that he had asked her to destroy it, it seemed that link would also be broken.

Jude sensed Steve's change of mood. She slipped out from under the covers and padded across to her desk. Steve watched the sway of her hips as she crossed the room. She picked up an index card, scribbled something on it and then went over to Steve's bag and tucked the card into the front pocket of his bag. Steve propped himself up on one elbow.

'What's that you're putting in my bag?'

'It's my friend's telephone number in London. Even if I've moved on, she will be able to give you my new contact details. Probably better if I don't phone you at Glisson Road every other day.'

Steve laughed nervously. 'No, probably not a good idea.'

Jude slipped on her dressing gown.

Steve watched her sadly. 'Is that it then?'

'I hope not. Just a brief comfort break. Back in two ticks.'

By the time Steve got back to Glisson Road, having trudged through the drifts of snow that had built up, he was slightly worse for wear in a number of ways. He ran himself a bath and soaked in it until the water became too cool. He then put on some clean clothes and loaded those still bearing traces of Jude's menstrual blood into the washing machine. He thought he'd have an early night and compose himself for Grace's return the following day, but first he needed something to eat. Lacking the energy to make a proper meal, he settled for some cheese on toast. As he was eating his meagre supper, the phone rang. Oh dear, he hadn't yet worked out what he was going to say to Grace. He went out to the hall to answer the phone, certain that she would sense that he'd been up to no good.

But it was Jon. 'Hey, man, how did it go with the poem conundrum?'

Not without a hint of self-satisfaction in his voice, Steve said, 'Problem solved.'

Jon chuckled. 'That's ace. So you must have given the hot chick a seeing to, then?'

Steve gasped. 'I did, but that's the exact opposite of what I said I was going to do.'

'Of course. That's the way it works. I'm proud of you. She showed her appreciation, I hope.'

'She certainly did!'

'Good man. No regrets, Steve. No regrets. It'll all be cool. See you around.'

Steve went back to his toast. He didn't buy into Jon's view of himself as some kind of Zen master of playing the field, but it was certainly true that talking to Jon had resulted in a satisfactory outcome. At least thus far. Whether Grace would buy into his revised account of the fate of his poem, the precise details of which he hadn't yet settled on, was another matter entirely.

Steve sat up for a while longer. He'd expected Grace to call, but perhaps she'd got tied up in something. Or perhaps she was waiting for him to ring. His conversation with Grace's mother the previous night had gone well, but he had no real desire to repeat it this evening. Anyway, Grace would be back tomorrow and he could do with an early night. He finished his glass of Aberlour and went up to bed.

Gideon and June had finally gone to bed, leaving Grace and Peter in the sitting room of Lane End.

Peter sipped his whisky. 'Just like old times,' he said sardonically.

Grace sat with her arms folded. 'Hardly.'

'I'm sorry. I wasn't planning to stay. Snow wasn't predicted on the weather forecast. It's massively inconvenient for me too. I'm flying to New York tomorrow, weather permitting.'

'I would have preferred to meet in Cambridge.'

'Me too. I didn't really want to drive all the way down to Somerset.'

'So you thought I'd be spending a nice Christmas on my own.'

'I thought you'd probably have Gary and Matt around. They practically lived at our place.'

'Why not have waited until the New Year?'

'I'm travelling a lot in January and I wanted to try and get this divorce business sorted out.'

'It doesn't make things easier for me having my parents involved. Since they provided us with the deposit for the house, they wanted to make sure that my rights were protected in the divorce.'

'I'm giving you the whole bloody thing.'

'They are simple people, Pete. They don't understand the way divorces work. You do also have a reputation as a sharp operator, something you have been quite keen to talk up in the past.'

'Oh, for goodness' sake. Everyone knows I make a distinction between business and family.'

'It may be thought that, for you, everything is business.'

'Do you know how much that sounds like an anti-Semitic jibe?'

'You know me better than that, Pete. If you need clarification, what I am saying is that you are the one who has dissolved the family that you and I constitute. Then you come barrelling down here to tell me, and more hurtfully, my parents that you will accept that you have committed adultery in proceedings and, in the interest of getting a quick divorce, you will sign across to me your share in the house. What's the hurry? I can't believe it's because you want to make an honest woman of Ginny.'

Peter didn't have an immediate answer. Grace laughed bitterly. 'Not like you to be lost for words.'

'I just think it would be kinder to everyone concerned if we drew a line under our relationship as quickly as possible, then we can all get on with our lives. Which means you can return to Cambridge and console yourself with shagging Steve Percival until he finds other female delights.'

'That's vile. In any case, why bring up Steve?'

Peter caught Grace's eye and said, with a triumphant look on his face, 'Because he's written to Ginny from Glisson Road.'

'Peter, you shouldn't attribute your own motivations to others. There is a perfectly simple explanation. Since I'm now paying the mortgage on my own, I thought it would be a good idea to have a lodger. Anyway, he hasn't actually moved in yet.'

'Even so, you need to watch him; he's a regular little Lothario.'

'I can take care of myself. Who I take into my bed is no business of yours. I have to say it's a bit rich your feeling jealous. It's not me who's been the serial philanderer.'

'Mark my words, he's a bit of an operator. You'll regret getting tied up with him.'

'I don't know what kind of nonsense Ginny's been feeding you, Pete. She exploited that boy until she found someone even more gullible to get her hooks into.'

'Look, there's no point prolonging this. I will let my solicitor know that you will be citing adultery on my part, which I will not contest, and then we can get everything off to the court.'

Peter stood up, knocked back his whisky and said, 'I'm sorry it ended like this. We had some good times.'

Grace wanted to say that she was only sorry that she hadn't kicked him out sooner, but confined herself to a gnomic, 'Yeah.'

Grace sat up for a while longer, waiting for Peter to finish using the limited bathroom facilities at Lane End. She sipped her whisky and reflected on the day. There was more to this than met the eye. Peter didn't make grand gestures for nothing. Ginny must have agreed to his mission. She couldn't help feeling that they were cooking up something between them, and it was only the vagaries of English law that put the lighting of the touch-paper in her hands. It would be good to get the ownership of the house trans-ferred to her under the auspices of the family court, of course, but her solicitor had advised her that she was in a strong position on that score. Her instinct was to resist being hustled into a hasty decision. Not that she had hopes of a reconciliation, but she wanted to make sure that she wasn't giving up something that would only become apparent once the divorce had gone through. She resolved to drag her feet until she had been able to take advice from those who knew about these things.

When she was sure that Peter was settled in his room, she tapped on the door of her parents' room and was relieved to find they were still awake, chatting quietly. She sat down on the edge of the bed. 'I'm so sorry. It's been ghastly, but thank you for all your support. I'm sorry to say I don't trust Peter and I want to take some time to think about his offer.'

Gideon was conciliatory. 'It must be hard for him too.'

June was having none of it. 'He's brought it on himself. We were the ones who provided the deposit for the house, and in the early days, it was Grace's earnings that paid the mortgage. If it were all worked out properly, I'm sure it would show that his share is really rather small.'

Gideon still wanted to give him credit. 'But he's admitted guilt and is prepared to make some kind of restitution. That seems a decent response to me. I think that Grace is right not to rush into a divorce.'

Grace was grateful for her father's support, even though it was almost certainly because he disapproved of divorce *per se*.

She kissed both her parents and said, 'I think I'll go to bed now. Night, night.'

Grace went to her own room, which, given the limited number of bedrooms in the house, was right next door to Peter's. It was odd to think that here they were, still married after ten years, having been living together until only a few weeks ago, now sleeping in separate bedrooms. Not that she was minded to go next door and kiss him goodnight. What she really wanted to do was to phone Steve. She couldn't now remember whether he was expecting to get a call from her or not. They had not yet had any time in which to develop mutual patterns of behaviour. In the end, she decided that she would not feel comfortable talking to Steve on the phone, conscious after Peter's earlier jibe, that he might be able to hear her side of the conversation from his room.

## Sunday, 29 December 1974

STEVE WOKE ON THE Sunday morning somewhat apprehensive about the day ahead. It was not lost on him that the return of one's lover ought to have generated more positive emotions, of joy and pleasurable anticipation perhaps. But his feelings of guilt at having succumbed to Jude's charms were complicating his reactions. He felt that Grace was bound to intuit something of what had happened, especially if, or more likely when, the conversation came around to the matter of his poem and Grace's demand to have her own copy. To take his mind off things, he decided to spruce the place up and to make the beef casserole so that it could simply be warmed up later that evening. By lunchtime the house was back to rights, taps and mirrors sparkling, carpets vacuumed, clothes folded and put away and the casserole cooking away in the oven on a low heat, filling the house with delicious aromas. He sat down on the sofa in the front sitting room with a cup of tea and a book, reasonably proud of himself.

He was wakened some time later, the day already growing dark, by Grace leaning over him and kissing him on the forehead. 'Hello, sleepy head.'

Steve leapt up. 'Grace, welcome home.'

He took her in his arms and kissed her on the mouth.

Grace sighed pleasurably and then, releasing herself from his embrace, said, 'I wasn't sure if you were in. There was a delicious smell coming from the kitchen, but all the lights were off and there was no reply when I called your name.'

'Sorry, I must have nodded off.'

'Sound asleep more like it. Late night last night?'

'No, quite an early one actually, but I was running around a bit this morning. Let's go through to the kitchen. I need to check the casserole and I'll make a pot of tea.'

A few minutes later, they were sitting around the kitchen table sipping their teas.

Grace said, 'I'll just have this tea and then I need to lie down for an hour or two. Perhaps you would care to join me?'

Steve thought he probably ought to. 'In that case I'd better turn the casserole off.'

Grace smiled. 'Good thinking.'

Sometime later as they lay in each other's arms, Grace said, 'I'm sorry I didn't let you kiss me down there. I'm not quite sure of the moves.'

Steve laughed. 'It's not ballroom dancing. There aren't pre-scribed moves. If you'd rather I didn't do that, I won't.'

'Were you expecting me to reciprocate?'

'No, of course not.'

'I'm afraid I'm not very experienced in that context. Even when things were going reasonably well with Peter, that kind of thing wasn't part of our repertoire.'

'Grace, making love with you is delightful. Neither of us should have to do anything we're uncomfortable with.'

'But I imagine you'd like me to take you in my mouth.'

Steve shrugged. 'Only if you wanted to.'

'I'm not saying I won't do it. I'm just not ready for that yet.'

'Of course. It's not an issue. Please don't get hung up about it. I'll leave it to you to tell me when you're ready. If you're never ready, that's fine too.'

'Thank you. I presume you got that kind of attention from your other women.'

Steve wasn't sure where Grace was going with this. Did talking about his other partners turn her on? Or was it just a way of establishing the lineaments of their sexual practice? He thought he'd better tread carefully.

'You make it sound as if I've been a bit of a Casanova. But I've only had two girlfriends and if it's any consolation, oral sex was not a significant feature in either of them.'

'Not even with Ginny?'

'No.' This wasn't strictly true. It depended on how you inter-preted the word *significant*. He was just hoping to deter Grace from pursuing the subject further.

But Grace now changed her angle of attack. 'Doesn't Jude count as one of your girlfriends then?'

Clearly she had inferred that his statement about oral sex did not include Jude. Nevertheless, obtusely continuing with his implied quibble about the status of his relationship with Jude, he said, 'Not really. We hadn't really got to the stage of considering each other boyfriend or girlfriend. It was a very brief relationship.'

'But it *was* an actual relationship?'

'Only if instances of casual sex with the same person constitute a relationship.'

'But from what you've told me, that's not quite how Jude sees things.'

'How she sees things is beside the point. Especially since she's London-bound.'

'When did you find that out?'

Steve could see exactly where this was going now. 'When I went back to my room to make sure I'd moved everything out.'

'You saw her?'

There was no point in trying to hold off the inevitable. 'Yes, I was hoping to get the manuscript of my poem back.'

There was a long silence, while Grace processed the implications of Steve's statement. 'So that's why you couldn't give me your poem. You'd given it to her.'

'Not exactly. It's more complicated than that. Until a few days ago I was under the impression that the poem no longer existed.'

That wasn't quite what Grace had been expecting. 'Really? Because?'

'Because I put it in the dustbin the first day I moved into Tenison Road.'

'Oh, Steve. Why didn't you tell me right at the start?'

'Because I was ashamed of what I had done and angry with myself.'

Grace now thought she saw how this was developing. 'But somehow the bin men failed to consign your poem to the flames because someone had rescued your poem, and that person was Jude.'

Steve nodded mournfully. 'Yes, exactly.'

'Why didn't she give it back to you right then?'

'At first, she didn't know it was mine. There was no name on it. Also, I had torn some of the pages. It took her a while to tape them together and put them in order.'

'Oh, Steve.'

'In the process, she said that she grew to like the poem. She actually works for a small publishing house.'

'But why didn't she mention it when she was sleeping with you?'

'I don't know. I think she was still trying to make up her mind about me.'

'What changed her mind?'

'You.'

Grace seemed surprised. 'Me?'

'Yes. She saw you in my room. The day you brought my mail from Ainsworth Street around and then the green-eyed god got to work.'

'Which manifested itself how?'

'The following day, when I went round to get my stuff, she came in and said that I'd stood her up the previous night.'

'Had you?'

'Yeah, it didn't seem quite right to mention it to you, in the middle of getting to know each other again. Unfortunately, she'd seen you through the window, taking your clothes off.'

'Oh, no.'

'So she took her own clothes off and demanded I make love to her.'

'Did you?'

'No, I didn't.'

'That was very self-controlled of you. I would have thought you'd do anything to get your poem back.'

'At that point, I still didn't know that she had the poem. It was only later in the conversation that she said that she'd found a poem in the bin and eventually worked out that I was the only person in the house crazy enough to write something like that.'

'Crazy?'

'Well, actually, she said something like the only one arrogant enough to write something so crazy.'

'She may have a point.'

Steve ignored this tentative alignment between Grace's and Jude's view of him. 'As you might imagine, I had been grieving over the poem and regretting my hasty destruction of it. So I thanked her profusely for having rescued it. But she said that she wasn't sure I deserved to have it back, given that I had so cruelly dumped her. I could also forget trying to find it in her room because it was now in her office at work.'

'Oh, dear. You do seem to be rather vulnerable to a certain type of woman.'

'She said I'd humiliated her. I told her that I didn't want to fuck things up with you. She said there was no need for you to know. I said it was a matter of ethics and self-respect. She then said she was going away for Christmas. I should give the matter some thought over the holiday and we could resume negotiations when she got back. At that point, I thought the issue was containable until you told me during our telephone conversation on Christmas Day that you wanted to see the poem, and failure to comply would incur your wrath.'

'Oh, Steve, I'm sorry. It was a somewhat ham-fisted joke. I didn't realise I was putting you under such pressure.'

'So, when I got back from London, I went round to Tenison Road and broke into her room.'

'That doesn't sound like the best way of fixing a bad situation. Do you have skills in that regard?'

'No, Garth did it for me.'

'Was he dressed?'

'Of course not.'

Despite Steve's discomfort, Grace was finding Garth's supporting role in his account somewhat amusing. 'It's just as well he spends most of his time unclothed, otherwise he'd pose a threat to the neighbourhood. But isn't it more than a little shady to break into another person's room?'

'I thought she might be lying about it being at her office.'

'Presumably, she wasn't lying, because then I doubt you'd be making this lengthy confession.'

Steve nodded.

'What would you have done if it had been there?'

'Destroyed it, properly this time.'

'Why?'

'Over Christmas at my mother's, I came to the conclusion that my original impulse to destroy the poem had been the right one. If I couldn't find it in her room, I would tell her that not only did I not want it back, but I was happy for her to destroy it.'

'Despite my wrath?'

'It was the only way to free myself from her.'

Grace squeezed his hand.

'But although I didn't find the manuscript of *Event/Horizon*, I did find another manuscript, a draft of a novel, written by Jude. At least, that was the assumption I made.'

'What did you do with this manuscript?'

'I took it.'

'Oh, dear. I'm starting to think that new Steve has lost track of his moral compass.'

'I suppose I thought there was some kind of equivalence. She had my manuscript and was setting conditions for its return, so if I had her manuscript, I was in a position to neutralise her conditions.'

'By having a manuscript swap?'

'Yes. The next day, while I was waiting for Jude to return from Manchester, I read her manuscript. It was good. But I was also starting to feel uncomfortable about having broken into her room.'

'As well you might.'

'But there seemed no way to avoid having to admit it.'

'Anyway, when she returned, she invited me up to her room, perhaps assuming I intended to meet her conditions. At one point she went out to the loo and, having lost my nerve, I took the opportunity to put the manuscript back in her desk.'

'So now you didn't have to admit to breaking into her room, but nor did you have a bargaining chip.'

'Exactly. But I still hadn't told her that I didn't want the poem back. I was counting on that breaking the hold she thought she had over me.'

'So when she came back, you told her.'

'Yes.'

'Then you ended up in bed with her, and *that* encounter, at least, involved oral sex.'

Grace had completely outmanoeuvred him. Sheepishly, he said, 'Yes. How did you know?'

'By wilfully refusing to classify Jude as one of your girlfriends earlier on, you were, in effect, confirming that your relationship with her involved oral sex. It's pretty obvious, really. But I am curious as to how you got to that stage.'

'She showed me that my logic was flawed.'

'Nicely played, Jude. Do you think I might like her?'

'I can't really answer that. But she is a bright girl.'

'All your girls are bright, Steve.'

'Are you annoyed with me, Grace?'

'Do you want me to do some wrath?'

'It's what I deserve.'

'Look, this all needs some careful unpicking. I'm grateful you've told me the whole story, or as much as is necessary. I don't suppose I expected it all to be plain sailing. We have to work out how we go on.'

'I'm so sorry. Grace, I'll move out if you want me to.'

'I don't want you to move out. I want you to give me a baby. But, in relation to that, I too have a confession to make. I enlisted my father to help me persuade my mother that having a relationship with a younger man was not anything to fear. My father, however, is a subtle man and I found myself confiding in him more than I had intended and telling him about my plans to become pregnant by you. Once he knew that, how could he not share the information with my mother?'

It was now Steve's turn to be exasperated. 'Oh, Grace, that's not what we agreed. I'm only glad I spoke to her on the phone before she found out. Otherwise I might have got a much frostier reception.'

'Oh, but she did know by the time you spoke to her. She's actually delighted. It's my father who has reservations.'

'I'm not sure that makes me feel much more comfortable.'

'My father is a sweetheart. If my mother had taken it the wrong way, we would certainly have had a struggle on our hands. Even if he disapproves, which he does, my father will not make difficulties. But that does mean that we now need to tell your mother.'

The thought that Grace might have intended something like this all along hardened Steve's resolve. 'I really don't think that's necessary.'

'But we'll be seeing her soon. Wouldn't it be best to prepare her?'

'I think we should stick to the original plan and tell her once we know you're pregnant. She's got enough on her plate with this move to Berlin.'

Grace could see from the pugnacious set of Steve's features that there was nothing to be gained at that moment by trying to persuade him to the contrary.

That night Grace and Steve had an early night, not for purposes of passion, those appetites having been sated earlier in the day, but because Steve was about to begin working with Gary. Over the Christmas break Grace had imagined that she and Steve would have some time together to get to know each other better as lovers and housemates before the Lent term began. She had been looking forward to some days of sybaritic excess interspersed with work on her lecture series, but this was now looking unlikely. While she was pleased that Steve had got a job and even more pleased that it was with Gary, she knew that the latter was a hard taskmaster and would probably demand total commitment from Steve. Still, it did mean that not only could she start on a reading list for her as yet unknown research assistant, but that there would still be time for hedonistic interludes.

She looked fondly over at the sleeping Steve, snoring gently under the bedclothes. What a strange boy he was, really rather innocent, but with a pleasing streak of amorality, ignorant about the world, yet surprisingly resourceful. She didn't suppose would keep him for long, but with luck she would keep him long enough. She leant over and kissed him on the forehead and felt his long eyelashes flutter on her cheek. She already felt protective, and indeed motherly, towards him, but she must do her best to restrain those impulses. The more she tried to mother him, the more likely he was to be attracted to women closer to himself in age. She should do her best not to make him feel that he was being kept on a short leash. What was it that Germaine had written in *The Female Eunuch*? Something about lovers, who are free to go when they are restless, being the ones to come back? That is what she needed to make Steve feel.

It would be difficult, though. Jude had definitely got under his skin. But if it really was true that she was London bound, then at least temptation would no longer be on Steve's doorstep. On the other hand, even though Grace had not met Jude and therefore had no real idea of what she was like apart from what Steve had told her, she very much doubted that Jude would destroy Steve's poem. If Jude was intent on keeping tabs on Steve, she was much more likely to preserve the poem and spin out its eventual return for as long as possible. It was, therefore, probably pointless for Grace to try and thwart communications between Steve and Jude, or any other potential lover. Not that she should encourage it either. But if he did feel the need to be away from time to time, she should resist subjecting him to any cross-examination.

It wouldn't be easy. The point was to make him feel comfortable enough with the arrangement to make her pregnant. If that meant giving him some leeway in respect of extracurricular sexual activities, so be it. Fortunately, it was already clear to her from the contortions that Steve had tied himself in when recounting his interactions with Jude that he had a lively conscience. If he did take solace elsewhere from time to time, he would no doubt suffer similarly complicated paroxysms of guilt, which was all to the good if the result was to limit the frequency of such divagations.

What curious creatures men were, seemingly unaware of, and yet so clearly guided by, the promptings of that rubbery protuberance between their legs, for the most part a shy and modest appendage, but of which men were immoderately proud. She reached down, feeling between Steve's legs, and smiled. It was in its dormant phase, curled up like a dormouse. She took it in her hand. Even as she did so, it began to flex and Steve stirred in his sleep. She smiled again. Poor boy, she had no doubt that if she woke it up, he would probably oblige her. It was not that she wanted another session; it was just that she wanted to know his body and this particular part of his body in its more private moments.

The next day, Grace was sitting in her study preparing her lecture notes when the phone rang downstairs in the hall. She was about to call out to ask Steve to answer it when she remembered that he had gone out to get something for the evening meal. She pushed her chair back, walked downstairs and, answering the phone, said, 'Hello?'

'Hello, this is Angie Barrett. I'm sorry to disturb you.'

'Hello, Angie, this is Grace, as I'm sure you realise. I'm afraid that Steve isn't here. Shall I get him to ring you when he gets back?'

'Thank you, that would be very nice. Can I give you my number, just in case he has mislaid it. He's not very organised about things like that.'

Grace laughed and wrote down the number that Angie gave her. Having read it back to Angie, she said, 'I'm very much looking forward to meeting you and Rob. I have, of course, been aware of you, in particular, for the last two years.'

'Well, that's partly what I was phoning about. I wanted to make sure that Steve had consulted you. When I mentioned to him in one of my letters that Rob and I were coming to Cambridge, I was, of course, thinking that we might be able to stay at Ainsworth Street with him and Ginny – '

Angie didn't quite know how to refer to the relationship between Grace and Steve. 'I'm sorry, Grace, I hope I haven't put my foot in it.'

'Not at all, Angie. Steve and I are in love. I know people are going to be shocked. I am quite a lot older than Steve. But that's the way it is.'

'I'm not shocked, Grace. The age difference is immaterial.'

'I agree, but I'm not sure that that's how others will see it.'

'Like who, for example.'

'Well, Steve's mother for one. She's coming to stay with us at the end of the week.'

'Mavis is delightful. You will get on with her fine.'

'So, you know her?'

'Yes, she's an extremely sensible woman.'

'Thank you for that, Angie. It does reassure me somewhat.'

'Grace, I was worried about Steve when he was with Ginny. I have no qualms about his being with you. I'm delighted. My hesitation earlier was because, until Steve's recent letter, I had no idea that you and he were together. If I'd known, I would never have prompted him to invite us.'

'Well, I'm glad it's turned out the way it has. I've wanted to meet you for a long time. I feel I know you already from all the things that Steve's said about you. And about Rob too. You have both been incredibly supportive of him.'

'I sometimes feel I could have been more supportive than I was.'

'I'm sure we all feel like that. I wish I'd been a bit sterner with him about his studies. But there we are. Anyway, you are both very welcome to stay, but I'm afraid we will only be able to put you up for two nights. I have just been appointed a university lecturer and I'm in a total panic about preparing my first lecture.'

'Oh, Grace, congratulations. Steve always said you were brilliant.'

'Perhaps living with me will give him a truer idea of my abilities. Anyway, when are you planning to come to Cambridge? I should say that we are already committed for the weekend of the eleventh and twelfth.'

'We were hoping to arrive on the evening of the seventeenth and leave on the morning of the nineteenth.'

'That's perfect. Shall I ask Steve to ring you?'

'Well, I don't think there's any need now that we've spoken.'

'Okay, if you're sure. I look forward to the seventeenth.'

'Me too.'

# Glisson Road

## Friday, 10 January 1975

STEVE WAS WAITING IN the booking hall of Cambridge railway station for the arrival of the six o'clock train from London. It was not until the more energetic commuters had passed through the ticket barrier that he spotted his mother. He ran towards her and, taking her overnight bag with one hand, gave her a big kiss. Outside the station Steve hailed a taxi and not many minutes later they pulled up outside Grace's house in Glisson Road.

Mavis said, 'Steve, I didn't realise it was so close to the station. We could have walked.'

'Grace insisted we take a taxi. She's dying to meet you.'

Indeed, Grace was already waiting for them on the doorstep. Steve ushered his mother through the gate and up the front path. Grace stepped forward. 'Mavis, I'm so pleased to meet you. Please come in.'

Mavis stepped into the hall and let Steve take her coat. She then followed Grace into the big kitchen-diner.

Grace said, 'We'll show you your room later, but first some refreshment. A cup of tea? Or something stronger?'

'Tea, please.'

'If you want to wash your hands while I'm making the tea, the door to the right in the hall is a cloakroom. Steve will show you.'

'No, I'm fine, thank you.'

Mavis sat down and smoothed her skirt over her knees. Steve sat opposite her.

Mavis said, 'This is a lovely house. Very convenient for the station.'

'That was the main reason we bought it. Peter commuted a lot.'

Mavis nodded. 'Of course.'

Grace poured the teas. 'I'm sorry to have to mention my husband so early on in the conversation, but there's no point pretending that he doesn't exist.'

Mavis said, 'I understand. I think it's better if we're frank with each other.'

Steve watched the exchanges between the two in silence and in something approaching terror.

Grace returned to the matter of the house. 'It would actually have been better for me if we'd been closer to the faculty buildings and colleges. But Fenner's, the university cricket ground, is right behind us and the Botanic Gardens are not far away. So, Glisson Road isn't without its advantages. Cambridge is, after all, quite a compact city.'

Mavis, however, was not finished with the subject of Peter. 'Is there any chance of a reconciliation with Peter? Sometimes men, and not only men, need to wander a bit, so they can return to base.'

Grace laughed. 'I can see that you are not one to beat about the bush, Mavis. This is not the first time that Peter has wandered, but it *is* the last time as far as I'm concerned. And no, there is no chance of a reconciliation. Peter actually had the cheek to invite himself down to my parents' place a day or two after Christmas in order to tell us that he would admit to adultery and cede his share of this house to me, if I agreed to a quick divorce.'

'That must have been upsetting, and not just for you. What did your parents think of that?'

'I'm not sure how much Steve has told you, but my father is a vicar. So he is not keen on the idea of divorce. Moreover, my mother never really liked Peter. On the other hand she received a very favourable impression of Steve when she spoke to him on the phone. So my parents are at sixes and sevens about it. I'm afraid that's entirely normal for them.'

'Does your mother have any particular reason for her antipathy towards Peter?'

Grace stood up and walked over to the sink, stared out of the window for a moment or two, then turned back to Mavis and Steve and said, 'I thought we might have had this conversation later this evening. But, you know, I think it is much better to have it now. However, if we are going to dispense with chit-chat, I think we should clear the teacups away and open a bottle of wine. Steve, could you do the honours?'

Steve leapt up, pleased to have something to do. Grace sat back down, while Steve struggled with a corkscrew and a bottle of claret. 'My mother considered Peter bumptious. He could be tactless, and I do think her use of the word bumptious contains a hint of anti-semitism. But the real reason for her antipathy, as you put it, is that she knew that Peter didn't want children and she was desperate to be a grandmother. You can guess from that that I am an only child.'

Mavis said, 'I see.'

Steve was now pouring the drinks and put a glass in front of his mother and handed one to Grace. He then resumed his seat, taking a large slug from his own glass as he did so.

Grace raised her glass and said, 'Before we get into more contentious matters, let us have a toast to welcome you to Glisson Road.' Mavis and Steve raised their glasses, but no one knew quite what form of words to use for the toast.

Grace took a sip of her wine and said, 'Mavis, I can see that you are far too incisive to find that a satisfactory explanation. So please feel free to ask whatever you want and we will do our best to answer truthfully.'

'Thank you, Grace. Well, I suppose I was just wondering whether your mother was still keen to become a grandmother.'

'Yes, she is.'

'Are you minded to oblige her?'

'I am, and to satisfy my own longings.'

'To which end you have recruited Steve?'

'You could put it like that. But I'd prefer to say that Steve and I have fallen in love and I have asked Steve if he would be prepared to be the father of my child.'

'Not to be your husband?'

Grace had been fearing this question. Leaving aside the inconvenient fact that she was still married to Peter and might be for some time until they formalised their divorce, Grace wasn't sure that she wanted to tie herself to a man in that way ever again. One of the attractions of Steve, from the point of view of becoming pregnant, was that she didn't see him as husband material. However, she had only just met Mavis, and such frankness might not be welcomed. She would have to tread carefully.

'That too if things work out that way, but I wanted him to know from the outset that I want to have a baby with him.'

Mavis turned to her son. 'What do you think of that, Steve?'

'Ma, I love Grace and I want to have a child with her.'

'But you're scarcely more than a child yourself. Grace is closer to me in age than she is to you.'

'So what? I haven't been looking forward to this conversation. I knew you'd be upset, but I didn't think you'd be so negative about it.'

'I'm not being negative. I'm just trying to understand the situation.'

Grace intervened. 'Mavis, I don't blame you for what you're saying. My father has said many of the same kind of things and has also invoked the deity. I realise the huge responsibility I am asking Steve to accept and that is why I do not think of him as being scarcely more than a child. I taught him for two years. He is one of the best students I have ever taught. His ideas are far beyond most of his contemporaries. I think I was falling in love with him all along.'

Mavis pursed her lips. 'Perhaps if you had treated him like you treated your other students, he would have done better in his finals. Do your college or university superiors know about your relationship?'

Grace looked as if she had been winded. 'We were not having a relationship when I was teaching him.'

'But he was already affecting your judgement.'

'Ma, please don't treat Grace like this. She was, and she is, a brilliant teacher. It was entirely down to me how I performed in my finals.'

Mavis ignored Steve's attempt to defend Grace. 'So you've had this same conversation with your own parents?'

Grace said in a small voice, 'Yes.'

'But they have not yet met Steve?'

'No, we're going to go down to Somerset together soon.'

Mavis sighed. 'I'm sorry to be so negative. Steve is my son, and I'm not sure I trust his judgement, mainly about himself. Like your own mother, I have dreams of being a grandmother, but I fear that Steve might let you down once you have had the child. As a consequence, I might well become estranged from my own grandchild.'

'Mavis, I promise you that if I do have a child with Steve, you will always have access to your grandchild, whatever happens.'

'It is easy to say that now.'

'I agree, but I mean it.'

Steve was aghast at his mother's behaviour. 'Ma, I promised Grace that even if you didn't agree with what we are planning, you would be kind and considerate. I've never seen this side of you.'

'That's because you don't really know me, Steve. You haven't really tried to get to know me.'

'Because you've never told me anything about yourself.' Steve was finding it difficult not to shout. He jumped up. 'I love Grace. I want to be with her. I'm going to be with her and I want to be the father of her child.'

Mavis took a handkerchief out of her bag, wiped a tear from her eye and then blew her nose. 'Do you think you could show me to my room? I think I need to lie down for a bit.'

Steve immediately dropped his voice, 'Yes, of course. I'm sorry if I was shouting.'

Grace remained silent, a thoughtful look on her face.

Mavis sniffed again. Steve went out to the hall and picked up her bag. 'I'm afraid your room is on the second floor.'

'Steve, I'm not yet fifty. I can handle a couple of flights of stairs.'

Steve went up the stairs ahead of Mavis and pointed out the guest bathroom next to her room on the second floor. Mavis walked into the room and looked around. 'What a lovely room! What a lovely house! I do not wish to pry, but do you have a room to yourself?'

'I do have a room on the first floor in which I can work. It also has a bed in it, but Grace and I share a bedroom. She has her own study at the back of the house; actually, it's immediately below this room.'

'Steve, I'm sorry if I have upset Grace. I just didn't feel that we could go through the weekend without having a proper discussion. I can go back to London first thing tomorrow morning.'

'That won't be necessary, Ma. Grace is tougher than that.' Steve wasn't sure if that was actually the case, but he would soon find out.

Mavis took her shoes off and said, 'I'll just spend a penny and lie down for half an hour. What time are we eating?'

'No special time, but let's say eight.'

On the way downstairs, Steve wondered whether he was going to be dealing with a tearful or furious Grace. But as he entered the kitchen, she said, 'Blimey, you didn't tell me she was an interrogator. She seemed to have worked out that it was all about my becoming pregnant without either of us saying anything explicit.'

'I'm sorry, Grace. I've never seen her behave like that before.'

'Well, I don't suppose it's easy bringing up a child on your own. I'm sure you have to develop a certain ruthlessness.'

'She said if you're upset, she'll go home first thing tomorrow morning.'

'Oh, phooey! I'm not really upset. I'm just not sure what the next step is. In the end whether we have a child or not is up to us. And that's what I said to my own parents.'

Steve retrieved his wine glass. 'Suddenly, I'm not so sure I'm brave enough to visit your folks.'

'Oh, don't be ridiculous. They're a pair of pussycats by comparison.'

'I thought Mavis was too, but now I find she's a lioness protecting her cub.'

'Well, you'll have to make it clear you're no longer an ephebe.'

'She won't know what that is. I certainly didn't, until you told me.'

'I'm not suggesting you use the term. You have to do it by your behaviour.'

'That doesn't make it any easier, especially when she's saying that I've never really tried to get to know her.'

'She probably feels you neglect her and she's probably right.'

'But that's not the sort of thing I can change overnight.'

'No, but you can have it as a goal. What time did you tell her we're eating?'

'I said about eight.'

'Okay, let's get on with the meal and do our best to have a nice evening. You may not believe this, but I really like her and I think we're going to get on fine. We both love you and want the best for you. I think she's just trying to make sure that I'm not exploiting you. I don't blame her. I will be doing the same for my child in years to come.'

'Our child, Grace…'

At that moment, Mavis walked into the room in her stockinged feet. 'Grace, I'm so sorry. You must be shocked at my behaviour. I apologise wholeheartedly for any implication that your behaviour was improper when you were Steve's supervisor. I know full well that for all that period Steve was with Angie. I think perhaps I'm really expressing the concerns I had for Steve when he was with Ginny. As a result, you've ended up being the lightning conductor for some of that tension.'

Grace walked across the room and put her arm around Mavis. 'You don't have to apologise. I know how difficult this is for you. It's difficult for all of us. But I also feel that you and I are going to be the best of friends.'

Mavis sniffed and wiped a tear from her eye. 'I know you will look after him. It's just that I feel I'm losing my boy.'

Grace hugged her again. 'You're not losing him, you're getting me as a daughter and with luck another small human being, whom we can all love.'

Steve, amazed at the sudden turn around, said, 'Right, shall we begin again.'

Later that evening, Mavis was lying in her bed in the guest room of Grace's house. She regretted having used some of her professional tricks on Grace and Steve, but she was impressed by how they had dealt with her contrived antics. She couldn't pretend that she approved of what they were contemplating, but she had formed a favourable impression of Grace and considered her a serious person. It was more difficult to assess Steve's motivations, simply because he was her son and emotional factors were involved. But she feared that he would eventually let Grace down. It pained her to entertain such thoughts about her own son, but she had thought for some time that he was not an entirely serious person. He'd always had his head in the clouds.

In the short term, however, it seemed as if Steve's new living conditions were very agreeable. How many twenty-one-year-old men had such comfortable quarters? Furthermore, Grace, while not as charming and vivacious as Angie and presumably not as beautiful as Ginny, was certainly no dowdy bluestocking. But it was odd to think of her only child and his former teacher sharing a bed in a room beneath hers. She wondered whether they would have the audacity to make love while she was a guest here in their house. Earlier she thought she had heard a squeal from Grace, but it could have been a sneeze, and after that just the quiet murmur of voices.

But how ridiculous to be lying there, wondering whether her son and his girlfriend were having sex. Generally, she was incurious about the sex lives of others. Because it had been an absence in her own life for so long, she'd needed a bulwark against resentment. In any case, she was of a generation and a class that kept such things under wraps. Times had changed, though, and the younger generation seemed to take a shameless delight in sexual matters.

Things were also changing for her, however. Not only was the Berlin posting a huge career move, but she too had acquired a lover. Rediscovering her own sexuality, making herself vulnerable once again, opening herself physically and emotionally to another person had been thrilling. However, it was also making her vulnerable professionally, perhaps clouding her judgement. Again the parallels with Steve's position were all too obvious. No wonder she was transferring her anxiety and apprehensiveness.

She had initially been irritated when Steve announced he was working the next day. Once again it seemed that he was giving no thought to her. But she had quickly realised that it would give her time alone with Grace. She was beginning to feel that she and Grace could reach an accommodation, which would help her to worry less about Steve and get on with her own life. It did feel a little like handing him over to a substitute mother, albeit one with whom he would be having a sexual relationship. But it would be as well not to pursue that thought too far.

## Saturday, 11 January 1975

STEVE RANG THE BELL affixed to the wall to one side of the double doors of the Festival Theatre. He was glad to be away from the house. He hadn't expected it to be easy, but nor had he expected his mother to come out with all guns blazing. In the end, however, Grace and Mavis seemed to have reached some kind of accommodation. Perhaps in his absence they would be able to get to know each other better and perhaps come to like each other.

A few moments later one of the doors swung open to reveal a mighty figure, who greeted Steve with an affectionate, 'Hello, petal. I wondered when we were going to meet again.'

'Butch, what are you doing here?'

'I jumped ship. Gary tempted me away from the Arts. I'm the Festival's stage manager.'

'Congratulations.'

'Last time I saw you, you were not in a good place. Thought I'd offer you a job on the crew. But it seems Gary nabbed you first.'

'Butch, it's lovely to see you.'

'And you, petal. Come in and I'll show you around.'

They passed through a small lobby, which opened out onto a horseshoe-shaped auditorium arranged on three levels with two tiers of boxes and a gallery. Ahead of them was the stage, which lacked both a proscenium arch and curtains. There was a small crew of painters slapping paint onto the large cyclorama at the back of the stage and carpenters lustily sawing and hammering. A radio was blaring out pop music, and there was much ribald chat as the crew got the theatre ready for its re-opening.

Steve looked around open-mouthed. 'Butch, I had no idea. The theatre is beautiful.'

'It is, isn't it? We're going to bring it back to life. At least for a while.'

'I feel so privileged that Gary's asked me to be his assistant.'

'As you should be. You'll learn more on this gig than three years at RADA if you approach it properly. That means no fucking about. Gaz has got a lot on his shoulders and he's going to need a reliable wingman.'

'I promise, Butch. I won't let him down.'

'You'd better, because if you let him down, you'll be letting me down too. I recommended you to him. He had his reservations. He asked me to track you down, though he found you before I did. So it sounds as if you've landed in the divvy?'

'Well, it's very nice living in Glisson Road.'

Butch chuckled. 'Hot and cold running everything, from what I hear.'

Steve blushed. 'Yeah, Grace is very generous.'

'A word to the wise, Gary cares about Grace. A lot. Don't mess her around either.'

Steve gulped. He knew that Gary and Butch were close, but he hadn't imagined that his domestic arrangements would be a subject of discussion between his new employers. 'I'll do my best, Butch. I respect her enormously.'

'You'd better do better than your best if you want to continue to work in this town.'

Steve could see that Butch wasn't joking. Where was the lovable hunk, who had shown him around the Arts and cheered him up when he was in the Slough of Despond? Was it just because he had now taken on an important role in a risky enterprise? Or was it because he was Gary's faithful *consigliere*? Rather the latter, Steve thought.

Butch turned to Steve and, towering over him, put one of his giant hands on each shoulder. 'Sorry to rough you up. This is a fraught enterprise with little chance of success. Every member of the team has got to pull his or her full weight. You may think that you're just Gary's bag-carrier, but you're more than that. He's hired you for your brain. If he falls, you've got to catch him. You've got to spot the landmines and be brave enough to shout out. If you find it getting hot, come and have a talk with me. Don't be afraid.'

Butch then crushed Steve to his massive chest and said, 'I'll show you to Gaz's cubbyhole. But never call him that. I'll let you know if and when that's permitted.'

Steve nodded and followed Butch to a small office on the far side of the auditorium. He tapped on the door and pushed it open. 'Young man to see you, Guv.'

Gary looked up from the desk he was working at and said, 'Steve, great – come in.'

Steve stepped inside and took the seat that Gary indicated. 'No need to hover, Butch. Come in and join us.'

It seemed to Steve that the little office was unlikely to accommodate a person of Butch's bulk and stature, and the idea that such a weighty body could hover was another improbability. In any case, Butch had other things to attend to. 'No, it's okay, Guv. Lots to do. Just to say that I've ordered sandwiches for twelve-thirty in the public bar of the Zebra. Will you two be joining us?'

'We'll see how we're going.'

Steve rather hoped that they would be joining the crew on their lunch break, but clearly the matter was not for him to decide.

Butch stepped back into the auditorium and began to harangue the crew as he walked towards the stage. For a moment, Steve saw the theatre as a wooden square-rigger, with Butch the first mate and Gary the captain. He tried to visualise himself as the midshipman, but after the talking-to he had just had from Butch, he felt rather more like the cabin boy.

Gary said, 'Push the door to, love.'

Steve did as requested and then regained his seat.

'Your notes on the scripts were very good and I agree with all the ones you have rejected.'

Gary picked up one of the piles and said, 'So we're agreed that none of these is worth looking at again.'

Steve laughed. 'Yeah, there were some real stinkers in that lot.'

Gary put the rejected scripts in the wastepaper basket. 'I'm pretty sure we said in the terms and conditions that we would not be returning scripts.'

Steve nodded. 'Yep, nor commenting on them.'

'Simply not got the time for all that if we're going to get this baby to fly.'

Gary picked up his notepad. 'There are about ten plays on the shortlist, but only two plays which we both think are possibles. Let's assume they're both through to the performance group. However, we need four finalists. So, we'll take it in turns to argue for one of the remaining eight plays on the shortlist. With luck, we'll end up with four we can take into production. I'll start.'

He leafed through the pile of scripts, picked one out and said, 'This one, *Standing Stoned*, would probably work quite well on our stage with no tabs and a cyclorama. Single set, small cast.'

Two hours later, they had worked through all eight, arguing the case for each back and forth. At first, Steve had been hesitant to express his views too forcefully. He knew time was short and he didn't want to draw out the discussion, but Gary seemed to be doing the exact opposite, at one moment arguing for a script and a moment later arguing against it, seemingly determined to take all day about getting the four scripts that would go into production. Steve began to lose patience with the process and became more polemical. He almost felt that Gary was goading him. Eventually, at twelve-thirty, Gary said, 'Okay, I think that we can safely say that we haven't got two more to add to the finalists' pile. *Standing Stoned* is a possibility, but only just. I think we're going to have to cast the net a bit wider.'

Steve was desperate for a break. 'What do you suggest?'

'I think we ought to extend the closing date and put out a call for a few more scripts. Can you contact the *Cambridge Evening News* and *The Stage*? And anyone else who will carry the announcement. Do you think you could do a press release and get it printed at XPress?'

'Yeah.'

'Do you have a typewriter?'

'Yeah. What will the new closing date be?'

'Well, let's see.' Gary peered at the calendar pinned to the wall above his desk. 'It's the eleventh of January today. So let's say that we extend the closing date to the end of February. The week of new writing performances isn't until the first week of May, which should give us plenty of time to cast and rehearse the four new plays. Can I leave that all in your hands?'

'Absolutely.'

'Good, let's get to the Zebra then or all the sarnies will be gone.'

Mavis came down late to breakfast to find Grace sipping coffee on her own and reading the Saturday *Guardian*. 'Steve still in bed?'

'Oh, no. He's already gone to work.'

'I didn't realise that theatre people started work so early.'

'They don't normally. It's the first day the full company has access to the building.'

'So it's a new theatre?'

'Not exactly. It's actually a very old theatre, but it hasn't been in use as a theatre since before the war. My friend Gary Lewis is bringing the Festival Theatre back to life. It's a very exciting project, but also a risky one.'

'If Steve had told me he was working today, I would have put off my arrival until this evening.'

'But at least it will give you and me more time to get to know each other.'

'I'd like that.'

'I understand your reservations about what Steve and I are planning. You just think that I am taking advantage of him. I suppose to an extent I am. But Steve is not as naïve as you seem to think. He is an intelligent young man, who is brave enough to plot his own way through life. He was never going to stick to the safe conventional career paths. He is tough and resilient. But he is also kind, often to his own detriment.'

'Steve tells me so little.'

'Perhaps because you discourage it.'

'I don't think so. Why would I do that?'

'Because those kinds of conversation involve the exchange of information, and you haven't been able to tell him about yourself. '

'What makes you think that? Is it something he's said?'

'No, it's something I've inferred.'

'I'm not sure where you're going with this.'

'When I was a graduate student in Berlin and Paris in the early '60s, I was recruited by the British security services to gather information on French intellectuals and academics with communist sympathies. The person I reported to was ostensibly an employee of the Foreign Office, but actually worked for another organisation entirely.'

'Should you be telling me this?'

'I mention it because it would not surprise me if your job at the Foreign Office was actually something to do with the security services. I don't expect you to confirm or deny my suppositions. But it would explain why the flow of information between you and Steve was even less comprehensive than normal between parent and offspring.'

Mavis was silent for a few moments, until, setting her jaw, she said, 'Does Steve know you were recruited?'

'No. It wouldn't be appropriate for me to tell him. I am still occasionally debriefed. Does Steve suspect what your work involves?'

Mavis laughed. 'No, I don't think so. How curious. You know I'll have to check out what you're saying.'

'Of course.'

'To be honest, I'm not sure if that makes me feel any more comfortable about your situation with Steve.'

'I realise that, but you must sometimes have felt that about your own situation.'

Mavis sobbed gently. 'Yes, I did. It's the reason I never found anyone else.'

'But Steve thinks you remained single for him.'

Mavis shook her head. 'What a fool I've been. No wonder he's so spoilt.'

'You haven't been foolish. It was difficult. But you must have been lonely.'

'I was. But…'

She hesitated. Grace remained silent, smiling steadily at Mavis.

'…I do have a friend now.'

'Well, that's marvellous.'

'Please don't tell Steve.'

'Alright, but wouldn't it be better if he knew?'

'Yes, but it's something that we can't be public about right now. It would probably impact both our jobs.'

'I understand. I will keep it to myself.'

'Thank you.'

'Steve said we could visit you in Berlin. We could come at Easter.'

'I'd love you to.'

Mavis took a sip of her now cold tea. 'Do you really want a child?'

'Yes, I want what you had.'

'Believe me, it is not easy combining motherhood and a career. It pains me to say this, but I don't trust Steve to support you at the moments when you will most need him.'

'I'm under no illusion that he will probably drift away at some point. I hope he doesn't. He is a lovely person. We could have a great life together. But he has a kind of magic about him. All kinds of intelligent, strong women, and some men, fall in love with him. He is constantly surprised by the effect he has on people. He doesn't expect it and he doesn't exploit it. Or if he does, it's in a rather innocent way. He was very hurt by Ginny, and I'm sorry to say, by me too. So he constructed this new persona, *new Steve* he calls it, and immediately a girl in the house he was living in fell for him. But *new Steve* is actually old Steve with a change of clothes. I think he thinks that he's more manly in new-Steve mode, but he's not. Then again models of masculinity have changed since you and I were younger, and for the better. Steve's not conventionally good-looking and he is a little naïve – or perhaps guileless might be a better way to put it. Even so, I am not the only woman to find him attractive, indeed sexy, to use the modern term. He is not short of admirers, but he remains oblivious to this fact.'

'I am not reassured by the picture you paint. It is not the Steve I thought I knew.'

'I want you to understand the situation. I will do my best to look after him, but I can't promise to make him stay with me. There are other forces at work, which are likely to overcome my best endeavours.'

Mavis was thoughtful. 'Did you know Angie?'

'No, but I knew of her. No doubt, she would be your preferred choice for Steve.'

'Well, she was.'

'I will be meeting her soon. She and her current boyfriend are coming to stay for a couple of nights.'

Mavis seemed surprised. 'Steve didn't say.'

'No, he's got a tendency to keep things under wraps.'

'Yes, he has.'

'It's probably no consolation, but I think Angie would be my choice for Steve too. I'll have a better feeling about that when I meet her. I'd rather her than Ginny. But I'm afraid to say that I don't think that he's entirely over Ginny, or ever will be.'

'Oh, Grace, I wish you hadn't said that.'

'Actually, so do I. The thought has only just crystallised in my mind. It's been floating around for some days. Steve showed me a recent letter to him from Ginny.'

'Yes, he mentioned to me that Ginny had written and wanted to send some drawings of her to him.'

'She's trying to exert some control over him from afar.'

'You make her sound like a witch.'

'Well, I do think she is something of the sort. In fact, I do feel that Steve's women, and that perhaps includes you and indeed me, are a certain kind of woman.'

'What kind? I'm not sure I understand you.'

'Well, at its simplest, we're all strong women. So perhaps we are all witches. Or something even more uncanny.'

Mavis nodded slowly. 'I still don't really understand what you're saying, but since Steve is out and since we have now broached the subject of Ginny, could you tell me what happened? Steve has told me very little.'

Grace got up from the table. 'I'm not sure. I don't want to go behind Steve's back, but I do understand that it's perplexing for you. Let me make another pot of coffee and I'll try and order my thoughts.'

A few minutes later with a fresh pot of coffee and a refilled plate of biscuits between them, Grace asked, 'What was the last substantial information you had about what was going on in Steve's life?'

'I came down for his graduation and he introduced me to Dr Doyle, who seemed a very nice man, and was complimentary about Steve.'

'Richard is a lovely man and a great scholar. Steve was very lucky to be taught by him. Richard is also a good judge of ability.'

'But Steve didn't do very well in his Finals.'

'Not everybody is cut out to be an academic. I think it was clear to us that even if Steve had got a First, he would probably not have completed his PhD. He had already decided to plough his own furrow. Did you also meet Steve's tutor?'

'No.'

'You probably would have got a somewhat different view of Steve from him. I take it you understand the difference between the role of tutor and the role of director of studies at Cambridge.'

'Yes.'

'Did you meet anyone else?'

'We had dinner with Angie's parents in the evening. They were delightful people.'

'So at that point things must still have been okay between Steve and Angie.'

'Well, I did detect some tension between them. But I was also trying to get over my own shock at what Steve was up to. It was news to me, for example, that he'd decided not to take up the job in the city with the German company he'd worked for before coming to Cambridge. Instead he got a job as a milkman. Fortunately, Angie's parents, or her father at least, treated it as a huge joke. But then he came out with this business about taking a production of *The Importance of Being Earnest* to Edinburgh.'

'Wilde doesn't sound like Steve.'

'The following day he told me that he'd just said that so as not to shock the Barretts. The play he wanted to do was one by Beckett, *Krapp's Last Tape*.'

Grace laughed. 'Much more Steve's thing.'

'But I have no idea about the transition from Angie to Ginny'

'I don't know all the details either. Steve needed a place to live near the dairy. But the only people he could find to share the house with him were Ginny and her then boyfriend, Jon, a notorious local hipster.'

'What happened to Jon?'

'Good question. I understand he's an electric guitarist and was offered a job with a band who were about to set off on a tour of the United States.'

'Leaving Steve and Ginny together in the house near the dairy.'

'Exactly.'

'With inevitable consequences.'

'Yes.'

'Did you meet Ginny?'

'I did. I bumped into Steve in a local pub one evening and I invited him and Ginny to supper to meet Peter, my husband, and Gary, whom Steve is now working for. The evening was a great success although I couldn't help noticing that Peter immediately focused on Ginny. Over the years we'd had our difficulties, but at that point he'd been behaving himself for some time. Or at least that's what I believed.'

'This was the period during which you and Steve became closer?'

'Well, only in the sense that he stopped being my student and became a friend. We discovered that we were both runners and used to meet up for early morning runs.'

'Mightn't Steve have read something into that?'

'I suppose so, if you mean it gave him the opportunity to see me in running gear. But it also gave him the opportunity to notice my bright red face and excess pounds. To be quite honest, the majority of undergraduates at Cambridge are male, and as a female teacher, one gets rather used to having one's body appraised by young males with a sense of entitlement.'

'So there was no sweet talk?'

'No.'

'What did you talk about then?'

'We talked about the poem Steve was writing. I was trying to persuade him to be more professional about his writing. But he's not one to take advice, not even when it comes from Rob, his best friend. Rob's also a poet, but with a much better understanding of the poetry world. He was and still is a great champion of Steve's work and managed to get an extract of Steve's poem accepted for an influential small magazine.'

'But the chap who ran the magazine had a heart attack and so the poem was never published.'

'Yes. To make matters worse, Angie and Rob both found themselves on the same PhD course in Edinburgh and fell in love.'

'Oh, dear, that must have hurt Steve.'

'It did. But he was able to take solace in the fact that he was in a relationship with a beautiful, enigmatic woman. In many ways Ginny was good for Steve. She too was trying to get him to be more professional. She even bought him a typewriter.'

'So you and she had a common aim?'

'Well, to the extent that we were both trying to help him.'

'Maybe he just expects women to sort things out for him. That's also probably my fault.'

'Mavis, you had to be both mother and father to him. Don't blame yourself.'

'But what you're saying is that Ginny wasn't the wicked fairy that I have been imagining.'

'I have no reason to feel particularly generous towards Ginny, but I think that's right. She was the one who encouraged him to give up the milk round and find a job which would give him more time to write. She also got him to help her do up the house they were renting. In return Steve encouraged her to get back to drawing and painting.'

'Ah, yes, he mentioned something about her art.'

'She had been at art school before she was discovered as a model.'

'But there was another side to her too.'

'Well, she seems not to have been an easy person to live with. She suffers from bouts of depression. She was also a user of drugs.'

'Did she encourage Steve in that direction?'

'I think he was already smoking cannabis.'

'Oh, dear. Do you think he's still taking drugs?'

'Well, I'm pretty sure he hasn't taken any since he's been living here. You can't be a university teacher without getting to recognise the distinctive aroma.'

'What about this girl, Jude?'

'I don't know, but in any case she's left Cambridge.'

'So you were seeing Steve quite regularly, but from your point of view he and Ginny were in a reasonably stable relationship. What happened to upset things?'

'I hold life drawing classes here and I invited Ginny to join us. It was only then that I realised how talented she was as an artist. But the other person who noticed was Peter. He'd studied at the Slade and felt himself to be an artist before anything else. Normally Peter didn't come to my classes. He considered it far beneath him, but when he saw Ginny's work, he decided to attend. Of course, the fact that she is supernally beautiful might also have had something to do with it.'

'I know that. I've seen the photographs in the newspapers. It's one of the things I find odd about this whole sorry story. What would such a woman see in Steve?'

'As I was saying earlier, Mavis, perhaps it's hard for you to see what an attractive man your son is.'

'But then she transferred her affections to Peter.'

'It might be easier to understand her motivations there. Peter is a charismatic, handsome man. He is also a product of the German Jewish diaspora, which I think is also the case for Ginny. But in the end, it's probably just because he's wealthy. Ginny appears to be one of those people who either doesn't work or doesn't see why she should work.'

'Presumably Ginny has a family somewhere.'

'An elderly, ailing father. They're not on good terms, but she nurses him when he's ill. So she was in London quite a lot and, of course, so was Peter.'

'How did their liaison come to light?'

'A friend of mine saw them together at the Frankfurt Book Fair. When they got back, I accosted them at our flat in London. I thought I might be able to shame them, but they were exultant. Ginny told Steve the following day that she was leaving him, and shortly after that, she moved into the London flat.'

'I'm so sorry, Grace.'

'I must admit I was feeling pretty sorry for myself.'

'Did you speak to Steve?'

'Just to tell him what had happened. Then I didn't see him until the day of the Cambridge 10K race for which we'd both been training. It was a filthy day, pouring with rain. Like a fool, I didn't watch my footing and hurt my leg. I finished the course, but in agony. Steve helped me back here and one thing led to another. I now felt doubly guilty and told him the next morning that we should step back from each other. I don't think he was pleased to hear that.'

'That's when he stumbled into Jude?'

'Yes.'

'If you do become pregnant by Steve, don't you think that kind of situation is likely to arise again and maybe more than once?'

'Yes, I do. I'm not going to tell him he's free to sleep with other women, but I'm not going to blame him if he does.'

'But isn't that very similar to the life you had with Peter?'

'Yes, I've thought that there is a pattern here.'

'If, or more likely when, Steve meets a new Ginny, you will then be in effect a single parent. I can tell you from personal experience that it's not easy. I know times have changed and perhaps your job will give you more latitude than mine gave me, but it will still be hard work, and you will be lonely.'

Grace was thoughtful. 'Yes, I see that.'

'Are you pregnant yet?'

'No, I'm in the process of coming off the pill, but by this time next year you will be a grandma, I hope.'

Mavis reached her hand across the table and covered Grace's with her own.

When Steve got home from the theatre, Grace was fixing some supper and Mavis was sitting at the big table with a glass of red wine in front of her. He pecked his mother on the cheek and then walked over to Grace and nuzzled her neck. 'Sorry, I'm so late. It's been a long day.'

'Some of it spent in the Zebra, no doubt?' Grace said over her shoulder.

'I did have a couple of drinks. It was kind of compulsory.'

Grace laughed. 'Of course. Team building.'

'That's exactly what Gary called it.'

'Well, you did much better than I expected. How did the script conference go?'

'Pretty exhausting, actually. We agreed immediately that there were two plays that were head and shoulders above the rest. But Gary wanted at least four titles for the new writing competition. So we spent most of the morning taking turns to speak in favour of each of the remaining scripts while the other did his best to reject his arguments. It took me a while to get the hang of it. It was a kind of devil's advocate procedure. But once I realised what Gary was after, I rather enjoyed it.'

'Did you agree on two other finalists?'

'No. There was one that at a pinch could make the cut. But Gary has decided that he wants to cast his net wider. So he's extending the deadline and has asked me to rewrite the ad calling for scripts and run it again in *The Stage* and the *Cambridge Evening News*.'

Steve poured himself some wine and sat down beside his mother. She pushed a bowl of crisps towards him and said, 'So, when you were talking last summer about taking a play to Edinburgh, you weren't joking.'

'I wasn't joking, but I didn't really know how to go about it. So I'll learn a lot working for Gary. He's asked me to be his assistant for the auditions and rehearsals of the shows he's personally directing.'

Grace said, 'Steve, that's amazing.'

'Yeah, Butch said I'd learn more than three years at RADA.'

'He's right.'

A thought occurred to Mavis. 'Didn't you tell me at Christmas that you were now writing plays rather than poetry?'

'I did.'

'So, presumably, that's why Gary asked you to assist him?'

'No, Butch recommended me. I haven't mentioned that I'm working on a play. I don't want to show it to anyone until I feel more confident about it.'

Grace turned around from her work on the supper. 'Not even me? Don't you think you owe me a sight of it, after not letting me see your poem?'

Steve squirmed. 'There's nothing really to see yet. Just disconnected lines of dialogue.'

Grace wiped her hands on her apron. 'My dear, this is the age of the Theatre of the Absurd. That's what theatre-goers want.'

'Well, there's disconnected and there's incoherent.'

'Steve, it's high time you realised that your inner critic will undermine everything you write. It's never going to be satisfied. So you need to listen to the people who already see something in your writing. People like Angie and Rob, and me.'

Mavis intervened. 'And me, Steve. Even though you've never shown me anything you've written, certainly not this poem which seems to have caused such upset in your life.'

'You wouldn't like it, Ma.'

'Why? Does it have sex in it?'

'Well, yes, but that's not what I was thinking of really.'

'What then? Drugs?'

'Yes, that too. But no, the ideas, the abstractions, the allusions.'

'If what you're saying is that I wouldn't be able to understand what you're writing about, who exactly are you writing for?'

'People like Grace.'

Grace laughed scornfully. 'Ha, you say that, but in the end you didn't even let me see the parts of *Event/Horizon* that I actually helped you with.'

Steve said, 'No one's seen it…' – suddenly realising that wasn't quite true.

Grace glared at him. 'No one. Apart from Jude. She's read it, hasn't she?'

Steve looked disconsolate. 'Yes.'

Mavis thought it best not to let on that she already knew something about Jude. 'Who's Jude?'

'A young woman with whom Steve's been having a series of one-night stands, which is not the same as a relationship, apparently. I think that's the way you put it, isn't it?' Grace turned back to the kitchen work surface and resumed peeling the potatoes.

Mavis turned to her son. 'Why did you show it to Jude, but not to Grace?'

Steve was beginning to regret having brought Grace and his mother together. He was also irritated now with Grace's jibes. 'I didn't show it to Jude. She found it in the bin of the house in Tenison Road and retrieved it. I didn't ask her to do so.'

'So, you've got it back?'

'No, she didn't give it back to me.'

'Why not?'

'Because I said I didn't want it back.'

'Why did you say that?'

'Mum, I really don't want to talk about all this.'

'I don't think you can just leave it like that.'

'Oh, alright, because I felt the poem was cursed. It just brought about bad things.'

'I've never thought of you as superstitious.'

Grace turned around again. 'Steve is trying not to tell you what the conditions were for his getting the poem back.'

Steve flashed another angry look at Grace. She really was stirring things.

But Mavis was not to be deterred. 'Well, what were the conditions?'

'Jude said she'd only give it back if I slept with her.'

'But from what Grace just said, this was a young woman you were already sleeping with?'

Steve ran his hand through his hair. 'Mum, this is the modern world. Jude and I were getting to know each other and that included sleeping with each other. Grace and I weren't in touch. Then Grace called on me and we decided to get back together. Grace gave me a book of her poems at Christmas and asked to see the final version of *Event/Horizon*. At that point, I didn't have the courage to tell her I'd destroyed it. It was only when Jude told me how upset she was that I wasn't going to continue the relationship with her that she told me that she'd rescued the poem. I was trying to work out how to get the poem back without jeopardising my relationship with Grace. So I broke into Jude's room, hoping to retrieve the poem. But it wasn't there.'

Mavis was shocked. 'Steve, that's not acceptable behaviour.'

'I know. That's the kind of thing I mean, about the poem. So I decided that the only way to deal with the situation was to tell Jude that I didn't want it back.'

Grace laughed. 'Then slept with her anyway.'

Mavis studied Steve closely. 'Did you?'

'Mum, I don't want to have this kind of conversation with you.'

'It's too late, Steve. We're having it. Did you sleep with her even though she no longer had any hold over you?'

Steve looked miserable. 'Yes, I did. I lost my way in the logic of the situation. I was just trying to minimise the hurt to everyone.'

Mavis shook her head sadly. 'You can't go to bed with every girl who sets her cap at you. Not when you've agreed to be the father of Grace's child.'

'Honestly, I feel terrible. I told Grace everything. I thought she'd forgiven me. I don't know what to say. Perhaps I should go up to bed and leave you two to sort my life out for me.'

Grace dried her hands and put her arms around him. 'Steve, this is difficult for all of us. But you're safe with me.'

Steve allowed himself to be embraced, but at the same time he was thinking that being safe with Grace was not what he'd signed up for. For some reason he couldn't put his finger on, he felt less safe with Grace than he did with Ginny.

Later that night as Grace was getting herself ready for bed, Steve, fully-clothed, lay on top of the bed sullenly watching her. There had been an awkwardness between them all evening. Finally, Steve said, 'What was all that about, when I came home from the Festival this evening?'

Grace had been dreading this conversation. She had almost immediately regretted having ganged up with Mavis against Steve when he'd come home from work. She didn't know what had come over her.

'I'm sorry, Steve. Mavis and I had already had a couple of glasses of wine before you got back.'

'But putting me on the spot like that. That's not going to make my mother feel better about us being together.'

Grace was carefully brushing her hair. 'Actually, Mavis and I got on very well while you were at work. I think she is reconciled to our plan and looking forward to being a grandmother.'

'How did you bring her around?'

'We just got to know each other better. I think she decided to trust me. Actually, we have quite a lot in common.'

That didn't make any sense to Steve. 'Like what? My mother's not an expert in European thought and language.'

'I'm not sure that's quite right, Steve. After all, she does work for the Foreign Office.'

'You're not suggesting that, just because she's a clerk or an assistant in the Foreign Office, she must automatically be up to speed about foreign relations?'

'I'm not going to spell it out for you, Steve. You're just showing how naïve and arrogant you are.'

'Well, if that's what you think of me, what on earth is the point of us being together?'

'Because that's not all you are. You are also a sweet, talented boy.'

'I am not a boy.'

'No, you are not; I'm sorry. It's a form of words, admittedly a form that could be thought of as belittling. It is something that women have had to get used to when we are referred to as girls, but I don't mean it like that. If you're a boy, I want to be your girl. At the same time I'm investing in everything that makes you a man. I'm relying on your virility and fertility.'

'So you just want me for my body?'

'What's so bad about that? How do you think it would make me feel if you said you just wanted me for my mind?'

Steve didn't have a ready response. He was still smarting from being called a naïve and arrogant boy and wasn't sure which part of the insult he objected to most. And what did she mean about not spelling things out for him?

The conversation faltered again. This was the first time that Grace had appreciated that Steve had a truculent side to him. It was apparent that she wasn't handling the situation very well. On the surface she and Mavis had got on well. But she was now regretting having divulged her past involvement with the security services. Why had she done that? Perhaps because it had seemed the best way at the time to indicate that they had something in common. She finished removing her makeup and started to undress, suddenly aware that Steve was watching her closely.

Normally she was a brisk undresser, but tonight it might make sense to prolong the process. She started to find reasons to pause at significant stages of undress, hanging a blouse in the closet, draping her bra over the back of a chair, finally slipping off her knickers and bending over to put her underclothes in the laundry basket, before padding around to the other side of the bed and leaning over him to retrieve her nightdress from under the pillow.

'Come on, Steve. Stop brooding. Get undressed and come to bed.'

Steve rolled off the bed and, with little of the artifice that Grace had shown during her own disrobing, got undressed. Even so, Grace found the sight of his slim, lithe body arousing. Of course, he was angry with her and would probably not be as sexually responsive as he usually was. But she wanted to show him that the earlier stupid conversation about Jude didn't matter. So it would be up to her to make the running.

## Monday, 20 January 1975

AFTER GARY HAD LEFT to go to his dinner, Steve sat in the bar of the Great Eastern Hotel watching the city types having evening snifters before heading back to their residences in the gin and Jag belt of East Anglia. He was in no hurry as he wasn't meeting Al until later. He let his mind drift over the actors Gary and he had auditioned today. He could see why Gary had insisted that he keep very full notes because it was quite hard now to differentiate one actor from another. The only one that stood out in his mind was a pretty, dark-haired girl called Becky, not so much for her acting ability, which, as far as he had been able to judge, was at least as competent as the majority of the candidates, but for her looks. She had been wearing tight jeans and an even tighter white T-shirt. Normally, one could only study the bodies of young women discreetly. But in the context of an audition, close study of the candidate was the whole point of the procedure. At one point, Gary had leaned across to him and said, 'Does she work for you, as a straight male?' Steve had taken a second or two before replying with feigned dispassion, 'Yes, she has a neat little body, but more importantly she enunciates and projects her voice. I could hardly hear what the two before her were saying.'

Gary had nodded. 'Yes, I agree. Thanks.'

He sat there sipping his drink, hoping that she would be one of Gary's picks, especially as Gary had asked several of the younger women, including the one who was now occupying his thoughts, whether they had any objection to nudity on stage. They had all said yes.

As he was thus pleasurably occupied, he was startled out of his reverie by a familiar voice. 'Steve, fancy seeing you here!'

He turned to see Ginny, looking carefully burnished, looming over him. For a moment, he didn't know what to say. The coincidence of bumping into Ginny, of all people among the millions thronging London seemed too improbable, but then he remembered that Ginny had remarkable powers of distorting the ordinary laws of causality.

'Ginny, what are you doing here?'

'Looking for a drink after a long session with my lawyer. What about you?'

'Recovering from a long day auditioning for the new season at the Festival Theatre.'

'My goodness, you've come on since the days of the box office at the Arts.'

'I'm just Gary's bag carrier and note-taker.'

'Ah, yes, Gary. I thought he had a soft spot for you.'

'I can't say I've noticed. He's a pretty tough boss.'

'Those are not incompatible states of mind, if you ask me. Do you mind if I join you? Or are you waiting for Gary?'

'No, please, take a seat. What can I get you to drink?'

'Gin and tonic, please.'

Steve caught the eye of a waiter and ordered Ginny's gin and tonic and another beer for himself.

Ginny sat down opposite him. Having studied him closely, she said, 'You're looking well. Clearly Grace is feeding you properly.'

Steve laughed. 'So far I've done most of the cooking. The only time she really cooked was when my mother came to stay.'

'Ooh, congratulations. How did that go?'

'It wasn't all plain sailing. My mother took a while to accept the situation.'

'The age gap?'

Steve thought it was better not to say anything about a baby. 'Essentially, yeah.'

'The thing is, Steve, you're ageless, both younger and much older than your biological age.'

'Really?'

'Well, you know the kind of nonsense I spout.'

'Not at all. I learned a lot from you.'

'What kind of women to avoid, I imagine.'

Steve laughed again. 'No, I'm still vulnerable in that regard.'

Ginny took a sip of her drink. 'I'm sure you're not referring to Grace here. Do I take it there has been someone else?'

Steve wasn't sure that he should be confiding in Ginny, but did so anyway. 'Grace and I didn't get together as a couple until a few days before Christmas. In the intervening weeks, I was living in a bedsit and became friendly with a girl called Jude.'

'Good for you, Steve. But that didn't last.'

'I had to make a choice.'

Ginny looked at him over her glass. 'Sometimes, what feels like a choice is no choice at all.'

Steve had forgotten how enigmatic Ginny could be. 'I've missed you, Ginny.'

'I miss you too, Steve. I hurt you, and I'm truly sorry about that.'

'You warned me right at the start, but I chose not to listen.'

'Even so, I should have been gentler with you.'

They both fell silent. Now that Steve looked at Ginny carefully, he could see that she had put on a bit of weight, which actually suited her, but under the makeup, she was very pale. After an uncomfortably long pause, Ginny said, 'Are you getting the train back to London?'

'No, I'm staying here tonight. We've got two more days of auditions.'

'Would you mind if we went up to your room? I'm not feeling too good.'

'Oh, Ginny, wouldn't it be better if I got you a cab to take you home?'

'I think I'm going to be sick. The thing is, I'm pregnant, and I've been suffering terribly with so-called morning sickness. I need a private bathroom and somewhere to lie down for a few minutes.'

Steve wasn't quite sure whether he actually believed her. Even if what she was telling him was true, he wished she hadn't entrusted him with the information. But whatever the case, she certainly didn't look well, and it would be cruel to deny her request. 'Okay, I'm on the third floor.'

He stood up and helped Ginny to her feet. He'd also forgotten how brittle her mood and health were. They walked to the lifts, Ginny leaning on his arm. A few minutes later, he opened the door to his room and she dashed into the bathroom and shut the door behind her. Steve sat down on a chair. This was a strange turn of events. He was meant to be meeting Al in Islington in an hour's time, but he could hardly leave Ginny in his room while he went out and had a few pints. With luck, the nausea would pass shortly and he could call a cab for her. He took his shoes off, got his book out of his bag, and lay down on the bed.

He had not read very far when the door to the bathroom opened and Ginny, wrapped in a bath towel, stepped into the room.

'Steve, I'm sorry, would you mind if I got into bed for a while?'

Steve felt he could hardly decline her request. He got off the bed and put his book on the bedside table. Ginny walked towards him, pulled back the cover, unwound the towel from her naked body, and got under the sheets. From the glimpse that Steve had of her torso, he would not have said she was pregnant. On the other hand, it could only be early in the pregnancy, and it did look as if her breasts were fuller and her belly not quite as flat as he remembered it. Whatever the truth of the matter, she still looked transcendentally beautiful.

'Could you pick up my clothes?'

Steve stepped into the bathroom. It didn't look as if she had had a shower, but for some reason, she had undressed. Picking up her underclothes, he noticed how silky they were. He folded her clothes and put them with her bag on the sideboard. He then went around to her side of the bed and put his hand on her brow. She was cold and shivering.

'Can I get you a warm drink? Should I phone Peter?'

'No, just get into bed and hold me.'

'Ginny, I can't. You're pregnant.'

'What difference does that make?'

'But we're not together now. What would Peter think?'

'He doesn't need to know; anyway, he's abroad. Nor does Grace.'

Steve hovered indecisively beside her. She threw back the sheet and, reaching her arms out, drew him down, pressing her naked breasts against his chest. The scent of her body swept over him. He buried his face in her hair. She said, 'Take your clothes off and hold me properly.'

As if hypnotised, he removed his own clothes and climbed in beside her. My God, how he'd missed the feel of her body, her silky skin, her improbable angles. She reached down and grasped his cock and said, 'Steve, I've missed you so much.'

'I've missed you too.'

'I know we can't get back together, but I want you to fuck me. Don't tell me I'm pregnant. It won't harm the baby and by definition you can't make me pregnant again.'

'Again?'

'In the sense that I'm already pregnant.'

Lying beside him a little later, she said, 'I don't get that kind of action at home.'

Still panting, Steve said, 'Nor do I.'

'But that's not what it's about, is it?'

'I've got no idea.'

Ginny remained silent.

Steve propped himself up on one elbow. 'Are you really pregnant?'

'Yes, I thought you might enjoy the fuller breasts. I realise they're still fairly meagre compared to Grace's.'

'Ginny, you are so beautiful. But you need to tell me what's going on here.'

'As soon as I saw you in the hotel bar, I knew I wanted to fuck you.'

'But, Ginny, you can't do things like that.'

'Why not?'

'We're involved with other people. You're expecting Peter's child.'

'They don't need to know.'

'Are you thinking this might happen again?'

'I don't entirely rule it out, but the circumstances are not often going to be quite so propitious.'

'Are you doing some astrology here?'

'That would be one way of looking at it.'

'Ginny, you scare me.'

'Steve, no harm is going to come to you.'

'So why did we break up?'

'We just had to. You must accept it.'

'But am I ever going to be able to make love to you again?'

'It's not impossible. Don't run ahead. Enjoy this moment.'

'I feel I've betrayed Grace.'

'I know. I have no idea what has passed between you and Grace, but I'd be surprised if she sees the relationship as one for the long haul.'

'Even so, I feel guilty.'

'Don't. You have no need to. If you really want to sleep with a woman, or a man for that matter, you can make it happen. You have earned the right.'

'Ginny, that's not the case.'

'Try it and let me know how you get on.'

'How am I supposed to do that?'

'If you mean, how to let me know, just send me a postcard. Write something on it like "The Great Eastern magic worked." Don't put your name. I will know who it's from. If, on the other hand, you mean how to try out whether what I'm saying is true, I'm afraid I'll have to leave it to you to work that out. My spelling it out won't help.'

'You've always known how to freak me out.'

'I know, but I don't wish you ill. You have helped me in ways you can't imagine. Perhaps one day you will find out. As to your reward, if you do decide to test out what I'm saying, bear in mind that such gifts are always double-edged. Never let yourself become the creature of your own power. Be thoughtful before using it. I will do my best to look after you. But even I can only do so much.'

Steve was feeling very strange listening to these words. Had she given him some acid? Or was it in her saliva? He felt that he had known her for all time. He believed that everything she was saying was meant in earnest. He also knew that he would never sleep with her again, but that in some way he would always have her.

They lay there for some more minutes until Ginny rose from the bed. 'I need a quick shower. Come in and talk to me while I'm sorting myself out.'

Twenty minutes later, Ginny was fully dressed and as prim and burnished as when Steve had first seen her in the bar. Steve was still wrapped in a towel. She bent down and kissed him. 'Steve, you are a lovely man. Thanks for helping me out.'

'I didn't do anything.'

'Oh, but you did, and blessings on your head for it.'

She strode to the door and left without a backward glance.

Steve looked at Al across the rickety table in the front bar of the King's Head in Upper Street and said, 'So how's the law going?'

'Tedious as fuck.'

'What did you expect?'

'Well, not gentlemanly chit-chat about Ronsard or Racine for sure, but cramming for professional exams has nothing whatsoever to recommend it. Just pure memory work, no analysis. It's all just a load of carbolic smoke balls.'

'What?'

'A famous case in contract law.'

'Blimey, it sounds a bit N. F. Simpson to me.'

'Totally. Or how about snail-flavoured lemonade?'

'No thanks. I'll stick to the Young's Special.'

'Anyway, what are you doing up in the smoke?'

'Auditioning actors for Six Characters, Mr Sloane, Mother Courage and some new plays that we haven't selected yet.'

'You're pulling my leg.'

'Seriously. I'm the assistant to a guy called Gary Lewis.'

'Blimey, the RSC and National Theatre guy.'

'Really? I didn't realise that.'

'What planet are you on, Steve? Anyway, how did you snag that gig?'

'He and Grace are best mates. Although I was actually recommended by a guy called Butch.'

'You're Sundance, I take it.'

'I suppose I am.'

'And how's life with Grace Abounding?'

'It's great. I had a little difficulty disentangling myself from a chick who lived in the bedsitter house. She understood us to be in a relationship. Didn't understand the concept of being in a series of one-night stands with the same person.'

'Oh, dear. Before you tell me more, let me get some more beers in.'

While Al was at the bar, Steve ran over in his mind what he could and what he shouldn't tell Al. He trusted him completely, but it was a lot to take in and he wasn't entirely sure that he even approved of his own behaviour.

Al returned with the beers. 'So where were we? A little disentangling operation. Was that successful?'

'Not entirely.'

'Ah, so there's an element of ongoingness.'

'Just so.'

'Is Grace aware?'

'Yes.'

'Yet you haven't been given your marching orders?'

'Well, there are extenuating circumstances.'

'Does that mean that things are still going on?'

'Let's just say they haven't been terminated, but there is a hiatus by reason of geography.'

'Such as?'

'She moved to London, but is still in touch.'

'Well, your old uncle Al could give you a hand here, distract her from the irresistible lure of the Percival.'

'It's not such a crazy thought, Al. I think you'd approve. I'll see if I can effect some kind of hook-up.'

Al was suddenly suspicious. 'If this chick is so hot, why are you trying to palm her off on me?'

'Because things are already complicated enough and I haven't got enough mental energy to handle a feisty redhead.'

'Are you sure she doesn't look like the back end of a bus?'

'No, she's a cracker and absolutely bonkers in the sack.'

'I'm not convinced, Percival.'

As ever, Steve had talked himself into saying more than he had intended. 'Well, to begin with, Grace has asked me to give her a child.'

'I presume you're talking about procreation here, not popping down to the local department store and buying one off the peg.'

'Exactly. Grace and I are going down to Somerset in a couple of weeks to stay with her parents and give them the good news.'

'When you say good news, you don't mean that Grace is already pregnant.'

'No, merely that we are at it, hammer and tongs, during her fertile periods.'

'Why not wait until the iron is glowing?'

'Why not indeed? Grace thinks we should be open about it. But to judge from the effect it had on my mother, I'm not so sure. Worse still, her old boy is a vicar.'

'Eek! Mavis took a dim view then?'

'Needed some convincing.'

'Age gap and all that?'

'More that yours truly was not someone to be relied upon.'

'Well, she has a point.'

'Fuck off, Al.'

'Jokes. I'm sure you'll have Grace's folks eating out of your hand.'

'There's another thing. I met Ginny last night.'

'Oh! Naughty, naughty. The full Monty?'

'Yep. She's pregnant too.'

'Hang on a moment. If you only tupped her yesterday, you can't possibly know it's resulted in a pregnancy.'

'No, she's already pregnant by Peter.'

'Oh! Naughty, naughty, naughty.'

'Indeed. If it hadn't been so lovely, I'd be feeling more miserable than I actually am.'

'You are your own worst enemy, Percival. You'd better hand over the redhead's number at once.'

* * *

Gary and Steve were sitting in the bar of the Great Eastern. Gary was drinking a large glass of Châteauneuf-du-Pape and Steve had a pint of beer on the go.

Gary said, 'Steve, it was good having you along. When we were reviewing the candidates this afternoon, your recall for individuals was incredible. As soon as I hear someone speak, I recognise them, but the name on paper makes no sense to me.'

'I suppose it's because I was spending more time jotting down your comments against each name in my notebook rather than actually assessing the person's performance. I hardly looked at some of them.'

'Well, that's useful food for thought. Do you think you'll be able to get your notes typed up for Monday?'

'Yeah, I think so. We've got guests this weekend, but I think they're pushing off before lunch on Sunday, and Grace usually spends Sunday afternoon and evening rustling up her Wednesday lecture.'

'So, how's it going at Glisson Road?'

'Fine. We had my mother to stay recently and she and Grace got on like a house on fire. We're going down to Somerset in a couple of weeks for me to be presented to Grace's parents. Actually, I'm terrified, but I did have a nice conversation with June on the phone.'

'You'll be fine. They're lovely people. They were accepting of me, even after I'd come out and that was nearly ten years before homosexuality was, at least, partly decriminalised.'

'I'm just worried they'll think that Grace has traded a handsome, successful publisher for a penniless boy. I'm so grateful for your taking me on as your assistant because it means I can at least present myself as having some kind of standing. It also means I can make a contribution to the household expenses.'

'Grace knows what she's doing and I'm sure you make a contribution in other ways. I had a drink with her last week and I don't think I've seen her looking so well for years. She said you'd been updating her sexual repertoire.'

Steve blushed. 'That's one way of putting it. I actually got the feeling that she was sex-starved and I hope she's now relaxing into a loving relationship.'

'Yeah, intimacy between her and Peter came to an end quite some time ago. He really didn't treat her very well. So it must be great for her to have a sexy young guy in her bed.'

'I can assure you it's great for me too.'

'Peter was a bastard. I imagine you don't have a very positive view of him either.'

'To be honest, I hardly think about him at all. I just wish Grace would get the ball rolling with the divorce. Apparently, he'd like to get on with it too, but it seems it's up to her to initiate proceedings.'

'What do you think's stopping her?'

'No idea, but I don't think it's residual affection.'

'What about you? Do you still have feelings for Ginny?'

'I'd be lying if I said I didn't, but they're very mixed. She could be weird and scary, whereas Grace is incredibly nurturing. Ginny was also high maintenance. But she did open my eyes to certain things.'

'Via the magic of LSD, according to Matt.'

'How did Matt know?'

'The bookshop guy told him.'

'That figures. Well, it was amazing and I trusted her completely throughout. She probably imprinted me somehow, but I'm not sorry I took it.'

'I'd like to talk to you in more detail about your experiences with acid. I'm thinking of doing Heathcote Williams's AC/DC. Do you know it?'

Steve shook his head. 'No, I'm afraid I don't.'

'I'll give you the play script when we get back to Cambridge. I'd like to have your opinion. Speaking of scripts, we've had some responses to the ad extending the deadline for the new writing competition. You could pick those up and start reading them when you pick up AC/DC.'

'Gary, if I haven't made it clear already, I'm really grateful for the opportunity you've given me. I will do my best not to let you down. Actually, when I said that to Butch, he said I'd better do better than my best.'

'You're doing fine so far. But the world of the theatre can be a tough place. Not everyone's cut out for it. It can play havoc with relationships. But don't worry, I'll let you know if you're not delivering. I'm afraid I have a reputation for being a tough boss.'

'Well, at least I'll know where I stand.'

'You certainly will.'

## Friday, 24 January 1975

ROB WAS LYING IN bed in the guest room of the house in Glisson Road watching Angie tidy her hair. 'This is a nice place that Grace's got. Old Steve has landed on his feet again, it seems.'

Angie put down her hairbrush and joined Rob in bed. 'It certainly is beautiful, but I thought Steve looked a bit subdued.'

'It sounds like he's got his hands full with the theatre job. Steve prefers to take a more relaxed approach to things.'

'Yeah, his boss sounds like a bit of a slave-driver.'

'But it's typical of Steve that with no real theatre experience he lands a job with Gary Lewis.'

'I don't think he knew who Gary Lewis really was before he took the job.'

'Also typical. Reading scripts for Gary, assisting him at auditions, apparently Gary wants Steve to sit in on rehearsals of the shows he's directing for this new season at the Festival. Most people have to struggle for years to get an opportunity like that. But that's what being Grace Mitchell's lover can do for you. She gives him an *entrée* to a world he could never enter on his own. Steve doesn't even seem to realise that Grace is one of the few Cambridge poets that Flynn respects.'

'I'm surprised you never mentioned it to him.'

'Well, we've only recently discovered he was in a relationship with her.'

'It does him credit then that he doesn't seem to be cynically exploiting the situation.'

'I don't think you can be both naïve and cynical.'

'Oh, come on, Rob, that's a bit harsh.'

'Well, how many people of our age find themselves having to choose between a beautiful catwalk queen and one of the best-connected intellectuals in the country?'

'I'm not sure I accept the choices facing Steve are bipolar. The dark beauty you are referring to seems to have abandoned him.'

'Whatever Ginny is up to, I think it more likely that she has only temporarily withdrawn from the field of battle and that the rivalry between her and Grace is still an active issue.'

'I'd like to remind you that the person who Ginny stole Steve from was me, not Grace.'

'Well, yes, I think you too are part of the weird constellation around Steve.'

'Oh, that's ridiculous. Steve and I were just young lovers. I had neither beauty nor connections to offer.'

'I don't actually accept that. You are beautiful in your own right and gave him access to a realm of wisdom that could only be of benefit to him.'

'Which he spurned.'

'I know it must rankle and I know you haven't entirely given up on him…'

'You talk as if Ginny, Grace and I are tussling over Steve or seeking some kind of endorsement from him. I have never heard anything so preposterous. We are all stronger than Steve.'

'Of course you are. But for a poet choosing a muse is a hazardous business. It is a terrible doom. It can destroy you. That's what I mean about the rivalrous constellation that the three of you form.'

Angie laughed. 'It sounds to me that you're getting yourself in the mood to pay homage to the Mighty Flynn.'

'As we all must.'

'Rob, enough of this. I think we have to accept that in this house we pay homage to Grace and that is exactly what Steve is doing.'

'I'm sure you're right.'

'Actually, it's hard to imagine there's a downside to Grace. She's even more delightful than I'd imagined from Steve's puppy-dog descriptions of her when we were living in Victoria Road.'

'She's certainly more buxom than Ginny.'

'Careful, Rob. I don't know that I'm altogether comfortable with the idea of your appraising Grace's curves. I'd say she's just nicely covered.'

'Well, clearly the extra curves don't stop her running.'

'But I bet she has to strap her top down a bit, though.'

'Who's being inappropriate now?'

'I'm just trying to point out that there's a happy medium between Ginny's skeletal *décolletage* and Grace's incipient embonpoint.'

'A point occupied by the fragrant Miss Angela Barrett, no doubt.'

'Indeed.'

Rob reached across to caress Angie's breast, only to have his hand slapped away.

'If you think the quickest way to a girl's heart is to cop a feel, you're sadly mistaken.'

'It's all this talk of the happy medium. I wanted to remind myself.'

'I'd say it's more to do with the amount you were drinking this evening.'

'Well, Steve and Grace were opening the bottles at a rate of knots.'

'I hope they don't drink like that every night.'

'At least he's not smoking dope, which was a major feature of life with Ginny.'

'No, that is a good thing.'

'Anyway, we've both had a busy week and a long journey down from Edinburgh. I thought it'd do us good to unwind a bit.'

'With a bit of hanky-panky?'

'Why not?'

'We're in someone else's house.'

'Which can only add to the piquancy. Surely paying homage to Grace doesn't preclude our normal intimate relations?'

'They might hear.'

'So what? Anyway, I'm sure they're still at the stage where they can't keep their hands off each other, so they're unlikely to be listening out for the creaking of our bedsprings.'

'Grace is a more mature woman. I'm sure she's not like that.'

'I wouldn't be surprised if that made her even randier.'

'Really?'

'Oh come on, Anj. We've even got our own bathroom.'

A little later, now indeed more relaxed, Angie returned to her concerns for Steve. 'He looked as if he had something on his mind.'

'Steve's always got something on his mind. That's what being a poet is.'

'You don't seem like that.'

'That's because I'm not the real deal.'

'Oh, let's not have that again, Rob. You're much more accomplished than Steve.'

'That's not what it's about. One can be accomplished, as you put it, published, successful in the eyes of the world, but still be a poetaster.'

'Nonsense. I don't want to hear any more of this talk. But what did you think of all that stuff about Steve throwing *Event/Horizon* in the bin and the girl upstairs rescuing it. Steve didn't look too pleased when Grace was telling us the story. He was pretty tight-lipped about the whole thing.'

'That's exactly what I mean. Only a real poet would throw away the poem he'd spent a year or more writing and wrecked his prospects for.'

'Only a real idiot.'

'No, it's something to do with courage.'

'What do you mean?'

'Well, he's doing the orphic thing, steeling himself not to turn around.'

'But surely it's the girl who's bringing the poem back from oblivion, not Steve.'

'No, the poem is Eurydice. The poem is just the trace, the husk of an earlier impulse. In a sense the poem itself is unimportant. Of course, it would be better if we had the poem, but it is more important that Steve retains that sense of temerity.'

'So what do you think the girl's up to? And don't try fitting her into your bloomin' constellation of muses.'

'I've no idea. Not every girl that Steve goes to bed with is a vital component of his psyche. No doubt we're all part of processes in other people's lives, which we only dimly understand. But she clearly recognised that the poem was a fine piece of work. And, yes, she's probably got the hots for him.'

'I wonder if Grace also thinks that?'

'No idea. Grace is no one's fool. But I think we're missing some part of the jigsaw puzzle.'

'Do you think Steve would confide in you?'

'I think he's more likely to confide in you.'

'Not about two-timing Grace, surely?'

'You never know. Maybe you can get some time alone with him tomorrow afternoon, when I'm with Flynn. I think Grace said she was going to be out too. So you could subject him to the old third degree.'

'I'm not sure. I think you ought to be the one to try and get some time alone with him. You're his best friend.'

'He just lets me think that. He doesn't really have friends. No one, well, no male ever really gets close to him. He's more comfortable with women. Anyway, tomorrow's Flynn Fest schedule is pretty packed and then we're heading back to Edinburgh on Sunday morning.'

'Rob, I'm not sure I want to be alone with Steve.'

'I'm under no illusion that you still have feelings for him. I know he has a kind of magic about him.'

'Nonsense. He's rather sad really.'

'Sadness worn in a certain way can be alluring.'

'I think you're garbling some quote there.'

'That's the kind of poet I am.'

'Stop it, Rob. I don't know what's got into you. You're constructing a set of dynamics which don't apply. I love you and I want to be with you for the rest of my life. I want to have your children. My parents love you too. My mother is so relieved that I'm no longer with Steve.'

Rob pulled her towards him. 'Babies? That's the first time I've heard talk of babies. Don't you think we should get our PhDs first and teaching posts, preferably back here in Cambridge.'

'Of course, you numbskull. I'm not suggesting you should impregnate me here and now.'

'Phew, that's a relief. But I'm happy to share those aspirations.'

Angie kissed him tenderly. 'No more Steve talk tonight. We're here for Flynn.'

'You're right. I'm looking forward to introducing you to him tomorrow evening at the party.'

Grace and Steve were lying in bed reflecting on the evening with Angie and Rob. Grace said, 'Are you okay, Steve? You seem a bit thoughtful.'

Steve shrugged. 'It's nothing.'

'It's clearly not. Come on, get it off your chest.'

'Well, I wish you hadn't told them about the business to do with the manuscript of *Event/Horizon*.'

'You never mentioned that there was an embargo on the subject. I thought you were quite proud of your behaviour.'

'I don't want to have to go into details.'

'Your friends are very nice people. I am sure they will treat whatever you tell them with discretion. Now that I've met them, I'd happily have them to stay here again.'

Struggling to cast off his sullen demeanour, Steve said, 'Thank you, Grace. It's lovely of you to say it, but actually I couldn't bear it.'

'You will never get over Angie, Steve, but the pain will diminish. Yes, Rob is everything that you aren't. But it's pretty obvious that he's also in awe of you and would like to be more like you.'

'I don't buy that for one moment. Rob is always ticking me off, in a way, for being so disorganised. If there's anything about me that he envies, it's that I'm living with you.'

'Well, he'd certainly done his homework, quoting extensively by heart from *The Abyss Looks Back*.'

'Yeah, creep.'

Grace laughed. 'Whereas, in fact, it's the bad boys I seem to like.'

'Have there been others?'

'That would be telling…'

'You've worried me now.'

'I'm glad to hear it. I can't have you taking me for granted. But enough of that. As I mentioned, I'm going to be out tomorrow afternoon. But at least it'll give you some time with your friends without me in attendance.'

'Rob's having a tête-à-tête with Flynn tomorrow afternoon.'

'In that case you'll have some time alone with your first love.'

'I'd rather not.'

'Don't be ridiculous, Steve. What could be nicer? Why don't you tell her about our plans to have a baby?'

'I thought we weren't telling people, apart from our parents, until we know you're pregnant.'

'But Angie and even Rob are a bit different, don't you think?'

'In what way?'

'Well, Angie was your girlfriend for two years.'

'That sounds to me like a reason not to tell her.'

'Okay, it's up to you. But if you do tell her, I'm not going to be upset.'

Steve wasn't sure what was behind this sudden change of approach. 'By the same reasoning, why don't we tell Ginny and Peter?'

'You know what? That's not a bad idea.'

'Really?'

'At Christmas, Peter offered to transfer to me his share in this house if I agreed to begin divorce proceedings. It's not like Peter to give away something he doesn't have to or to have to publicly admit to adultery. I can only assume he wants to marry Ginny.'

'Sorry, Grace. I can't follow your logic here.'

'I've been holding off starting the divorce, not because I hope to get back with Peter, but because I just want to thwart him. But what's the point? If he's prepared to give up his share in this house without a court enforcing it, it must be to his pecuniary advantage somehow. I can only think that has something to do with Ginny. Her father's wealthy, isn't he?'

'I have no idea. He's a doctor and lives in Hampstead, so he's probably not exactly hard up. But I still don't understand where you're going with this.'

'I think I'll write to him and agree to move the divorce along on the terms he proposes. I will also let him know at the same time that you and I are in a relationship and that we're hoping to have a child.'

'Do you think that's wise?'

'What can he do? He'll hate the idea that you're living in what he probably considers his house and sleeping with his wife. Even though he didn't want children, it's still seen as a symbol of virility. Even if he changed his mind, it's highly unlikely that Ginny could be persuaded to bear a child.'

Ever since his encounter with Ginny in the Great Eastern Hotel, Steve had been struggling to make sense of what she had told him, but all his attempts had foundered on the inevitable feelings of guilt. But now everything snapped into focus. Peter had denied Grace a child. His departure meant that she could now conceive if she could find a willing partner. While her enlisting of Steve was the most direct way of fulfilling her biological urges, it was also a swipe at Peter. However, that was founded on the presupposition that not only did Peter not wish to be a father, but that a woman like Ginny would be seriously lacking in maternal impulses. That was now clearly not the case.

The realisation of this fact would be devastating to Grace, and her idea of appending the news that she and Steve were *trying* to have a child would invite the riposte that Ginny was *already* pregnant. No, the knowledge that Ginny was pregnant must be kept from Grace for as long as possible and certainly until she herself was pregnant. He must deflect Grace from her determination to inform Peter of her arrangement with Steve.

'Grace, this all feels very provocative. I'm in favour of your proceeding with the divorce. But let's keep the pregnancy thing under our hats until it's a reality. We don't want to tempt fate.'

'I just want to be able to imagine the look on Peter's face.'

'That kind of gesture never works, and as often as not backfires. I would prefer our sessions of unprotected sex to be for the purposes of bringing a new life into the world, not as a way of settling scores.'

'Steve, this is a side of you I am not familiar with. What happened to the charming, feckless youth? Where did the serious paterfamilias come from?'

'I don't know. I've been thinking about what my mother was saying about me and I don't want to be that person, the person that lets other people down. I want to be better than that. I know that I'm not going to be able to change overnight, but I'm going to try.'

Grace didn't entirely believe the fine words. She was aware of Steve's lively conscience and his tendency for self-recrimination, so she felt that there must be something more than just the fruits of meditating on Mavis's comments prompting this new pomposity. But at the same time, she recognised that there was truth in what he said.

'Okay, you're probably right. But I don't think it will harm to tell Angie and Rob.'

Now that he was privately querying Grace's motives, he also saw that by widening the circle of those that knew they were planning to have a child, Grace was not only attempting to mark Peter's card, but also Ginny's and Angie's. There was an element of pre-emption involved, which in effect said *Hands off, he's mine* to the other two women in his life. Steve had the uncomfortable feeling that Grace was exploiting their intention to have a child. But he didn't blame her. Few people's motives were entirely pure.

'I don't know. I think we should stick to our original plan. I would really rather not be alone with Angie. I still think she has some scores to settle with me. You didn't say anything about having a meeting today when we invited them.'

'It's a date of longstanding, but I didn't want it to be the reason not to have Rob and Angie to stay with us. It's nothing to be alarmed about. It's normal. In the same way that Rob has got a meeting with Jeremiah Flynn tomorrow without Angie.'

'Yeah, that's because he's one of Flynn's bum boys.'

'Steve, it does you no credit to speak about your friend like that. Could it be that you are more jealous of Rob for his closeness to Flynn than for the fact that he's in a relationship with your first love?'

Striking a petulant note that he knew was unbecoming, Steve said, 'Well, for all he's done for me, he's never introduced me to Flynn.'

'Would you like to be introduced to Flynn?'

'I'd like to be acknowledged.'

'We all would, but isn't the best way to let him see your poetry. Surely that's what Rob did.'

'Flynn was Rob's teacher.'

'I'm sorry that you had to put up with me.'

'I don't mean it like that.'

'Have you read any of Flynn's poetry?'

'Of course.'

'Have you read any of mine?'

'You know I have.'

'You have yet to comment on my work. Unlike Rob.'

'I'm sorry. It just made me despair. It's everything I can't do.'

'Not good enough, Steve. You have to support your assertions with examples. Encomia like that are worthless. You may be right, but you have not made the case. I really have let you down if I have managed to have you under my wing for two years yet you haven't even got that simple point clear in your head.'

'Grace, it was like it was written in fire. It hurt me to read it. I did read it, but I felt it was undoing me.'

'I'm still not accepting this. But let us go back to Flynn. Would you like to be introduced? He's a good friend of mine. We could have him round for supper. But think carefully how you want your first encounter with him to happen. Or whether you really do want to meet him. He is a severe man. He doesn't mince his words.'

## Saturday, 25 January 1975

ANGIE STOOD ON THE doorstep of Grace's house and watched Rob setting out for his meeting with Jeremiah Flynn. When he had disappeared from view, she stepped back into the house and went through to the kitchen. She found Steve washing up the lunch things.

She sat down at the table. 'I'm glad we got some time together.'

Steve dried his hands and joined her at the table. 'Me too. Shall we go to bed?'

'How dare you!'

Angie had not meant to be so curt, but the proposal had touched something deep inside her, making her think for a moment that the struggle for Steve's devotion was not yet totally out of the question, despite her assurance to Rob to the contrary. It was as if Steve had sensed this because, yes, a part of her did want to go to bed with him.

Steve did not seem perturbed by her response. 'Grace has more or less said that it would be okay, so long as I don't tell her.'

But Angie had now regained her composure. 'I don't believe you. But even if it's true, what good would it serve? I just wonder what's going on here.'

'You could carry me off to Edinburgh.'

'You're being absurd. You can't treat people like this. You had your chance.'

'But I didn't realise how things would turn out.'

'Too bad. We had a lovely time together, but now we're with other people and on completely different trajectories.'

'Which are intersecting at this very moment.'

'I know you think you can have sex with whoever you're with at any given moment. Maybe there are people who accord you that privilege. But I am not one of them.'

'You can't blame me for trying.'

'I can. It shows that you don't take relationships seriously.'

'But I do. That's the problem.'

'Did you sleep with the woman who rescued your poem?'

'Yes.'

'When you were already with Grace?'

'It's complicated, but yes.'

'Doesn't deceiving Grace trouble your conscience?'

'Yes, but she accepts these things. I don't want to explain why right now. I'd rather leave it to Grace.'

'She's a remarkable woman.'

'She is and I love her and trust her.'

'And she loves you?'

'After her fashion. She certainly enjoys the sex.'

'Do you enjoy sex with her?'

'Yes, but she is inexperienced and afraid of letting go.'

'Unlike Ginny presumably?'

'Indeed.'

'You must hate her. Ginny, that is.'

'Not at all.'

'You're not hoping to get back with Ginny, are you?'

'What's hope got to do with it? But if you're asking me if it's likely, I'd have to say no.'

'Steve, you've turned into a very strange man. I feel like you're not really the person I knew when we were students.'

'I'm the same person, but I've changed.'

'Was it the drugs?'

'I don't think drugs change you. Perhaps they open a door.'

'Are you still smoking dope and taking acid?'

'No, Grace doesn't approve.'

'Well, good for Grace.'

'You never really approved either, did you?'

'No, but that wasn't the reason we broke up. Did you enjoy making love with me?'

'It was beyond compare. We are made for each other.'

'Steve, don't say things like that.'

'Don't ask the question then.'

'Anyway, I don't believe you. I don't let go either, nor am I very experienced. I'm just like Grace.'

'Not at all. You're very different.'

'I'm younger, I suppose.'

'You are, but it's not that. There's something about you, a way of understanding the world. I wanted to learn from you. I *did* learn from you. But the understanding was beyond me.'

'And that's why you left me?'

'I stayed; you left.'

'Leaving aside your quibble, I get Ginny, Grace and me. But I don't see how Jude fits into your story.'

'Nor do I.'

Steve and Rob were sitting in the front room. The two women had already gone up to bed. Before they had done so, Rob had been entertaining the company with an account of his afternoon with Flynn, which had been supplemented by some slightly less adulatory observations from Angie on proceedings at the evening event. Rob had clearly informed Flynn at some point during the day that he and Angie were staying with Grace, because Flynn had asked him to pass on his regards and congratulations to her. Grace noticed the sullen expression that passed across Steve's face as the regards were duly delivered.

When the women had left the room, Steve said to Rob, 'Grace has got a nice collection of malts here. Could I offer you a nightcap?'

Rob, feeling pleased with his day and the reassurance he had received from Flynn that he was not forgotten, said, 'Why not? We don't have an early start tomorrow.'

Steve fixed them a couple of Laphroaigs and resumed his seat.

Rob took a slug of his drink and then said, 'So tell me about this woman who rescued *Event/Horizon*. Did you sleep with her?'

'Yeah.'

'And?'

'There's nothing to tell really. She and I were living in the same house. When I moved in, I decided that I'd had enough of the poem and put it in the rubbish bin at the back of the house. The bins were rather full and I didn't do a very good job of pushing it down. Jude saw the pages of the manuscript, when she put her own rubbish out, and took them up to her room.'

'Wow! What was your reaction when she gave them back to you? One of relief, I imagine. Did you immediately count the pages to make sure they were all there?'

Steve groaned quietly under his breath. 'It's not as simple as that. I don't actually have the manuscript.'

'Who's got it?'

'Jude. I told her I didn't want it back and gave her permission to destroy it, properly this time.'

'Can't you just ask for it back?'

'Then I'd have to sleep with her…'

'I thought you said you'd slept with her.'

'I had, but that was before I knew she had the poem.'

'So what was the problem?'

'Because by then I was back with Grace.'

'*Back* with?'

'When Ginny went off with Peter, Grace and I had a bit of a thing, but decided it was too soon to treat it as a proper relationship.'

'But more recently, you decided it was back on?'

Steve nodded.

'Jude was left high and dry?'

'Kind of.'

'So now she's punishing you by not giving you back your manuscript?'

'No, she's not making any demands. I think she's just waiting for me to fall into her arms.'

'Is that likely?'

'Maybe. The fact of the matter is that Grace and I are in a relationship of convenience. I get a beautiful place to live in and further on down the line she gets a baby.'

'What?'

'She wants me to be the father of her child.'

'You're winding me up.'

'No, that's the deal. Theoretically, we're only telling our families at the moment. But you and Anj are practically family as far as I'm concerned.'

'You're intent on doing that?'

'Yeah, we've already told my mother. Next weekend we're going to Somerset to meet her parents.'

'How do you feel about that?'

'I'm terrified. I've already spoken briefly with her mother on the phone. That went okay. But her old boy is a vicar, disapproves of divorce and the like. The chances that he will approve of Grace having a child with a former student who is at least fifteen years younger than her are remote.'

'How did this all happen?'

'I don't know. I seem to be at the focal point of some whirlpool of crazy events. I've stopped trying to swim against the riptide. I'm conserving my energy and hoping I stay afloat. I don't know why it's all happening.'

'Because you're a born poet, as all true poets are.'

'Bollocks!'

'You can rail against it, but it's your fate, even if you never write another line of verse.'

'Oh, I don't buy into all this nonsense. I was just pretending to be a poet. I knew I was no good.'

'It has absolutely nothing to do with conventional ideas of quality. People like you remake the conventions. You should have come to the Flynn fest.'

'Rob, Flynn would destroy me.'

'I'm not so sure about that. He might not like you or your work, but I don't think he could destroy you because you operate beyond his immediate sphere of influence.'

'Rob, you are a great mate. I am endlessly grateful to you. But I'm not operating in any sphere. I'm having a great time living with a beautiful woman and learning about the theatre.'

'After living with a previous beautiful woman.'

'Yeah, who walked out on me and left me mouldering in a shitty bedsitter.'

'Where you had a fling with yet another woman.'

'Who fell for a persona I briefly adopted.'

'What was the persona?'

'I called him new Steve. He was a kind of Jack the Lad. Try it on with any chick.'

'Okay, so what's the approach? Do you just go up to a girl and say, let's go to bed?'

'Yeah, more or less. The thing to do is to act as though it's a matter of course and to accept that you're likely to be rejected. But don't show any fear or doubt, even though that's exactly what you're feeling.'

Rob shook his head despairingly.

While the two men had been pouring their malts, Angie had caught up with Grace on the first floor landing. 'Grace, thank you so much for allowing us to invade your home.'

'It's been a pleasure. I've wanted to meet you for a long time. Steve was always talking about you in his supervisions.'

'And he was always talking about you when he returned from them.'

'Well, I'm sorry if you feel I've stolen him from you.'

'It wasn't you. To be quite honest, I feel you've rescued him.'

'From a certain former model?'

'Exactly.'

'If you're not too exhausted from having hobnobbed with the Flynn fan club, have you got five minutes for a chat?'

'Of course.'

'Let's go into my study. We don't want to be surprised by one of the men.'

Grace led Angie into her study and invited her to take a seat.

Grace also sat down and, pursing her lips, said, 'You're not shocked by the fact Steve and I are having a relationship?'

'Not at all.'

'I'm quite a lot older than him.'

'I don't see that as a problem.'

'But many people do – Steve's mother for one.'

'You've met Mavis?'

'Yes, we had her to stay last weekend. She was quite upset to begin with.'

'My impression of Mavis is that she's an entirely sensible person.'

'I agree, but what really upset her was that we told her we are planning to have a child together.'

Angie was unable, for a moment, to disguise her own surprise, but realising that this was one of the missing pieces of the jigsaw puzzle, said, 'Oh, that's… wonderful.'

'Steve didn't mention it this afternoon?'

'Well, at one point, he seemed about to say something significant but then he clearly thought it might be better if it came from you. I had been going on a bit about the delights of Edinburgh and the imminent publication of Rob's first collection of poems.'

'It doesn't shock you?'

'Well, of course, I'm surprised. But since separating from Steve last summer, many things to do with him have surprised me. I sometimes wonder if the person downstairs is the same person I was living with.'

'He does seem to believe that he has become or has created a persona called new Steve.'

'Leaving aside the rather unimaginative name, that would describe the situation, though not explain it.'

'Do you think I'm being foolish in choosing Steve to father my child?'

'Grace, I wouldn't presume to judge. I don't know the circumstances.'

'I mean do you think that Steve would make a good father, biomechanical matters aside.'

'Well, the Steve I thought I knew certainly would. I mean, he has a sweet disposition and is sensitive to others. Whether he has the stamina for the long haul is another matter.'

'I don't expect him to stay with me forever, and I won't require him to make a financial contribution. But I do want him to be more than a sperm donor and to have his name on the birth certificate. I want us to be open about what we're doing, which is why I'm a little disappointed that he didn't mention it to you this afternoon. On the other hand, you are his first love and I recognise that he still has feelings for you.'

'All the more reason why he should have told me. So far as those residual feelings are concerned, it's time he realised that I am with Rob and when I come to have children, it will be with Rob.'

'You can imagine, though, that the idea of Rob as the father of your putative children would plunge Steve into a gloom every bit as much as the news of Rob's publishing success will, or has.'

'Those two boys are ridiculous. Of course they're best friends, or say they are. But they are also intense rivals. Steve is envious of Rob's success. But Rob thinks that any success he's had is because he works so hard, whereas things just happen to Steve because, from Rob's point of view, Steve is the real deal, the real poet.'

'Poor Rob, but what a nice man he is. Not something you could say about Steve.'

'I'm hesitant to agree with the latter typification. I only wonder, if you think that, why choose him to be the father of your child?'

'Because, despite what I just said, he is to hand, and because I don't have time to find an alternative, who would also be a reliable life partner. Steve is helping me out and for that reason, I don't expect to keep hold of him, though I would be delighted if I could. I also recognise that he will probably find temptations elsewhere.'

'I see, but even so, Steve has a talent for letting people down and seldom repays encouragement, as I know only too well.'

This last remark seemed to nettle Grace. It was one thing for the present incumbent to lightly disparage Steve, quite another for a former lover to offer such opinions. Grace felt a gentle recalibration was in order and that Angie needed disabusing of the idea that she was the grit in the oyster of Steve's poetic talent. 'The person who has really let me down here is Peter, my husband. Peter is also the person who interposed himself between Ginny and Steve. I don't wish to minimise the feelings between you and Steve, but it is Ginny who got under his skin in a way that you and I probably never could.'

Angie was not insensitive to the rebuke, but ploughed on. 'You're surely not suggesting that he and Ginny are likely to continue their relationship at some level?'

'I'd say it's unlikely. Peter is an insanely jealous person. Then there is the absence of proximity. But I do think that at some level she has captured him forever.'

'But just now you said he would find temptations elsewhere.'

'Yes, the person who occupies that role at the moment is Jude, the woman who rescued the manuscript of *Event/Horizon*.'

Already knowing the answer to the question she was about to ask, Angie said, 'Do you think he's slept with her?'

'Oh, he's definitely slept with her, several times. Whether he's likely to sleep with her again is an open question, but I certainly don't rule it out.'

'Oh, Grace, that's so horrible for you.'

'Not really, but I'm not going to give him *carte blanche*. I want him to feel he's transgressing each time he wanders.'

It was as if Grace somehow assumed that Angie and Steve must have actually made love earlier that day and was now absolving Angie from any guilt she might feel. Because at that moment Angie certainly felt that she had transgressed, if only in thought.

Later, up in the guest room, as she waited for Rob to rejoin her, she reflected on the conversation with Grace. Angie wondered whether the whole point of the conversation had actually been to establish some kind of pecking order among the women in Steve's retinue. In which case Angie was clearly in the trailing position. On the other hand, it also seemed that Grace did not consider herself to be the undisputed head. That role seemed to have been accorded to Ginny. But, as in the conversation earlier in the day with Rob, what remained unclear was how Jude fitted into the picture. No doubt it would become apparent in due course.

Yet Angie could not believe that Grace viewed her own prospects in such bleak terms. More probably, she just wanted someone else close to Steve to know that she had no illusions about him and, it seemed, she trusted Angie enough to be that person. Angie felt sorry for Grace, but was also curiously impressed by her strength and composure. Using Grace's terminology, it was also evident to Angie that the person who had got under her own skin was Steve, something she had always suspected, and which, in the wider view of things, must be a matter for regret.

## Friday, 7 February 1975

STEVE FIDGETED IN HIS window seat all the way from Paddington to Castle Cary, unable to concentrate on his book. From time to time, Grace patted him on the knee reassuringly. 'It'll be fine. Try not to fret.'

They were on their way to spend the weekend with Grace's parents in Somerset. In their programme of coming out to family and friends as a couple, Steve had been dreading this encounter most of all. He wasn't sure if it was because Grace's father was a vicar, albeit now retired, or because the very fact that he was retired put him in the same age group as his one surviving and very elderly grandparent, his father's mother. Grace had made it clear that Gideon had long ago given up trying to convince her how misguided she was in having renounced the faith into which she had been born. He would probably have found adherence to another monotheistic religion preferable to atheism. But in an increasingly godless society, he had withdrawn into his own devotions and now put his efforts into prayer.

The train pulled into Castle Cary. As they were getting their bags down off the rack, Steve said, 'How do I address your father? Is it Father Gideon? Or Reverend Mitchell?'

Grace laughed. 'Well, of course, I call him Daddy. I don't think I've ever used his Christian name. But you can just call him Gideon. Or if that makes you feel uncomfortable on first being introduced, call him Mr Mitchell.'

Steve nodded. Grace gestured through the window. 'That's him there, next to the light blue Morris Traveller.'

Steve followed her gesture and saw a tall gaunt man scanning the carriages of the train, which was grinding to a halt. When it had finally stopped, Grace and Steve stepped onto the platform and a few moments later Grace was introducing Steve to her father who immediately said, 'Oh, please call me Gideon.'

Gideon took their bags and put them in the back of the car. Grace said, 'Steve, you sit in the front. Not so much legroom in the back.'

Steve didn't feel he could refuse, but would have preferred to sit in the back, fearing that the front seat would expose him to more extensive conversational duties.

Gideon started the Morris and they set off for Lane End. Once they were cruising along the country lanes, Gideon said, 'Do you know this part of the world, Steve?'

'No, this is the first time I've ever been here. I'm afraid I'm not well-travelled.'

'Nevertheless, you probably know London like the back of your hand.'

'Well, certain parts. Borough, Bermondsey, Elephant and Castle.'

'So you're a real Londoner?'

'Yes, I suppose so. I loved being so close to the river.'

'Did you go to school locally?'

'Yes, I got a scholarship to the City of London School for Boys.'

'So you're an Old Citizen?'

'I am, but I don't really have much to do with the old boys network.'

'Does your mother still live there?'

'We have a flat there, but my mother is living in Berlin. She works for the Foreign Office and was posted there a couple of weeks ago.'

Grace leaned forward from the back seat. 'Daddy, you can give Steve the third degree when we get back to the house.'

'I'm sorry, Steve. It's not often we get a real Cockney down here.'

Steve laughed. 'It's okay. I'm proud of being a Cockney, even if I no longer sound like one. CLS drummed that out of me. Not that I'm aware of ever having heard the sound of Bow bells. Too much noise most of the time. And other church bells as well, probably from St Paul's.'

'Ah, Great Tom, isn't it?'

'I'm not sure what you mean.'

'The bell that chimes on the hour at St Paul's is called Great Tom. There is an even bigger bell called Great Paul, but that is only rung on special occasions.'

'Okay.'

'I'm sorry, Steve. You can probably tell I'm very nervous. June wants us to make a good impression.'

Steve laughed again, deciding already that he liked Gideon. 'Gideon, I'm the one who needs to make a good impression.'

'Oh, you have, my dear fellow, you have.'

Fortunately, this excruciating conversation was brought to a halt by the Morris turning into the gates of Lane End. At the sound of the car's tyres crunching on the gravel, June came to the front door, which was set into a little porch.

The car was unloaded and Grace introduced Steve to her mother. June and Steve shook hands and then June said to Grace, 'My dear, your young man is even better looking than he sounded on the phone.'

Grace laughed. 'Can you tell if someone's good looking on the phone?'

June could tell she was being mocked. 'Of course you can. But I grant you that certain details have to be filled in later.'

Grace put her arm around Steve and said, 'You can see my parents are completely barmy. But they're also very lovely people and I'm sure we're all going to get along fine.'

Steve wished he could be sure of that, though he feared that he would fail to come up to expectations at some point.

But on this first evening, the mood was welcoming. June had a warming supper ready for them, and Gideon opened a nice bottle of red wine. After supper, Steve offered to wash up, but June wouldn't hear of it. 'You've had a long journey and it's already late. I suggest we go to bed and hope that the weather is good enough tomorrow to show you something of the village and environs.'

Steve followed Grace upstairs to her bedroom. She opened the door and said, 'Welcome to my maiden bower.'

Steve stepped inside the room and looked around. Not much had changed in this room, it seemed, since Grace was at school in the fifties. There were framed school pictures and certificates, gymkhana rosettes, a hockey stick and lacrosse stick in the corner of the room, chintz curtains and matching bed throw. Two small bookcases flanked a desk in front of the window. In the far corner a huge doll's house surmounted a rickety chest of drawers.

Grace looked embarrassed. 'What are you thinking?'

'I love it. It gives me a sense of your past.'

'Peter hated coming in here. He particularly hated the doll's house.'

'From the outside it looks like a fine example of the type.'

'My father made it. He's good with his hands.'

'Then it also has sentimental connections.'

'Exactly. For the same reason, Peter hated the bed too.'

'Well, the bed is a bit narrow and he is quite a big guy.'

'It wasn't bought with the idea of accommodating me and a large male of the species.'

'So it's as well I'm not particularly big.'

'But you're not as small as you think either. Anyway we have business tonight so being close together can only be good.'

'Grace, I am not going to make love to you tonight.'

'Oh yes, you are, my fine fellow. This is what you signed up for. I'm right in the middle of my fertile period, as you know from last night's activities. So you're on duty for the next four nights.'

'I don't want to upset your parents. They have been so nice.'

'You're not going to upset them. They know how babies are made. Anyway, you didn't have any such qualms when Mavis was staying with us. In fact, I think you rather relished it.'

'This is a much smaller place than the Glisson Road house.'

'With hugely thick walls. Steve, I want a baby and you have volunteered for the job. If I have to dance around the room in my old school uniform to get you in the mood, that's what I'll do.'

Steve threw himself on the bed. 'Okay, it's a deal. Get the gymslip out.'

They woke late the next morning. When Grace climbed out of bed and opened the door to go to the lavatory, the smell of frying bacon and freshly brewed coffee drifted into the room. Steve lay there feeling very content, letting his gaze take in the details of the room that he had missed the previous night. Soon Grace returned, wrapped in a towel. She was carrying another towel which she tossed to Steve. 'I'm afraid the shower is a bit of a fiddle. It's a plastic curtain around the bath. And the hot and cold taps are a bit idiosyncratic. I'd recommend adjusting them before you step into the bath otherwise you'll either scald yourself or freeze.'

Later over a fried breakfast, Gideon outlined the plans for the day. In view of the inclement weather, the walk they had hoped to take to show Steve the locality and its stunning views was not really viable. So he had booked lunch at the local pub, which was very close and would only involve limited exposure to the elements. He thought Steve would find the local brew extremely tasty. June wanted to know if Steve was keen on Scrabble. She thought if people weren't too sleepy after the pub lunch a couple of rounds might be fun. Steve said he was familiar with the game, but certainly no expert. After that, June said, if anyone was still hungry, there would be a cheese board with local cheeses, cold meats and fresh bread.

Gideon was not wrong about the beer. Steve got a taste for it and consumed three pints during the lunch session, though Grace said it was actually four pints. Whatever the exact number, the ale affected his Scrabble performance negatively and he came last. The winner by a long way was June, with Grace the runner-up. Gideon averred that it was well-known that women had an advantage over men when it came to language. His tongue freed by the beer, Steve wondered why the advantage should be limited to language, a comment which earned him a sharp look from Grace. His Scrabble performance might not have been impressive, but he had thoroughly enjoyed sitting with these lovely people, who were in some sense his family now, with a small glass of port to hand, the fire roaring in the grate and the wind howling outside.

After the game, Gideon went up to have a nap and June and Grace went out into the kitchen. Steve, assuming they were embarking on preparations for the evening meal, offered to give a hand. But he was chased out of the kitchen, Grace suggesting that he might find the back sitting room, which doubled as a library and had its own fireplace, a nice place to read quietly. Not wishing to intrude on what he now understood to be a mother and daughter heart-to-heart, he did as he was told and made his way to the library. It was well stocked, but only if you were a cleric or theologian. Nevertheless, he soon found a section devoted to local folklore and archaeology and settled down to a pleasant read.

After half an hour or so, June came into the room carrying a tray of tea things. 'Would you mind if I joined you? I've got a fresh pot of tea here and some nice biscuits.'

Steve leapt up and cleared a space on the small table. 'Of course not. I'd be delighted.'

June put the tray down and sat in a small armchair. 'I thought we could get to know each other better. Grace has gone upstairs for a nap.'

Steve smiled and nodded, while thinking that this was the conversation he had been dreading.

June poured the teas and passed him a cup and saucer. 'You probably think I'm going to give you a bit of a lecture. I can assure you I'm not. I am delighted that Grace is getting away from that man, but I am sorry that he also stole your girlfriend. I imagine you miss her and still have feelings for her.'

He had not expected discussions about his suitability as a father to start with an enquiry about his feelings for Ginny. He would have to tread carefully. 'Of course, I was upset at first, but I'd always known that the relationship with Ginny wouldn't last. She told me as much right at the start.'

'Ah, yes, Ginny. I believe she is very beautiful.'

'Also very unpredictable and subject to bouts of depression.'

'You'd known Grace for two years before you and she got together?'

'She taught me. I saw her at least once a week in term time, occasionally more.'

'There was no talk or hint in that time that you had feelings for each other?'

'There was no talk or hint, but perhaps there were thoughts, at least on my side. She is so beautiful and so brilliant. I couldn't believe my luck that I got to spend an hour a week in her company.'

'She says you are a poet.'

'So are half the undergraduates at Cambridge.'

'But you wrote a book-length poem.'

'Yes, but I'm still not sure that makes me a poet.'

'She thinks it does. She is, after all, a considerable poet herself. She has won a number of awards.'

'Yes, I saw some of them on the walls of her room. I have never won a single award.'

'There is still time.'

'June, Grace has been so supportive, but I don't think I can live up to her expectations.'

'I think you can, Steven, and I want you to try.'

Suddenly, Steve sensed that they weren't talking about his poetry. 'I love her. I want to be with her. Clearly, I'm younger than her and have not yet established myself in a career, but I will do my best to look after her.' He remembered saying something similar to Butch, who'd replied that it had better be better than his best.

June took a sip of her tea. 'Grace has put her trust in you. She has exposed herself. She made a mistake with Peter …'

'She hasn't made a mistake with me, Mrs Mitchell.' Steve's eagerness not to be tarred with the same brush was more obvious in the tone of his voice than he would have wished.

'June, dear, please. I'm not accusing you of anything. I'm warning you what Grace can be like. She can be impulsive, spiteful. You are the one who is vulnerable. She could throw you out. You have no rights in the relationship.'

'I don't think she's like that at all.'

'You haven't known her for very long. She's very strong and very determined and quite manipulative.'

'I'm sorry, I can't agree with that assessment.'

'What I'm trying to say is that if things get difficult, I'd like you to think that you could ask us – Gideon and me, but particularly me – for help and advice. You will always be welcome here.'

'June, you've worried me. I don't see any of that being necessary.'

'I didn't mean to worry you. I only wanted to say that we… that I am delighted that you have come into Grace's life. But you are a young man and you are taking on a weighty responsibility. I am trying to say to you that I am your friend and if things do get hard or confusing, as long as I am alive I will do my best to help you.'

Steve's head was spinning, but he managed to say quietly, 'Thank you, June. I am grateful for what you are saying. It is just a little unexpected.'

'I'm sure it is. But you must see that you are being set a series of tasks. Men always think they are doing the choosing and assessing, but I hope you won't mind me saying that this is simply not the case. We, and by we I mean women, do the choosing and assessing. Sometimes we ask you to do the impossible just for the hell of it or as a test. I am proud of my daughter and I don't know Ginny, though I think from what I do know that I understand what she's about, but I wouldn't be surprised if whatever indignities are heaped on Peter as a result of his association with Ginny, he will find his situation more bearable than the one he had with Grace.'

'Peter mistreated Grace?'

'Yes, because he was powerless.'

'He's the boss of a successful publishing company.'

'Pshaw! That means nothing. He wouldn't have got it going without Grace. I daresay Ginny will now play a similar role as backstop.'

'But if Peter is powerless, what does that make me?'

'You are stronger than you think. Your mother has done a good job. But I am here to help too.'

Steve wished people would stop helping him. Yet, much as he was alarmed and bewildered by the things that June was saying, he was also immensely grateful to her, sensing that she foresaw things which would challenge him in ways that, right now, he could not comprehend.

He went over to June and knelt down beside her, bowing his head. She rested her hand on his head and he felt a surge of electricity run through him. He looked up at her. She was smiling at him radiantly. Then almost as suddenly, the radiance faded and he felt elated but very tired.

June said, 'Go upstairs. Grace is waiting for you.'

Steve rose and without another word left the room.

On the train on the way back to London the following afternoon, Grace said, 'That wasn't so bad, was it?'

Steve squeezed her hand. 'No, it was amazing. Your parents are really lovely people.'

'They love you too.'

'I find that hard to believe, but I suppose apart from showing how crap I was at Scrabble, I didn't blot my copybook too much.'

'I should have warned you about the Scrabble.'

'When I was reading in the library yesterday afternoon, your mum came in and we had a very weird chat.'

'I thought you were rather pensive when you came upstairs, until other matters occupied you.'

'She was extremely supportive and welcoming to me, but she was also quite critical of you.'

'Mothers and daughters, Steve. Not something you would have come across.'

'She said that Peter would have an easier ride with Ginny than he had with you.'

'Ah, that. She probably went on to say that I can be impulsive and manipulative.'

'She did. And that you can be spiteful.'

'Oh, she really was giving you the treatment.'

'She more or less said that if I was finding things tough, she would do her best to help me.'

'Presumably she meant tough with me.'

'I don't know what she meant. I said that I didn't see that as being necessary.'

'That's very loyal of you Steve.'

'I wasn't trying to be loyal. It's what I think.'

'Well, thank you anyway.'

'She also said that men think they do the choosing, but it's actually women who do the choosing. Sometimes they make men do things just for the hell of it. But she thought I was stronger than Peter, which seems absurd to me.'

'Well, I agree with her there.'

'Then she touched my head and I felt a surge of energy go through me. It really freaked me out. But then I felt very calm, and she told me to go upstairs and see you. I know this is stupid, but is she a kind of witch, not in a bad sense?'

'Perhaps witch is a rather loaded term. Let's just say that she's a wise old woman.'

'Did you tell her it was your fertile period?'

'No, but she probably guessed. Why?'

'It felt a bit like sex when she touched me, in the sense that she knew it was the right time for us to make love.'

'Everything feels like sex to you, Steve. You see my old school gymslip and it turns you on.'

'One hardly needs to be a Freudian analyst to know that uniform fetish is pretty common.'

'If that's what it takes to keep you at it, I'd better see if there are any to be had in Cambridge, preferably a slightly larger size, though. I was conscious that my old one was doing a poor job of containing me. I was rather flatter-chested in those days.'

'I found that aspect particularly gratifying.'

'I could see that. I must say it's been quite a voyage of discovery finding out what turns you on. Although, it'd probably be easier to take the apophatic route and list the things that don't. I'm sorry that the landscape of my own sexuality is so barren.'

'I wouldn't say that. You are just more reserved. I'm sure we'll get there.'

'It's not that I'm not prepared to dress up for you or go down on you, as you know. But that's what makes you tick, whereas I have no idea what makes me tick.'

'We should dig into that a bit more, then.'

'But not now, and certainly not here.'

'Well, that sounds like exactly the place to start.'

'Steve, I am not going to have sex with you in this train compartment, if that's what you mean.'

'I think your mother would want us to.'

'That's crazy. She would be horrified.'

'I'm not suggesting we tell her that her magic worked, but the next stop isn't for ages. We can pull the blinds down.'

'You're not serious? What if a ticket collector comes along?'

'We'll show him our tickets.'

'I am not taking my clothes off on this train.'

'Well, we'd only need to do that if we were simulating sex, as they do in the movies. But we'll be dissimulating. In other words having sex, but not looking as if we were.'

'How would we do that?'

'We could arrange our clothes to allow access without removing them completely. Well, you'd have to take off your knickers and sit on my lap.'

'Steve, I am not a contortionist. Nor am I the sort of woman who sits on a man's lap.'

'All the more reason to give it a go.'

'You're serious, aren't you? I don't think this is my fantasy. It's your fantasy of what my fantasy is.'

'Perhaps. But after all, it is one of your fertile days, and we may be too tired by the time we get home.'

Grace tapped her lips with the tips of her fingers. 'Have you got the tickets to hand?'

Steve pointed to the breast pocket of his shirt.

'Okay, but if we end up in court for public indecency, I will turn you into a frog.'

Much to Grace's surprise, the scheme worked to the satisfaction of both of them without undue contortions being required and without any intrusions from British Rail employees. Once Grace had caught her breath, she stood up and slipped her knickers and tights back on. Apart from a flushed face, she looked the demure senior academic again and said, with evident pride, 'Okay, that was really rather enjoyable.'

Steve, adjusting his own clothing, said, 'Nothing like a little jeopardy to season an everyday dish.'

Grace pouted. 'Careful, Percival. I am not an everyday dish.'

## Friday, 21 February 1975

STEVE PUSHED OPEN THE doors of the Great Northern and went inside. He spotted Garth at a corner table and went over and joined him. 'Hi Garth, so what do you need to talk to me about that means you've had to put some clothes on?'

'I'm doing a mutual friend a favour. But first let me get you a pint. IPA?'

Steve nodded and while Garth was at the bar tried to work out how many mutual friends they had. None would have been his first guess. Unless you counted Garth's partner in nudity, Kelly, who was hardly a friend of Steve's. The only other acquaintances they had in common were the other residents of the Tenison Road house, Jason, Susan and, of course, Jude. But Jude had moved to London. Steve decided to stop guessing and wait until Garth returned with the beers.

When he got back to the table, Steve said, 'So has the landlord found tenants to replace me and Jude?'

'Yeah, a couple of cool chicks. The one in Jude's old room seems happy to do a bit of naturist socialising.'

'Blimey, Garth, a bit of a result for you there.'

'Yeah, the word's getting about. I don't know what stopped you joining us for our starkers soirées.'

'Time of the year, really. If I'd stayed until the spring, I might have been prepared to get my kit off, but it's just too cold at this time of year. Anyway, which mutual friend are we talking about? We don't have that many.'

'Jude, of course. You and she were really getting it on.'

'Passing ships, Garth. She moved out and we lost touch.'

'She said she gave you her address in London on a scrap of paper, but she figured you'd probably lost it. In any case, she's moved.'

'So you've been in touch with her?'

'She dropped by the house the other day and asked me to give you this.'

He took a packet wrapped in brown paper from his shoulder bag and handed it to Steve.

'She said a note with her new address and telephone number is tucked inside the book.'

Steve stared at the packet in a kind of reverie. It bore his name in a bold florid hand surmounting two kisses.

Garth looked at him. 'Aren't you going to open it?'

With some difficulty, Steve focused his thoughts. 'If you don't mind, I'll open it when I get home. It's just a book we were talking about and I don't want to lose her new address.'

When Steve got back to the house, he was pleased to find that Grace was still out. He went up to his study and started to carefully open the packet, doing his best not to tear the paper. He hadn't needed to open it to guess what it was, but what now surprised him was to find not the loose-leaf typescript of *Event/Horizon*, but a typeset and bound edition of his poem. He leafed through the pages. At a glance he could see that the typesetting was of a high standard. He turned to the imprint and saw that it was published by Labrys Books, a publishing house hitherto unknown to him. Tucked inside the front cover was an envelope also bearing his name. He opened the envelope and read the note it contained.

Dear Steve,

I hope you like the enclosed copy of *Event/Horizon*. I am now enrolled at the London College of Printing and produced this edition on an Arab letterpress machine. I did all the typesetting and printing and a friend did the binding. We produced an edition of ten copies. The text is as accurate a rendering of your typescript as I was able to make. Please let me know you have received the book safely. This very limited edition has cost me many hours of work. Not that I am complaining. Your poem deserves to be read in a fine edition. My new address is at the head of this note. Please do not be angry with me for having contacted you. I am not asking for anything in return. Perhaps only that you be brave enough to show this book to others, including Grace. With love, Jude.

Steve was stunned. The book was a beautiful object. He honestly did not feel that his work deserved to have such care lavished on it. Jude said in her letter that she did not expect anything in return other than a letter to acknowledge safe receipt of the book. On the face of it, this was just a token of courtesy or good manners, but by not expecting anything in return, it made the sense of obligation almost limitless. She had also asked him to show it to Grace, as if that weren't in itself an obligation. It would be immensely foolish of him not to show it to Grace, but it would also make it clear to Grace that her rival was still keeping tabs on Steve from afar. On the other hand Grace would no longer be able to chide him for not having shown her the poem.

He lay down on the bed and read a few pages of the book. As an object, the book was beautiful, but he was not so sure about the poem. He no longer recognised it as the work of his own hand. He felt simultaneously embarrassed by it and unequal to it. Once again, as he had towards the end of his time in Ainsworth Street, he felt that it was something alien, something that had a life of its own. He may have created it, but it was not his.

He heard the sound of the front door opening and a bag being dropped in the hall. A few moments later Grace walked into their bedroom and bent down to kiss him. 'Heavy day at the Festival?'

'No, I got off early today. Gary was going up to London. I met Garth for a pint.'

'Who's Garth?'

'The guy who lived upstairs from me in Tenison Road.'

'Oh, yeah, the nudist who taught you how to pick locks.'

'Yeah.'

Grace kicked off her shoes and lay down beside him. 'Was he coaching you in other areas of misconduct?'

'No, he gave me this.'

Steve handed Grace the beautiful letterpress copy of *Event/ Horizon*.

Grace leafed through it. 'Oh, Steve, this is beautiful. Who made it?'

Steve handed her Jude's letter, which she quickly read. 'Well, well, what a remarkable young woman. She's got you bad, hasn't she?'

'Grateful though I am for the book, it all feels a bit manipulative and oppressive.'

'Yes, I think she knows how to get to you.'

'I wish Rob could see this.'

'Write to her. Thank her for the book, tell her you showed it to me and that I'm very pleased. Ask her if you can have another copy for Rob, who was a crucial influence in the gestation of the poem. The worst she can say is no.'

## Friday, 28 February 1975

STEVE PUT THE DRINKS on the table and took a seat. 'Thank you for making the letterpress edition of *Event/Horizon*. It looks amazing.'

'Well, thank you for supplying me with a worthwhile text to set.'

'In a very indirect sort of way.'

'Which is how most things happen, I find.'

'Thank you for agreeing to provide a copy for my friend Rob.'

'One good turn deserves another, don't you think?'

Steve had rather feared that there might be some strings attached. 'Jude, I am not going to go to bed with you.'

Jude laughed. 'Sadly I've got too much on today for anything like that.'

'Okay, so what brings you up to Cambridge?'

'Well, apart from seeing you, I've had a job interview this morning.'

'For a job in Cambridge?'

'Yes. The job hunt wasn't going too well in London and then I was asked if I'd be prepared to rejoin Vanguard.'

'I thought you hated your boss.'

'I did, but he's gone. Vanguard has been taken over by Inflexion, who've been making a number of acquisitions. The new guys kicked him out and they're considering me as his successor. There are plans to expand the operation considerably.'

Jude noticed Steve's furrowed brow. 'You look as though you've seen a ghost. Are you alright?'

Recovering his composure, Steve said, 'Yeah. Have you got the job?'

'They're going to let me know in a few days. So I might be back in Cambridge soon. How do you feel about that?'

Actually, Steve had very mixed feelings, but it would be unworthy of him under the circumstances to hint at his reservations or be anything other than positive. 'I'm pleased for you. Jobs are hard to come by at the moment, even with a good degree. So, if the old boss is gone, who interviewed you?'

'The big boss of Inflexion.'

'Peter Newman?'

'Yeah, you know of him?'

'I actually *know* him.'

'Really?'

'He's the guy who stole my girlfriend.'

'Ginny?'

'Yeah.'

'Oh, so he's *that* Peter.'

'What do you mean *that* Peter? I don't think I ever mentioned his name.'

'The Peter who figures in the handwritten notes you inadvertently or perhaps purposely tucked into the manuscript of my novel.'

Steve wasn't quite sure how to play this latest piece of information.

'Your novel?'

'Yes, the one that was in the drawer of my desk. I assume you came across it when you were looking for your own manuscript.'

'What makes you say that?'

'Because you told Garth you needed to get something from my room and he picked the lock for you.'

'Ah, yes. I'm sorry. I was desperate to get *Event/Horizon* back. I know you said it was in your office, but I thought there was a chance that you were lying.'

'But why did you leave your notes for me to find?'

'I didn't actually do it on purpose. Garth let me into your room the day before you got back from Manchester. I thought I'd take your manuscript and use it as a bargaining chip to get mine back. But while I was waiting for you the next day, I read your draft and thought it was really good. I was particularly interested in the central relationship structure you'd set up and wondered whether I could plot the people from my own complicated relationships onto the characters in your draft. But then I heard you come through the front door, and in a bit of a scramble, I stuffed the whole sheaf of paper into my bag and followed you upstairs.'

'So when did you put it back in the desk?'

'When you went to the loo.'

'Ah, yes. I'd forgotten that. When I found your notes, I thought you must have put them there on purpose and it was your way of keeping things open between us.'

'No, I'm an idiot and I was in a total panic. I completely forgot about my notes. Anyway, the notes were just nonsense.'

'Not at all, it suggested to me ways that I could improve the book. I can see that I ought to have introduced confidants for the three main protagonists.'

'Jude, it's a great piece of work. You should finish it.'

'It's juvenile, a love triangle, too much explicit sex.'

'It's 1975. No one's going to bat an eyelid.'

'That's not what bothers me. I don't want to do a Cambridge *Fear of Flying*. Female author proving she can be raunchier than the boys, peppering her prose with vulgar obscenities.'

'You can remove the offending words, or just imply them. The book is well-written. I think you should send it to an agent.'

'So you're permitted to disavow your manuscript, but I'm not?'

'Your novel is actually good.'

'How about this then? If you think that, why don't you edit my manuscript? What do you say?'

Steve sighed. 'There's more to editing a novel than spotting the odd vulgar expression. But in any case, I've got my hands full with my theatre duties.'

'Take as much time as you need. The manuscript is in the package with the copy of *Event/Horizon* for Rob.'

She pushed the package towards him.

That evening, back at Tenison Road over a glass of wine, Grace said, 'How did it go with Jude? Did you have to go to bed with her?'

'Of course not, it's the middle of the day. Where would we have gone?'

Steve realised he was putting a little too much heft into his response because, of course, the thought *had* crossed his mind. Jude had been wearing a diaphanous blouse and a pair of tight blue jeans. In Jon's parlance, she had looked decidedly hot.

Grace saw the flicker of emotion cross Steve's face and, regretting her quip, said, 'Sorry, Steve, just joking.'

'It's okay. You have every right to be suspicious. There *was* a quid pro quo attached to her giving me another copy of her edition of *Event/Horizon*.'

'Is it something you can tell me about?'

'She'd worked out that I'd read the draft of her novel.'

'How did she do that?'

'When I was reading it, I decided to make some notes. Stupidly, when I put the draft back in her desk, I forgot to remove the sheet of notes.'

'That does seem rather like a fairly major Freudian slip.'

'Yeah.'

'So what's the quid pro quo?'

'She wants me to edit the novel, take out the fucks and blowjobs.'

'What?'

'She doesn't want to be the Cambridge Erica Jong.'

Grace laughed hollowly. 'Are such vulgarisms a feature of *Fear of Flying*?'

Steve was surprised that Grace hadn't read the book. It had been one of the biggest publishing sensations of recent years. 'They're more than a feature; they're intrinsic to the book. If you were to take them out, you'd end up with not much of a book. You might almost say that the book's vulgarity is its real selling point.'

'But Jude's manuscript is rescuable?'

'Yes, it is.'

'Did you agree to take on the task?'

'I didn't actually say I would, but the manuscript was in the package that contained the copy of *Event/Horizon* for Rob, so the ball's in my court.'

'Do you feel it has some merit despite the crude vocabulary?'

'Yes.'

'Would you let me read it?'

'Of course, but I'm sure you've got better things to do.'

'It's not that I'm not busy, but it's clear to me that I need to catch up with the way things are now.'

'You might be a little shocked.'

'If I am, it will have been worthwhile.'

'There's something else you should know. She was up in Cambridge for an interview at Vanguard Books, her old firm. It's now owned by Inflexion. She was interviewed by Peter.'

'Did she know you knew Peter?'

'No, but she does now.'

'Hmm, I'm not sure if that's good or bad. Of course, it's good for Jude that she might get her old job back. But I don't like the idea of Peter having a reason for being in Cambridge on a regular basis.'

'I'm not sure how likely that is. Jude said that Inflexion is on the acquisition trail, snapping up smaller publishers.'

'I wonder how he's managing to do that. The last information I had about Inflexion's cash flow was that it was very iffy. I wonder if it has something to do with his wanting to get on with the divorce.'

'I really don't know how these things work.'

'Do you think Jude would be likely to say that she knows you?'

'I got the impression she didn't think it would enhance her application.'

'Yes, I can see that. Still, for any number of reasons, it's all a bit disconcerting.'

# Berlin

## Sunday, 2 March 1975

IT WAS SUNDAY AFTERNOON. Grace and Steve were sitting in the front room; Grace working on her next lecture and Steve sifting through the pile of scripts that had come in since the extension of the closing date for the new writing festival. Grace was finding it hard going. It had been a mistake to finish the bottle of wine with their lunch and she was thinking of making a pot of tea when the phone rang. She put her notebook to one side and got up. Calls were seldom for Steve.

She reappeared in the room a few minutes later. 'It's for you. It's the Foreign Office.'

Steve stood up with a puzzled look on his face and went out into the hall and picked up the receiver. 'This is Steve Percival.'

Grace watched from the doorway with a mounting feeling of concern. She heard him say, 'Yes, I am the son of Mavis Percival.' Then she heard him say, 'How? When?'

He picked up a biro and scribbled something on the phone table notepad. 'Yes, yes, I understand. I will let you know when I'm there.'

He put the phone down. Grace, stepping towards him, said, 'Steve, what's happened?'

Steve looked blank. 'Mavis has had an accident. She was knocked over, a hit and run driver. She's in a coma.'

'Oh, Steve, that's terrible. What are you going to do?'

'I'm going to fly to Berlin. The chap who phoned, Fortescue, is booking me on the afternoon flight tomorrow. I'll go down to London now and stay the night in the flat.'

'I'll come with you.'

209

'Thank you, Grace, but you've got work. There's not much either of us can do. We'll just have to hope the doctors have got things under control.'

'Well, I'll see if I can postpone my last lecture until next term and then I could come out later this week after I've given Wednesday's lecture.'

'Thank you, but don't make any arrangements until I've got out there and have a better idea of what her chances are.'

With a sob, Grace embraced Steve, saying, 'This is terrible.' They clung to each other until Steve, gently prising himself free, went upstairs to pack a bag.

While he was packing, Grace was turning over in her mind the conversation she had had with Mavis when she had been staying with them. It had been clear to Grace that Mavis's job was not as anodyne as Steve seemed to think. She had almost immediately regretted revealing to Mavis her own past involvement with the security establishment, which had not been without its own complications. Now she had almost certainly put herself back on their radar by that error of judgement. In Mavis's line of work, accidents were seldom accidents. But what particularly worried her was that Steve had absolutely no idea what he might be getting into. But wouldn't she just be making matters worse if she shared her concerns with him?

The fact of the matter was that West Berlin was a dangerous place, especially for a rather guileless person like Steve. It would be easier if she were with him, but she couldn't really travel before she'd given her last two lectures of the term. Not if she didn't want her academic career to founder just as it was getting going.

At that moment, Steve reappeared in the living room with his bag. 'Right, I'm ready. No point hanging around.'

Grace stepped towards him and brushed back the lock of hair that always fell down over his forehead. 'Pre-flight check. Have you got your passport?'

Steve pulled a funny face. 'No, I'll just go back up and get it.'

'Before you go, how much money are you taking with you?'

'I've got twenty pounds.'

'Steve, that's not enough. You don't know how long you're going to be there and you don't know that the Foreign Office will get your ticket home. I'll give you another thirty pounds.'

'I don't want to take your money.'

'Don't be ridiculous. It's our money. Turn it into travellers cheques at Heathrow. If you don't need to use them, we can pay them back into your bank account.'

It took Steve some time to find his passport. By the time he came back downstairs again, Grace had decided to level with him.

'Steve, we need to have a serious talk before you go.'

Steve looked startled. What had he done?

'I know you're in a rush, but we need to sit down and take some time over this.'

Steve sat down, now even more worried.

'When your mother was here and you had your first session at the Festival, she and I had a long talk and got to know each other much better.'

'Yes, I could see that.'

'What I am about to tell you is very much against the rules, so you are going to have to use this information very carefully. It is not to be shared with anyone else, including, when she gets better, your mother. Do you understand?'

Steve nodded.

'I want more than that, Steve. Tell me you will not share this information with anyone else, ever.'

'I promise.'

'Okay. Your mother's job with the Foreign Office is just a cover. She actually works for the security services.'

'Did she tell you that?'

'Not in so many words.'

'How do you know then?'

'Because I too used to work for the security services, albeit in a more informal role.'

'When?'

'When I was a postgraduate student in Berlin and Paris.'

'You were keeping an eye on subversives?'

'I'm not going to tell you what I was doing. The point is, you are going to a place where you won't be able to trust anyone or believe what you are being told, including from our own side. At the same time, you mustn't let the people you are dealing with know you think that.'

'So you think what happened to my mother wasn't an accident?'

'Until the hit and run driver is tracked down or your mother comes out of the coma and can give her side of the story, I think it is safer to assume that. But, I repeat, you mustn't say this to the people who will take you to see your mother or to your mother if she is conscious by the time you see her.'

Steve ran his hand through his hair. 'Okay, if I find anything to support your hypothesis, I'll phone you and ask your advice about what to do next.'

'Don't do that.'

'What? I shouldn't phone you?'

'You have got to act as if any telephone call you make from Berlin, particularly any call to me here, is being listened to.'

'You think your phone is being tapped?'

'It might be now.'

'Now?'

'I've already said, I can't go into details.'

'How am I meant to communicate with you if I can't phone you?'

'On the contrary, I want you to phone me as often as you can. But we must limit the conversations to endearments, chit-chat and medical bulletins about your mum. The soppier the conversations, the better.'

'Supposing I come across something that supports your theory, how do I let you know?'

'I am going to give you two names and a Berlin telephone number. Before you leave this house, you are going to memorise them. You are not, repeat not, to write this down. If you feel you are in danger or you need to get some information back to me that is not to do with your mother's state of health, but is evidence of my suspicions, then ring this number. You will then ask if you are speaking to Armin. If you get a positive response, you say that it is Peter calling, make sure to pronounce it as a German would. Ask him if he can meet you in the usual place and get him to give you a time.'

'Where is the usual place?'

'In front of the lion enclosure at the Zoo. But never explicitly say this. Just the usual place. You will be carrying a copy of the current issue of Time magazine. Make sure not to fold the front cover back on itself. Only make this arrangement if you need some help. Armin will help you and get a message back to me. I will join you in Berlin as soon as I can, but it's probably not going to be until Thursday week at the earliest. With luck, Mavis will be out of her coma long before that and on the road to recovery and this will all turn out to be a bad dream.'

'I hope so, but you've worried me now.'

'I'm sorry, Steve. It's not something I wanted to do. But you need your wits about you. Perhaps I'm overreacting, but it's better to be safe than sorry. Right, we're going to have a cup of tea before you go, and I'm going to test you on what you've got to remember.'

Grace tested Steve twice before she would let him leave the house. They embraced tenderly before he opened the front door, reluctant to let each other go. Steve wiped a tear from Grace's eye. 'I'll phone you when I get to the flat.'

Grace nodded dolefully. 'But remember only lovey-dovey chit-chat.'

As Steve exited passport and customs control at Tempelhof Airport the following evening, he saw a smartly dressed man holding a placard with Steve's name. Fortescue had told him that he would be met at the airport by a Foreign Office colleague who would take him to his hotel and, in due course, take him to the hospital where his mother was being treated. He walked across to the man with the placard and said, 'Hi, I'm Steve.'

'Hello, Mr Percival. I hope you had a smooth flight. My name is Jeremy Collingwood.'

'Please call me Steve. The flight was fine, thanks. What is the latest news of my mother?'

'No real change, I'm afraid. It's too late to go to the hospital today. I will take you to your hotel now and collect you first thing tomorrow morning. Please follow me, I have a car waiting outside.'

'I don't have a hotel booked. I was hoping I might be able to find a hostel to stay in until I could get the key to my mother's flat.'

'The department has booked you into a hotel where we get special rates for our visitors.'

'I'm sure the kind of hotel you're talking about will be beyond my budget.'

'Please do not worry about that. The costs will be met by the department.'

'Thank you. That's very kind, but I'd still like to stay at her flat, once I've located a key.'

'I will check tomorrow if that is possible.'

Steve was about to ask why it shouldn't be possible, but they had now reached the drop-off area, where an anonymous-looking four-door Opel was waiting for them. Collingwood opened the nearside rear door and invited Steve to get in. He then walked around to the other side and climbed in. Leaning forward, he said, 'The Hotel Treibel, please, Jennings.'

The driver said, 'Yes, sir,' and drove towards the exit.

Steve was not unfamiliar with German cities. He had worked for nine months in Frankfurt before going up to Cambridge and had also visited Mainz and Heidelberg while there, but this was his first time in West Berlin. As they drove through the rainy streets, he was struck by the sheer scale of the city.

When they arrived at the hotel, Collingwood said 'You can knock off now, Jennings. I'll make sure there are no hitches with Mr Percival's reservation and then I'll make my own way home.'

'Right you are, sir. Same time tomorrow morning?'

'Yes, please.'

In the lobby, Collingwood said, 'I know you speak German, but if you give me your passport, we will get through the registration process much quicker. We use this hotel quite a lot.'

Steve handed over his passport and let Collingwood do the honours. All Steve had to do was sign the register, once all his documentation had been checked. The desk clerk handed over a key with a large fob and took Steve's bag. That done, Collingwood said, 'You must be starving. We can eat in the hotel restaurant or we can find somewhere a bit more *gemütlich*.'

'To be quite honest, the meal on the plane was sufficient. But I could do with a drink.'

Collingwood nodded. 'Could do with one myself. There's a nice little *Kneipe* around the corner, which will be much more informal than the hotel bar.'

It was still pouring with rain, but Collingwood borrowed an umbrella from the doorman of the hotel. A few minutes later, Steve had a large Pilsner in front of him and Collingwood a tumbler of Chivas Regal on the rocks, which he raised, saying, '*Prost*.'

Steve returned the toast and took a deep draught of his beer. Feeling immediately more relaxed, he said, 'Thank you so much for sorting things out for me. I wasn't really expecting it.'

'It's the least we could do.'

'Could you tell me more about what happened?'

'There's not much more to tell, I'm afraid. Your mother was crossing a road near her flat on Saturday night. It was a filthy night, much like tonight. A speeding car knocked her over. A passer-by saw it happen but was unable to get the car's registration number. Couldn't even say what colour the car was. He checked your mother and realised that she was alive but unconscious. Somebody else went into a bar and asked them to call an ambulance which took her to the Martin Luther Hospital in

Wilmersdorf. We didn't get to hear about it until the small hours. The next morning we set about trying to track you down.'

'What do the doctors say about her condition?'

'They are hopeful, but can't promise anything. We'd like to get her back to the UK, but the advice seems to be that moving her would be inadvisable right now. How long can you stay?'

'As long as necessary. Which is another reason why I think it would be better if I were to stay at my mother's flat.'

'I promise to consult with my superiors and get back to you on that tomorrow.'

'Thank you, Jeremy.'

'Would you mind me asking when you last saw your mother?'

'Less than two months ago. She came up to Cambridge and stayed with me and my girlfriend.'

'That would be Dr Grace Mitchell?'

'Yes, is that relevant?'

'No, it's just the details your mother left with our administration office.'

Collingwood took a sip of his Scotch. 'You knew that your mother was being posted to Berlin?'

'Yes, she told me at Christmas.'

'And you know what her job is?'

Conscious of the warning that Grace had given him, Steve said, 'Well, I know she works for the Foreign Office, but I don't know what she actually does. Are the police trying to find the driver?'

'They are, but they haven't got much to go on.'

'How many people actually saw the incident?'

'Four. They have all provided statements. There may have been one other, but that person didn't stay around to help or answer questions.'

'Isn't that somewhat suspicious behaviour?'

'Well, this is West Berlin. It is an anomalous place. Some would call it bohemian, others anarchic. The Americans had their draft dodgers until quite recently, but in West Germany if you don't want to do military service, all you need do is move to West Berlin. So the place is stuffed full of hippies and avant-garde artists. Need-less to say, such people are not keen to help the police.'

'Was my mother on her own when she was knocked over?'

'That is what we understand from the people who have provided statements. Why do you ask?'

'I'm just surprised that she was out on her own at night in bad weather in a city that was still new to her. Do you know where she had been or where she was going to?'

'I'm afraid not.'

'You are a colleague of hers?'

'Yes, in a manner of speaking.'

'What does that mean?'

'Well, the UK government has quite a large presence over here. One doesn't know all one's colleagues, especially not recent postings.'

'So could I talk to someone who did actually work with her? I'd just like to know what state of mind she was in.'

'I'm not sure that's going to be easy or possible to arrange.'

'Do you mean the only person I can speak to is you?'

'Well, not as such, but in practice that will probably be the case.'

'I don't understand.'

'I'm afraid I can't spell it out for you. I can understand you're upset and angry. But I can assure you that the matter is being looked into very thoroughly. Look, with luck, they can bring your mother out of this coma and then we can get her back to the UK. Until then, make yourself at home here. Berlin is a fascinating place. You can contact me at any time of day or night.' He passed Steve a card. 'These are my contact details.'

Steve took the card. 'Thank you, Jeremy.'

Collingwood took an envelope from his inside pocket and put it on the table. 'Changing the subject, the UK's exchange controls are a bloody nuisance. Even with the department picking up the tab for the hotel, I doubt that you were able to pull together enough cash to last more than a few days. So there's a float in that envelope. Don't spend it all at once, but if you do start to run short of cash, let me know. We may be able to help with a bit more.'

Steve did not pick up the envelope. He felt he was being manipulated. The fact of the matter was he had no idea who Collingwood really was, or indeed whether he really worked for the British government. 'Jeremy, I really don't think I can accept cash from you. I feel I might be compromising myself.'

'Steven, it's not my money. It's HMG funds. Berlin works on hard cash.'

'I am grateful. I do in fact already have some German currency on me, so can I offer you another drink?'

Collingwood stood up. 'That's very kind of you, but I really must go. I'll call for you tomorrow morning at ten o'clock.'

Steve stood up and the two men shook hands. Once Collingwood had departed, Steve opened the envelope and counted the notes. There were 150 Deutschmarks, almost the same amount that Grace had given him to buy traveller's cheques with. Was he being bribed? He ordered another beer and drank it, deep in thought.

Back in Glisson Road, Grace was lying in bed, wondering how Steve was getting on. She had been reading and was just about to turn the light out, when the phone rang. She jumped out of bed and ran downstairs. Picking up the phone, she said, 'Steve?'

'Grace, sorry to phone so late.'

Grace had been hoping that he might ring, but she was also worried that he might forget to keep the conversation on the meaningless endearments level.

'It's okay. I was still awake. Shall I ring you back? This call must be costing a lot.'

'The Foreign Office are paying my hotel bill until I can get the key to Mavis's flat. They didn't say anything about use of the phone in the room, but I'm not intending to overuse it. It'll just be nice to be in touch with you for the days I'm here.'

'When will you be able to visit Mavis?'

'Tomorrow morning, I hope. I'm being picked up.'

'That's good. Give her a kiss from me.'

'I will. I suppose I'd better go now. I don't want to find out that international phone calls aren't actually covered by the *Halbpension* arrangement.' He didn't mention the wad of cash he'd been given.

'Quite, let's speak again tomorrow, if possible.'

'Yes. Grace, I miss you.'

'I miss you too, darling. Let's hope they can bring Mavis out of the coma soon.'

The next morning, when Steve came down from his room in the Treibel, Collingwood was already waiting for him in the lobby of the hotel.

'Good morning, Steven.'

'Morning, Jeremy.'

'How did you sleep?'

'Very well, thanks.'

'The car is waiting outside. The hospital is in the Spandau area.'

'Is that near where the accident happened?'

'No, the ambulance took her to the nearest German hospital, but once she was stable, it was thought better to move her to the British Military Hospital in the Spandau area.'

'Why was that? Are there better facilities there?'

'Well, one wouldn't want to make that kind of comparison. But let's just say that it is more secure and all the staff are British.'

It was Steve's first view of Berlin in the daylight. He was struck by how much less dense it was than London. As they swept along the broad thoroughfares, Collingwood chatted amiably, perhaps sensing Steve's anxiety about seeing his mother in a coma. Eventually, they reached a modern multi-storey building in a leafy and sparsely inhabited part of the city. There were British military guards at the gate, who waved the car through after a cursory check of Jennings's pass.

Collingwood said, 'Get yourself a cuppa, Jennings. I don't know how long we're going to be.'

He then invited Steve to step out of the car and follow him into the hospital itself. They walked up to the second floor and came to a halt in front of a set of double doors. Collingwood rang the bell and a few moments later a staff nurse opened the door to them. Collingwood introduced Steve and then said, 'I will wait downstairs for you.'

Steve was grateful for his sensitivity. The staff nurse said, 'My name's Jenny. Your mother's in a side room. As you probably know, she is unconscious and she is attached to several machines. But it is nothing to be alarmed about. You can hold her hand and talk to her. It is thought that patients in a coma can sometimes hear people speaking to them and the voices of family members and friends are particularly comforting.'

Jenny took Steve into Mavis's room. Steve had readied himself to see her hooked up to various monitors and drips, but he hadn't expected to see her head swathed in white bandages. He sat down beside her and took her hand. It was cool and limp. He said, 'Ma, it's Steve. I came as quickly as I could. The Foreign Office people have been very good. Grace sends her love.'

For a moment he thought that the rhythm of her breathing quickened in response to his voice, but it soon dropped back. At that moment the door opened and a white-coated doctor came in. 'Hello, I'm Doctor Saunders. You must be Steve.'

Steve stood up. 'Yes, thank you for coming to speak to me. What is the outlook for my mother?'

'I'm afraid it's very hard to say. Sometimes people just come out of the coma a day or two after the injury. But I'm afraid her chances of a good recovery diminish for each additional day she remains in a coma. We detected that there was a build up of pressure in the brain and we took steps yesterday to reduce that. But we have yet to see any positive signs.'

'I realise, this is a military hospital. Will I be able to visit on my own, or will I have to get Mr Collingwood to accompany me?'

'I believe he is sorting out a pass for you now. You are welcome to come on a daily basis, but it would be more convenient to come in the afternoon. In that respect, we're just like a normal hospital. Jenny will give you the ward telephone number. Please stay as long as you like today. If you have any further questions, Jenny will find me.'

They shook hands and Saunders left the room. Steve sat down beside his mother again and took her hand once more. Despite the tubes and lines she looked peaceful. He actually couldn't remember the last time he'd seen her asleep. He wondered if he would ever hear her speak again. Self-consciously at first, even though there were only the two of them in the room, he began to talk to her, telling her how much he loved her, grateful for the way she had brought him up and how she had encouraged him to get to Cambridge, apologising for having neglected her since he had been there, and assuring her that he would make her proud of him one day. The more he talked, the more he had the sense that she actually could hear him. Eventually, he ran out of self-recriminations and told her he would come back the following afternoon. He kissed her tenderly on the cheek and then went to find Jenny to let her know he was leaving.

Jenny said, 'I'll give you Mrs Percival's things. I've put her clothes in a laundry bag. They will need a wash. Her raincoat will need to go to the dry-cleaners. I've put her small personal effects in her handbag. We removed her jewellery before operating. I'm afraid one of the earrings is missing. It must have come off in the street.' Jenny handed Steve the laundry bag and the small leather handbag.

'Thank you, Jenny, for everything.'

'Where can we get hold of you if there is any change in Mrs Percival's condition?'

'I am staying at the Treibel Hotel, but I'm hoping to move to my mother's flat. You didn't notice if there were any keys in the handbag, did you?'

'I didn't notice any.'

Down in the lobby, he found Collingwood, sitting on a bench reading a newspaper. Collingwood folded the newspaper and stood up. 'Did you get to speak to one of the doctors?'

'Yes, Saunders.'

'Ah, yes. Good man. What was the news?'

'Not much change apparently. They did some procedure yesterday to reduce the pressure on the brain. He also said that the longer she remained in a coma, the less favourable the outlook.'

'I see. Well, let's hope the procedure did the trick and we'll find her sitting up in bed tomorrow.'

'Thank you, Jeremy.'

'I see they've given you Mrs Percival's effects.'

'Yes, I'm hoping the key to her flat is in her handbag.'

'It won't be. The police took it and her passport when they were trying to establish her identity. The department is now in possession of both. However, I am afraid you will not be able to have immediate access to her flat. Our security people are checking it at the moment. They expect it to take several days. I will let you know when you can move in. Please make yourself comfortable at the Treibel in the meantime.'

'Why are the security people checking the flat?'

'I am told it is routine in such cases. It is nothing to be alarmed about.'

To Steve's way of thinking, that very phrase was reason enough to be alarmed.

Collingwood ran him back to the hotel and said that he would pick him up just after midday the following day. Steve went up to his room and lay down on the bed. When he awoke, he remembered that Jenny at the hospital had given him his mother's possessions. She said that she'd put her rings and the one earring that she had been able to find in his mother's handbag. He opened the handbag and carefully emptied the contents onto the surface of the desk. The first thing that struck him was that the rings were not the solitaire diamond engagement ring and the gold wedding ring that he was expecting to find. He was no expert, but he would have said the rings in the bag were costume jewellery.

He examined the other objects. There was a lipstick, mascara, a powder compact, a comb, a small pouch of tissues, a change purse containing both German coins and a small number of notes, a small silver propelling pencil, a tube of mints, a small square dispenser for aspirins, a couple of tampons, and a small leather-covered pocket diary with pop-rivet fastener. He opened the diary. It was still early in the year, so it did not take Steve long to scan the entries for the year to date, which in any case were notably few. The most recent entry was one for the previous Saturday, the day of her accident, which simply read "S 17:30". He now recalled that he'd seen a similar entry earlier in the year. He leafed back through the pages and found a similar entry for the first of February, which by one of the vagaries of the calendar was also a Saturday and must have been only shortly after she had arrived in Berlin. He wondered who or where S was or whether S indicated some regular meeting or event. He scanned forward to the first of April and noted that both the first Saturday in April and the first of April itself were blank, but pencilled in over the Easter weekend were the words "Steve & Grace?" So there was no doubt that this was indeed his mother's diary. He put the diary on the table and then carefully searched through the inner pockets of the bag, but they were empty. Not that he was expecting to find a set of keys. He knew that they together with her passport had been handed to the department.

Somewhat troubled by the thought that the time given for the diary entry the previous Saturday was by all accounts not too long before the time of her accident, he resolved to raise the matter with Collingwood the following day. He then lay on his bed and read until he nodded off. Waking a couple of hours later, he looked at his watch and saw that, allowing for the time difference, it was the time of day that Grace got home. He dialled her number and was pleased to hear her voice. 'Steve, how are you? Did you get to see Mavis?'

'Yes, they've moved her to the British Military Hospital. I spoke to the consultant. He said they'd conducted a procedure to reduce the pressure on her brain. He's hopeful that the treatment will be beneficial, but said that for every successive day she remains in a coma, the worse her prospects are.'

'Will you be able to go again?'

'Yes, because it's a military hospital, there's restricted access, but they've given me a pass. A chap called Collingwood from the embassy has been running me around. I asked if I could move to Mavis's flat, but apparently that won't be possible for a few days. I'm not sure what the hold-up is. How are you?'

'Busy, busy. But fortunately, the end of term is not too far off. I'm planning to come out the day after my last lecture. Even if Mavis has come out of the coma, I imagine it'll be some time before she's able to look after herself.'

'It'd be lovely to see you, but you don't have to come.'

'Steve, I want to come. I want to be with you and I want to help.'

'Grace, I miss you. It's so good to talk to you. I'll try and ring around this time tomorrow evening.'

The next day, Steve raised the matter of the entries in his mother's diary with Collingwood, particularly the timing of the one for the day of her accident, but he was unable to cast any light on it. Thereafter, Steve settled into a fitful routine. He would spend the morning exploring the different areas of West Berlin, eventually meeting up with Collingwood and Jennings for the run to the hospital in the early afternoon. He would sit with his mother for half an hour or so and then Collingwood would drop him off at his hotel. Occasionally he went out to a local bar in the evenings, but mostly he watched German television and read. At nine o'clock, if he was in, he would phone Grace.

On the morning of Monday, the tenth of March, a week to the day since he had arrived in Berlin, he received a call from Colling-wood.

'Steven, would you be free to meet for some drinks tonight?'

Steve, who had been beginning to tire of his own company, readily agreed.

The waitress brought their drinks to the corner table in a cellar bar. Steve raised his glass and said, 'Thanks, Jeremy, for asking me out.'

'Not at all. Berlin can be a lonely place. How's the German going?'

'I'm a bit rusty, but it seems to be coming back. Even though I haven't been speaking much German over the past three years, I've been reading a lot.'

'Berlin is very different to Frankfurt, though, and not just the accent.'

'Yes, so it would seem.'

'You're finding your way around okay?'

'Yes, I'm getting the hang of West Berlin. But I realise how much of the historic city I'm missing, being confined to the Western sector. I thought I might take a look at East Berlin.'

'Really? Have you done your homework?'

'As I understand it, Westerners are allowed to travel to East Berlin for the day without a formal visa.'

'You are correct. You have no qualms about that? It's not on every tourist's agenda.'

'I've been studying German language and literature since I was twelve years old. It seems strange now that I'm finally in Berlin not to take a look at what was in effect the heart of the historic city.'

'I understand. But before we move onto other matters, are things to your satisfaction at the Treibel?'

'Yes, the hotel is fine, but how long is it going to be before I can move into my mother's flat?'

'Not immediately, I'm afraid.'

'Could you explain to me what the problem is?'

'Not in so many words.'

'Look, Jeremy, you've used that phrase or something like it quite a lot in the week I've known you. The other thing is that, apart from the very laconic Jennings, you are the only colleague of my mother's that I have been permitted to meet. That suggests to me that there is something not entirely straightforward about all this.'

'Steve, before you rush ahead with this line of thought…'

'No, Jeremy, hear me out. I've been doing quite a lot of thinking since I've been here and I've come to the conclusion that you actually work for the security services. That probably means my mother did as well. Which would explain why I never really knew what her job involved. If all that is true, then maybe the hit and run was not an accident but was an attempt to kill her by the East Germans, the Stasi.'

'Honestly, Steve, they tend not to work like that.'

'But you're not actually rejecting my line of reasoning.'

'I'm neither confirming nor denying.'

'Which is pretty much what members of the intelligence community say when asked awkward questions.'

'Okay, I was planning to build up to this slowly, but in your incisive way you have leapt ahead. So I will tell you as much as I can. But before we go any further, I want you to promise me that you will keep everything I'm now going to tell you to yourself.'

Steve was about to say that Collingwood wasn't the first person to try to extract that promise from him. But it was clear from Collingwood's demeanour that this was not a time for flippancy. He nodded. 'I promise.'

'Well, as you have surmised, your mother is an experienced member of our organisation. She was here to take an active part in an operation that had been in the works for some time. We don't think her accident was connected to the operation, but it would be foolhardy not to act as if it were. So we have had to rethink.'

'Why are you telling me this now?'

'Because we didn't know much about you before, and now we think you can help us.'

'Me?'

'Yes, we would like you to deliver a package…' Collingwood paused. Steve already knew that it couldn't be as simple as that. '… to a person in East Berlin.'

'Why me?'

'Because you're new here. Our *friends* will not have built up a profile on you yet. They are relentless but a bit plodding. We need to get one of our agents out of East Berlin, and to do that, we have to get some travel documents into this person's hands. The documents will be fakes, of course, but so good that they will convince all but the most assiduous on border guards.'

'Who is this person?'

'It is better if you don't know that. Your job will be to give the package to an intermediary. Western tourists go into East Berlin every day, as you pointed out. They enter via Checkpoint Charlie or get the U-Bahn to Friedrichstraße and then enjoy the delights of East Berlin. The Ossis make you change your D-Marks at a very unfavourable rate and you can't bring out any Ostmarks you haven't spent. But otherwise it's quite straightforward.'

'If it's so easy, why doesn't someone, who knows what they're doing, go?'

'Because any known station hands will be followed very closely, which will complicate the handover of the documents.'

'Why won't they follow me?'

'Because they have no idea who you are. You are just another student tourist. That is the reason why we have not let you occupy your mother's flat, so we could preserve your anonymity. If in fact her accident was deliberate, then it may be that the flat is being watched. That is also why we have kept you sequestered from other colleagues. The fewer people who know you are here, the better.'

'Because you can't actually trust your own colleagues?'

'Once again, I'm not actually saying that. It just makes sense to take every precaution.'

'Look, Jeremy, you're a nice bloke. I enjoy your company, but, to be honest, how do I know you are who you say you are. Why should I trust you?'

'I don't have a good answer to that. I don't know what would convince you. Would it help if I were to tell you that I too was an undergraduate at St Radegund's, a few years before you, of course?'

'You were at St Rad's?'

'Yes. I also read Modern and Mediaeval Languages.'

Something occurred to Steve. 'What would you say Dr Doyle's favourite Goethe poem was?'

Collingwood thought for a moment. 'Hmm, probably *Willkommen und Abschied*, which begins *"Es schlug mein Herz, geschwind, zu Pferde!"'*

'Okay, I'm convinced.'

'Phew! That was a tough one.'

'Is that why they gave you the job of minding me?'

'You don't miss much, do you?'

'So is there an element of danger in what you want me to do?'

'I'd be lying if I were to say there was absolutely no danger. But really, the risks of any unpleasantness are extremely low. In, out, shake it all about.'

Steve was doubtful. 'Okay.'

'Does that mean, okay you'll do it?'

'No, it means: tell me more. How do I know who I'm meeting?'

'You will be meeting a girl, who will be known as Inge for this operation . Inge is a student at Humboldt University. You will spend two or three hours looking at sights and then you will go to a bar. We will give you the name and location of the bar if you agree to take on the operation. You will have in your bag a hardback book which will have some travel documents sewn into its cover.'

'What will the book be?'

'You will find that out tomorrow.'

'Tomorrow?'

'One step at a time. On arrival in East Berlin, you will buy a copy of the *Berliner Zeitung*. You will also be carrying a copy of an illustrated book of post-war East Berlin architecture, which we will provide. When you are in the bar, you will make sure that the cover of this book is visible, but keep the hardback volume in your bag. Inge will use the architecture book to identify you. She will ask if she can join you at your table. Do not use your real name when introducing yourself to her. She will be expecting you to call yourself Tom. Once you have exchanged some passphrases, which we will provide later and which ostensibly will be in relation to something in the *Berliner Zeitung*, she will take you to her flat where you will have sex. You will thank her for her services, pay her, making sure to leave the adapted book. At no time during the encounter will you make reference to the book. You will then go back to the Friedrichstraße station and return to West Berlin.'

'That's it?'

'That's it. What do you think?'

'Why do I have to have sex with this girl? Does she know about that aspect of things?'

'It is quite likely the Stasi bug her flat or will have watchers outside. If they are, we want them to think of her as someone feathering her nest by having sex with Western tourists. They certainly don't approve of such things, but it's not quite the same as being involved with Western agents. It would arouse suspicion if you didn't have sex with her. You have to understand the way the Stasi work. They document everything. If they have blurry photographs of a young couple making love and tape recordings of a passionate encounter, they will be satisfied this is a matter of moral turpitude, not an attempt to undermine the state.'

'I'm not sure I can have sex with someone I don't know and pay her for it.'

'We have done a little bit of poking into your life. One thing you seem quite ready to do is to have sex with women you hardly know at all.'

'Are you talking about Jude?'

'I really couldn't say, but I don't think the behaviour is limited to only one person. I grant you that you are not in the habit of paying for sex, but any money involved will be HMG's and not yours.'

'Earlier on you likened the encounter to the Hokey Cokey; in, out, shake it all about. But this seems much more like: in, shake it all about, out. Admittedly, in that order, it plays havoc with the scansion and the rhyme, but it's the out bit I'm worried about.'

Jeremy laughed. 'My choice of song title was inapt. Getting out will be the easy part. So do I take it you are agreeing to do the run?'

'I don't know. How long do I have to make up my mind?'

'Five minutes.'

'I can't make a momentous decision like this in five minutes.'

'You have to. Time is of the essence. The more time passes, the less likely we are to get our agent out. I will order some more drinks. I need your answer when I get back.'

In the event, Steve agreed, if only because he felt he was standing in for his mother. Not that he thought his mother would have had to sleep with someone as part of her involvement in this operation. How was he going to be able to square things with Grace? Tell her it was for Queen and Country? But from what Collingwood was saying, that was exactly what he would not be able to do. Nor did he believe Collingwood about the relative lack of risk, or about the lightness of any sanction, were he to be caught. In fact he was already scared. Where was new Steve when he needed him?

## Wednesday, 12 March 1975

As STEVE BOARDED THE northbound U-Bahn train at Spichern-
straße two days later, he was tempted to turn back and tell Collingwood that he had changed his mind. After all, who exactly was he
doing this for? Collingwood had implied that he was helping out on
an operation that his mother had been involved in, but that could
easily be a line he was spinning. Even if she had been involved, it
was unlikely that she had been employed as a courier.

To make matters worse, the weather was abominable. Sheets of
icy rain, driven by a cutting and capricious wind, poured from the
leaden sky. Despite the cagoule that Collingwood had provided him
with, Steve was already soaking. It seemed to him that surely even
the most obsessive architecture buff would have postponed a tour
of modernist buildings in East Berlin until the weather improved.
Not to do so was surely to invite closer scrutiny. But Collingwood
had been insistent. The run could not be deferred.

Then there were the risks. Collingwood had said it was very
unlikely that he would be searched at the crossing point. He probably wouldn't even be asked any questions. But Steve had felt that
his assertion had been less than convincing. Steve's confidence had
been further shaken when Collingwood had produced a copy of a
Captain America comic to put in his bag together with the book
containing the travel documents for the agent and the architectural
guide. Apparently the comic would almost certainly be impounded
if his bag were searched, on the grounds that it was a glorification
of American values. Steve wasn't sure how this made things better.
Collingwood had blithely opined that such publications had a high
value in the East and would distract the guard from looking too
closely at the other books in Steve's bag. Actually, the magazine
would be for the guard's later personal delectation. Steve would be

ticked off and then sent on his way. Nothing else would be scrutinised.

Steve assumed that security professionals knew what they were
doing, but even so he was a little startled that the adapted book he
was carrying was an edition of Nietzsche's *Jenseits von Gut und Böse*,
*Beyond Good and Evil*, as it was known in English. Was this some kind
of silly joke? Wouldn't the border guards think it strange for an
English man to be carrying such a thing and decide to look at it
despite the business with the Captain America comic? Collingwood
assured him they wouldn't. It would be obvious that he was a
student. Even if they were to examine it closely, they were unlikely
to detect the documents sewn into its binding. Once again there
was that weasel word *unlikely*.

While Steve was still trying to estimate the precise degree of
likelihood, the train pulled into the Wittenbergplatz station. Unable
to quell his fears, he changed to the U1 line and travelled on to the
Hallesches Tor stop, changing there to the U6 line. Soon the train
was pulling into the Bahnhof Friedrichstraße – the crossing point
for those wishing to visit the East. For a moment he considered
staying on the train as it traversed the ghost stations of the Eastern
sector on its way back to Leopoldplatz and safety in the West. But
he knew if he did that, he would be unable to face Collingwood,
and more importantly, unable to face himself.

Still dripping wet and with a mounting sense of trepidation, he
got off the train and went up to the checkpoint, where there were a
number of small booths. He had hoped that the crossing might be
busy, but on this particular day the border guards seemed to out-
number visitors. He was ushered into a short queue. A few moments later a border guard was asking for his passport, which he
had ready in his hand. The guard studied the passport carefully.
'*Engländer?*'

'*Ja.*'

'*Sie sprechen Deutsch?*'

'*Ein bißchen.*'

The guard nodded and said, '*Herein*,' indicating that Steve should
step into the small booth to one side of the barrier. The guard
followed him in and pulled a curtain across the opening.

Making no attempt to speak English, the guard said, 'Please
empty the contents of your pockets onto the table.'

Steve put the contents of each pocket onto the table: his wallet,
his keys, a none-too-clean handkerchief, a pen, his notebook. Steve
was conscious that his hand was trembling slightly as he laid each

item down. When he had finished, the guard asked him to take off his cagoule and his coat.

Steve put his bag down, took his cagoule and coat off and laid them on the table. The guard then indicated that he should raise his arms. When he had done so, the guard patted him down, looking, no doubt, for anything in a shirt or trouser pocket. Satisfied that these were empty, he then checked the pockets of Steve's coat. Finding nothing there either, the guard picked up the wallet, which was lying on the table, and opened it. He counted the notes. Steve was glad that Collingwood had recommended that he take only forty D-Marks, five for the visa and the twenty-five he was obliged to change at parity for Ostmarks, the remaining ten D-Marks for emergencies.

The guard then flicked through the notebook. Collingwood had suggested that Steve take one and write in it the names of some of the sights he was apparently going to see, as well as a number of simple German words and phrases. The guard seemed surprised. 'Café Moskau?'

Steve nodded. 'It's an architectural masterpiece. I am visiting several other modernist buildings today.'

'In this weather?'

'It's the only day I have.'

'I think you are underestimating the Berlin weather.'

The guard closed the notebook and, noticing the bag on the floor, asked Steve to empty its contents on the table. Steve pulled out the hat and gloves, the copy of *Jenseits von Gut und Böse*, the guide to modernist architecture and finally the Captain America comic. Completely ignoring the Nietzsche, the guard picked up the architectural guidebook and, glancing at it, said, 'Architecture student?' Steve nodded, hoping that he wouldn't be required to supply further details. He felt that if he tried to offer an explanation, his voice would betray him. But at that moment the guard noticed the copy of the Captain America comic he was still holding in his hand. The guard put the architecture book down and grabbed the comic from him. Without even looking at it, he said, 'No, no. You cannot bring such filth into the DDR.'

He threw the comic into the bin. 'Anything else?'

Steve, still unable to speak but thankful for Collingwood's prescience, handed the guard the bag. The guard turned it upside down and felt in the outer pockets. He then looked steadily at Steve for a few moments, as if trying to read his thoughts. Steve wasn't sure whether to meet his gaze or stare at the floor. Was defiance or

submission a better strategy? But before he had come to a conclusion, the guard had picked up his passport, stamped it, inserted a
slip of paper and, handing it to him, said, 'You can go. Don't lose
the slip of paper. You will need it when you exit.'

For a moment or two, Steve stood rooted to the spot before
repacking his bag, putting his coat and cagoule back on and returning wallet, keys, notebook and handkerchief to his pockets. As he
did so, it occurred to him it might seem more authentic to protest
about the confiscation of the comic, but he resisted the urge and
left well alone. The guard continued to watch him until he was out
of sight. On the upper concourse, Steve bought a copy of the
*Berliner Zeitung* and a street map. Before tucking them into an outer
pocket of his bag, he glanced through the paper to see if there
were any productions of Brecht plays running in East Berlin and
was not sure if he was relieved to find there were none. The passphrase he was to slip into the conversation, apparently derived
from his reading of the newspaper, was *Mutter Courage*, in reply to
which his contact would supply the words *Das Leben des Galilei*.

A few minutes later, emerging from what Collingwood had told
him was called the Tränenpalast and taking a moment to get his
bearings, Steve struck south towards the grand thoroughfare of
Unter den Linden. It was still raining, but less heavily. The first
thing on the list of sights that Collingwood had suggested was the
view of the Brandenburger Tor stranded in the middle of the no-
man's land between east and west. Steve stood at the barrier looking across the Pariser Platz, only now realising how near and yet
how far he was from the safety of West Berlin. He took several
deep breaths, drawing the acrid, cold air deep into his lungs,
noticing that he was still trembling. A few minutes later feeling
somewhat more stable, he turned to begin his progress along Unter
den Linden. But before he did so, he quickly scanned the pedestri-
ans in his vicinity. Collingwood had said he might be followed. Did
he recognise anyone from the Tränenpalast? Had anyone noticed
his trembling? He thought not.

He set off, walking slowly, peering through the rain at the faded
but monumental buildings that lined what had been Berlin's premi-
er street. He looked at his watch. He had two hours before he was
due at the Am Dreieck bar, off the Prenzlauer Allee. Soon he was
passing the gloomy bulk of the Humboldt University buildings and
then, after crossing the Kupfergraben channel of the river Spree by
the Schloßbrücke, the even bigger bulk of the Berliner Dom.
Continuing along what was now Karl-Liebknecht-Strasse, he

looked up at the 1960s space-age TV tower, its gigantic antenna surmounting a globe, incongruously looming over the mediaeval St Marienkirche church.

Cutting across under the TV tower, he walked through the vast expanse of Alexanderplatz, a triumphalist vision of the future, passing the Haus des Lehrers with its Mexican-style mural, the neighbouring domed congress hall and eventually reaching the ultra-modern Café Moskau. It was a little over an hour since he had emerged from the Tränenpalast. He could do with a coffee and decided to step into the Moskau. It would be a relief to get out of the wind and rain. He took his cagoule off, hung it on a hook and, catching the eye of a waitress, ordered a coffee, a bowl of soup and a roll.

While he was waiting for his order to arrive and mindful of Collingwood's admonition to check as frequently as possible whether he was being followed, he scanned the spacious café. He was not the only one taking refuge from the elements, it would seem. Everywhere in the dining room, coats and umbrellas dripped and steamed. But did he recognise anyone from the environs of the Tränenpalast?

The trouble was that the more he studied the other patrons of the café, the more he thought he recognised several of them. After a few jittery moments, he realised that what was throwing him was that everyone seemed to be wearing the same kind of clothes. The Fernsehturm, the Café Moskau itself, and the view of the Kino International cinema building on the other side of the road from the café might testify to the futuristic aspirations of the German Democratic Republic, but the apparel of its citizenry did not share those aspirations.

In an unsuccessful attempt to shake off a rising sense of paranoia, he pulled the copy of the *Berliner Zeitung* from his bag and scanned the front page to decipher what passed for news in a totalitarian state. His reading was interrupted by the arrival of his coffee and soup. Both were tasteless but, nevertheless, welcome.

He had been planning to continue down Karl-Marx-Allee as far as the Kosmos cinema, another of the buildings in his architecture guide, but now looking at the street map he could see that if he did so, not only would he be cutting it fine to get up to the Am Dreieck in Prenzlauer Berg at the agreed time, but by then he would also be soaked to the skin. He therefore decided to abandon the detour to the Kosmos and go directly to Prenzlauer Berg. He'd rather be early and reasonably dry than late and soaking wet.

Leaving the Café Moskau, Steve retraced his footsteps back towards Alexanderplatz, eventually turning right on Karl-Lieb-knecht-Straße. Soon he found himself in Rosa-Luxemburg-Platz. He stopped for a few minutes to study the neo-classical façade of the Volksbühne Theater before continuing on his way to the Prenz-lauer-Allee.

The Am Dreieck was tucked away in a side street and it took Steve some time to find it. The exterior of the bar looked distinctly shabby but inside it was warm and busy. A matronly waitress greeted him with a cheerful *Scheisswetter* and asked whether he was on his own. He said he was meeting a friend later. Although Steve was clearly a foreigner, the waitress seemed to feel that this was not worthy of remark and led him to a table in the corner of the room. He was pleased to see that there was somewhere to hang his ca-goule and had a good view of the main entrance. After glancing at the menu, he ordered a Berliner Weisse beer and a Bratwurst. Mindful of the routine that Collingwood had taken him through the previous day, Steve also pulled the architectural guide, now rather wet and dog-eared, from his bag and placed it prominently on the table in front of him. He also extracted his copy of the *Berliner Zeitung* and settled down to resume his reading.

It was late afternoon and the café was beginning to fill up. Steve realised that in his anxiety to find the bar, he had not checked for some time whether he was being followed. He scanned the bar now. The only other solo drinker in the bar apart from Steve himself and, therefore, the person most likely to be an observer was a sour-looking middle-aged man in a badly-fitting jacket and drab tie. Herr Drab also had a newspaper spread in front of him, the indispensable accoutrement of the solo drinker it would seem, and only occasionally raised his eyes from it.

But had Herr Drab already been in the bar on Steve's arrival or had he arrived subsequently? Annoyingly, Steve was not sure. The only thing that somewhat reassured him was the fact that Herr Drab did not look as though he had spent the last couple of hours trudging through the rain. The other troubling matter was that there were no female drinkers, nor did it look like the sort of place where a woman would feel comfortable on her own. These thoughts, however, were dissipated by the welcome arrival of his beer and *Wurst*.

Shortly after Steve had finished his snack and ordered another beer, the gender imbalance of the bar was somewhat righted by the arrival of three young women. While divesting themselves of their sodden outer garments, the women exchanged some lively repartee with the waitress and, after a brief debate about where to sit, occupied the table next to Steve's. Soon the waitress brought the drinks for both tables. Clearly something about Steve's studied colloquialism in thanking the waitress drew him to the attention of his new neighbours. When the waitress had returned to the bar, one of the girls leaned across and asked him in German where he was from. For a second Steve considered claiming to be from Frankfurt, but thought better of it and replied in German that he was from London. One of the girls complimented him on his German. He looked pleased.

The girl furthest from him said, 'What are you doing in this part of East Berlin?'

'I'm on vacation in West Berlin, but I'm interested in modernist architecture and I wanted to see the new buildings in East Berlin.'

The third girl said, 'You chose a bad day for it.'

'Yes, the weather is almost as bad as in England.'

The girls appreciated his quip and the first one said, 'Are you a student?'

Steve, disappointed that it wasn't obvious, said, 'Yes.'

The first girl said, 'We're students too. Why don't you join us?'

Steve would have liked nothing better, but it would make things awkward when his contact arrived. 'That's very kind, but I'm waiting for a friend.'

This statement provoked a certain amount of mirth and the girls returned to their conversation. Clearly this was a man with options.

Half an hour later, Steve was still waiting for his contact to appear and was on his third glass of beer. He was beginning to wonder if he'd got the time of the meeting or the name of the bar wrong. He looked around the bar, which was fuller now. He was relieved to see that the headcount of women had increased, but all of the female newcomers were with male companions. He was not quite so happy, however, to see that Herr Drab was still studying his newspaper intently. In the many scenarios that he had gone through with Collingwood, none had covered what to do if he really thought he was being followed or if his contact failed to show.

While he was mulling his options, there was a kerfuffle at the next table as the girls stood up and embraced each other. Two of them put their now slightly drier coats on and one of them said to the girl nearest Steve, 'I don't know what you see in that Rudi. Come back with us.'

She replied. 'No, I'm sure he'll be here soon. See you tomorrow.'

Her friend was not convinced. 'I bet he stands you up.'

When the two girls had left the bar, the girl who was waiting for Rudi said to Steve, 'So it looks like we're both waiting for a friend.'

Steve laughed. 'Yes.'

The girl said, 'Would you like another drink while we're waiting?'

Before he could answer, the girl had already caught the waitress's eye. A few minutes later fresh glasses of Weisse arrived and another tick was added to the beer mats.

The girl raised her glass. 'Prost'

Steve clinked his glass against hers and took a sip of his beer.

'I'm Inge,' she said.

Feeling somewhat foolish, Steve suddenly realised that he had been sitting next to the girl he was supposed to be meeting for the best part of an hour. The fact that the three girls had arrived together had led him to discount any of them as being his contact, even when two of them left. But Steve saw that this was in fact a clever way of deflecting attention and he now felt a bit foolish, even more so when he realised that Inge was waiting for him to provide his cover name. After what must have seemed like a very suspicious pause, Steve managed to introduce himself as *Tom*, not yet feeling at home in his alias.

'What are you studying, Tom?'

'Architecture. What about you?'

'History. I'm a postgraduate student at Humboldt University. I guessed you were studying architecture from your guide to DDR architecture. I see you're reading the *Berliner Zeitung*. Do you find it interesting?'

She was clearly reminding him that she was now waiting for his passphrase, which, if overheard, could pass for a reference to something in the newspaper.

'It's the first time I've read it. It seems very serious compared to *Bild*.'

'Which is filled with sex and lies, I believe. We don't see it on this side.'

'Whereas in the *Berliner* I have just read a very good review of *Mutter Courage* at the Theater am Schiffbauerdamm.'

'Do you like Brecht? There was also a very good production recently of *Das Leben des Galilei*.'

'That is one of my favourite plays.'

'Mine too.'

She had responded with the correct pass phrase. With a good deal of trepidation, he said, 'I'm sorry. I was thrown by the fact that you came with friends.'

'Even in East Berlin it's not easy for a woman to go into a bar on her own.'

'Of course.'

'Right, let's get down to business. You are a sex tourist from the West and I am supporting myself through my studies by picking up men and having sex with them in exchange for western currency.'

Steve nodded. 'Yes, I understand.'

'In a moment we are going to start kissing and we'll make it so obvious that it'll get us thrown out.'

'Isn't it a bit dangerous to draw attention to ourselves in that way?'

'We want any informants in the bar to corroborate what Stasi microphones might pick up back at my room.'

Collingwood had said as much, but for some reason he felt he should show some surprise. 'You're being bugged?'

'It's best to assume that. You will make no mention at any time of the object you have brought for me, which you will leave in my room. We will, however, haggle over money. I will ask you for fifty Ostmarks and you will say that you only have twenty-five. I will say for that you will only get a handjob. You will say you also have ten D-Marks and I will say you can have whatever you want for that. Of course you will not have to pay anything. I am not actually a prostitute.'

'I realise that you are not a prostitute, but the money is not mine and I would like you to have it.'

'I do not want payment. It would call into doubt my motives for doing this. I do not want to discuss it further.'

Chastened, Steve said, 'Okay, I understand.'

'Good. Well, when we have completed the haggling scene, you will ask me to undress and I will then give you a blowjob, that's the correct term, isn't it? You will say very clearly so that the microphones pick up what you're saying that it was the best blowjob you've ever had. Even if that is not the case. We will then make love in more conventional ways. I will make a lot of noise and so should you. At the end, I will cry. You will get dressed and leave, remembering to put the book you have brought on the table. You will on no account refer to it. You will then go immediately to the Friedrichstraße station and cross to the West.'

'Do we have to have sex? Couldn't we pretend?'

'Tom, unless you are a very good actor, I think pretending is harder than doing it for real. If you are worried that I might be infected, I can assure you that as far as I know, I am not. This is not something I routinely do.'

'What do I say if I am interviewed at the Tränenpalast?'

'You will say that you have been seeing the sights and having a drink. The border guards will probably not have been alerted at that stage. The Stasi are thorough, but slow.'

'You must be taking a huge risk.'

'I am.'

'But why?'

'It's better if I don't go into that. If we ever meet again, maybe I will tell you.'

'Do you hope to be a *Republikflüchtling*?'

'I hope for more than that, but if all else fails, yes.'

Steve took a swig of his beer and noticed that his hand was trembling.

Inge said, 'Are you ready for this?'

In a moment of truthfulness, Steve said, 'No, not really.'

For the last few minutes, Inge's tone had been stern and no-nonsense, but now she softened. She put her arm around his shoulders and, kissing his cheek, whispered, 'If it's any consolation, I will try to make sure you have a good time.'

With that, she put her left hand between his legs and whispered, 'Touch my breasts. Be bold.'

Under almost any other circumstances, Steve would have been delighted by a young woman inviting him to touch her breasts and to be bold about it. But as things stood, he did not feel that he could give the matter the attention it deserved.

She then kissed him on the lips and slipped her tongue into his mouth. He felt himself hardening and breathed in the scent of her body. She then slipped her hand inside the waistband of his pants and grasped his cock. Suddenly he felt much more engaged than seemed appropriate in a public place.

She sensed his tension and, relaxing her grip, said with a small laugh, 'Maybe better to save it for the Stasi.'

But at that moment the waitress had spotted what they were up to and started to shout at them. Inge muttered some choice explet-ives back and asked for the *Rechnung*. The waitress got her notepad out of the front pocket of the short apron she was wearing and started scribbling. Steve, whose erection had vanished as quickly as it had arrived, said to the waitress, 'I'm sorry. I'll pay for both tables.'

The waitress harrumphed. 'You're a silly boy. That's not the only thing you'll be paying for this evening. You'll probably get something else that you didn't bargain for.'

Steve glanced at the bill and then got his wallet out, making sure to leave a sizeable tip.

As they were getting up to leave and putting on their coats, the waitress said to Inge, 'I don't want to see you in here again, my girl. Take your filthy trade somewhere else.'

By now, quite a few of the drinkers were looking in their direction, including Herr Drab. Steve felt himself blushing.

Out on the street, it was still raining, but perhaps not with the earlier intensity. Inge said to Steve, 'I recognised the guy by the door. I'm pretty sure he's an informant. If he follows us, we'll need to lose him. There's a park just up here. We'll go in there. We should have a good view of the footpath from the kids playground.'

She led him into the park and then over to the playground, where they concealed themselves beneath the struts of a children's slide. Standing so close together, she noticed that Steve was trembling. She put her arm around him. 'You're new to this, aren't you? They should have sent someone with more experience.'

'They said I wouldn't have a security profile yet.'

'Yes, that makes sense. You'll probably have one after this evening, though.'

She kissed him tenderly on the neck. 'You'll be okay. The ones who tremble are the brave ones. I can see you're a quick learner.'

At that moment, they heard footsteps on the path. Inge put her fingers to her lips and a few moments later, they saw Herr Drab hurrying along. When he came abreast of them, he peered through the railings of the park. Had he heard something? It seemed unlikely that he had spotted them. The few streetlights near that part of the fence cast very little of their weak, yellowish light into the park and visibility was further reduced by the rain and mist. In fact, after looking left and right, he unzipped himself, extracted his cock and pissed copiously into the bushes. Then, after rearranging his clothing and listening carefully for a few moments, he hurried on, splashing through the puddles on the pavement.

Once Inge felt certain that he was out of earshot, she said, 'We're going to have to take a detour. We don't want to bump into him further up the road.'

Inge led Steve by a series of backstreets to where she lived. It was a pre-war house in a sad state of disrepair, bullet marks still pocking the grimy stucco. Inge opened the front door and stepped into the entrance hall. There were no carpets, the wallpaper was torn and stained and there was a pervasive smell of damp. They went up to the second floor and Inge unlocked the door to her room and switched the light on. She took her wet coat off and hung it on the back of the door. She then pulled her boots off. While she did so, Steve looked around the room. Inge had done what she could to make it more homely, with a colourful throw on the bed and stylish posters on the walls. She had even painted the woodwork. Nevertheless arrangements were even more primitive than they had been in Tenison Road.

Inge caught Steve's eye and, putting the side of her forefinger to her lips to signify silence, gestured to him to take his cagoule and shoes off. After putting them beside hers to dry, she raised her right hand and, bringing it down like an orchestral conductor counting in a group of musicians, said, 'My standard rates are fifty marks, *Liebling.*'

Realising that they were now in role, Steve said, 'I was told the going rate was fifteen to twenty marks. Twenty-five if oral was included.'

'Well, you were told wrong. For twenty you'll only get a handjob.'

'What about if I gave you twenty-five?'

'Two handjobs.'

'I also have ten D-Marks.'

'I'd need to see the money first.'

Steve mimed taking notes from his wallet and slapped his hand on the table as if handing over the cash.

'You are an *Arschloch*, my little *Engländer*. But okay, whatever you want.'

'In that case, could you undress, please?'

Inge flashed him a conspiratorial smile and began to remove her clothes, revealing her pallid, skinny body. Steve suddenly realised that she was standing in front of the window and the curtains were undrawn. He mimed drawing the curtains with his hands, but she shook her head. 'Your turn, *Engländer*. Or are you planning to remain fully clothed?'

Steve started to remove his own clothes, struggling comically with his wet jeans. More than a little embarrassed that he seemed not to be achieving an erection as readily as he had in the bar, he stood facing her with his hands clasped over his genitals. She smiled again and gestured to him to come towards her. They embraced standing up and he was relieved to feel his cock beginning to respond to the feeling of flesh on flesh. But the idea of being watched by observers peering through telephoto lenses from the other side of the street seemed to be preventing him getting to the point where his performance would warrant a starring role in a Stasi porn movie. Inge released him and, whispering in his ear, said, 'I'm sorry, I'm not very good at this.'

He whispered back, 'No, it's my fault. I'm too nervous at the thought of being filmed.'

She kissed him on the neck and said, 'Let's get into bed. I'll warm you up.'

Steve, dispirited and already feeling like a failure as a courier for the foreign intelligence service, was only too happy to comply. Once in bed, she pulled the covers over their heads so that the microphones wouldn't pick up what she was saying, and said, 'You do not have an erection. Are you homosexual?'

'No.'

'Then you don't find me attractive? My breasts are too small?'

'No, your breasts are lovely.'

'Or you find oral sex disgusting?'

'No, Inge. It's the thought of being watched. Or maybe I'm just afraid.'

Steve was feeling miserable. He was jeopardising the operation because of an attack of nerves rendering him impotent. Some James Bond he was!

Inge had an idea. 'We need something to help us relax. I have some Goldbrand Doppelkorn.'

She threw back the covers and went over to what must have been her cooking area and opened a cupboard. Steve watched her, admiring her slim body and neat breasts, but dismayed that his own body was still being so unresponsive. She returned with two shot glasses and a bottle of clear schnapps. Climbing back into bed, she poured two measures, knocked hers back and gestured that he should do the same. He swallowed the schnapps, spluttering slightly. After they had downed a second round, she put the bottle and the glasses on the bedside table and said, 'I will not touch you down there. I just want you to kiss my breasts.'

Steve rolled over and did as she had asked. He took each one in turn in his mouth, working on the nipples with his tongue. Then, moving down her body, he parted her legs and opened her with his tongue. Soon she was arching her back and moaning quietly, finally coming with a series of small screams.

Steve rolled off her and whispered, 'I thought we were meant to be making a lot of noise.'

Inge put her arm around him. 'That was too precious to waste on the Stasi. Thank you. But I see you are now warmed up.'

Indeed, Steve's cock was now ready for showtime. Without further comment, he penetrated her in a more conventional way, which she greeted with a delighted yelp. He told himself that it was not that he was trying to make up for his earlier flaccid performance, but in fact it was precisely that. He thrust powerfully and came with a throaty chuckle. In role, Inge said, '*Sehr gut, Engländer.*' Then out of role, whispered, 'Oh, Tom, that was lovely.'

He held her tight. 'For me too.'

Sometime later after two more carefully orchestrated and much noisier couplings, Inge said she would make some coffee. She hopped out of bed and went across to the kitchen area, returning a couple of minutes later with the coffees.

When they had finished their coffee, Steve, pulling the blankets over their heads once more, said, 'Can I contact you again?'

She hugged him. 'That is not a good idea. In fact, you should not come to the East again. I think you will find that in a few days or so, you will be on the blacklist.'

'But what about you?'

'My options are rather limited. I would just like to become a university teacher, but I have a feeling I will be barred.'

'Can they do that?'

'That and much more. They will blackmail me or threaten to end my studies.'

'Oh, Inge, I'm so sorry. Can you tell me your surname?'

'No. Inge is not my real name. Please don't tell me yours. For all sorts of reasons, we are unlikely ever to meet again. But you are a brave guy and you are doing a good thing. It has been lovely to have this time with you.'

'Inge, I want to take you with me.'

'That is not possible. Nor would it do either of us any good to develop feelings for each other. You could get hurt.'

'You mean by the Stasi?'

Without explicitly confirming his supposition, she continued, 'Which is why you must leave now. I will show you to the Prenzlauer Allee. I recommend you take the S-Bahn from there to Bahnhof Friedrichstraße.'

Inge said she needed to use the lavatory. While she was out of the room, Steve slipped the ten D-Mark note from his wallet and tucked it into the architectural guide, which he slipped under Inge's pillow. By the time she returned, he was fully dressed. He watched her put her own clothes on and tie her hair back. Noticing how he was watching her, she smiled sadly at him for a moment and then sliced her right hand through the air to terminate any further developments of that kind.

Back in role, Inge said, 'Well, *Engländer*, I hope you feel you got good service for your ten D-Marks.'

Steve winked at her but said in role, 'I've had better. But thanks anyway.'

Inge punched him lightly on the arm, laughing quietly.

As they put their coats on, Steve noticed that Inge slipped the Nietzsche book into her shoulder bag. He said nothing.

At the tram stop, she kissed him passionately, saying she would never forget him. He could see that she was crying. After a moment, she turned and walked off into the freezing, misty night. Steve felt utterly forlorn.

On the tram to Bahnhof Friedrichstraße, Steve's feeling of loss was gradually replaced by elation. Apart from his initial failure in front of the window to respond to Inge's ministrations, he felt he had acquitted himself reasonably well. Perhaps it was the very real frisson of danger and the knowledge that they were being taped that had intensified the experience. Or perhaps it was simply the fact that Inge was an amazing lay.

Back at the Tränenpalast, Steve's self-congratulatory mood was soon punctured when he realised that the border guard who had searched his bag on the way in was now on duty on the exit control point. Even worse, the guard had recognised Steve and was waving him over to his booth. Steve briefly contemplated trying to pretend that he hadn't noticed the gesture, but rejected the idea on the basis that that was just likely to result in closer scrutiny.

In the booth, the guard said, 'Well, *Herr Architekt*, how was your day?' The tone was friendly, but there was not even a hint of a smile on his face.

'Good, thanks. Sore feet, though.'

'Did you get to the Café Moskau?'

'Plenty of other places too.'

'Such as?'

'The Haus des Lehrers, the Volksbühne Theater and the TV Tower.'

'That is not such a long walk and you do not look as wet as someone would be who has been looking at buildings all day in this weather.'

Steve thought it better not to mention the Prenzlauer Berg area and racked his brains to remember some of the other buildings he had glanced at in the architecture book. 'I also got down to the Kosmos cinema and walked up to the Friedrichshain park. But I got lost a few times.'

The guard nodded. 'Open your bag, please.'

Steve did as he was asked, and the guard looked inside the almost empty bag, which now only contained the street map and the very crumpled newspaper. The guard frowned. 'Something's missing.'

Steve's heart skipped a beat. Surely the guard hadn't made an inventory of the contents of his bag. Before Steve had managed to come up with a halfway credible explanation, the guard's face lit up. 'Of course, you had an architectural guide. What happened to that?'

Thank goodness, it wasn't the Nietzsche he'd noticed. Regaining his composure, he said, 'I mislaid it at one of the cafés I stopped at. It was near the end of the day, so I decided not to go back for it.'

'What was the name of the café?'

'I'm afraid I didn't notice.'

'But you could tell me the name of the street it was in.'

'I don't know that either. I'd got lost and I just needed to get out of the rain.'

The guard did not seem convinced. 'There was something else too.'

Terrified that the guard would now remember the Nietzsche book and in a moment of inspiration, Steve said, 'Yeah, you impounded my Captain America comic.'

The guard narrowed his eyes, now marginally less suspicious. 'Ah, yes, filth.'

He then asked Steve to empty his pockets. Steve put the contents of his pockets on the table and the guard picked up his wallet and opened it. Cursing himself under his breath, Steve noticed the bill from the Am Dreieck sticking out from one of the slots in his wallet. The guard pulled it out and studied the receipt. 'Perhaps this is where your book is. The Am Dreieck.'

Doing his best to keep the fear out of his voice, Steve said, 'I don't think so. I went into several bars and cafés.'

'But you got as far as Prenzlauer Berg. You didn't mention that.'

'As I said, I managed to get myself completely lost.'

The guard then pulled out the remaining Ostmarks from the wallet. 'You cannot take these out of East Berlin.'

Steve had been expecting this but, already knowing the answer and hoping to divert the conversation to other matters, said, 'Aren't you going to change them back to D-Marks?'

'You should have bought something. You could have fucked a woman for this amount. In my experience, coming back with an empty wallet is normal for a boy of your age. So I wonder how you have been spending your time.'

Steve said, 'I told you. I was looking at buildings.'

'I am not sure I believe you, *Herr Architekt*. I interview a lot of people and there is something not quite right about your story.'

The guard picked up a clipboard and leafed through several sheets of paper. After a few moments, tapping one of the sheets with his finger, he said with a chuckle, 'Well, well, *Herr Architekt*. I see that I made a note here that you also had ten D-Marks in your wallet when you entered the DDR. But now there is no sign of the Western currency. So it looks like you have been active on the black market and yet you have nothing to show for the transaction.'

Trying to hide the anxiety he was now feeling and recalling that the guard had implied a few moments ago that sex tourism was normal, Steve decided it was time for new Steve to put in an appearance. 'She said that I could have whatever I wanted for Western currency.'

The guard roared with laughter. 'I've underestimated you, *Herr Architekt*. I hope you gave her one up the arse for her troubles.'

Deciding that it was better to go with the grain of the guard's suppositions, Steve said, 'It's normal, isn't it?'

The guard roared with laughter once again and started filling out a docket. 'This is a receipt for your Ostmarks. They will be available to you the next time you visit us.'

Steve took the counterfoil. 'How long is this valid for?'

The guard shrugged. 'Indefinitely.'

With that, the guard stamped his passport, handed it back to him with his wallet and let him through the barrier. Only when he was on the other side of the barrier did Steve realise that the guard had retained the receipt from the Am Dreieck.

The next morning, as arranged, Jeremy was outside the Treibel just after lunchtime to take Steve to the hospital. This would give them an opportunity to talk about the previous day's operation.

'Any unexpected difficulties yesterday?'

Steve saw no advantage in giving an excessively detailed account. 'No. They confiscated the American comic, but only gave the most cursory look at the Nietzsche book.'

'Were you followed?'

'Not as far as I could tell, but there was an informant in the bar.'

'How do you know?'

'The girl told me.'

'How did that go? Not too distasteful, I hope.'

'No, she was very nice. The thought that we were probably being observed, maybe even filmed, did somewhat affect my performance, at least initially. I never thought I'd fail to deliver the goods when being offered sex by a naked young woman. But I managed to get my act together after a couple of hits of Doppelkorn.'

'Come, come, Steve, if you will excuse the expression, I am sure you acquitted yourself very well. And the book?'

'She took me to the nearest tram stop and I noticed that she'd put the book in her shoulder bag. I guess she was taking it to the person it was really meant for.'

'Indeed.'

'Is she in danger?'

'I'm afraid she is. She is a very brave young woman. With luck, if she is hauled in, it will be for living off immoral earnings, as it is called in our home jurisdiction, the penalty for which is considerably less harsh than that for aiding and abetting a *Republikflüchtling*. There are plans to try and get her out, but as you can see, it is not easy.'

'If there is anything I can do to help…'

'You have done a great deal. For now it is best if you lie low and care for your mother. But perhaps we will come back to that thought in the future.'

They had now reached the hospital. Steve went up to the ward while, as usual, Jeremy waited in the reception area. Jenny said there had been no real change in Mavis's condition, but to Steve's eye, she looked smaller and greyer. He took her hand and told her something of his visit to East Berlin. He looked forward to telling her more about it when she had recovered. Once again he had the sense that she could hear him, even though there was little outward evidence.

\* \* \*

Later that evening, Steve phoned Grace. He'd been too exhausted, both emotionally and physically, to phone the previous evening. When she answered, she sounded bright and elated.

'Steve, I'm sorry I was out when you called last night.'

Steve decided that nothing was to be gained by admitting that he hadn't actually tried to ring. 'Celebrating the end of your first lecture series?'

'How did you guess?'

'I wish I could have been there.'

'I'm sure you were enjoying yourself in East Berlin.'

'It was a very strange experience. It was like being on another planet just a stone's throw from our own. East Berlin is an odd combination of modernist architecture and Wilhelmine buildings still showing signs of war damage. The streets are potholed and full of noddy cars belching smoke and making a fearful racket. There is a very visible security presence and, from what I understand, an invisible one too. The crossing by underground is an intimidating experience. They asked me to step into a booth and empty my pockets and bag. I also had to take off my jacket and submit to a body search.'

'Which you passed presumably.'

'Yes.'

'Then they force you to convert 25 D-Marks at a one to one parity. But they don't let you take out any Ostmarks you haven't spent.'

'Ah, the delights of autarky. And how is Mavis?'

'The same. I went in again today. There was no change that I could detect. I did think she looked a little thinner. I do get this feeling that she knows I'm there. I hold her hand and talk to her, tell her what I've been doing.'

'Oh, Steve, I'm so sorry.'

Steve felt a lump in his throat. 'They keep saying that she's no worse, but I can't help thinking that she's not going to come round.'

'Don't give up hope. I will be with you on Saturday.'

'Grace, you don't have to come. You've got so much else on your plate.'

'I want to be with you and I want to see Mavis. The ticket is booked. My BEA flight gets in at five-thirty.'

'It'll be lovely to see you. I'll meet you at the airport.'

'Then you can show me the delights of West Berlin.'

'I'd love to, if I knew what they were.'

'Being with you will be delight enough.'

The call finished with the usual endearments, and Steve went to bed in a more positive frame of mind, at the back of which the only shadow was the knowledge that he had once again been unfaithful to Grace albeit for, he hoped, noble ends.

The following morning on the way to the hospital, Steve said to Collingwood, 'I thought you'd better know that my girlfriend is coming to join me. She'll be arriving on Saturday.'

Collingwood was thoughtful. 'Ah, I see.' Realising that this was perhaps not the most positive way of greeting the news, he added, 'That'll be nice for you.'

'Yes. I was just wondering what I can and can't tell her.'

'I'm afraid you can't tell her anything.'

'Does that mean the operation isn't over yet?'

'I can't say.'

'Look, Jeremy. I helped you out and put myself at risk. You could at least give me a bit of leeway.'

'I would like to, Steve, but we have to operate on a need-to-know basis.'

'Does that mean that I can't even tell Grace that I've been to East Berlin?'

'I don't see why you can't tell her that. But you can't tell her what the real purpose of the visit was. If you did, you might be jeopardising the safety of other people.'

'But seeing that I've done my bit, can't I now move to my mother's flat? I think Grace will think it strange that I still haven't been provided with the key.'

'Yes, I see your dilemma. Let me make some enquiries. I will phone you later this evening.'

Later that evening, as Steve sat in his room at the Treibel, the phone rang. It was Collingwood. He'd had discussions with colleagues, and it was felt that there was now no reason why Steve shouldn't move into his mother's flat. Collingwood would take him there after the visit to the hospital. He should have his bag packed and have checked out of his room. There would be nothing to pay.

## Saturday, 15 March 1975

GRACE TOOK A SIP of her wine. 'This is a nice place Mavis has.'

Steve wasn't so sure. 'I haven't got used to it yet. They only let me move in yesterday. I don't get much of a sense of my mother.'

'Her things are here, aren't they?'

'I'm not sure they are. I don't recognise the clothes in the closet or the things in her bedside cabinet.'

'Really?'

'It's like a stage or film set. Okay, she hasn't been here long, and presumably she didn't bring much with her. But I don't recognise the style of the clothes. The only item of clothing that I could say was hers was the nightdress that was under the pillow. It was the one she was wearing at Christmas. The rings they gave me in the hospital were definitely not her wedding and engagement rings.'

'Is there anything that would connect the flat with her?'

'Only minor things. There was a copy of *The Times* from the day of her accident. There's a packet of Earl Grey tea in the kitchen cupboard. It's her favourite tea. There are also two letters sent to her from London, which I found in the pocket of her dressing gown.'

'Who are the letters from?'

'I don't know. They're just signed with the letter S.'

'What kind of letters are they?'

'They're love letters. Rather creepy ones actually. I didn't really like reading them.'

'Would you mind if I read them?'

Steve fetched the letters from the desk and handed them to Grace. She opened the first and read quickly.

Darling Mavis,

How are you settling in? Berlin is a marvellous city, isn't it? I am so much looking forward to showing you around, although I expect that by the time I get out there, you will already be an old hand.

Our last night together in London at your flat was for me the acme of fulfilled desire. How could I have suspected that there was such a passionate woman underneath that reserved exterior, nor imagined the more intimate delights of that *terra incognita*. It seems to me that the spark between us had been there for many years, but people like us just did not do that sort of thing. I cannot wait to take you in my arms again and kiss you.

Write to me soon and tell me how you are.

With love and affection, S.

She put that letter to one side. 'Reading other people's love letters, especially one to a parent, is never going to be easy. It's a good idea not to try and read between the lines.'

Steve nodded glumly. Grace picked up the second letter.

Darling Mavis,

Thank you for your letters and for the photo. You look stunning. I am missing you too. I am sorry that I had to cancel my travel arrangements at such short notice. There was a bit of a crisis at work.

So this is just to say that I have booked my flight for 1st March. It gets into Tempelhof at about 5.30 pm. I note that BA, as I suppose we now have to call BEA as was, is soon moving to Tegel. How sad! There is something so monumental about Tempelhof, but no doubt modern jet liners need much longer runways.

I look forward to our long weekend together. I can't wait to see you. Good though the photograph is, it cannot compare to the real thing.

With love and affection, S.

Reflecting on the conversation that she had had with Mavis when she had visited them in Cambridge, Grace now felt uncomfortable knowing that she was in possession of a piece of information in that regard that Steve was not privy to. She had promised Mavis that she would not mention it to Steve, but things had changed now with Mavis's accident.

'You've no idea who this Mr S is?'

'None at all. I didn't know she had a special friend.'

'Well, it seems she did. Mavis told me when she was at Glisson Road about a special friend, but she asked me not to tell you. I think she guessed you'd be upset and wanted to make sure that the relationship was more than just a fling before telling you. I think recent developments mean that the promise I made her no longer holds.'

Grace watched Steve carefully. How would he react? Steve took a moment to digest the information, but remained calm. 'Did she say anything about this man?'

'No, I did get the impression that he might be a colleague, but it was not said explicitly.'

'Okay. But the thing that really troubles me is that it sounds like this person was coming to Berlin on the day that Mavis had her accident.'

Grace nodded. 'Coming specifically to be with her. So why wasn't he with her when she had the accident? Or if he was not with her at that point in time, why didn't he contact the authorities? Has Collingwood mentioned anyone?'

'He did say that there was one witness to the accident who didn't wait to give a statement to the police and no one seems to have any leads as to whom this person was.'

'I suppose we could be putting two and two together and getting five.'

'Yes, but there is another thing. The copy of *The Times* is from the day that Mavis was knocked over and I get the feeling that no one has been in the flat since that weekend.'

'And?'

'I mean how does a copy of *The Times* come to be in Mavis's flat in West Berlin on the very day on which it's published in London? I don't suppose London papers get to Berlin until a day or two later at the earliest.'

'Which means that the person who brought it arrived on that same day.'

'Exactly. That's what S says in his second letter, and it also ties in with an entry in her pocket diary, which has "S 17.30"'

'It ought to be relatively easy for someone like Collingwood to get the passenger manifests for planes coming in from London that day. But before we rush into sharing our concerns with him, let's think this through. Could I have a look at the copy of *The Times*?'

Steve fetched the newspaper and Grace spent some time leafing through it. 'Well, I can see that the crossword is half done.'

'That must be S's doing. My mother was an expert crossword solver. If she'd got her hands on it, it would have been completed. She didn't quite finish them in the time it took her egg to boil, but it was close.'

'Has Collingwood given you any idea what Mavis's role was here?'

Steve was tempted to tell Grace what Collingwood had told him when trying to persuade him to take on the East Berlin run. But that was likely to lead to further questions. 'Not really. Although everything seems to be very hush-hush.'

Grace nodded. 'It's easy in a place like this, and especially when one is in touch with the intelligence services, to let feelings of paranoia colour everything. I agree there's a bit of a conundrum here, but I'm sure your mother's accident is being looked into very carefully. I think we should put our own investigations to one side for now. Apart from anything else, we might be making things awkward for Mavis when she recovers.'

Steve thought this made sense. 'Yes, I hadn't thought of that.'

'Anyway, we've got other work to do.'

Steve was puzzled. 'Work?'

'Making a baby. We're towards the end of this month's fertile period. So it's time to get your kit off.'

'I'm afraid I'm not feeling very horny at the moment.'

'I haven't come all the way to Berlin to be told *Not tonight, Josephine.*'

'I'm sorry, Grace. Can't it wait until the morning?'

'Well, well, this is a turn-up for the books. Steve Percival turning down the offer of sex. I suppose I'm going to have to take my clothes off. It seems to be the only thing that gets you going.'

Grace started to unbutton her blouse.

Steve laughed, but he was no longer sure that this was still the case after his dismal showing in East Berlin.

Later as they were having a restorative cup of tea, Grace said, 'I've got a lot of my old haunts to drag you around, but some of them are now on the other side of the Wall. So, I'd like to have a long day in East Berlin next week. Would you be up for that?'

Steve was not sure that he really was. But how could he refuse without going into explanations?

'Of course, but why don't you show me around the Western zone first?'

Which is what she did. Steve had to admit that Grace's knowledge of the city was a great deal more detailed than his own. His own explorations had been limited to morning strolls in the vicinity of the hotel. He told himself that it was because he had been organising his days around his early afternoon visits to his mother at the British Military Hospital. But it was also true that after those visits he normally returned to his room at the hotel to read and write or occasionally to watch television, rather than sample the fabled nightlife of the city. The couple of sessions with Collingwood in the local *Kneipe* hardly counted. Otherwise he had done no socialising, unless one counted his encounter with Inge as such. Nor, despite Grace's arrival in the divided city, was he able to snap out of this withdrawn mood.

For some reason, he now felt awkward and diffident in matters of intimacy, treating her with stilted deference. It was almost as if he had gone back to being her student rather than being her lover. He told himself that it must be because he was feeling guilty about Inge or that he felt uncomfortable making love in his mother's bed, while she lay in a coma in a nearby hospital with diminishing chances of regaining consciousness. Grace sensed some of this and was gentle with him, coaxing him out of this mood without ever directly referring to it. Soon in her nurturing embrace, he began to thaw out emotionally and become more responsive. He started to feel once again that he had never loved anyone so much. He didn't care if they never returned to Cambridge. Why couldn't they just stay in Berlin forever, making love and enjoying what Grace had referred to as the delights of the city?

She certainly seemed to be remarkably well-informed about those delights. He asked her when was the last time she'd been in Berlin. She'd laughed, brushing off the question by saying that she couldn't remember, but not for quite a while. It seemed churlish to press the point, when with Grace to guide him, he now finally got to sample some of those delights, the famous bars and clubs of the Western zone, and a couple of the more infamous ones too. It was exhilarating and not just because it provided him with a delicious glimpse of what Grace must have been like fifteen years previously. With each successive day away from Cambridge, she seemed to become younger, more lighthearted, more capricious, more like the person he had seen in the photos on the mantelpiece in her study.

Not surprisingly, the transformation wrought by the Berlin milieu also revitalised their lovemaking. Profoundly grateful to her for helping him rediscover his former prowess, he was unable not to feel a little disappointed in himself. He'd always thought of himself as bold and adventurous but, if he were honest, recent events had shown that self-assessment to be delusional. No doubt he could take a certain amount of pride in his exploits in East Berlin, he supposed. But if he had not bought fairly heavily into Collingwood's frankly specious case that he would be acting as some kind of surrogate for his mother, he probably wouldn't have gone at all. Whatever the truth of the matter, it now looked as if he would soon be making another visit, this time initiated by Grace. He just hoped that he didn't encounter the same surly border guard, who had given him such a hard time on his previous visit.

The Friedrichstraße station was much busier than it had been on Steve's first crossing. Many more of the checkpoints were manned and there were queues at each one. Because Steve was worried that he might already be on the Stasi blacklist, he said he'd go first. Not that he put it to Grace in those terms. But it would be awkward if she went first, sailed through without any difficulties and he was then stopped. It might not be immediately apparent to Grace what had happened to him. He doubted that the famously brutal border guards would be helpful under such circumstances.

In the event, though, his passage through the checkpoint was a good deal quicker and simpler than the first time. He reached the open area beyond the booths and turned to see how Grace was getting on, expecting to see her smiling face coming towards him. But there was no sign of her. She must have been asked to step into the curtained-off booth. Maybe the *Grepos* had a policy of interviewing every nth person. He couldn't think what else might be the problem.

As he waited for her to emerge, one of the guards who patrolled the open space between the booths and the exit to the upper concourse approached him and told him, none too gently, not to loiter. Steve explained that he was waiting for his girlfriend to come through.

The guard said, 'Which checkpoint?'

Steve pointed to the one he himself had come through, and the guard stomped over to it to check with his colleague, returning a few moments later. 'She's been denied entry and escorted back down to the platform.'

'But why?'

'We cannot discuss such things.'

'How do I rejoin her?'

'You will have to exit and then return through the outward control area.'

253

'But she will be worried about me.'

'I think it is you who should be worried about her.'

Steve rushed up to the main concourse and got into the queue for the exit checks. He was impatient, but it wouldn't do to show it. With luck he would be waved through. Alas, his luck was out. The guard who looked at his passport and visa slip could see that he had only entered the DDR a few minutes previously.

'Leaving us so soon, Herr Parsifal?'

'My girlfriend has been denied entry and I need to get back to her.'

'There are still the formalities to go through. I see from your passport that you visited us a short while ago. So you will know that you cannot take your Ostmarks to the West.'

'But I haven't had a chance to spend them yet.'

'Those are the rules. We will add it to the unspent credits from last time.'

Steve pulled the recently acquired twenty-five Ostmarks from his wallet and thrust them at the guard.

'Patience, Herr Parsifal. We will keep your money safe. Maybe you should find a new girlfriend. We have some nice girls here in East Berlin. But perhaps you already know that.'

Steve was taken aback by these last words and found himself saying, 'I'm perfectly happy with my English girlfriend and need to get back to her.'

This only brought forth a sour chortle from the guard. 'Perhaps you should ask *Mutti* what she's been up to.'

With that the guard stamped Steve's passport and allowed him through.

Steve found Grace standing disconsolately on the westbound platform. They embraced and Steve kissed her tears away. 'What happened?'

'I'll tell you later. Let's just get out of here for now.'

As they travelled back to the West in silence, Steve replayed in his mind the insinuations of the guard at the exit checkpoint. Was he intimating to Steve that the authorities knew about his time with Inge on his previous visit? But if that were the case, why let him through? Who was he referring to as *Mutti*? On the face of it, it was a comment about Grace, who was indeed quite a lot older than him. But it was also possible that the reference was to his own mother.

Emerging at Ernst-Reuter-Platz, they decided not to go straight back to the flat and stepped into a nearby café, needing something a bit stronger than coffee. When the waiter had brought their beers, Grace said, 'You must have realised from what I was saying the night you were leaving Cambridge that I spent some time here in the 1960s. I was actually here immediately before and for some time after the Wall went up in 1961, doing research at Humboldt and at the Freie Universität.'

Steve wrinkled his brow. 'You never mentioned it before.'

'For most of the two and a half years we've known each other I was teaching you French literature and thought. But perhaps it didn't occur to you that I did the same combination of languages as you for my first degree. Consequently, it might not surprise you to know that my PhD thesis was on the German roots of French existentialism and phenomenology. So I decided to come to Berlin to do some research.'

'Shouldn't you have gone to Freiburg instead?'

'Well, yes, that was where Heidegger and Husserl taught, but Berlin had other attractions, not least that it was cheaper and there were generous grants and bursaries available.'

'This was before you were in Paris?'

'Yes. Anyway, I got to know some of the people who ran the student escape committees. You've got to remember that the Wall went up virtually overnight, and there were several hundred students who were actually attending the Freie Universität but lived in East Berlin. Committees were formed to try and help such students escape to the West. In the early stages, the preferred option was to produce fake passports rather than to dig tunnels. But of course, that needed couriers to deliver the documents to the person hoping to escape, and it made sense for the couriers to be legitimate members of the university but not German nationals.'

Steve was a little perturbed by the parallels. 'You were one of the couriers?'

'Yes. To begin with the system worked well. Later on, the East Berlin authorities introduced the temporary visa system which pretty much put a stop to the false passport technique.'

Steve hoped that wasn't still the case although he still had no idea whether his own single exploit had had a successful outcome. 'Were you ever detained?'

'No. I was lucky in that respect.'

'So how did they come to have a file on you?'

'Well, the escape groups did get infiltrated and there were informants. But the main reason was that I wrote some articles for *Stern* magazine about the crackdown on academic freedom in East

Berlin, which included hints about what I'd been up to. That appears to have eventually incurred the wrath of the Stasi.'

'So, you became *persona non grata*.'

'So it seems. I had no idea. I'm sorry, Steve, I was so much looking forward to going to East Berlin with you. Still, at least you've been over on your own.'

Even as this conversation was unfolding, Steve had been coming to the conclusion that in view of the earlier events at the Friedrich-straße U-Bahn station, it was absurd to keep the fact of his own activities as a courier from his lover, especially as she had now confessed her own involvement to him. Who, after all, was the arbiter of the need to know? Steve had not entered into any formal contract. He did not really know how the Official Secrets Act worked, but he assumed that he would have to have signed something for it to be effective. Everything had been done on an alarmingly informal basis with Collingwood, who had convinced him of his bona fides by claiming to have been at St Rad's, an assertion that Steve had no way of checking. For all he knew, Collingwood and Jennings were actually the bad guys. The thought had been gnawing at him for some time that he was being duped, or at the very least played.

Now, reflecting once again on the insinuations of the border guard when he turned back, he was starting to think that had he actually made it out of the station to the upper concourse on the eastern side, he might very well have been detained at that point and whisked off to be interrogated rather than simply denied access.

On the other hand, once he broached the matter with Grace, he was almost inevitably going to have to confess to another kind of infidelity, even though this one had been, in effect, out of his control.

'Grace, I wasn't going to tell you this, because I was sworn to secrecy. But when I went to East Berlin the other day, it was for purposes not unconnected with the reasons for your own visits there in 1961. In fact, I was expecting to be the one declared *persona non grata* and wondering how to square it with you.'

Grace said, 'Well, well. Would you like to tell me more?'

Steve proceeded to give a very compressed account of how Mavis had been running an operation to extract a valued agent from East Berlin which had been thwarted by her accident. The official line was that it was just an accident, but it seemed that, for operational reasons, it was being treated as something more deliberate. That in turn suggested that there had been some kind of leak in the organisation, which was why he had not been allowed to stay in Mavis's flat for the first two weeks of his stay in Berlin.

It also seemed to have occurred to someone, perhaps Collingwood, that Steve might, on his mother's behalf, as it were, help out by taking on the role of courier. He would not hand the documents over to the agent himself, but to an intermediary in East Berlin. It had been important, therefore, to limit the number of people who were aware that Steve was Mavis's son or that he was connected to members of the British security services. Consequently, Collingwood and his driver Jennings were the only members of the British security apparatus with whom Steve had had any contact.

Grace interrupted Steve's account. 'Do you trust Mr Collingwood?'

'Not entirely. But he seems very plausible, and I have not been able to detect any inconsistencies in what he says. He claims to be a former member of St Rad's and does seem to know the college intimately. At the time, I assumed that that was why he had been detailed to mind me.'

'Presumably, he is skilled in matters of plausibility. Do you think he might be the one working for the other side?'

'It did occur to me. He seemed to know a lot about me and, which was more surprising, you.'

A cloud passed across Grace's features and she did not respond for some moments. 'Well, the innocent explanation for that is that your mother's connections would have been vetted by MI6. The more worrying implication is that he is privy to Stasi intel.'

Thinking back to the border guard's comments earlier on, Steve said, 'Yes, I wondered about that too.'

'So why did you agree?'

'Well, time was of the essence. If they – we didn't move fast the agent would be picked up.'

'Of course. Put your mark under deadline pressure.'

'Presumably there were no hitches getting into East Berlin?'

'Only a minor one. Though now I look at it in the light of what you're saying, it might have been a way of identifying me to the Stasi.'

'How come?'

Steve rather regretted having been so frank, but if he couldn't trust Grace, who could he trust? 'I had to have three things in my bag: a gazetteer of East Berlin architecture; a hardback German edition of *Jenseits von Gut und Böse*; and a copy of a Captain America comic, all of which were supplied to me by Collingwood. He said the comic would probably get confiscated, but it would distract from the other things in my bag, particularly the Nietzsche, which was the book in which the documents were concealed.'

Grace nodded. 'But, of course, the comic could also have been a way of saying to the border guards: *This is the courier. Let him through. We want to find out where he goes.* Because it couldn't be known in advance what time you'd cross over or which guard would deal with you.'

Steve had only just reached the same conclusion and said, dolefully, 'What an idiot I am!'

'You're not, Steve. These are murky waters and you're dealing with people very experienced in these matters. But it is only a hypothesis and is not necessarily the case. We do need to keep it in mind, however. Presumably the contact was a girl?'

'Yes. How did you guess?'

'It's a fairly standard ploy, a version of the honey trap.'

'Her name was Inge. She said that's what the Stasi might force her to do.'

'Or perhaps had already made her do. So I suppose you had to go along with being the wide-eyed innocent and hand over the documents to her after she had fucked you, both of you doing it in the line of duty.'

'Yes, I'm sorry, Grace. I did suggest that we simulate sex, but apparently the Stasi would be more likely to believe I was a western sex tourist if they had convincing tape-recordings and photographic evidence'

'Well, at least you save dissimulation for me.'

Steve was puzzled by this remark. 'What?'

'You know, on the train back from Somerset, having sex but not looking as though we were. Anyway, how did you get on?'

'The whole thing was terrifying. The weather was terrible, freezing rain all day long. I was supposed to be a student of architecture, but not even the most hardcore building nut would have done the rounds of landmark buildings that day. I nearly missed the initial contact because she arrived at the bar with two friends. Then she seemed to think that it would be a good idea if we got ourselves thrown out of the bar.'

'For canoodling?'

'That's putting it mildly. She seems to have been doing it for the benefit of an informant in the bar.'

'The things people are reduced to doing to survive in a totalitarian state.'

'Yeah. We had to hide in a park until we'd made sure we'd lost the informant. So by the time we got to the house in which she had her room, we were both soaked through.'

'No doubt the clothes came off pretty quickly.'

'It was freezing. The house was a shithole, the front wall pock-marked with bullet holes.'

'I remember those old buildings. So then you had to get down to business. I hope she gave you a good time?'

'I don't suppose you'll believe me if I tell you I couldn't get it up to begin with.'

Grace couldn't help laughing. 'Oh dear, Steve. That really is letting the country down. But you, or maybe she, persevered?'

Steve looked completely miserable. 'A bit of both, I suppose.'

'A bit of how's-your-father, more like.'

'Do you think I've fucked things up?'

'Well, fucking certainly seems to have been involved, but whether you were doing the right thing or not depends on who you were actually doing it for, not on who you believed you were doing it for.'

'If by that you mean that Inge was a Stasi operative, why not just arrest me at the Tränenpalast and stop the passport getting through to its intended recipient?'

'Perhaps the Stasi knew an operation was on, but not the identity of either the agent or the intermediary. But if they followed the British student with the Captain America comic, he would lead them to the intermediary, who in turn would lead them to the agent. Or at least to a dead letter drop, which they could watch until the agent picked up the package. Once they had established the identity of the agent, they could arrest and interrogate both. What was your impression of Inge?'

'I wouldn't have said she was a professional.'

'Do you mean in the how's-your-father department or the world of espionage?'

'Either.'

'So what do you think she was?'

'She said she was a research student at the university, possibly doing history. Of course she might have been lying, but she said she was a student when she was still with her friends. So I think that was likely to have been the case.'

'Leaving aside what your yardstick for either kind of profession-alism is, it does seem that she was putting herself in danger. At the very least, she was threatening her professional ambitions in a society from which it is almost impossible to escape without powerful connections, and indulging in an activity that was perhaps contrary to her values and beliefs.'

'Yes, why would she do that?'

'For love, I imagine.'

'For love of whom?'

'Not for you, my bonny boy, though I'm sure she was relieved that she had someone as lovely as you before whom to abase herself. No, I would say she is in love with whoever the agent is. Since she is a research student, I'd put money on it being her professor or supervisor. Just like you and me in fact.'

'You're upset, aren't you?'

'No, once again, I'm glad you told me. But I wonder how long this can go on for? Was she attractive?' She knew she was demeaning herself by asking this last question, but the devil had got into her.

'Not really. She was skinny and pallid. Badly nourished, I'd say. Not particularly fragrant.'

'In other words, as sexy as hell, very much in the Ginny mould, lack of fragrance aside.'

'Grace, that's cruel.'

'I know, but sex and danger can be a potent cocktail.'

'Well, if you know that, perhaps you're not as innocent as you like to make out.'

'I'm sorry, Steve. I want you to myself at least until you give me a baby.'

'That's what I want too.'

'My darling, I don't think insight into your own motivations is your strong point.'

'Grace, why are you doing this?'

'I just want you to give me a baby, but you seem to be shagging every girl you bump into.'

'That's unfair.'

'I know, but I'm afraid that one of them will make off with you before you've got me pregnant.'

'Honestly, I will do my best, better than my best, but it's not the sort of thing you can just turn on. There are many other variables.'

'I know. Sorry. Shall we have something to eat? Just so we can justify another drink.'

Later, when they had finished their Wiener Schnitzels, Grace said, 'I'm sorry about that earlier on. I hope it's not a side of me you see too often. I've never really thought of myself as needy.'

'You're not being needy. You're anxious.'

'You're right. About all sorts of things. Not just whether I can have a baby, but Mavis, you, the situation you're in here as well.'

'Yeah.'

'I'm still processing all the things you told me earlier. I know it might sound a bit paranoid, but I think that we shouldn't talk about these things when we're at the flat.'

'You think it's bugged?'

'It could be. I think we should stick to things that have nothing to do with the situation here, other than Mavis's condition.'

'Do you mean that we should stop making love too?'

'It's a bit late for that. We've already had several nights of full-on shagging.'

'I don't think I like the idea of Collingwood listening in to our couplings.'

'I doubt it'll be him. Anyway, after your session with Inge, you should be getting used to performing for an audience. But talking of Mr Collingwood, do you think you could arrange for me to meet him? I'd like to get a sense of him.'

'I did suggest it before you arrived. He said he didn't think it was a good idea.'

'Well, that's very impolite of him. Let's get back to the flat and give him an earful of our shrieks and moans then.'

'I thought you said he wouldn't be listening himself?'

'I've just decided that he's exactly the type. Let's give him a command performance.'

## Saturday, 22 March 1975

BUT IN THE EVENT, Grace was to meet Jeremy Collingwood sooner than either of them had expected.

The next morning, after they had had breakfast and were trying to decide what to do with the day after seeing Mavis, the phone rang. It was Collingwood.

'Steve, I'm sorry to say that your mother's condition has significantly deteriorated. I will be over to the flat in fifteen minutes to take you and Dr Mitchell to the hospital.'

'Okay, thank you, Jeremy.'

Grace could see from Steve's face that something bad had happened. 'Steve, what's going on?'

'That's Collingwood. Mum's taken a turn for the worse. He'll be here in a few minutes to take us to the hospital.'

'Oh, Steve, I'm so sorry.'

'I'm feeling so guilty that we didn't go in yesterday, once we'd abandoned the East Berlin visit. I've visited her nearly every day since arriving.'

'Steve, it's not your fault. You've been very attentive. Our absence yesterday is not connected to her decline, if that's what it is. Let's not jump to conclusions.'

By the time they got down to the entrance of the apartment block, Collingwood was already there and gave a masterclass in charm.

'Dr Mitchell, I am so pleased to meet you. I thought it best to leave you two together for the first few days of your reunion.'

'Thank you, Jeremy. Please call me Grace. We are not within the precincts of Cambridge University now.'

'Thank *you*, Grace. I am aware of your academic publications as well as your poetry, which I find very impressive, formally precise, syntactically cunning, to which you bring an astonishingly hip vocabulary.'

'Goodness me, Jeremy. May I quote you?'

'Be my guest. But to more serious matters. Steve, I need to prepare you for this. The doctors don't think your mother has much time left. I know you both saw her the day before yesterday. Jenny tells me her condition was stable yesterday, but she seems to have declined overnight.'

Steve took a deep breath, but said nothing.

They stepped onto the street. Jennings had kept the engine running and a few seconds later they were speeding towards the British Military Hospital.

At the hospital, Collingwood said, 'You know your way up. Jennings and I will stay here as long as is necessary.'

Steve thanked him and led Grace up to the ward. Jenny greeted them at the door of the ward. 'Steve, Grace, this is not looking good. She is having difficulty breathing. But do try and talk to her. Dr Saunders will join you shortly.'

For a moment, Steve thought he might not have the courage to go into her room. But Grace took his hand and led him in. Both of them were shocked at how much her condition had changed. Her skin was grey and she was groaning quietly. Previously, she had seemed calm, but now she was clearly distressed. Steve took her hand. 'Mum, it's Steve. Grace is here too.'

Grace went around to the other side of the bed and took her other hand. 'Hello, Mavis. We came as quickly as we could.'

At the sound of their voices, Mavis seemed to stop struggling. Grace looked across at Steve. There were tears in his eyes. 'Mum, I love you. We both love you. Thank you for everything you've done for me. I'm sorry I didn't tell you about what was going on in my life. But I have found Grace now and I promise to look after her as well as I can, and if we are lucky we will have a baby…'

Whatever else he was going to say was lost in a sob.

Grace filled the silence. 'Mavis, I will look after your beautiful boy. I love him more each day.'

At that moment, Doctor Saunders arrived. Steve was about to get up, but Saunders put his hand on Steve's shoulder. 'Stay there. I think you can see that she hasn't got long left. But now that you are here she seems calmer. I'm sorry, there's really nothing more we can do.'

He looked at the readings on the machines attached to her. 'She is not so distressed now. Don't tire yourselves out. Take a break from time to time. Get a cup of tea. Jenny will fetch you if there's a change. I will come back in an hour.'

But in the end he came back sooner. It became apparent not long after he had left the room that her vital signs were beginning to fail, life was leaving her body. She took a series of shallow, croaky breaths and then stopped. The machines beeped one by one. Steve dropped his forehead onto Mavis's hand and sobbed for several minutes. Grace left her side of the bed and stroked Steve's back gently. Saunders came into the room and said, 'Step outside for a few moments, and we'll make her more presentable.'

Outside in the corridor, Grace said, 'Oh, Steve, I'm so sorry. At least we were here.'

But Steve could not speak.

Grace cradled him all night, rocking him in her arms. She had never seen him so utterly miserable. She thought back over the last couple of days, and then over the last few months. For ten years or so, her life had been remarkably uneventful, the life of an apparently happily married, hard-working academic. But since bumping into Steve in the Six Bells on Covent Garden the previous summer, she seemed to have been on some kind of emotional roller-coaster. She had separated from her husband, decided to have a child on her own, and become a university lecturer. Now, most unexpectedly of all, she was back in Berlin and embroiled in a way of life that she thought she had left far behind. It was odd to find that even after all these years, she was still *persona non grata* in the DDR. In some odd way, it thrilled her. She had heard old hands in the espionage game say that once you tasted the excitement, you never really got it out of your blood.

The fact was that things happened around Steve. He gave the impression of being oblivious to the effect he had on people, particularly women. But now that the one woman who had been his lodestar and his anchor had gone, how would he cope? Was she, Grace, strong enough to occupy that role in Steve's life? Could she be both his lover and a substitute for his mother? Well, if she wanted him to be the father of her child, she would have to be.

Suddenly, there were all sorts of practical problems to be addressed: a funeral, getting back to Cambridge, and, in due course, sorting out Mavis's flat and her will. And not forgetting the completion of the divorce from Peter, which would then leave her free to marry Steve and provide a safe harbour for her orphaned lover.

## Friday, 28 March 1975

STEVE WASN'T SURE HOW he got through the next few days. Grace did her best to comfort him. But in some ways having her there made it worse. He just wanted to curl up into a ball and cry his eyes out, but her presence meant that he had to do his best to put a brave face on the turn of events, and arrangements had to be made.

Collingwood explained that German laws relating to death were strict. There was much more official intervention. The first thing to be decided was whether Steve wanted Mavis's body repatriated to the UK or for the funeral to take place in Berlin. Steve pointed out that Mavis's only close living relative apart from himself was her mother-in-law who was elderly and bed-bound and unlikely to be able to attend a funeral service, even in Britain. So he thought it made sense to have the funeral in Berlin. Collingwood also explained that cremation whilst not unknown in Germany was far less common than in Britain. Steve was clear that she would have preferred cremation and that since she had no formal religious affiliations or beliefs, secular arrangements would be appropriate. Collingwood pulled some strings with the local authorities and arrangements were made for the cremation for the forthcoming Friday.

At ten-thirty on the appointed day, a cold grey morning, Collingwood picked up Steve and Grace from the flat. On the drive to the crematorium, Collingwood asked if Steve was going to say a few words. Steve was taken aback.

'But there won't be anyone there apart from us.'

Collingwood said, 'Actually, there will be some people from the department, including my governor, and the British Consul General. The Yanks asked if a couple of their people could attend. Of course, I should have cleared it with you first. But your mother was highly regarded. I think that there might be some German colleagues, too.'

Steve was horrified. 'But what am I going to say? Especially to a group of people I don't know and who don't know me.'

'You don't have to say anything. My governor will say a few words on behalf of the department. There may be one other contribution. It's fitting some words are said on such occasions. Everyone there will have known your mother in some capacity. They are grieving too. But I think it would be appreciated if you could say something. Just talk about your mother as you knew her.'

Steve turned to Grace, who had remained silent through this exchange. 'What do you think?'

'You should say a few words. No one wants to have to do something like this. You will regret it if you don't.'

'But I haven't prepared anything.'

'Just let the words come to you.'

'What if the words don't come? I'll look like an idiot.'

'They'll come. Your heart will overflow.'

They had arrived at the crematorium. Jennings dropped them at the main entrance, where two bulky men in overcoats were checking the IDs of people arriving for the funeral. Collingwood led Steve and Grace into the small chapel. A crackly recording of a Bach cello suite was playing over the public address system. Steve was surprised to see that there were more than twenty people there. He was now in a state of shock. Collingwood led them to the front row that had been left clear for the immediate family members and friends. He then said, 'May I join you? If you don't think it inappropriate I will be acting as the informal celebrant.'

Grace was grateful to Collingwood. She could see that Steve's nerves needed steadying.

A few minutes later, the funeral director approached Collingwood and nodded as if to say that everything was ready. Collingwood walked to the lectern and began speaking.

'Ladies and gentlemen, we are gathered here today to honour the life and work of Mavis Cicely Percival, née Daniels. Mavis was a colleague and friend to many of us here and she will be greatly missed. This will be a simple secular service, as she would have wished. There will be a memorial service in London in due course to celebrate her life and work more fully. I will now ask Gilbert Hardcastle to say a few words.'

Collingwood returned to his seat and Gilbert Hardcastle took over the lectern and offered a few words of regret. He praised the quality of Mavis's work and her qualities as a colleague without giving any indication of what that work was or providing any anecdotes that might give an insight into her character. Steve understood the constraints that Hardcastle was operating under, but it was as if he had never really known Steve's mother.

When Hardcastle had returned to his seat, Collingwood regained the lectern and said, 'I would now like to ask an old friend of Mavis's to say a few words.'

A somewhat grizzled but handsome man from a few rows behind Steve and Grace rose and went to the lectern.

'Ladies and gentlemen,' he began, in a German-inflected accent, 'I cannot tell you how devastated I am by this sad turn of events. But rather than dwell on the present, I would like to say something about Mavis when I knew her in 1948.'

Steve could scarcely comprehend what the speaker was saying. 1948? Before he was even born.

The speaker continued. 'Some of you will know that Mavis first came to Germany in 1947, initially working at Wolfsburg in the British sector of Germany, helping to get the VW plant going again. She was then posted to Berlin in 1948 shortly after the Soviet blockade started. It was round the clock work, British planes landing at Gatow, American planes at Tempelhof and French planes at Tegel.

'Inspired by the example of Ernst Reuter and Willy Brandt, both anti-Nazis and anti-communists, I had stood as an SPD candidate in the first post-war municipal elections and been elected for the Pankow area of Berlin. As an energetic young councillor during the blockade, I was keen to make sure that my constituents got the food and heating rations they needed. Meanwhile Mavis's job at Gatow was to liaise between the military authorities and the civilian administration. In my efforts to help my constituents, I was probably an extreme nuisance to Mavis. But despite this we became friends.

'At the same time as being a city councillor, I was also completing my PhD on the period of German Romanticism at the university. One of the consequences of the blockade was that the Freie Universität was established in December 1948 in the American sector of the city. I was invited to transfer to the new university. But not only was my constituency in the Soviet sector, but so too were the libraries and archives that I needed for my academic work. So I decided to postpone any decision to transfer until I had been awarded my PhD.

'Mavis, not surprisingly, was disappointed in my decision. She wanted me to complete my PhD at the Freie Universität, and then for both of us to move to London. She said I would have no trouble getting an academic post in the UK. But I felt I had a duty to my constituents and to my city. No doubt Mavis and I were as obdurate as each other and perhaps if we had tried to compromise, we might have found a way to keep the relationship going. But, to cut a long story short, we soon went our separate ways. Shortly afterwards, I heard that she had met a very nice English soldier who was stationed here. In due course they got married in London and had a son, Steven Percival, who is with us today.

'For reasons that I need not go into here, while my political career foundered, my academic career prospered at what was now called Humboldt-Universität zu Berlin, and I eventually became a professor.

'That might have been the end of the story, but then, totally unexpectedly, a couple of years ago, Mavis and I met at a conference and we found that the spark that had existed between us had never quite gone out. We met several more times and were planning to be together. There is no need for me to go into how I am able to be here today. Some of you will already know. And then this happened, and I have lost her once again.'

For a moment, he lost his composure and had to stifle a sob before continuing. 'Mavis was a marvellous woman, a doughty foe of totalitarianism, a true friend to Berlin and Germany, and a fine example of English civility and humane professionalism. I will miss her terribly.'

The speaker returned to his seat and, bowing his head, removed his spectacles and pretended to clean them.

Throughout his eulogy, Grace had been squeezing Steve's hand. She realised that what was already going to be an awkward task for Steve had just become very much more difficult.

She whispered in his ear, 'Are you okay? I'm sure everyone would understand if you felt you were unable to speak.'

Collingwood also turned towards Steve, his head tilted slightly, as if to check that he was still prepared to go ahead. But Steve was trying to process what the previous speaker had just said: that his mother had been in Germany and Berlin at critical moments in recent history; that before his father she had had a lover, whom, in a parallel universe, she might have married, and who was now speaking at her funeral; that her knowledge of German and German politics was probably considerably more extensive than his own; that she had, to some extent, albeit briefly, resumed a relationship with this dignified and eloquent figure, whose name he did not know, and who had just praised his mother in a speech which Steve couldn't hope to emulate.

Nevertheless, despite the polished performance, something didn't add up. The whole thing felt very contrived, as if it were for the consumption of others, not for the immediate mourners. Then he remembered the letters in Mavis's flat. Was this his mother's lover? But if so, why were the letters posted in London? Unless the professor was already based there. Was he therefore the person who had flown in from London on the day of the accident, bringing with him the copy of that day's *Times*? Even more worryingly, was he the person who had absconded from the scene of the accident?

Suddenly he realised that Collingwood and Grace were looking at him, waiting for him to say whether he was going to be able to speak or not. He let go of Grace's hand and walked slowly towards the lectern. He faced the congregation, his mind a blank.

'Ladies and gentlemen, thank you for coming today to honour the memory of my mother. In all sorts of ways, it seems you probably know her better than I do. Perhaps it will come as no surprise to most of you that I had no idea what her job entailed and I suppose that is how it must be. It does me no credit to say that I'd assumed she must have a rather boring, unimportant job. Now I find from the person who spoke before me that she was actually doing immensely important work long before I was born. Well, perhaps not that long. In fact, at rather the age I am now. I am conscious that my own contribution to the greater good has thus far been negligible.'

Steve was suddenly aware that he was talking rather more about himself than about his mother. He glanced over at Grace, but she just smiled encouragingly at him.

'The thing about Mavis is that she did all that and brought me up, effectively, on her own. I don't remember her ever complaining. She never got cross with me. She helped me with my schoolwork, without actually doing it for me. She behaved as if the scholarship I got to the City of London School for Boys and the place I got at Cambridge were down to my own efforts, when in fact both achievements were down to her tact and gentle pressure. She always knew what I was thinking, but never pre-empted what I was about to say. She was neat and modest and strong beyond belief. I will miss her so much.'

He could say no more. The emotion overwhelmed him. He knew he ought to finish what he was saying in a tidier way, but he no longer had the composure to do so. He waved his arm pathetically in thanks and walked back to his seat. As he slipped in beside Grace, Collingwood patted him on the arm and said, 'Well done. Magnificent.'

Grace squeezed his hand. 'That was lovely. She would have been so pleased.'

The Bach cello suite resumed and the coffin slipped away. Once the curtains had closed again, Collingwood stepped up to the lectern and said, 'The department has laid on some refreshments in a private dining room at the Treibel Hotel. Do please join us there in half an hour if you can.'

People started filing out. Several opened cigarette cases and lit up in the colonnade outside the chapel. Steve realised that his position as chief mourner meant that he would now have to shake hands and hobnob with and thank people for coming. He would have to be gracious and stoic, but that was not how he was feeling. He felt angry, undermined, cheated. He wanted to howl and keen and beat his sides with his hands. He didn't want to be civilised and grown-up.

But already the Consul General, with a flunky whispering in his ear, was bearing down on him. 'A fine encomium, my boy. She would have been delighted. I am afraid that I can't join you for refreshments at the Treibel, but I would be very happy to entertain you and your lady at the consulate while you are here if you would care to be in touch with my office.'

Steve swallowed his anger and said, 'Thank you, sir. We're so pleased that you could make the time to attend the funeral. It means a lot to us.'

The flunky steered the consul to the limousine that was waiting for him, handing him a sheaf of papers as he settled himself in the spacious back seat.

Suddenly, Steve knew he could do it. He shook hands and hobnobbed and thanked people he didn't know for coming and accepted praise for the deftness of his speech.

Finally, the German professor came across to where Steve and Grace were standing. From the corner of his eye Steve saw that Collingwood was standing on the other side of one of the columns of the colonnade watching attentively.

'Steven, please allow me to introduce myself. I am Dieter Müller. May I congratulate you on your touching words. They brought tears to my eyes. You are a fine son.'

'Thank you, Professor. I was also touched by your own words. I learnt much in that short space of time that I had not previously known about my mother.'

'I hope you did not feel that I was being indiscreet.'

'No, it is perhaps in the nature of the job that she did that her only son would know less about her life than colleagues and former acquaintances.' Steve could not bring himself to use the word *lovers*.

But if the German professor sensed any disparagement he did not show it. 'Steven, please introduce me properly to your delightful companion.'

'My apologies. This is Dr Grace Mitchell, lecturer in French literature and thought at Cambridge University and fellow of Newnham College.'

'Dear lady, I am very pleased to meet you. I am a great admirer of your work.'

Grace shook the professor's hand. 'As I am of yours Professor Müller, and equally pleased to meet you.'

Steve, who until that moment, had felt that he had been faking the hobnobbing quite well, spluttered, 'Do you mean you two know each other?'

Grace laughed uncomfortably. '*Of* each other. To some extent our subject areas overlap.'

The professor said, 'They do indeed. But Steven, I also wanted to thank you for what you have done for me.'

'I'm sorry, Professor. I am not sure what you mean.'

'I understand that I have you to thank for bringing the travel documents to East Berlin, which have allowed me to escape the clutches of the Stasi.'

Steve was aghast. 'You mean they were for you?'

'They were indeed and I am very grateful.'

But before anything more could be said in this public place, Collingwood intervened.

'Professor Müller, I hope you are going to join us at the Treibel. If you are, please travel with us. There is plenty of room in my car. I will sit up front with the driver.'

'Thank you, Collingwood. I would be delighted to accept your offer.'

Steve said little in the car on the way to the hotel. Collingwood sat up front with Jennings and Grace sat in the back seat between

Steve and the Professor, who kept up the academic banter with her, asking what she was working on now and if he would be permitted to see an uncorrected proof copy of her book. He would be very happy to write a puff for it.

Meanwhile, Steve was trying to equate the urbane goatee-bearded figure of Professor Dieter Müller with the image of the agent that he had had in his mind when he had crossed to the East on that rainy day. What kind of crucial, perhaps secret, information would a professor of literature have that would be useful to the British security services? On the other hand, it seemed that Grace had been right when she was wondering what might have been Inge's motivation to risk so much without any benefit to herself. It did indeed look as if she had been doing it for her teacher.

But if what Müller had said in his speech were true, his mother had also been in love with him, albeit before Steve's birth. More perplexing still, the professor had gone on to hint that the love between them had recently been rekindled. But this did not square with the letters that Steve had found in his mother's dressing gown pocket. Neither the professor's first name nor his surname began with the letter S, and unless the S represented some pet name that was used between him and Mavis, then those hints were unfounded. Especially since on the first of March, he would still have been stuck in East Berlin and not in a position to fly in on the afternoon flight from London that day. So, either his mother had been carrying on two love affairs at the same time or there was something bogus about Müller's statement.

Collingwood, aware that Steve might be having difficulty processing today's revelations, turned around in his seat. 'Steve, how are you feeling?'

'Pretty weird, actually.'

'I am not surprised. When we get to the hotel, can I have two minutes of your time?'

'Of course.'

'Could you suggest to Grace that she take Dieter up to the dining room? They seem to be getting on well. Academics do seem to gravitate towards each other.'

Steve nodded, but privately he was far from happy about entrusting Grace to Dieter.

Steve had never seen Collingwood so nonplussed before. 'I'm sorry about Müller. He went completely off *piste*. I was against letting him speak, but the governor fell prey to his charm. Even so, he was meant to confine himself to generalities, not provide detailed testimony.'

Steve was in no mood to accept Collingwood's apology. 'Not only was I not prepared for revelations in connection with my mother that concern me so directly, but I feel you also ought to have let me know that he was the person for whom I carried the false passport across. It rather compounded the shock.'

'I am sorry, Steve. It was not my decision.'

'You talk about restricting information on a need to know basis, and then Müller shouts something like this from the hilltops. He says in effect that he and my mother had resumed a relationship from before I was born and were planning to be together in the UK.'

'You are right. All I can say is that you should reflect on the hilltops aspect of what you have just said.'

'Well, perhaps I can ask *you* to reflect on the fact that whoever swept my mother's flat before you allowed me to take up residence there seems to have missed the two letters in her dressing gown pocket, love letters from London signed by someone signing himself S, who was flying into West Berlin from London on the day of her accident and who brought with him a copy of that day's *Times*. Not only does this not fit with Müller's assertion that they had become lovers again, but it also potentially points to the person who made off at the time of Mavis's accident.'

Collingwood was silent for a few moments. 'I see. This is all most unfortunate.'

'I'll say it is. I feel like you've been jerking me around.'

'Steve, it's not like that, but I can't give you a fuller explanation of what actually happened.'

'Well, I'm glad you accept that I haven't been told the truth.'

'All I can say is that the deception is intended for consumption elsewhere.'

'Jeremy, that is not good enough and I am going to ask Müller a few questions.'

'Steve, I beg you not to do it over the funeral baked meats. Müller is leaving West Berlin in the next few days. But I will try to set up a *tête-à-tête* with him for you tomorrow.'

'I am not a vindictive person, but if you don't set up this meeting and if I don't get a better explanation, I will make a bloody nuisance of myself.'

'I understand. Shall we go up? You will be missed.'

\* \* \*

Without having exchanged further words on the way up, Steve and Collingwood entered the private dining-room where a buffet for a small number of people was in full swing. Grace had managed to shake off Müller's attentions. He was now talking to Collingwood's boss. Grace handed Steve a glass of Sekt and said, 'What did Collingwood want?'

'He wanted to apologise for letting Müller speak at the funeral. He was personally against it, but he was overruled by his boss. According to Collingwood, Müller didn't stick to his remit.'

'Yes, it does seem a little reckless to expose oneself that way only days after having got out of East Berlin.'

Something occurred to Steve. 'Did you recognise him?'

Grace looked uncomfortable. 'Not with a beard and long hair. He looks quite different in the author photos in the books of his that I've seen. But once he'd told us his name, I could see the underlying likeness.'

'Were you surprised?'

'Of course I was. It's a huge event in the world of letters and even weirder that he has a connection to Mavis.'

'Do you believe what he said about her?'

'Steve, we have to be very careful here. In these situations, it's difficult to know what's true and what's not.'

'You may be right, but I'm afraid I asked Collingwood whether he could arrange for me to have a longer talk with Müller. I'd like to find out more about that period when he claims to have been with my mother during the airlift. Collingwood said he'd see what he could do. But apparently Müller is leaving West Berlin in the next few days.'

'I think you should be very cautious. Would you like me to accompany you?'

'No, I think I'd rather do it on my own, if you don't mind.'

Grace seemed somewhat relieved. 'That's fine. I think it's probably better that way.'

## Saturday, 29 March 1975

WHEN STEVE ENTERED THE bar, his first thought was that Müller had not yet arrived. He scanned the tables, but was unable to spot a trendy older man with luxuriant salt and pepper hair and a raffish beard. It was only when he saw a rather more conservative looking, clean-shaven man with neatly slicked-back hair waving at him, that he realised that in the intervening twenty-four hours Müller had transformed his appearance.

'I'm sorry, Professor Müller, I did not recognise you.'

'I find that reassuring. I only grew the long hairstyle and the beard for the fake passport and to make it more difficult for the border police to identify me. But I also needed to get a West German passport after the funeral yesterday, and I didn't want to be immortalised as a bearded old hippie.'

Müller may have been reverting to his default style, but Steve wasn't sure it was an improvement. Müller signalled to the waitress and, when she arrived at the table, ordered two beers.

'Steve, thank you for joining me. But I am sad to see that you have not brought Grace.'

'She sends her apologies. She is catching up with some work. Recent events have interrupted her preparations for next term's lecture series.'

'So you have chosen an eminent intellectual to be your partner.'

'I would say that she has chosen me, Professor Müller.'

'Please call me Dieter. I hope you will not mind me observing that she is several years older than you.'

'It's a long story, which I'd rather not go into here. Suffice it to say that I was one of her less able students.'

'I am sure that is not the case. No doubt you are engaged on postgraduate studies which will, in due course, result in a valuable contribution to the field.'

'No, I'm sorry to disappoint you. I am no longer a student.'

'*Ach was!* I do not believe that for one moment. It is thanks to you that I am now in West Berlin.'

'I am happy to have been of service, but intellectual abilities were not really called for.'

'Maybe not, but bravery was.'

'No doubt bravery was also involved in your own situation. Have you had to leave family members?'

'I never married or had children, much to my regret. My parents are long dead, as is my only sibling. That was why I was watched so closely and prevented from travelling to academic conferences in the West. I was seen as a defection risk.'

'I can see that not having close family might make defection easier, but you must also have had to leave possessions behind.'

'Well, the DDR is not as materialistic as the West, but I have had to leave my library, which grieves me. Even in the consumerist paradise of the West, I doubt that I will be able to build it up again to its previous extent. I am too old now and, in any case, I come to the West without a penny to my name other than the hundred marks I have been granted by the West German government.'

'So what will happen to your books?'

'I have donated most of them to the Humboldt University library, unofficially of course. I have distributed the remainder, which include a number of the more valuable titles, among my closest students, in the hope that at some point in the future, we will all be reunited.'

'But what about your notes and unpublished papers?'

'Yes, another tragedy. In the case of the most important papers, I was able to have them copied and distribute copies to trusted collaborators. I was also able to share some drafts with scholars in the West. The mail censors are not that interested in the love affairs and the squabbles of the Jena set. But my *Zettelkasten*, which is the real engine of my research, was a much bigger problem. Are you familiar with the *Zettelkasten* method?'

'I can construe the word. Slip box, I suppose, but I have no idea what the method is.'

'Card-index file would be a better translation, but the method is in the way one links the cards. I borrowed the idea from a West German colleague. How do you keep your own notes?'

'Basically, I have a notebook on the go all the time and I write things in it, in no particular order.'

'What Lichtenberg called a *Sudelbuch*, which for some reason is translated into English as waste book. But do you ever find yourself not being able to find a reference or citation in one of your books?'

'Frequently.'

'That is what the *Zettelkasten* system is designed to overcome. Through the use of a classification system you link cards one to another. Of course, it takes quite a lot of time to set up and then you have to be consistent in your note taking habits. It can become an obsession. My archive fills several boxes.'

'So have you had to leave your *Zettelkasten* too?'

'Once again, I have entrusted some of them to my best students. But Mavis brought back the two most important ones.'

'Not through the Tränenpalast, surely?'

'No, we took advantage of an occasion when she was being driven in an official car through Checkpoint Charlie to attend a conference in Weimar. They searched the car pretty thoroughly on the way back, but were not interested in notes about August and Caroline Schlegel.'

'So does that mean that my mother visited you in East Berlin?'

'Yes, a number of times.'

'Do you still feel vulnerable here in West Berlin?'

'I certainly do. However, I will be on my way to Scotland tomorrow.'

'*Scotland*?'

'Yes, I have been honoured to be named an extraordinary fellow of Edinburgh University.'

'Congratulations. Scotland is an interesting place.'

'Do I detect a note of pity in your voice that I have not been invited to your own *alma mater*?'

'Not at all. It's just that its culture is fiercely different from England. You may also find the accent in Edinburgh a little challenging at first.'

'Is this an example of the English exceptionalism that one hears so much about? Let me remind you that we talk about the Scottish Enlightenment but not the English Enlightenment. When there were only two universities in England, there were five in Scotland, and of ancient foundation. Herder and Goethe were hugely influenced by the early poems of Walter Scott and Macpherson's *Ossian*, even if it was a farrago. There is a famous passage in Goethe's *Werther* where the spirit of *Ossian* is invoked at length. It is also clear the influences went in both directions, as can be seen from Scott's translations of early works of Goethe. I am looking forward to many happy hours poring over manuscripts in the National Library of Scotland, which have hitherto been unavailable to me, in furtherance of this research.'

'I apologise. You can see I am no scholar. Nor am I particularly well informed about the constituent countries of my own nation.'

'No doubt nationhood is a convenient illusion. It has certainly been the curse of the German-speaking territories of the Holy Roman Empire, which itself was neither holy, Roman, nor an Empire, as Voltaire quipped.'

Steve already regretted locking horns with an internationally renowned scholar and attempted to bring the conversation back to more personal matters. 'But to return to your remarks of yesterday, it is clear that you went back a long way with my mother. That was indeed news to me.'

Müller looked troubled. 'I am sorry, Steve. Had I known, I would not have included those details in my speech.'

'Well, I was at first shocked, but then it kind of made sense. My mother never spoke about her work or her life before she met my father. Could you tell me more?'

'There is not much to tell. What would you like to know?'

'Were you lovers?'

'Yes, we were deeply in love.'

'Did you resume the relationship more recently?'

'Yes, though there were impediments, as you can imagine. But it was wonderful.'

'Surely she was followed and your accommodation was bugged or under surveillance?'

'You are not the only one who can outwit the Stasi.'

'I'm not sure I did.'

'I'd rather not go into details, but we never met at my apartment. Once again, friends and colleagues were very helpful.'

In the light of the love letters from S, Steve thought that Müller must be lying. But maybe it was a case of like mother, like son. Maybe his mother's resumed affair with Müller had been conducted on the same basis as Steve's encounter with Inge. Just a part of the job. He was also surprised that Müller was so confident about being able to evade surveillance. That was not what one heard about the Stasi.

'But isn't it likely that there was an informant in your circle?'

'Possibly, but one becomes adept at spotting such bad apples.'

'So you were not going to join my mother at her flat in London?'

'I am sure that we would have spent some time there. She, in turn, might well have come up to Edinburgh from time to time. I can imagine that your reaction might not have been entirely positive, but of course we were unable to include you in our discussions. I am sure, however, we would have sorted it out.'

Steve was not so certain, but nor was he about to pursue the point. 'Yesterday in your oration, you said that while your political career foundered, your academic career prospered, and it was around about then that you and my mother broke up. Would you be prepared to give me more details about that period?'

'Absolutely, but let's get some more drinks first.'

He called the waitress over and ordered more beers.

'I was elected a city councillor in the 1946 municipal elections for the SPD, the Socialist Party, the equivalent, more or less, of your Labour Party. Despite massive backing from the Soviets, the SED, effectively the Communist Party, had not done very well. So for a time there was a semblance of democratic municipal government. A vote was held condemning the blockade, which was carried by the non-communist majority.

'A subsequent meeting of the council at the town hall was surrounded by thousands of pro-communist protesters, organised by the SED, outraged by this outbreak of democracy. The protesters broke into the building and smashed it up, threatening councillors, allied officers who were observing the debate, journalists and Western police officers. Many of these individuals were then held hostage until early the next day. It became clear to many of us that democratic government in the east of the city was impossible and plans were put in place to hold new elections in the West.'

This was all new information to Steve. 'So why didn't you stand in those elections?'

'Because they didn't cover the eastern boroughs. But there was another reason. It was made clear to me by the East Berlin authorities that if I wanted to complete my PhD, I should give up my political aspirations. Which, I'm afraid, is what I did.'

'You could have moved to the Freie Universität.'

'Yes, I could have. But I was at the university founded by the von Humboldt brothers. Why would I move to an upstart institution with no record of academic excellence? Had you been encouraged to move from Cambridge University to the local technology college, you would get some idea of my reluctance. It was also made clear to me that if I kept my mouth shut politically, I would progress up the ranks quite quickly. I'm not proud of what I did, but it seemed the best option at the time. At that stage, no one saw the Wall coming. In fact, there was a naïve hope that Stalin would agree to a treaty with a unified but demilitarised Germany, and the Allies and the Soviets would be able to withdraw. Stalin even drafted a document, but Adenauer turned it down.'

Steve could see that he was going to have to improve his knowledge of the politics of post-war Germany. 'But my mother disapproved of your decision?'

'Not so much for political reasons, as for personal ones. She had been offered an important job back in London and wanted me to go back with her. She said I could continue my studies there. But I wasn't sure how easy that would be and feared that a German might be treated none too well so soon after the war in a city which his country had bombed. Also my English was not as good as it is now. I suppose I was just frightened. If I could have seen what was coming in the shape of the Wall, I might have thought differently. I also told myself that the relationship with me would restrict Mavis in the organisation she was joining. So she decided to break off the relationship. I am not blaming her for the decision she made. We both put our professional ambitions before love.'

'Thank you, Dieter, for being so frank with me. I had no idea of any of this. She never spoke about it.'

'An inevitable consequence of the work she was doing.'

'I suppose so. Would you mind me also asking why the British security service was prepared to arrange your escape? I am sure your work on the Jena set and its links to the Scottish Enlightenment deserves to be finished in the tranquil surroundings of the National Library in Edinburgh, but I cannot believe that British official resources have been deployed to that end.'

'I am afraid that is one question I cannot help you with. At least not for some time. If we remain friends, I am sure that, in due course, I will be able to tell you something.'

'I understand.'

'I am glad we had this talk. I think it was perhaps better without Grace. It means that I have been able to be franker than would otherwise have been the case. But I do hope to get to know her better on the conference circuit in the UK.'

In the time that Steve had been living with Grace, she had attended no scholarly conferences, so the possibility of Müller and Grace encountering one another in such settings seemed remote. Even so, he was not delighted by the prospect. But it would be churlish not to respond positively to Müller's hopes. 'I am sure she is excited by the thought of working with you in the future. From what I understand, her recent lecture series has been very well received.'

'You are a lucky man, Steve Percival. That woman has a fine intellect and is a brilliant writer. How did you charm her? I would love to know your secret.'

Steve laughed. 'Yes, I occasionally have to pinch myself. I'm not sure exactly how I ended up with her.'

'Perhaps it is precisely because you take such things for granted that she does not feel oppressed by you. I understand from Collingwood that you have a way with women. Which seems to have come in handy in delivering the travel documents to my student.'

This troubled Steve. He had been told that Müller would not know who the intermediary was because a dead letter drop would be involved. But Müller's comment seemed to imply that there had been a face-to-face handover. Hoping to draw Müller out, he said, 'Will your friend be okay?'

'I cannot say for sure. She knew the risk she was taking. I am sorry to say that several of my students will be under scrutiny. While that is to be regretted, it also gives her some protection. With luck, the Stasi, if they were already monitoring her, which is by no means certain, will just consider her to be a young woman keen on befriending young men from the West, not an entirely unusual occurrence. She may get pulled in for questioning, but if she keeps her nerve, she should be okay.'

Steve thought it ill became Müller to downplay the risks for his students and for Inge in particular now that he was safely in the West.

'You spoke of bravery earlier, but I wasn't running the kind of risks that your student is.'

'I am not sure that is entirely the case. You volunteered for a dangerous assignment.'

This statement further unsettled Steve. Collingwood had assured him the penalty, had he been caught, would have been negligible. Affecting a sang-froid he didn't really feel, and hoping that Müller had not detected this moment of uncertainty, Steve said, 'It was only because I had no obvious connection with the British security people and I was to hand.'

'Being to hand is a very Heideggerian quality, if I may say so.'

Steve was finding Müller's smugness intolerable. 'Perhaps if Heidegger had spent less time as an apologist for the Nazis, he might have come across the expression: to a man with a hammer all problems look like a nail.'

Müller smiled. 'The hermeneutical hammer, no doubt. Perhaps you are more of a moral philosopher, Herr Percival?'

'I am not any kind of philosopher, Professor Müller. But I am grateful for your time. I need to get back to Grace now.'

Müller gave Steve a sidelong look. 'Does Grace know about the girl you delivered the documents to?'

Steve pondered his reply for a moment. Clearly, Müller knew precisely who the intermediary was and what had transpired. Perhaps he was working on the assumption that Steve would keep such information from Grace, a detail that he might be able to exploit at some point in the future. Steve's inclination was to tell him to get lost. But he resisted the impulse. 'You might not believe me, but yes, and in considerable detail.'

Müller now laughed uproariously. 'Oh, well played, Herr Percival. I can see we are going to get along fine.'

Back at the flat, Steve found Grace sitting at the desk in the small bedroom, scribbling furiously in an A4-lined pad. He threw himself on the bed. 'How's it going?'

'Surprisingly well, actually. It is quite liberating not to have a library at hand. I just have to trust my memory. Of course, my memory may be faulty, but it means I don't interrupt the flow of my argument by looking something up. I can check the facts later.'

'I think we all have to write into the unknown.'

'Get you, *cher poète*.'

'I'm not saying that's what I do. I wish I could. It's what I gleaned from Blanchot's *Le Livre à venir*.'

'When did you read that?'

'I borrowed it from your study. I'm sorry, I should have asked.'

'No, that's fine. I believe I suggested you read it last summer. I'm glad to see you eventually get around to your assignments.'

Steve ignored this dig at him. 'Have you been beavering away since I went out?'

'Not all the time. I made some calls to Cambridge. I hope Collingwood's masters don't mind too much. I had to talk to the faculty secretary and the college to let them know when I'll be back. I also had a chat with Gary to check that all was well with the house.'

'He has a key?'

'Yes, always has had. I trust him completely.'

'Of course.'

'He sends his condolences.'

'That's nice of him.'

'Actually he said he'd like to have a brief chat with you, if you're up to it.'

'Did he say what about? Have I screwed up?'

'No, everything is fine. But he did say that he'd had to get someone in to replace you. He wanted to let you know so you didn't find out when you got back.'

'Of course. I rather expected that.'

'He also wanted to consult you about one of the late submissions to the new writing competition.'

'I wasn't able to read them all before I set off for Berlin. I made him notes for the ones I'd read.'

'Which he appreciated. He largely agrees with your assessments. However, there was one script which didn't have full author details. Just a name and a telephone number. He tried the number several times, but there was no reply. He wondered whether you might have an address or another way of contacting the author.'

'Did he say what the title of the piece was?'

'Something about a fault. Ring any bells?'

'Yes, I'm afraid it does if the title of the piece was *The Fault's in the Set*.'

'That's it. Was it one you read?'

'No, one I wrote.'

'One you *wrote*? You wrote one of the plays. How come Gary doesn't know that?'

'Because I submitted it under a pseudonym. I didn't want to influence him one way or the other by submitting it under my own name. The telephone number is my mother's flat.'

'Oh, Steve, you are a dark horse.'

'To be quite honest, I'd forgotten all about it. Do you think he'll be annoyed?'

'Only one way to find out.'

'I was hoping for a bit more reassurance than that.'

'Be bold, Steve. You're the one who's been jousting with the Stasi.'

'Gary's much scarier than an East German border guard.'

'Don't be ridiculous. He's a pussycat. Phone him now. I'll go out if you want.'

'No, stay. You might have to put me back together again afterwards. Where was he when you spoke to him?'

'He was at home.'

Steve went out to the hall, picked up the telephone and told the operator that he wanted to make an international call. The operator asked Steve to hold while she routed the connection through to the UK. After a considerable pause, Gary came on the line.

Steve took a deep breath and said, 'Hi, Gary. This is Steve. Grace said that you'd like a word.'

'Hi Steve, thanks for calling. But first, I'm so sorry to hear about your mother. You must be devastated. Matt and I send our condolences.'

'Thanks. It is all a bit unreal. At least I got to see her and although she never regained consciousness, I had the feeling that she knew I was there.'

'Well, it's good that you've got Grace there with you.'

'Yeah, I think I would have gone to pieces without her.'

'I don't want to add to the upset, but I'm afraid I've had to get someone to replace you. I thought I'd better let you know. It's pretty busy here, as you can imagine.'

'Of course. I understand completely. How's the season going? Did you get *Six Characters* to fly?'

'No. It was a bit of a clunker. I think your idea of differentiating the levels of reality by setting it in a TV studio and updating the text was a good one. If only we'd had more time. But *Mr Sloane* is going well. It helps that it has a smaller cast. All four of them are working well together. They were also the best actors in *Six Characters*. Sally, who's playing Kath, is brilliant, even though her character is a fair bit older.'

'I'm glad to hear *Mr Sloane* is working. I'm sorry to have missed both shows, especially having had a bit of input into both.'

'Well, with luck you'll be back for *Marat/Sade*. Please do drop by when you're back. You never know, we might find something for you to do.'

'Thanks, Gary. Anyway, Grace said that you wanted to talk about one of the submissions.'

'Yes, your notes were great, by the way. There were a few pieces that must have come in just before you left for Berlin which are, reasonably enough, without notes. One of them is called *The Fault's in the Set*, by a guy called George Dent. But I can't get through to him on the number he provided and there's no address given. Can you cast any light on the matter?'

'Yes, I can. I'm George Dent.'

'*You're* George Dent?'

'Yes, I'm sorry. I shouldn't have done it like that. I just didn't want to put anyone in a difficult position.'

But Gary was still getting up to speed. 'You wrote *The Fault's in the Set*?'

'Yes. When I saw the sort of thing that was being submitted, I started playing around with an idea that I thought might work on the Festival stage. But then I got cold feet about talking to you about it, so I chickened out and put a pseudonym on it. Then with all this stuff with my mother, it completely slipped my mind. I'm sorry. It was very unprofessional. You have every right to be annoyed with me.'

'The only reason I'm annoyed with you is that you didn't consult me. I might be tough with actors, but I treat writers very gently. Even if you'd produced a piece of rubbish, I hope I would have been encouraging. But, in any case, this is a good piece. Not that it doesn't need tightening up in places.'

Over the crackly connection, Steve wasn't sure if he'd got Gary's drift. 'Are you saying you like it?'

'Yes, so far as I'm concerned, it's one of the winners. I want to produce it. When are you planning to get back to Cambridge?'

'In a few days' time.'

'Good. I'm afraid I'm going to be asking for a bit of a rewrite. Nothing too drastic, but on the other hand I'd like you to help cast the piece and advise me during rehearsals. Does that work for you?'

Steve could hardly believe what he was hearing. 'Yes, yes. I don't know what to say. Thank you, Gary. I'm so grateful.'

'So it does look like we'll be working together again after all. Look forward to seeing you next week.'

Steve hung up and said to Grace, in wide-eyed amazement, 'Gary wants to produce my play.'

'Steve, that's wonderful. I only wonder why you don't trust the people around you a bit more.'

'I don't know. Maybe because I don't trust myself.'

'So, in the usual Percival way, you lose one job, but immediately get a better one.'

'I'm not sure about that. He says that he wants me to do a rewrite.'

'Steve, that's the deal. Don't get all hoity-toity about it.'

'Sorry.'

'So you really had abandoned poetry for playwriting. I didn't believe you that day I came round to Tenison Road.'

'Which you were quite right to do. I only started writing *Fault* when I was assisting Gary with the auditions in London.'

'That was a quick piece of work.'

'It's a very short play.'

'I hope you're going to let me read it.'

'Yes, of course.'

'I don't know what's of course about it. Had it not been for Jude I wouldn't have been able to read the final version of *Event/ Horizon*.'

'Yes, okay, okay. But I don't think you'll like it.'

'Why is that?'

'Because it has female nudity in it.'

'I'd be more surprised if it didn't. The female nude I take to be your specialist subject.'

'I think I justify it in the play. It's not gratuitous. Gary didn't mention it as a problem.'

'I don't think Gary is averse to creating a bit of a scandal. It might get more bums on seats.'

'Well, I'm just letting you know in advance that you may disapprove.'

'Thank you for your consideration. How did you get on with Professor Müller? Did he comment on my absence?'

'He was sorry that you weren't able to join us, but thought that it would enable him to be franker about certain matters.'

'Was he?'

'Well, he went into considerable detail about his relationship with Mavis. I suppose I have to accept his account of the period when she was in Berlin before she met my father. If it's true, it shows that Mavis was already doing important work in 1947 and 1948. But I am more doubtful about the idea that they had renewed the relationship in the last couple of years, especially in the light of the letters from Mr S. He was also frank about having put his academic career ahead of his political convictions.'

'Such things are not unknown even in our own polity.'

'I guess so.'

'Did he cast any light on the operation to exfiltrate him?'

'Rather too much, I thought. He thanked me for the role I played. But what particularly worried me was that he seemed to know that the intermediary was one of his female students. I was under the impression from Collingwood that a dead letter drop was involved. If, however, Müller knows who it was, then either Inge took the package to him directly or he's been given her identity by another source.'

Grace was silent for a moment. 'I hope it is not the latter. Not that there is much comfort in a breach of protocol either.'

'Müller accepted that several of his students would fall under suspicion and might be pulled in for questioning. But he felt that if the girl in question kept her nerve, she'd probably be okay. He didn't seem all that concerned. The worst that might befall her was a reprimand for loose morals.'

'I think it's difficult for us in the privileged environment of the West to imagine what it's like to live and work in a totalitarian state.'

'He doesn't seem to have any close family, which was why he wasn't allowed to attend conferences in the West, and has been considered a defection risk for many years. He seemed more upset by having to leave his library than by the possible consequences for his closest students.'

'Without condoning his callousness, any scholar would grieve at the loss of his or her library.'

'He's given the most important volumes to the Humboldt, unofficially, of course, and the pick of the rest to chosen students.'

'But presumably he's also had to leave his papers?'

'Yeah, but he had copies made of the most important ones and distributed them among his students. He also managed to get some out to scholars in the West.'

'Did he mention any names?'

'No. Anyway, he seemed more concerned with something called a *Zettelkasten*.'

'Ah, yes, the secret weapon of the Teutonic mind. What did he do with that?'

'It seems that Mavis brought out the most important part in the boot of her official car. I must say I find that detail hard to believe, but I guess he wouldn't have said it unless there was some possibility of corroboration.'

Grace was thoughtful. 'That really would be the crown jewels. I wonder where those notes are now.'

'Scotland probably.'

'Why do you say that?'

'He's on his way to Edinburgh soon. He's been elected an extraordinary fellow of the university.'

'How fascinating! A pity that one of the Cambridge colleges hasn't been quicker off the mark.'

'Speaking for myself, I'd rather not consider the possibility of bumping into him on Parker's Piece. He can stick to the Meadows in Edinburgh as far as I'm concerned.'

'Speaking of Cambridge, we need to book our flights back.'

'Collingwood's already done it.'

'For both of us?'

'Yes.'

'If you want to know what I think doesn't feel quite right. It's Collingwood's employers picking up the tab for everything.'

'They must feel they have an obligation to Mavis.'

'Clearly they do, but I think it's you they have their sights on. They're trying to recruit you. I recognise the signs.'

'Grace, I'm not a spook; I'm a poet.'

'A playwright now, I believe.'

'I've written a play. That doesn't make me a playwright. Whereas once you're a poet, you're not allowed to abandon the calling.'

'I will remind you of that someday.'

'But in any case, I am not a spook. I'm completely hopeless. I get myself tangled up in all sorts of ridiculous situations, mainly with women. I'm effectively a kept man. I got a so-so degree and my career prospects are nugatory.'

'Exactly the kind of person they're after. You really don't know yourself, do you? You're basically decent and trustworthy, but with a streak of amorality. You are self-effacing, but determinedly bloody-minded. You resist being managed or mentored, but take what you need from those around you. You're not someone who takes the straightforward route, but you reach your goal somehow. You don't toe the line, but you're not a reckless revolutionary. Basically, you're a maverick or maybe a free spirit.'

'Thank you for that pen portrait. Do you think I should listen to their offer?'

'That's entirely up to you. But I can tell you, it's quite hard to get off the merry-go-round once you're on it.'

'Yes, I already get a sense of that.'

'While you're adding to your portfolio of jobs, let me remind you of the first one you took on, which was getting me pregnant. You might have noticed this morning that I started my period. So that's one area you're not delivering on. I think I'm going to have to put you on a no-sex diet for the next ten days until my next fertile period. That includes no sneaking off to East Berlin for a quickie with Inge.'

Steve laughed. 'What was that you were saying just now about not taking the straightforward route, but reaching my goal?'

'I'm serious Steve. I want a baby. If you don't get a move on, I might have to find someone else to oblige.'

'Müller?'

With a cry of fury, Grace picked up a magazine that was lying on the desk, rolled it up, and started beating Steve with it.

## Monday, 31 March 1975

STEVE OPENED THE FRONT door to his mother's Southwark flat and ushered Grace into the narrow hallway. They dropped their bags and Steve said, 'Right, cup of tea first. Have a look around while I'm making the tea. Thank goodness we thought to buy a pint of milk.'

By the time the tea was made, Grace had made a tour of inspection of the small flat and was now sitting at the kitchen table. 'Steve, this place is lovely. But I seem to recall you said it was a council flat.'

'Did I? Well, *council flat* has more street cred than *flat in an early nineteenth-century house*.'

'So Mavis wasn't a tenant. She presumably was a leaseholder.'

'I suppose so. I never looked into that sort of thing.'

'Well, you're going to have to now. Not least because, if there's a mortgage still running, you'll have to make monthly repayments. There'll almost certainly be an annual service charge too.'

'Probably best to sell it then.'

'That all depends. It might make more sense to hang on to it. I'm sure we can work something out on the financial front.'

'I'd rather not think about that kind of thing right now.'

'Of course not. I'm sorry. It's just that you'd led me to expect something a bit grittier, when in fact it's rather delightful.'

They sipped their tea. Grace admired the teacups. 'All her things are so lovely. She had a good eye for quality and style.'

'Yes, that's what I meant about the Berlin flat. You can look in her wardrobe later, you'll see what I mean.'

'Are you sure you want me to do that?'

'Well, you're going to have to at some point because we can't keep her clothes for ever. It'd feel a bit creepy. It'd be better to give them to a charity shop. But I'd rather not be the one to pack them up. Of course, keep anything for yourself if it's your kind of thing.'

'Okay, we'll see.'

They sat in silence for some time. Grace realised that Steve must be finding it difficult. He might have been suspicious of the anonymity of her flat in Berlin, but here virtually every object in the flat was a powerful reminder of his mother's absence. Eventually, she said, 'I liked your bedroom. Leaving aside the lack of lacrosse rackets, hockey sticks and gymkhana trophies, it's very similar to mine.'

Steve laughed quietly. 'No doll's house or framed certificates for winning poetry competitions.'

'No, but some rather nice diecast toy cars. I see you have a Morris Traveller in pride of place. Gideon would be pleased to know that.'

'I wanted to get rid of all that stuff, but Mavis wouldn't let me.'

'Nor will I. What's your equivalent of my gymslip?'

'No idea. It did occur to me, when I was here at Christmas, that Mavis had probably kept my school blazer. But even if it still fitted me, I can't imagine it would give you a thrill.'

'That just shows how well you know me!'

'You may well be right. Anyway, I'm afraid you won't be surprised to know that there's no food in the flat. I can go out and see if I can find an open shop. Or we could go to the local pub and have a pint and a pork pie.'

'I'm not that hungry. The food on the plane was plenty for me. What I do need is a bath. Is there any hot water?'

'Should be. I put the heating on when we came in.'

'Are we sleeping in your room?'

'No, we'll use Mavis's. My bed is even narrower than the bed in your childhood bedroom.'

'Are you sure?'

'Yes, it'll be a bit weird, but I don't want to create a shrine. I'd prefer to remember her in other ways.'

'I think that's much the best approach.'

While Grace soaked off the journey in the bath, Steve left a message for Sheena Ferguson, his mother's colleague, letting her know that he would be staying in the flat for a couple of days. Shortly after he'd hung up, the phone rang. Steve considered not answering it, but then, thinking that it was an odd coincidence, finally picked up.

'Steve, this is Sheena. I'm sorry I didn't get to the phone in time.'

'Oh hi, Sheena. I presume you know about Mavis's death.'

'Yes, Steve. I am so sorry. She was a marvellous woman and a great friend and colleague. It is such a terrible thing to happen just when she'd got the posting she'd always wanted. But I expect you knew all that.'

Actually, Steve hadn't known that it was specifically the posting she'd always wanted. But now, after his encounter with Dieter, it made much more sense. 'Thank you, Sheena. I just wanted to let you know that Grace, my girlfriend, and I will be staying at the flat for a couple of days before we go back to Cambridge.'

'Thank you, Steve. Actually, I'd assumed that. Jeremy rang to let me know which flight you were on.'

'Collingwood?'

'Yes. He thinks very highly of you.'

'Well, that's very kind of him, but I didn't really do much.'

'That's not what I hear. Anyway, I wonder whether you would have time to pop into the office while you're in London. There are one or two things we need to sort out with you.'

'We were thinking of heading back to Cambridge the day after tomorrow.'

'Tomorrow is fine for me. Could you manage eleven-thirty? We're only ten minutes' walk from Mavis's flat. Have you got pen and paper and I'll give you the address?'

Steve jotted down the address Sheena gave him on the pad that lived next to the telephone. 'Can I just check that eleven-thirty is okay for Grace?'

'I'm afraid I need to ask you to come on your own. There are some private matters to discuss. I'm sure Dr Mitchell will understand.'

Steve was so nonplussed by Sheena's forthright manner that he immediately agreed. He remembered that his mother had said that Sheena was not one to be trifled with. Having achieved what she wanted from the phone call, Sheena said, 'Thank you, Steve. I look forward to seeing you tomorrow morning.'

Steve was still sitting on the chair by the phone table musing on the conversation when Grace emerged from the bathroom swathed in towels. 'I've left the water for you.'

'It's okay, I don't need a bath.'

'I would prefer my bedmate to have washed the dust of travel off his lissom body.'

'Oh, come on, Grace, it's not your fertile period yet. I thought I was meant to be saving my seed.'

'Who said anything about making love?'

'That's the only time you insist on my having a bath or a shower.'

'Careful, my bonny lad, or you might find yourself sleeping in your own truckle bed tonight.'

Steve started to undress in the hall. 'Well, when you put it like that…'

'Enough of this bravado. When you come to bed, could you bring a glass of water, please?'

Steve spent so much time in the bath, mulling over the conversation with Sheena, that by the time he had dried himself and joined Grace in the bedroom, she was apparently asleep. Too sleepy himself to unpack his bag, and thus eschewing nightclothes, he slipped under the bedclothes, pleased to find that Grace was also naked. He put his arm around her, caressing her breasts and pressing his torso against her curved back. But that was the limit of his pleasure for now. Stirring in her sleep, Grace mumbled, 'You took too long. I'm already asleep. You'll have to wait until morning.'

Steve realised it was futile to quibble over the contradiction of saying you were asleep if you actually were, and was soon asleep himself.

# Tuesday, 1 April 1975

STEPPING INSIDE THE ANONYMOUS-looking building the next morning, just before eleven-thirty, at the address Sheena had given him,
Steve was reflecting on how readily Grace had accepted that she
would not be joining him at this meeting. Having signed in at the
reception desk and been given a lanyard with the word *guest* printed
prominently on the plastic label, Steve was asked to take a seat.
Sheena would come and collect him shortly.

He didn't have long to wait. A few minutes later, the double
doors that led into the reception area swung open and a small, late
middle-aged woman with iron-grey hair entered. A thin smile
broke her otherwise severe features and she said, 'Steve, thank you
for coming to see me at such short notice. I hope Dr Mitchell was
not too put out.'

'No, no, I think she welcomed the chance to do a bit of
shopping.'

Sheena laughed and said, 'Please follow me.'

A little later, having travelled up several floors in a lift, Sheena
ushered Steve into a spacious office. She invited him to take a seat
on a sofa in front of a coffee table, while she picked up a folder
from her desk which stood in front of a large window. 'Coffee?'

Steve nodded. 'Black, please.'

Sheena flicked a switch on an intercom and said, 'A pot of coffee
for two and a plate of biscuits, please, Tracey.'

Having ordered the coffee, she walked over to the armchair, set
at right angles to the sofa on which Steve was sitting, and sat down.

'I know I have already expressed my condolences, but I'd like you
to know that Mavis and I have been colleagues and friends for
many years and I too am still trying to come to terms with her

death. I do not want to try to rival your own grief, but I am more upset than I can say.'

'Thank you, Sheena. I must admit that I am still feeling numb.'

'Thank goodness you have someone to comfort you. Mavis told me how pleased she was that you and Dr Mitchell were now a couple.'

'Can we call her Grace? It feels weird to be calling her Dr Mitchell as if I were still an undergraduate.'

'Of course. I also understand that Grace is aware of the line of work Mavis was in.'

'She seems to have understood well before me.'

'Yes, well these things are not easy and do not sit well with our everyday relationships.'

'I am starting to realise that.'

'So to be perfectly brutal about it, you will realise that your mother died on active service. It is not thought that the accident was a deliberate attempt to kill her, but nor can we rule it out. Enquiries are still ongoing. We require our officers, when taking part in the kind of operation with which your mother was involved, to lodge with us certain documents in the event of such developments.'

'What kind of documents?'

'A will, personal letters to family members and a statement dealing with financial and property matters. There is also a set of keys to her flat, which we have been holding.'

She handed him the folder containing the documents. 'It's probably best not to try and absorb all this now. If, when you've read the documents, you feel you need the advice of a solicitor, I can direct you to one who works with us quite regularly. However, any solicitor should be able to help you. You will see that the flat now passes to you. You are also the beneficiary of a life insurance policy. Things have been so arranged that you should be able to pay off the outstanding mortgage with the proceeds from the life policy without a large estate duty bill. If you run into difficulties on this front, please do get back to us. We can almost certainly help. If everything works out, you should end up as the owner of your mother's flat and have a reasonable amount in the bank. You won't be a millionaire, but you should be in a reasonably comfortable position. Do you have any questions?'

'My mother said that you had been looking after the flat in her absence. Will that continue?'

Sheena laughed. 'Well, I personally wasn't bringing the milk in, if that's what you mean. But yes, the department was taking care of things there while she was on active duty. I am afraid that will now cease. You will have to make your own arrangements to make sure bills are paid and any obligations as a leaseholder are met. We can certainly give you a bit of time to get to grips with all that, though.'

There was a knock on the door, and an assistant came in with the coffees. She put the tray on the coffee table and said, 'Is there anything else, ma'am?'

'Yes, could you bring me the documents for Mr Percival to sign? They're on my desk.'

Tracey went over to the desk and returned with several sheets of paper. 'Thank you, Tracey. That'll be all.'

When Tracey had left the room, Sheena slid one of the documents across the coffee table towards Steve and said, 'This is to acknowledge receipt of your mother's will, a personal letter to you from her and a statement of her financial affairs. Please confirm that that is what is in the folder and then sign the document I have just given you where it is marked. Here is a pen.'

Steve took a sip of coffee and then glanced through the contents of the folder. Not wishing to prolong the rigmarole, he scribbled his signature in the appropriate place.

Sheena retrieved that sheet and then said, 'So now we have to have a rather more difficult conversation. Before we do, I want you to know that I promised Mavis that if anything happened to her, I would do my best to keep in touch with you and offer help if ever it were needed. She was worried that your family connections were rather limited. She even spoke in terms of my taking on the role of godmother, purely in a secular sense. Does that surprise you?'

'Well, I don't wish to seem ungrateful, but yes.'

'Let me explain. I have known you since you were a baby, but you do not know me because those encounters declined as you grew up. Despite that, if anything had happened to your mother during those years, I would have become your guardian. Of course, you are now an adult and capable of making your own decisions, but your mother asked me to continue to act as an informal advisor and mentor.'

Steve was mystified by where this conversation was going. Sheena noticed the look of discomfort on his face. 'I apologise for this cumbersome preamble. I can see you are feeling embarrassed, but I can assure you, if you would be kind enough to hear me out, that I am the one who has the embarrassing admission to make.'

'Of course. I know my mother would not have given me your name and contact details without trusting you completely. It's just that I have become wary of situations where it seems that other people are making plans for me.'

'As you should be. It depends, of course, on who it is making the plans. Let me ask you this. You have met Professor Müller, twice now, I believe. On the second occasion you were *à deux*.'

'Yes, that's correct.'

'What were your impressions? Be candid.'

Steve hesitated, not knowing where an honest reply to this line of questioning might lead. 'Frankly, I didn't take to him.'

'I see. Could you expand on that view?'

'I resented the way he took over my mother's funeral. She may well have had a relationship with him in 1948, but that did not give him the right to grandstand in the way he did.'

'I have seen a transcript of what he said and he praised Mavis handsomely.'

'But it was very much about him.'

'Inevitably, much of what we do in this business can never be talked about.'

'I suppose so. But I also find his assertion that he and she had got back together sickening. For a start, I don't believe it.'

'Do you have reasons for this lack of belief?'

Steve sensed he was on thin ice here, but decided to press ahead anyway. 'When I was finally allowed to go to my mother's flat, something didn't feel quite right about it. It felt like a stage set. Yes, there were one or two of her things there, but it seemed as if it had been assembled to look like her flat. I searched around to find things that would confirm that it was hers. I found two letters in the pocket of her dressing gown that were certainly addressed to Mavis at that apartment, but there was no sender name or address and only an initial for the valediction.'

'What was the initial?'

'The letter S.'

'Thank you. Did you read the letters?'

'Yes, they were love letters from someone in London. In the second letter, the writer said that he would be arriving at Tempelhof on the afternoon of the day which turned out to be the one on which she had her accident.'

'Do you think that happened?'

'Yes.'

'What makes you think that?'

'There was also a copy of *The Times* for that day in the flat. That means the newspaper arrived in her flat before she went out on the trip during which she was knocked over. I doubt that copies of *The Times* are routinely available in Berlin on the day they are published in London. Someone must have come in on the afternoon plane from London and brought it to the flat. That interpretation would fit with the information in the second letter from S. I also discovered that there had been a witness to the accident who had not waited around to be interviewed by the police. I wondered if this might have been S and for some reason, he didn't want to be caught up in something that would require him to make a statement. I was also curious as to why this person wasn't being sought by the police.'

'This is all by way of answering my question about why you don't believe that Mavis and Müller were having an affair and that therefore there was no reason for him to make such a statement at her funeral?'

'Yes.'

'Perhaps she was conducting two relationships simultaneously, or perhaps one of the relationships was just for show, as it were.'

'That's not the kind of person Mavis is, was.'

'Are you that kind of person?'

'No.'

'But you had sex with the young lady known as Inge in East Berlin.'

'Well, yes, but I was asked to.'

'Does it not occur to you that Mavis may have been asked to do the same thing?'

'Why would she need to do something like that?'

'To persuade Müller to betray his country, then, in recognition of the services he had rendered, to help get him out. Which meant that S had to be very circumspect. Have you any thoughts as to who S might be?'

'No, I don't know any of Mavis's friends.'

'You know one?'

'Who?'

'Me.'

The world had now completely turned upside down for Steve. 'You're S,' he said, almost in a whisper.

'Yes. Your mother and I were lovers, only very recently, I'm sorry to say, though there had been a spark between us for many years. Does that disgust you?'

'No, not at all. I think it's wonderful, and so sad that you and she didn't have longer together.'

'Thank you, Steve. Yes, I was the person who came in on that afternoon flight and went to the flat with my copy of *The Times*. And yes, I was the person who disappeared into the Berlin mist once I realised that others had called an ambulance.'

'Why did you disappear?'

'Because if it had become known that I, as the director of the department, was spending an illicit weekend with my lesbian lover, who was also the person running the operation to get Müller out – an operation in which that person was posing as Müller's lady love and which had taken a couple of years to organise – our friends would have smelt a rat. So I had to make sure not to be identified at the scene.'

'Did Müller know that Mavis wasn't really in love with him?'

'Who knows? It's not a question we can easily ask him.'

'Why weren't you with Mavis when she got knocked over?'

'You think I ought to have taken the hit too? You may be right. But the simple answer is that I'd gone back into the bar to call a cab.'

'Do you think it was a hit rather than an accident?'

'As a matter of fact, I do, but I doubt if the police will come up with any hard evidence.'

Sheena handed him another sheet of paper. 'Now that I have given you some insight into the operation your mother was involved in, I need to ask you to sign this document. It is a summary of what people call the Official Secrets Act. Actually, signing it doesn't bind you any more or less than the provisions of the Secrets Act do anyway. You can be in breach of the Act even if you don't sign it. The reason we ask you to sign it is that it shows that you understand that what we do here is of importance to the security of the country. I realise that you have already done some work for us without formally signing anything, but that is because we were improvising frantically in the wake of your mother's accident.'

Steve read the document, but still he hesitated. 'I don't mean to be impertinent, but doesn't your conduct in this affair raise a number of questions? I don't mean in terms of sexuality, but in terms of professional conduct.'

'You are quite right. There is an ongoing internal review. It could cost me my job. In this work, it is difficult to conduct normal, loving relationships.'

'That is partly what is troubling me. Grace and I are trying to have a baby.'

'I know. Mavis was delighted, eventually.'

'Well, you know I was her student and she is quite a lot older than me. So that already introduces complexities into the relationship. If I am not able to talk freely with her, I can see things becoming even more difficult.'

'I am not about to give you explicit permission as to what you can and can't tell her. I think you know that she has already signed one of these forms and has been of service to us on occasion. So I will have to leave it to the pair of you to be sensible about this.'

With this partial concession, Steve signed the document.

'Thank you, Steve. I do hope you and I can keep in touch on a personal level. I will never forget Mavis. I see your mother in you. Please consider me a port in a storm. Never be shy about having recourse to me.'

'Thank you, Sheena.'

'Do you have any last questions?'

'Was it Jeremy who told you that I'd found the letters?'

'Yes.'

'Does that mean that if I hadn't, you and I wouldn't have been having this conversation?'

'We would have been having an abbreviated version relating only to *post mortem* arrangements and the offer of help on a personal level. There certainly wouldn't have been any confession of my affair with your mother.'

'Have I screwed things up by expressing my suspicions to Jeremy?'

'Well, it has been slightly uncomfortable for me to have to own up to my sexuality. But actually that's a good thing. It has also led to a couple of people being reprimanded for not having done their jobs properly in sweeping your mother's flat.'

'Is one of those people Jeremy?'

'No, we have high hopes for Collingwood.'

Sheena stood up. 'Well, I think that's enough for today.'

Picking up the folder she had given him, Steve stood too. He put his hand out to shake Sheena's hand. She stepped towards him. 'Come, come, now that we understand each other better, let me give you a hug.'

Steve was considerably taller and stooped down to allow himself to be embraced. 'Thank you, Sheena. It has been so good to meet you.'

Grace had still not returned from her shopping expedition when Steve got back to the flat. He really had no appetite to read his mother's will or look at the statement of financial affairs, but he did want to read the letter from her, even though he did so with some trepidation.

Dear Steve,

If you are reading this letter, it means something unfortunate, but not entirely unexpected, has happened. You will by now know more about those circumstances than I could foresee when I was writing this letter. I hope it has not been too distressing for you.

I am writing this shortly after staying with you and Grace in Glisson Road. I am sorry I was so sceptical about what you and Grace were planning. Of course I was and am actually delighted by the prospect of becoming a grandmother and so much sooner than I had ever imagined. Sadly, the fact that you are reading this letter means that I will not be around to meet my grandchild. It seems so unfair.

However, I do not want you to think that I have had a tragic life. Though your father and I were only together for a relatively short time, we had a strong and loving relationship. Nor could I have asked for a finer son. You have been loving and supportive, and I am very proud of you. Despite some of the things I said to you in Cambridge, I know that you will be a good father yourself. Grace has made a sensible choice. She is right when she says that in a number of important ways you are more mature than your years. During that weekend, Grace and I got the measure of each other, I think. I can assure you that I like and admire her. But just because she is a strong, independent woman, it does not mean that she will not need your help and support. It may require more of you than you can possibly imagine at this point. You will need to face the obligations you are taking on with cheerful good humour.

You will also now have a much clearer idea of what my professional life has involved. And no doubt you have also got to know my dear friend and colleague, Sheena Ferguson. As a matter of fact, if something had happened to me when I was younger, she would have become your guardian. So, in a sense, even though you have not really known her, she is your informal godmother. Even if she weren't, you can trust her completely, especially in practical matters to do with my will or financial affairs. She is a single, childless woman, married to the service. She will probably try to convince you that you are perfect material for the service yourself. I would advise against this. It can become all-consuming. But in the end, it is your decision.

Although it was hard when your father died and I have been a single parent for many years, recently, when I had begun to think it was too late, I became romantically involved with another person. It was wonderful to find that I could still give and receive physical love from a like-minded soul. I cannot name names in this letter and I would caution you against making too hasty an assumption about who this person is. But it is not the person with whom my professional duties have reunited me in the last two years. All I can say here is that this relationship has given me deep joy. I cannot imagine the circumstances under which the identity of this person might come to light, but if they come to pass, please accord my lover the deepest respect.

Steve, I love you so much. I am sorry to leave you so soon. But I do think you have good people around you, who will care for you. Have a good life and tell your children about me.

With endless love, Mavis

Steve began to cry uncontrollably. His body was racked with sobs. He was still sobbing when Grace came in fifteen minutes later. She dropped her bags and said, 'Steve, what's happened?'

He gestured at the letter. Grace picked it up. 'May I read it?'

Steve nodded.

A few minutes later, Grace said, 'Oh, Steve, that is such a beautiful letter. What a brave woman. She must have known the risks.'

Grace sat down beside him and wrapped him in her arms. 'You've got me. We have each other. Whenever we feel that things might be going wrong, let us remember Mavis's words.'

Steve nodded again. He did not yet have the strength to comment. Grace thought a change of mood was called for. 'I'll put the kettle on.'

Over the cup of tea a few minutes later, Steve started to emerge from the abyss of sadness he had slipped into. Eventually, he said, 'The fact that she must have written that letter in the cold light of day, before she left to go to Berlin, is what horrifies me the most. It must have been like facing a firing squad.'

'Yes, but she was a woman of great composure. The fact is the war that started in 1914 is still not over. There are still casualties on both sides. In that sense she is a war hero. She knew the risks she was taking.'

'Yes, Sheena, whom I thought was a kind of housekeeper who kept an eye on officers' affairs when they were overseas, turned out to be the director of the department.'

'Hang on. You weren't seeing Sheena Ferguson, were you?'

'Yes, she sends her regards. Which, I assume, means that you know of each other.'

It took Grace a moment or two to regain her composure. She now regretted even more her frankness with Mavis about her own earlier involvement with the intelligence services. In a slightly strained voice, she said, 'We do. Well, well! I imagine that was a different kind of conversation from the one you thought you were going to have.'

'It was. In all sorts of ways. I don't think I can unpack it all right now. Do you mind? I'd just like to go and lie down.'

Later, over a couple of glasses of wine, Steve told Grace about the life insurance policy arrangement to pay off the mortgage, meaning that he would become the owner of the Trinity Church Square flat once probate had been granted. But he'd decided earlier on not to broach more ticklish subjects and left the account of his meeting with Sheena at that.

Grace took a sip of her wine. 'Gosh, Steve. That's a bit of a transformation in your circumstances. I suppose that means you'll be ditching me and filling the place with hot chicks.'

Steve looked horrified. 'No, I need you more than ever.'

'You do now. But you're already getting fed up with me badgering you to get me pregnant.'

'I'm not. I'm sorry about this morning. When you came back from the loo, I got a bit of a shock seeing you in my mother's dressing gown. I was also rather nervous about going to see Sheena.'

'Then I'm the one who should be apologising. I should have thought about that. It's one thing to sleep with you in your mother's bed, quite another to jump you when I'm wearing a familiar article of her clothing. I can see that must have been weird. But we'll be back at Glisson Road tomorrow. We can defer the hanky-panky until then.'

'Maybe.'

But in fact the wine soon worked its magic. Grace asked to see his school photos. Steve said they were in the drawer of the desk in his bedroom. They sat on his bed, leafing through the album, Grace alternately cooing and laughing. Before long they had put the album to one side and undressed each other, only transferring to Mavis's bed after they had made love in the confines of Steve's childhood bed.

# The Festival Theatre

## Monday, 14 April 1975

GARY PUSHED THE PLATE of biscuits towards Steve and took a sip of his coffee. 'You've got a real gift for dialogue. *Fault in the Set* is a great little play. But, with only two characters, perhaps it's a little compressed. I was wondering if we could introduce another character so that we get a different take on the husband and wife relationship.'

'That's an interesting idea, but before we get too deeply into *Fault*, I'd like to show you something else, which is not much longer but has a bigger cast.'

'I don't think we should be jumping around. Your juxtaposition of TV addiction and the male gaze in *Fault* is deftly done. There's nothing like a bit of on-stage nudity to ruffle feathers in the local press. We could certainly do with bigger audiences, even if they contain a few Mary Whitehouses.'

'Well, I can offer you nudity on stage in this new work too, but not TV addiction.'

'Have you got it with you?'

'Yes, it's only five thousand words. It's called *Palace of Tears*. You can probably read it quite quickly.'

Steve got the script out of his bag and passed it across to Gary who said, 'Okay, give me half an hour. Go and get yourself a coffee at Hank's.'

When Steve got back, Gary was sitting at his desk in the little cubbyhole he called his office at the Festival and said, 'You're right, *Palace of Tears*, without being a lot longer, is a bigger play. There's much more going on in it. My general approach is not to change horses in mid-stream. But in this case, I think I'm going to break the rule of a professional lifetime. But that also means that we're going to have to pull it from the new writing festival, I'm afraid.'

Steve suddenly wished that he hadn't been so determined to persuade Gary to look at something that was still very rough around the edges. Gary noticed the look of disappointment on Steve's face. 'Don't worry, you're not being demoted. It's just that I don't think we can rehearse a play with this many characters for only one performance. If we can get a working script in the next few days, I'd be prepared to schedule it for the week after the new writing festival.'

Steve didn't know what to say. He'd expected a flat no. He certainly hadn't expected such a positive response. But Gary was still ordering his thoughts. '*Palace of Tears* has clearly been written while you've been away, and in the light of your own personal tragedy. However, the script in its current state is not quite the finished product yet. Art is a form of alchemy; the raw experience requires transmutation.'

'Yes, this is essentially a first draft and I'd like your help to sharpen it and make it work on stage.'

'Which I will be delighted to do. But I wonder if you're ready to make such personal material public so soon after the death of your mother.'

'I'm going to say yes, although I do appreciate that writing a play is one thing; seeing it performed quite another.'

'Another point of concern is that, from what little I know of your mother's tragic accident, the play is, to some extent, based on an actual event. What I don't know is how far the intelligence services setting is real or imagined.'

Steve smiled. 'Well, let's just say I can neither confirm nor deny such suppositions.'

'So we might be getting into hot water? Not that I am against a tussle with the authorities, but I don't want the Festival Theatre Company to be on the receiving end of a defamation suit from specific individuals. So before we go ahead with casting and rehearsals, I need you to supply me with a written disclaimer in your own hand that all names, characters and incidents in this play are fictitious.'

Steve, much to his own surprise, found himself agreeing to this condition.

Gary said, 'I'm sorry to be so pettifogging, but I have to think about my backers. But at least we don't have to run the gauntlet of the Lord Chamberlain anymore.'

'That's fine. I understand. I can do it now.'

'No, give it to me first thing tomorrow. Can you meet me for breakfast at Hank's?'

'Sure, what time's breakfast?'

'Let's say nine-thirty. I also want you to add one or two scenes.'

Steve was more alarmed by this request than the provision of a disclaimer. 'What do you have in mind?'

'You mention, quite far into the play, that Wolfsburg and Honoria are lovers, but you don't *show* the relationship. If you don't feel you want to do that, cut out the reference. It's gratuitous. Currently, the play opens with Wolfsburg and Jena having just had sex. But I think it would be stronger if the opening scene was between Wolfsburg and *Honoria* having just had sex. It will then be clear to the audience from the start that the subsequent relationship between Wolfsburg and Jena is fake. To be honest, I'm not sure the Wolfsburg/Honoria relationship works. It feels like it comes from a completely different play. But it's up to you. You're the playwright. Do you think you could rustle up something by tomorrow?'

'Maybe. But I'm not sure how explicit I can be.'

'Don't think in those terms. Make it truthful to the story you're telling and then let me judge if we can stage it or not.'

'Okay. How much nudity can we have?'

'Same answer. You can have as much as you like, as long as it's a function of the dramatic situation that the relevant characters are in. The audience also needs to be shown that Bertie is the mole, not merely told, and that he has been or is about to be arrested. How you achieve that is up to you. But I think we need to leave the audience feeling that the tragedy of Wolfsburg's death has had some beneficial consequences.'

Steve was amazed at Gary's grasp of the play's structure after one reading and his sense of the much better play that lay within his clumsy first draft. 'I'll do my best, but that's quite a lot of new material for the speed that I write at.'

'Get as much as you can down on paper and we'll go through it at Hank's tomorrow.'

'Is that it?'

'I'm afraid not. I have some other suggestions to make, quite radical, even crude ones, I'm afraid.'

Steve had been about to get up and head back to Glisson Road to set to work on the things that Gary had suggested while they were fresh in his mind, but now sat back with an apprehensive look on his face. The word *radical*, in particular, set alarm bells ringing. 'What do you have in mind?'

'Well, earlier on you asked me how much nudity we could have and I said as much as the dramatic situation justifies. But there's another issue for a small company like ours. We have to work with the actors we already have in the company. We have neither the time nor the money to recruit new actors. Sally is the obvious person to play Wolfsburg. It's a part she can really get her teeth into. If she's required to get her kit off, she won't object. She's a trouper, and the play is, after all, about how espionage instrument-alises people and their relationships. But we need to give her a bit of protection. She's not as young as she used to be.'

Steve nodded. 'That's fine. I didn't have any particular actors in mind when I was writing the piece.'

'Good, so we'll give her a *negligée* and light the scene tastefully.'

'Great. You're the director. I wasn't thinking *Oh! Calcutta!* anyway.'

'But, having said that, I do feel that the play needs a proper bit of nudity. If you recall, that's essentially why we selected Becky when we were doing the auditions.'

'Really?'

'Yeah, I asked you if her looks worked for you as a straight man. I judged your response to be enthusiastically positive. She also said she'd be prepared to do nude scenes.'

'She wasn't the only one we asked that question.'

'No, but she's the one I chose for those purposes.'

'So why not cast her as Wolfsburg?'

'Because she doesn't have the heft for the part. She's too young.'

'What's the solution then?'

'I'd like you to rewrite the scene between Tristan and Inge to show that they have a sexual relationship.'

'But Tristan and Inge are, in effect, just couriers. They're what are called cut-outs – not in the sense of being two dimensional, but in the sense that Inge doesn't know who the package comes from, and Tristan doesn't know who it's destined for.'

'I understand that's how things work in real life; but this is art. Wolfsburg and Jena, who are apparently former lovers, are both using others in the interests of their respective ideologies. Tristan is up for as much sex as he can get, but that is not the case with Inge. She really is in love with Jena and she is prepared to use her body and sacrifice her own prospects to help him get to the West. Hers is a selfless love, and this makes her the victim of the situation and therefore the tragic centre of the drama; not Wolfsburg, even if she is eliminated by the Stasi. I'm sorry if I'm treading on your grief here, but that's how I see the play.'

'Nor Tristan?'

'Most definitely not Tristan. He is an amoral hustler on the make.'

Steve was rather winded by this view of Tristan. 'But he's not.'

'I want you to make sure that he is. I want you to write against the grain. You don't want people saying it's just a piece of lightly disguised autobiography.'

'I wish people would stop saying that.'

'Come on, Steve. I don't know what went on in Berlin and I don't want to know. But we don't want to give the critics a stick to beat you with. We certainly don't want to invite the attentions of interested parties who could put a spoke in our wheels.'

'But I'm not sure how I make it about Inge's predicament.'

'Work it backwards. Assume the last scene shows her being arrested by the Stasi. She is going to prison for a long time. Her academic career is over. She will never see Jena again and she will never get out of East Berlin.'

'For fuck's sake, Gary. That's a completely different play.'

'No, it's not. It's the play that's implicit in what you've already written. Everyone in your first draft is pretending to be someone they're not, except Inge. You need to show that. The audience's sympathies need to be with Inge.'

'How do I do that?'

'Currently, you open with a love scene between Wolfsburg and Jena. I'm suggesting you open with a love scene between Wolfsburg and Honoria. Then follow that with the one between Wolfsburg and Jena. It's asking a lot of Sally, but she'll do it. Nor am I sure who best to cast for the part of Honoria. But we'll work that out. By contrast, you have Tristan and Inge meeting in a bar and Tristan handing the package over to Inge. But that scene doesn't earn its keep. Nor does it allow us to exploit Becky's great young body. Drop the bar scene and focus on Tristan and Inge in bed together back at her apartment. She is not sleeping with Tristan because she has fallen in love with him. Nor is it in the hope that he can help her get out. She's doing it to help Jena get out. Being a freelance prostitute is her cover if she is picked up by the Stasi.'

Suddenly, Steve saw it all. 'Gary, that's brilliant. But I'm not sure I can rewrite it in that way, not overnight, anyway.'

'Believe me, Steve, you can.'

'If I can, then it's your play.'

'No, it's not. I'm only helping you shape what's already there. I'm happy to have an acknowledgement. But let's see where we are tomorrow morning.'

Steve got up to go. As he did so, Gary said, 'Don't forget that disclaimer. No disclaimer, no go, I'm afraid.'

Steve gulped. 'Of course.'

He walked back to Glisson Road in something of a daze. He really hadn't expected Gary to give *Palace of Tears* any consideration at all. But his initial pleasure in Gary's positive reaction to the play was overlaid by the anxiety that he would be unable to adapt it to Gary's requirements. Or even worse, that he might not actually want to take it in the direction that Gary had sketched out. For he was by no means certain that it was within his powers to realise on stage a lesbian relationship between two mature women. It was not just because he was neither a woman nor middle-aged, though that came into it. It was because the models for the two characters were his own mother and the senior colleague in the department, informally appointed to be his guardian, something of which Gary was completely ignorant. It felt as though he was betraying a confidence. He wished now that he'd never put in that line about Wolfsburg and Honoria being in a lesbian relationship.

Nor was he entirely comfortable about making explicit that the mole in the West Berlin station was Bertie, the character he had based on Collingwood, even if only someone who had already identified Wolfsburg with Mavis and Honoria with Sheena would, by a process of triangulation, be able to accurately identify the model for Bertie. In this case, the discomfort was compounded by the fact that he didn't really think that Collingwood was a double agent. It was just that he had met very few of the West Berlin officers, and Collingwood was an undeniably exotic character in his own right. He should never have been so blithe about his readiness to provide Gary with a disclaimer. Unfortunately, he would have to do the work that Gary had asked for and just hope that he was underwhelmed by the new material.

Just about the only thing he felt comfortable with was the promotion of the part of Inge. At least that gave his imagination something to work on, even if it was only the prospect of glimpses of Becky's unclothed body. Fortunately it was still early in the day and Grace wouldn't be home until the early evening. Not only did that give him time to work on the new scenes, but also time to consider how he was going to present the situation to Grace. She still had no inkling of *Palace of Tears*.

* * *

Grace put the manuscript down. 'When did you write this? We only got back a couple of weeks ago.'

'Grace, you've been on another planet since we got back. Anyone would think that it was your mother who had died.'

'That's a horrible thing to say, Steve.'

'Well, you seem to have switched off from me completely.'

'I've been working on my lectures.'

'Which hasn't stopped you going up to London a couple of times.'

'I have other responsibilities, not all of which I can fulfil in Cambridge.'

'I really don't know what that means. But I don't see why that should affect our love life. You haven't let me touch you in the last week or so.'

Grace glared at him. 'It was the wrong time of the month, and I've had a lot on my plate.'

'From what I understand, it's not impossible to conceive at other times of the month. I know I'm only an informal sex-worker, but I have needs too.'

'Steve, are you shaping up for a fight?'

'No, I'm just saying that there are times when you are so focused on what *you're* doing that you fail to notice what the person you're living with is doing.'

Grace crossed her arms angrily beneath her bosom and chewed her bottom lip. 'How come we're suddenly talking about our relationship, when we're meant to be talking about your play, your new play, one I didn't even know about because, once again, you didn't tell me about it. I do not think I'm the one at fault here. If you feel you're not getting enough nooky at home, I'm sure there are plenty of girls in Cambridge who will do the imperious Steve Percival a favour.'

Steve pulled his horns in. 'I'm sorry, Grace. I'm in uncharted territory. I showed Gary the first draft at Hank's this morning. He made some suggestions and I've spent the rest of the day redrafting the play along those lines. I'm feeling a bit weird because it doesn't feel quite like my own play at the moment.'

'Steve, there's little doubt that this is your play. Not only has it got plentiful helpings of your trademark female nudity, but it's set in the very place you and I have just returned from, and the scenario is not a million miles from the events in which you found yourself caught up. With or without Gary's additions, the play is brilliant, but you can't put this on stage. Just giving your characters codenames is not going to throw people off the scent. Sheena Ferguson will be down on you like a ton of bricks, not just because you're lightly fictionalising a real intelligence operation in Berlin, but also because you're making the characters based on Sheena and your mother into lesbians.'

'They were.'

'I have no idea why you would say such a thing. But if that is the case, then there is even greater reason why you and Gary shouldn't go ahead with this.'

'Look, I'm sorry, but there were other things that passed between Sheena and me when we got back to London, which I didn't tell you about because I was feeling so upset.'

'So what is it that you didn't tell me about?'

'Sheena and Mavis *were* lovers. Sheena was with Mavis when she was knocked over. Not at that precise moment, but she was the person seen walking rapidly away who didn't provide a statement.'

'My God! So the letters were from Sheena.'

'Yes. So now she's the subject of an internal enquiry because she shouldn't have been there.'

'But who else knew about the letters?'

'Unfortunately, I blurted it out to Collingwood when we got back to the Treibel from the crematorium. Because I was furious with the way Müller had been allowed to exploit Mavis's funeral.'

'Oh dear, Steve. You should have realised that Müller was under instructions from Collingwood, and, therefore, from Collingwood's boss, who we now know is Sheena.'

'Yes, I see now that Jeremy was trying to tell me that in so many words. Müller's speech was intended for the Stasi, all part of the smoke and mirrors. But I was too angry to take in what Jeremy was saying and I was just intent on making a nuisance of myself.'

'Which you did by telling him about the letters. Suddenly, you were charging around like a bull in a china shop, suggesting that *Mr S* was in some way involved in Mavis's accident.'

'Yes. Jeremy obviously knew that Sheena had been in Berlin, and was, I assume, covering for her. But he hadn't known about the letters from S because his team, who had swept the flat before we moved in, failed to find them in the dressing gown pocket.'

'So then he had to let Sheena know that you were in possession of letters to Mavis from a certain S. Even if he hadn't known about their relationship beforehand, he might infer it now.'

'Yes, it can't be a nice feeling to be outed in this way.'

'All the more reason why you shouldn't go ahead with this play or, at least, not in this form. I've only skimmed it, but you do also seem to be suggesting in the play that Bertie is a double agent. Do you really believe that Collingwood is a double agent?'

'No. I left issues like that open in my first draft. I didn't make the nature of the relationship between Wolfsburg and Honoria explicit. The idea that there was a mole in the organisation was only hinted at and not attached to any particular character. Nor did the first draft end with Inge being led off to the Stasi cells. Gary seemed to feel that the audience should be clear that Inge was the only honourable character. So that's what I've been working on all afternoon.'

'Yes, well, he certainly knows about how plays work. But did you tell him anything about the background to your script?'

'Not really. He realised that it had been prompted by the death of my mother and the time I spent in Berlin. His main worry was that while writing something like this might be therapeutic, seeing it acted out on stage might not be such a positive experience.'

'He makes a good point. I'm just surprised he didn't go into your motivation in a bit more detail or didn't get some kind of formal clearance from you.'

'Well, he did ask me to provide him with a written disclaimer that all names, characters and incidents are fictitious to protect the Festival Theatre.'

'That is sensible from his side of things. But it won't necessarily stop *you* getting into trouble. I don't think the Special Branch officers who come knocking on our door will be convinced by any disclaimer.'

'Oh, come on. We don't live in a police state.'

'There are more subtle means of control. I think you could be getting yourself into trouble. I'm serious. You should be very careful.'

# Tuesday, 15 April 1975

WHEN STEVE WOKE THE next morning, he was exhausted and anxious. In the light of Grace's comments and without having allowed himself to think about what Gary's reaction might be, he had toiled through the night removing most of the material that he had spent the afternoon adding to the play until his fingers were nearly bleeding from the typing. After all, Grace had a more privileged view of the people and events that had inspired the play than Gary did. A portrayal of the relationship between Mavis and Sheena would be a violation of his mother's memory and Sheena's confidence in him. Nor should a character that some might identify with Collingwood, however remote the likelihood, be shown as a double agent, an allegation for which he had not a shred of evidence. There was already enough betrayal and double-dealing going on in the play without that particular narrative strand. He had also, at Grace's prompting, removed the codenames. He realised now that both the Wolfsburg and Jena codenames could be used by those with some knowledge of these matters to identify the underlying models. About the only thing he had retained from Gary's suggestions was the enhanced role of Inge and her arrest by the Stasi at the end of the play.

It did not escape him, however, that he had done what he always did and revised the text almost to the point of extinction. What was left was schematic in the extreme and unlikely to satisfy Gary, even if he managed to resist taking umbrage at Steve's wholesale rejection of his suggestions. Anyway, he was far too tired to worry about that now, and perhaps there was an outside chance Gary would be prepared to reconsider *Fault*.

As he lay there, becalmed in self-loathing, the bedroom door opened and Grace, a concerned look on her face and a mug of coffee in her hands, entered the room. 'What time did you come to bed?'

'About five, I think.'

'You must be shattered.'

Steve grimaced. 'I am.'

'What were you doing?'

'I took on board what you said and rewrote the play.'

'Oh, Steve, I didn't mean you to sit down and tear into a rewrite there and then. I was just asking you to take time to consider what you were planning to put into the public realm.'

'There was no time. Gary wants to see the rewrite at Hank's this morning and, if he approves, give it to the cast later today for a read-through tomorrow.'

'How radical is the rewrite?'

'I took out virtually everything you objected to, the Sheena character, the lesbian relationship, the Collingwood character.'

'Oh, Steve, I'm sorry. I should have kept my mouth shut.'

'No, you were right. I got carried away by Gary's vision of the play. But it would have been my name on it and I would have felt like a shit.'

'But I know what you're like, you've probably reduced it to something completely abstract. Would you let me read the overnight version?'

'No, I'm sorry. I'm not even sure I've got the courage to show what's left to Gary. He's going to be hugely pissed off. Frankly, I'm terrified. My confidence has completely evaporated.'

Grace sat down on the edge of the bed and took Steve's hand. 'Steve, look at me. You'll be fine. You're the guy who ran documents into East Berlin.'

She leaned over and kissed him on the cheek. 'Gary's a sweetheart, really. Have a shower and get yourself down to Hank's.'

While he was in the shower, Grace speed-read the new version and was relieved to see that Steve had made the play a much less obvious account of recent events in Berlin. In particular, it presented Jena, the character based on Müller, as a much less complex character than Grace actually thought he was, a suspicion that thus far she had kept to herself.

An hour later, Steve pushed open the door of the café and stepped into the warm, welcoming fug of Hank's. Gary was already there, tucking into a fry-up. He waved Steve over. 'What do you want?'

Steve glanced at the menu and said, 'Scrambled eggs on toast.'

'Coffee?'

'Please.'

Gary gave the order to the waitress and then said, 'Did you manage to do the new scenes? If you have, let me read them while you're eating. Don't say anything. Don't try to defend it or excuse it. Just let me take it in.'

Steve fished the new draft out of his bag and slid it nervously across the table to Gary who, pushing his now empty plate to one side, started to read. This felt much worse than any supervision Steve had ever submitted to and he was pleased when the waitress arrived with his breakfast. Gary was still reading methodically through the script by the time Steve had finished his scrambled eggs on toast. But at least he felt a bit more human now. He pushed his chair back and, casting a furtive glance at Gary, indicated to the waitress that he'd like a refill of coffee.

As the waitress filled Steve's cup, she nodded towards Gary and said, 'Late with your homework, love?'

Steve laughed, 'Yeah, that's about the strength of it. I had to pull an all-nighter to get this done. I think I'm going to get detention.'

The waitress giggled girlishly and took the coffee pot back to the counter. Steve let his gaze drift around the room. He just wanted this to be over. Then he could go back home and get some sleep. It had been a mistake to submit *Fault* to the new writing competition and an even greater mistake to mention *Palace of Tears* to Gary. He sat there, squirming at the thought of what must be going through Gary's mind.

Eventually, Gary finished reading the typescript. He put the pages together and, steepling his fingers, said, 'Okay.'

Steve watched him silently. Not just a *beta-minus*, but a full-on *gamma*, it would seem.

Gary was now rubbing his chin. 'Yes, I think it works. I'm impressed that you threw out most of my ideas, but pleased that you kept the most important one. Inge, or Freya as she is now called, is a fully three-dimensional character. Becky will have something to work with. The whole play is also better without the codenames. Congratulations.'

Steve wasn't sure he'd heard correctly. 'You're going to do it?'

'Of course. I can see you have poured every last ounce of your being into this. Now you need some sleep. Go home and sleep all day if you need to. I'll take your typescript and get copies made for the cast. We'll meet tomorrow, ten-thirty at the theatre. I'll introduce you. You'll know some of them, by name at least, from the auditions we did in London. Then it's over to you, I'm afraid. I'll throw the meeting open so they can ask you questions about their respective parts and the context of the play. It should be fun.'

Steve felt that *terrifying* might be a more accurate word.

## Wednesday, 16 April 1975

STEVE WAS FEELING NERVOUS. What would a group of professional actors think of his script? He had arrived early in the hope of a word with Gary before the meeting started. But of Gary, there was no sign. Steve considered waiting in Gary's cubbyhole, but on reflection, thought it might be considered an act of *lèse-majesté*. So he walked through to the backstage area and looked into the prop room to find Butch having his breakfast.

'Hello, petal. You've come to see Uncle Butch?'

'It's always lovely to see you, Butch, but I was looking for the guv'nor.'

'He'll be in shortly. He had to go and see the bank manager. They're being difficult about the cash flow situation.'

'Oh, dear. Is it a serious problem?'

'Nothing that full houses to see your play won't sort out.'

'Butch, I don't like to think that the survival of the Festival Theatre is dependent on my play.'

'Gaz wouldn't be putting it on if he didn't think that it was going to get the punters in.'

'Honestly, I had no idea that there was a financial dimension to the play.'

'Petal, there's a financial dimension to everything. Anyway, stop hovering. Sit down and have a mug of coffee.'

Steve did as he was told. When Butch had poured the coffee, he said, 'I was sorry to hear about your mum. It just doesn't seem fair.'

'Thanks. I'm still in a state of denial.'

'She'd be so proud of you having your first play put on and directed by Gary Lewis.'

'I'm not so sure. Yes, she'd be impressed that Gary was directing it, but I think if she knew what the play was about, she'd disown me.'

'But I thought Gaz said she'd inspired it?'

'Yes, in the sense that I was in Berlin, she was in a coma and I had a lot of time on my hands. But I'm pretty sure she would have disapproved of the subject matter and the treatment.'

'Well, of course, I didn't know her. I do know, though, that Grace thought highly of her. And talking of Grace, how are you two getting on?'

Now was not the time to go into the difficulties they seemed to be having since they'd got back from Germany. 'Grace is amazing. I can't believe how lucky I am.'

'I gather that she's chosen you to be the father of her child.'

Steve was surprised. 'Who told you that?'

'Gaz, of course. I thought it was common knowledge.'

'Well, it's not a secret, but with one thing and another, I'd rather lost track of who knew and who didn't. Also, to be quite honest, we're not having a lot of luck in that department at the moment.'

'Does that mean you're not putting in the spadework?'

'I bang away on request. I'm not complaining. I've never had so much sex, but it is getting to be a bit of a chore.'

'Should you be telling me this?'

'You're the only person I have no secrets from.'

'I'm not sure that's wise, Steve. Not that I'd ever betray you or stitch you up on purpose. Nor am I the right person to give you tips on how to spice up your sex life. Refined ladies like Grace are not my speciality.'

Steve laughed. 'I'm sure anyone would love to be in bed with you, Butch.'

'Careful, petal, you might find yourself in a situation you can't handle with talk like that.'

'You know what I mean.'

'I'm sorry to say I do, but that's life isn't it? But if you want a tip, forget that you're trying to give her a baby. Just make her feel like the most loved person in the world. That means until you've succeeded in impregnating her, don't go sneaking around other back stairs.'

'Okay, duly noted. One further thing before the meeting starts, what can you tell me about the company? Is there anyone I need to look out for?'

'Nice enough bunch, on the whole. A couple of them are a bit wet behind the ears. Sally and David are troupers. They will do a great job for you. I've been impressed by John, a new face to me. That little Becky is a bundle of energy. She could be good if she learns to channel her energy. The only one you might need to look out for is Larry. He's the big name and expects to be treated as such, but his star is waning. All the same, there'll be a section of the audience who'll come in just because his name is on the playbill.'

'Thanks, Butch, that's useful. The person here who's wettest behind the ears is me. I don't need to tell you I'm pretty terrified of this meeting.'

'Don't be, Gaz'll look after you.'

Butch looked up at the clock on the wall. 'Anyway, you'd better get out there. Meeting's about to start. Let's grab a drink together soon. I want to hear more about Berlin.'

Steve went round to the rehearsal room to find it was still empty. After a few minutes Gary entered the room. 'Morning, Steve. How are you feeling?'

'Okay, so far. I've just had a coffee with Butch. He's been calming my nerves.'

'It'll be fine. It's your play. Just tell the actors how you see it.'

Gary took a seat and opened a folder. Clearly, he had more important things to attend to than settle Steve's nerves while they waited for the cast to arrive.

When, at last, everyone was seated, Gary called the meeting to order. 'Good morning, everyone. Thanks for being on time, near enough. We've got a lot to get through. I've called this meeting to introduce Steve Percival, the writer of *Palace of Tears*. This is your chance to ask him any questions you have about your part or the context of the play. So I hope you've all read the script.'

Gary introduced each actor in turn to Steve. A couple of the younger faces were familiar to him from the auditions in London, and he recognised the one Butch had called Larry from the television. Introductions completed, Gary said, 'Right, who'd like to go first?'

There were a few moments of shifting in chairs and throat clearing until a middle-aged man with greying temples said, 'Hi, Steve, I'm David and I'm playing Siegfried. Could you give me some idea of Siegfried's background and motivation? In my reading of your play, which is a great piece of work, by the way, he has turned against the regime. But presumably he has condoned it for many years; otherwise he wouldn't be a professor?'

Realising that he was about to talk for probably the first time in his life about something on which he was the undisputed authority, but grateful that it was one of the actors Butch had called a trouper, Steve said, 'Thank you, David. That is a very good question. Being an intellectual in the world's most surveilled society is not easy. When I was developing the play I sketched out Siegfried's backstory. During the war, he had been an anti-Nazi and an anti-communist activist. After the cessation of hostilities, he returned to his studies and became active in the SPD, the German equivalent of the Labour Party. In the first post-war elections for the Berlin city council, he was elected as the representative for the Pankow area, which is now a borough of East Berlin. But after the Berlin Airlift of 1948, he realised that democratic politics in East Berlin were no longer possible and stood down to concentrate on his academic work. So, yes, he turned a blind eye to the developing situation in East Germany. But his real weakness is that he has an eye for the ladies.'

Gary took over. 'Thank you, David, for getting the ball rolling with a typically thoughtful question. I would like to add a few points about surveillance. After Steve and I had finished working on the script yesterday, I had a meeting with Richard Croft who is designing the show and Tony Buttermere, who will be lighting it. The action of the play alternates between East and West Berlin. However, because of our limited resources and the fact that we don't have a house curtain here, we are constrained to a single set. Richard has asked Tony to light the West Berlin scenes in warm, bright tones, and the East Berlin scenes with pools of yellowish light and areas of shadow towards the wings and upstage. Richard is also going to construct a platform on either side of the stage. This will mainly affect Reg, Bill and Harry, who play the Stasi officers and the Stasi informant.'

A rather eager looking young man raised his hand, 'Since we are touching on the Stasi parts, could I quickly ask whether you want us to use German accents or to play the parts straight?'

'Thank you, John. Good point. Straight, please. You could use English class or regional distinctions, but no *Ve haff vays of making you talk* stuff.'

'*Jawohl, mein Herr!*'

Everyone laughed. John was clearly a live wire. Presumably, every company of actors was required to have a resident joker on hand.

Gary waited until the group had settled down before continuing. 'So when the trio just mentioned are not actually listed as being in an East Berlin scene, they will be on the platforms, wearing headphones and wielding binoculars to give the impression that surveillance is constant.'

But if John was a joker, he was a thoughtful one. 'Not the West Berlin scenes, though?'

Gary clearly hadn't considered that aspect of the presentation. 'Well, that's a good point. Perhaps Steve will know from his research how far the tentacles of the Stasi reach. It is clear from the script that Siegfried's defection is an attempt to set up a network of agents in the British university system. If they can do that, then operating in West Berlin must be considerably easier.'

He turned to Steve for his view. Steve had really done no research, but he didn't want to undermine what little confidence the company might have in him.

'The East German state definitely has a foreign intelligence service, but unlike here in Britain where MI5 and MI6 are independent entities, it is ostensibly a department of the Stasi. The word Stasi is an abbreviation for *Ministerium für Staatssicherheit*, which translates directly as Ministry for State Security. The foreign intelligence department of the Stasi is known as the HVA, which is an acronym for *Hauptverwaltung Aufklärung*, a rather opaque term, which translates less directly as the Main Directorate for Reconnaissance.'

Gary interrupted. 'Thank you, Steve. I think we'll just stick to the term Stasi.'

'Of course. I just wanted to confirm to John that the East German security apparatus definitely has the means to conduct operations in the West, including in the UK. They are certainly capable of compromising vulnerable individuals. Whether they are capable of tapping phones or bugging apartments in West Germany is another matter. But in West Berlin, it certainly pays to be circumspect.'

Gary nodded. 'Okay, so it looks as if we should show that there is a level of surveillance for the West Berlin scenes too.'

John had one further point. 'I play the Stasi colonel. Are the Stasi uniformed officers?'

Having only personally dealt with the border police, Steve wasn't sure. 'The Stasi has a military structure, but agents and informants, especially those outside the jurisdiction, would be in civilian clothes. I did, however, envisage the Stasi characters in the play as being in uniform.'

Gary said, 'We'll discuss that with Richard Croft, but that seems to make sense.'

Steve was surprised that Gary had cast John as the Stasi colonel. He was much younger than Steve had imagined the character. But then, Gary's options must be rather limited if he was hoping to draw only on the actors who were already members of the company.

Becky, whom Steve recognised from the auditions, put her hand up and said, 'I'm playing Freya. Could you tell me something about her motivation?'

Steve flashed Becky a shy smile. 'I'm afraid you've caught me out there. Freya started off as a small part, just an intermediary, but somehow the character took over and demanded a bigger role. With Gary's help, I turned her into the most complex character in the play. At the start of the play, she seems to be using her sexuality to obtain better grades from Siegfried. But when she encounters Tristan, it looks at first as if we are now observing the flowering of a love affair between two young people manoeuvred into working informally for their respective spy organisations. They talk to each other about whether there is a way that she can get to the West. She goes with Tristan to the Friedrichstraße U-Bahn station, the so-called Palace of Tears, where we observe a tender farewell between her and Tristan. But in the next scene, we see a very similar farewell played out between Siegfried and Freya. It's not entirely clear which man she is lying to. For the purposes of the play, I think it's important that this is undecidable. Both readings should be possible. Nor should this uncertainty be resolved when, towards the end of the play, she is arrested by the Stasi and led off to what will be the start of a long prison sentence.'

Gary intervened. 'It's good for us to understand that the Palace of Tears is also a hall of mirrors. No one is quite what he or she seems to be.'

There was a murmur of assent from the cast. Once it had subsided, Gary continued. 'Larry, have you got anything to ask about Tristan's motivation?'

Larry might be a fading TV actor so far as Butch was concerned, but his reaction to Gary's question seemed to suggest that it was beneath his dignity to have to ask questions about his part. 'I have to say I'm a bit puzzled by Tristan. All the other characters, for good or ill, have an overt or covert goal. But Tristan seems to allow others to set his agenda for him. In particular he seems to take a passive role. It seems improbable to me that someone like that would be selected for what is potentially a dangerous operation.'

Gary's crinkled brow suggested he was wryly amused by Larry's stance. 'Oka-ay. Steve, can you help Larry here?'

Steve got the feeling that the last person Larry wanted any help from was the very inexperienced author of the play. Steve's first impulse was to challenge Larry's view. But on second thoughts, he realised that it would probably be better to let Larry run with that particular interpretation.

Steve took a deep breath and said, 'I hope all the characters are susceptible to multiple interpretations and maybe Tristan is more resourceful than he looks. But your interpretation has considerable merit, Larry. Tristan definitely presents as an innocent abroad, someone who doesn't really understand other people, particularly women.'

With a scarcely concealed smirk on his face, Larry said, 'Tristan's a drip. Why write the part that way?'

Steve was at a loss to know how to respond to this challenge to his authorial competence. He looked over at Gary, who, as inscrutable as ever, showed no signs of coming to his aid. He was aware that everyone was looking at him expectantly, but his mind was a blank. Suddenly, the awkward silence that had developed was broken by Becky saying, 'I don't see Tristan like that at all. He's a new man, sensitive to women. He is careful not to take advantage of the charade of intimacy with Freya that he and she are playing out, by letting her set the limits. He does not touch her breasts until she asks him to. I think the reserve he displays makes that a sexy scene rather than a bit of crude groping.'

Steve noticed that Becky was blushing. He thought he might be too. Grateful to her for her intervention, he said, 'Thank you, Becky. That is also a valid interpretation. I think we can see his reserve as a strength.'

Steve looked over at Gary again and noticed that he was now chuckling. 'Thank you, Becky and Larry. You've touched on an important issue here, which we need to sort out. I wonder, Sally, if you have any thoughts along the same lines for Gertrude, since you have one rather intimate scene with Siegfried. The stage directions in the first scene ask for some moments of nudity for your character. How do you feel about that?'

'To be frank, I've had my tits out on stage more times than I care to remember. I don't say it gets any easier. David and I have worked together quite a lot and I know I can trust him to be proper. I must say I question whether it's absolutely necessary. Steve does seem rather keen on unveiling the female body on stage.'

Gary turned to Steve and said, 'What have you got to say to that, Steve?'

Given that Gary had encouraged him in that direction, Steve assumed that he would also defend the policy. But he remained silent, staring up at the back of the auditorium. Irritated, Steve's first impulse was to agree that the nudity wasn't necessary, but even as the words formed in his mind, he realised that to cave into the pressure would be to lose control of his own play. Suddenly, he was angry.

'Sally, when I was writing the play, I was trying to be honest to the characters. I had no particular actors in mind for the parts. Indeed, as the play went through successive drafts, some characters dropped out and the relationships between the remaining characters became more tightly focused. I think, to answer the previous point first, it's wrong to see Tristan as lacking a clearly defined goal. All the other characters are already fully chipped-in players in the Cold War game of poker. Tristan is the new kid in town and has to find a way of navigating this new world. That is a time-honoured method of setting up a dramatic situation, and, of course, the town in question is Berlin, a divided city. Going from West Berlin to East Berlin is like going through the looking-glass. So many of the things that happen in the West are mirrored in a darker key in the East. But the darkness leaks back into the West, or perhaps was there all along.

'We are familiar with the idea that sex is commodified, but it is also weaponised, particularly in the contested space of Berlin. On a small stage we can only imply the actual weapons of mass destruction ranged on either side of the superpower rivalry, which is also a cultural rivalry between democratic capitalism and autocratic communism. But culture is not monolithic; it is multi-stranded. Each strand, whether it be sport, art, or fashion, is in effect a proxy for the overarching rivalry. Sex, too, has a cultural dimension. It seemed to me that portraying weaponised sexual relations on stage was the most potent way of communicating that idea to the audience.

'Yes, nudity on stage is still shocking, even in 1975. So is the explicit depiction of sexual relations. I am not an actor myself, and I can only marvel at how brave you all are. However, I do understand your reservations about that scene. If you feel uncomfortable with the scene the way I have written it, then I will drop the stage direction indicating that Gertrude crosses the stage naked. But in that case I will also drop the matching scene in East Germany between Tristan and Freya.'

Steve fell silent and looked around the room. He might be fully clothed himself, but, at that moment, he had never felt so exposed. His justification of onstage female nudity by appealing to super-power rivalry was incoherent and deserved to be derided. Aware that he was trembling, he awaited the inevitable chorus of outrage and disbelief. But suddenly the room was full of laughter. There were even a few cheers.

Sally stepped towards him, embraced him and then kissed him on the cheek. 'I'm sorry,' she breathed in his ear. But almost imme-diately, she was displaced by Larry who, not to be outdone it seemed, offered his hand to Steve. But as Steve offered his own hand, Larry fumbled the grip, leaned into him and, just before he stepped away, said between clenched teeth, 'Pretentious cunt.'

The smile which had greeted the actors' laughter now froze on Steve's face. It was clear that his attempt to appease the company's box office draw had completely backfired. But as he watched Larry returning to his place at the back of the room, he realised that he was being embraced again, this time by Becky. 'That was amazing,' she said breathlessly.

One by one, the actors resumed their seats and when everyone was seated, Gary, who had remained in his own seat throughout this outburst of emotion, said, 'Thank you, Steve, that was a very inspiring defence of artistic integrity. Clearly, we will have to take extreme care with both those scenes. But for the moment we will leave the stage directions as they are in your script.'

John said, 'Are we going to read through now?'

Gary was already standing up. 'No, I think we have done enough here today and some of you have a performance this evening. We'll start the read-through tomorrow. Ten-thirty, please. Steve, is that okay for you?'

Steve nodded, still smarting from Larry's verbal assault.

Some minutes later, Steve, in a daze and reflecting on Larry's animosity, was walking back down Newmarket Road in the direc-tion of the Four Lamps roundabout when he heard footsteps behind him, and a moment later, Becky drew level. 'Steve, I just wanted to say privately that I thought you handled the meeting very well. Your script is brilliant and I'm very excited to be cast as

Freya. It's a great part for me. I've only had small parts so far. This is something I can really work on. Have you got time to talk about it over a cup of tea?'

Steve had nothing planned for the rest of the day other than pulling something together for supper. He looked at his watch. The pubs were just opening. 'Actually, I could do with a proper drink. The Champion of the Thames is just around the corner in King Street.'

Becky nodded enthusiastically. 'Even better.'

Over their drinks in the pub, Becky said, 'I hope you don't mind me hijacking you like this. You must be fed up with a bunch of actors trying to *improve* your play.'

'No, not at all. You all know much more than me about what works and what doesn't on a stage. I'm a complete novice.'

'It doesn't seem like it to me.'

'Well, it's very kind of you to say so, but actually I was terrified.'

'I thought you looked thoughtful and self-possessed.'

'In that case I must be a better actor than I think I am.'

'The way you dealt with Larry and Sally was brilliant. They do like to try and run a show.'

Steve thought it better to keep Larry's jibe to himself. 'They were very charming to me at the end of the discussion.'

'They had to be, but if I know those two, they're actually furious that you got the better of them.'

'Honestly, I wasn't trying to get the better of them. I was just trying to explain how I thought the play worked. Well, maybe I was trying to establish myself against Larry.'

'You were right to. He is a devious person.'

Was it possible that Becky's motives in asking to have a private chat with him might not be entirely innocent? Still very much on his guard, he said, 'But I thought Sally's concerns were entirely justified. I don't think I'd feel very comfortable taking my clothes off on stage.'

'Oh, you'd get used to it.'

'I doubt it. I used to sit as a life model for a girlfriend, and that was bad enough, even though she'd already seen me plenty of times with my clothes off.'

'So you stopped sitting for her?'

'Yeah, but not because of my disquiet. We broke up.'

'Oh, I'm sorry. Was the break-up painful?'

'It was, as a matter of fact, but I'd rather not talk about it.'

'I'm sorry to be so intrusive. It's just that you write very well about relationships.'

'Becky, it's lovely of you to say that, but could we confine our discussion to the play?'

'Yes, I'm sorry. Can I ask you some questions about Freya?'

'Of course.'

'Did she seduce Siegfried or was it the other way around?'

'Siegfried exercises a kind of *droit de seigneur* over female students; a phenomenon that is not unknown in our own educational system. Despite this, it does appear that Freya is actually in love with him, at least at the beginning of the action.'

'So, having sex with Tristan is something she's doing to please Siegfried – not in a creepy way, but to help him escape?'

'Yes, she's sacrificing herself. Or the possibility of having an ongoing physical relationship with him.'

'Has she already had sex with Siegfried?'

'Well, that's an interesting point. We are not shown that, but I think it is implied.'

'It all seems a bit unnecessary. They're already taking a risk, so why not just hand the documents over without more ado?'

'Effectively everyone in East Germany is being monitored or observed. It's easier to deceive the Stasi if you confirm their pre-suppositions. The idea is that Freya is seen to be committing a lesser crime than the one she's actually committing.'

'But Freya is arrested.'

'That was always the likely outcome, but at least she is arrested for being a freelance sex-worker, not for helping a British agent escape.'

'Siegfried isn't British.'

'An agent is anyone who works informally for an intelligence agency; whereas a salaried member of an intelligence agency is an officer. Confusingly, in general parlance, both are considered to be spies.'

'I hadn't realised that.'

'So the play is about betrayal?'

'That's certainly an element, but what I was really thinking about was the existential horror of not being able to trust anyone and the risk of giving your heart to someone in that context.'

'That's why the scene in the Palace of Tears when Tristan is leaving to return to the West is so emotional. Are Freya's tears real?'

'Are your tears real when you weep on stage?'

'The tears are real, but I'm acting.'

'Okay, but don't you have to summon up some sadness in your-self to get the tear ducts to open?'

'Yes. Not everyone can do it. But it's easier if the part is well-written.'

'So, it's the same for Freya. In a sense she is an actor, but she also feels sadness because the connection between her and Tristan has maybe awakened something in her.'

'That it's Tristan she really loves, not Siegfried?'

'What do you think? And while you're thinking about that, let me ask you a couple of questions. Do you really think the nude scenes are justified or would you rather not have to do your scene with Tristan in that way?'

'Honestly, it doesn't bother me at all. That's not because I've got a great body. I've got all the insecurities most of us have. Bum too big, tits not big enough. Worrying about whether I'll be on my period the week of the performances. But you know, once I'm on stage, I'm concentrating so hard I forget all those things.'

'So you're fine with the scene?'

'Well, since you ask, I wish Larry wasn't playing Tristan.'

'Why?'

'He's a creep.'

'Really? In what way?'

'He's one of those actors who like to unsettle you, throwing in an ad lib, not hitting his mark, making a joke in the wings, as you're waiting to go on. The worst thing in a bedroom scene is that he'll probably be doing a surreptitious bit of groping.'

'Oh that's appalling. Why is it tolerated?'

'Well, he's been on TV quite a lot. He was in *Colditz*. But he's not getting that kind of work anymore.'

'I thought it was Sally who had the reservations?'

'She was standing up for me. She has no problems with David. He is a complete gentleman.'

'Yes, he does come across as such. I must say Larry is rather older for the part than I would prefer. It seems a strange choice by Gary. I suppose in a small company the options are limited.'

'John could do it.'

'He was the one cracking all the jokes?'

'Yeah. John *is* a joker, but he behaves when he's working. Actually, I think he'd be perfect for the part.'

'He's not your boyfriend, is he?'

'No, I wish he was, but he's gay.'

'Becky, you're not leading me up the garden path here, are you?'

'No, I promise. I didn't expect the conversation to get around to the suitability of actors.'

'I'm not sure I can do anything about it. But, whatever happens, I'd rather you kept this conversation to yourself.'

'Of course, I hope you don't think badly of me.'

'No, not at all. But I'm a bit out of my depth in such matters. To be quite honest, not only am I beholden to Gary, but I also find him rather intimidating.'

'He scares everyone. You don't get to be a director of his standing without being a tough nut.'

'I suppose so.'

As he was getting the supper ready later that evening, Steve was starting to regret having been so indiscreet with Becky. Had she been setting him up? Was she a trouble-maker? But the conversation had at least enabled him to reflect on the kerfuffle that had blown up in the meeting with the actors. Whether it was what Becky had intended or not, Steve was quite sure now that he distrusted Larry.

He was musing thus and slicing courgettes, when he heard Grace's key in the lock. A few moments later she entered the big kitchen, slumped down on a chair and kicked off her shoes. Steve dried his hands and went over and kissed her. 'Tea or wine?'

'Wine, please. And since I am still not pregnant yet, a full glass of Claret, none of your half measures.'

Steve poured two glasses and handed the fuller one to Grace. 'How was your day?'

'Knackering. Faculty meetings are enough to make one scream. But I don't want to talk about that. How did the session with the actors go?'

'It started well enough. They asked intelligent questions, which I was able to answer. It was good to get an idea of the extent to which a particular personality fitted my mental image of each character. The chap who's playing Tristan, for example, is much too old for the part.'

'Older actors can play younger roles. Look at Ian Lavender in *Dad's Army*.'

'I suppose so, but he was also the only one to be critical of his character. I mean, what's he want me to do? Rewrite it for him?'

'What's the actor's name?'

'Larry Saunders.'

'Well, no wonder. He's a big name on TV. People will come to the show, just to see him.'

'I'd rather they didn't in that case. I get the feeling that he will sabotage the whole thing.'

'Did you raise your concerns with Gary?'

'No, he had other things to do.'

'Will you?'

'Maybe.'

'Well, then, stop fretting about it. But the rest of the meeting went okay.'

'Yes, and no.'

'What's that mean?'

'I was asked to justify the scenes involving some nudity.'

'How did you respond to that?'

'I just talked a load of cobblers about going from West Berlin to East Berlin being a bit like going through the looking glass, the same city but everything different and then that led on to remarks about superpower rivalry and culture being a contested site in which sex is weaponised and a load of other tosh.'

'They cheered you to the rafters, no doubt?'

'Well, there were some murmurs of approval.'

'So what's the problem? Apart from the fact that the postgraduate programme in this university is really missing a bullshitter of your calibre, Steve.'

'I think the discussion about nudity was a proxy for a discussion about something else. I'm not sure what, but there's something going on between the actors.'

'If that's what you think, you need to raise it with Gary.'

'I'm afraid he'll tell me to butt out.'

'If he does, he does. Put it out of your mind for now and let's have a nice evening together.'

'Thanks, Grace. You're always so sensible.'

'It may seem like it to you, but I'm not so sure that's the case.'

The next day the cast read through the whole play for Gary and Steve, both of whom were making notes. By twelve-thirty they had got to the end and Gary let everyone go, only asking Steve to join him for a drink to discuss the session. He suggested that they avoid the Zebra, the regular resort for crew and cast members. So for the second day running, Steve found himself in the Champion of the Thames for the purposes of discussing his play.

Gary brought the beers over to the table and sat down. 'Sorry, I had to leave so promptly at the end of yesterday's session. I'm having the devil of a time with the bank.'

Steve took a sip of his beer. 'Butch said that there were cash flow problems.'

'Yeah, but I think I've plugged the gap for now. One of our backers has agreed to guarantee the overdraft.'

'Wow! That's a relief.'

'It doesn't mean we're entirely out of the woods, but it buys us some time. But I'm afraid it still means that I can't pay you anything.'

'That's okay. The person who's the executor of my mother's will has been able to let me have some money pending probate.'

'I hope you're not talking about large sums because, if you are, you might find me asking you to be a backer as well as a playwright.'

'I'm afraid it's only £500, but I can make that go a long way with Grace's help.'

'So how are you two getting on?'

'She's been amazing. I don't know how I would have got through the last six or seven weeks without her.'

'She says she's trying to have a child with you.'

'Yes, I feel a bit awkward talking about it. I know how special she is to you.'

'But not so special that I would have felt happy about being the father of her child, which I believe she was considering at one point. But it does entitle me to wonder whether you know what you're getting into. It's quite a responsibility you're taking on.'

'I wish I could say that I did know what I was getting into, but the truth is I don't. In some ways, the fact that she says that she doesn't want me to commit indefinitely doesn't actually make it easier. At the moment, especially since I seem unable to hit the target, as it were, it just seems like a daydream.'

'If you want the relationship to work, you need to stop feeling like that. But let's move on to today's read-through. How did it feel hearing professional actors reading your words?'

'To be honest, it was a sobering experience. I thought it was a bit of a car crash. The actors were, on the whole, great. The problem was with the writing. Some of the lines were real clunkers, stilted and difficult to get your tongue around. And there were several speeches which were far too long, lectures rather than part of an exchange. I've marked my copy of the script at those points and I'll try and fix them tonight.'

Gary took his own copy of the script out of his bag and handed it to Steve. 'I agree. I've marked lines on my own script that need fixing.'

Steve glanced at the first few pages of Gary's copy and said, 'Looks like there's not much of an overlap between us.'

'You're the author. Just because I've marked a passage, it doesn't mean you have to change it. The writing is your prerogative. But I wouldn't have said that the lines that need fixing amount to a car crash.'

Nor did Steve. He was using the discussion about textual emend-ations as a way of tiptoeing towards what he really wanted to say.

Taking a deep breath, he said, 'I think there's also a problem with the casting.'

Gary raised his chin combatively. 'But now you're straying into the area of my prerogative.'

'Yes, I know. So, I raise the matter with considerable trepidation.'

'As well you might. But go on.' The tone was curt, but was it possible that there was a hint of a smile playing around Gary's lips or was that a sneer?

'I don't think John is right for the part of the Stasi colonel. He speaks the lines well. He's got a good voice, but he looks wrong.'

'It's the theatre, Steve. We have makeup and lighting. John knows how to act like an older man. He's a good actor, and I'd like to make full use of his talents. I know you don't know the full com-pany, but who would you cast in his stead?'

'Larry.'

'Larry! He'd never accept that part.'

'But surely you decide who plays which part.'

'Of course, but Larry's the only *name* we've got in the cast. On the other hand, you are an unknown playwright. So we need something to bring the punters in.'

'I didn't think that Larry read the part of Tristan with any enthusiasm at all. He made the relationship with Freya seem completely unconvincing.'

'In that particular I agree. But I see no solution. What do you suggest?'

'He is better suited to the part of the Stasi colonel, and John could play Tristan. Just in terms of types, it's better that way around.'

'But Larry would jib at the lesser part.'

'I can expand it. In an earlier draft, I did actually write two scenes which prominently featured the Stasi colonel, but dropped them from the draft you saw. I could reinstate them.'

'I'm not sure. You probably dropped them for a good reason.'

'Because at that stage, I didn't see it as a stand-alone play. I thought it might be part of the new writing festival. But even with a bit of stage business and scene changes, I think the current version of the play runs too short.'

'That is a concern. So what do you have in mind?'

'I will make the textual changes we identified between us, and I will reinsert the dropped scenes with the Stasi colonel.'

'How long is that going to take you?'

'I'll have it ready for breakfast at Hank's tomorrow morning.'

'Are you serious?'

'Yes, I'll work all night. We can present it to the company, but really to Larry, as something that has been written to showcase his talents.'

'Okay, but I'm not promising to go with the new version until I've read it. If you can deliver the goods, we'll get it to the copy shop by nine and pay their rush rates to have the new scripts back for the ten-thirty read-through.'

Steve stood up. 'Okay, I'd better get on with it.'

Gary looked up at him. '*Bon courage, mon brave!*'

## Thursday, 17 April 1975

As STEVE SAT WITH Gary the next morning in Hank's, he could hardly keep his eyes open. Gary called the waitress over and said, 'A very strong black coffee and scrambled eggs on brown toast for my young friend here. The usual for me.'

While the waitress attended to their breakfast orders, Gary said, 'Did you get any sleep at all?'

Steve nodded. 'Yeah, from six to eight. Although it might have been better if I'd just powered through. But I wasn't sure I'd have enough energy to get through the day if I didn't have at least a couple of hours.'

'Well, you don't have to worry about that. After our drink last night, I phoned around the company and postponed the meeting. I thought it better to deal with Larry on a one-to-one basis without the rest of the company present. So I'm going to meet him for lunch.'

'Does that mean that you don't want me to join you?'

'Yes, if you don't mind. It means I can present the situation as one in which I've leaned on you to improve the script and write a better part for him. I know that's not the case and really it's your idea. But I hope you'll trust me on this as the way to get a better outcome.'

Steve was only too happy to agree to Gary's proposal. The last thing he wanted was a tussle with Larry. 'What if he says no?'

'Well, in the end it's my decision, but it would be better if he were on board with it. Sometimes it's harder to deal with fading stars than with the real A-listers. That means you can go home now and get some sleep. If he buys into the deal, then we can resume the read-through tomorrow with the cast changes and present it as an accommodation we're making for him.'

337

'What about John?'

'He'll be delighted.'

'And Becky?'

'I think she'll be delighted not to have to do a bed scene with Larry. He has a bit of a reputation. Not that she's raised any objections. This part is a big opportunity for her. But let's not get ahead of ourselves. Have your breakfast and I'll look at the new scenes while you're eating.'

It didn't take Gary long to decide that the expanded role for the Stasi colonel gave him just enough leverage to persuade Larry to see the recasting as a perquisite of his star billing. As Gary and Steve walked down Newmarket Road to the Festival, he said, 'Well done. You are definitely king of the overnight rewrites. I'll phone you this evening to let you know how it went.'

The call, when it came, was something of an anticlimax. Gary said that Larry had taken the bait and accepted the cast change with lordly complaisance. Gary had then spoken to John, who had been very excited to take on the Tristan role. He had then let the rest of the cast know about the changes. Becky, in particular, had been enthusiastic about the change and asked Gary to thank Steve.

Grace had been aware that Steve had pulled another all-nighter but, not realising that the company read-through had been postponed, she was surprised to find Steve cooking in the kitchen when she got home. He explained what had happened. As she sipped her wine, she said, 'You and Gary make a good team.'

'If by that you mean when he says *jump*, I say *how high?*, then yes, we do.'

'There's more to it than that. I don't suppose you ever worked all night on an essay for me.'

'True.'

'But what made you think that this John chap would be good for the Tristan part?'

Steve judged it better not to mention the true sequence of events. 'I had a chat with Butch and he thinks highly of him.'

'For other reasons, I imagine.'

'Possibly, but Butch is determined to make the Festival Theatre season a success, and he's a theatre person through and through. Anyway, the key to it was getting Larry to agree. So, I expanded the Stasi colonel part. I think he's probably now got the most lines of any of the characters. I think that's all he cares about. According to Gaz, Becky is delighted because Larry has a bit of a reputation for having wandering hands.'

'Oh, how horrible to have to work with someone like that.'

'Yeah.'

'So you call your boss Gaz now?'

'Well, not to his face. Not yet. But we're getting there.'

'Let me know when you're admitted to the inner sanctum. We'll open a bottle of champagne. Even I am not allowed to call him that.'

'You're kidding?'

'It's a boy's thing. Anyway, we have other reasons to open a bottle of champagne. I've finally got the decree absolute.'

'The what?'

'Peter and I are now officially divorced. The house is mine and I'm free to get on with my life.'

Steve flinched slightly at the fact that the freedom pertained to her life and not their lives together. While the phrase did not preclude him, it did not actually include him. But no doubt he was being oversensitive. She had just reached for a stock expression.

'Congratulations. I didn't know things had advanced to that point. When you and I last spoke about it, you were still suspicious of why he was so keen to divorce.'

'Yes, but then I realised I was just being petty. Whatever his reasons, it's a relief to have the situation settled. I didn't keep you up to date because you had so many other things to deal with.'

Which was certainly the case.

# Friday, 18 April 1975

THE SECOND READ-THROUGH the next day proceeded without a hitch. There was scarcely any comment about the cast changes or the new scenes. Just before they broke for lunch, those members of the company not in the cast of *Palace* joined the meeting. Gary had requested a full company meeting to outline the schedule for the next few weeks. He announced that the plan was to have the first night of *Palace* on Saturday, the seventeenth of May. That gave them only a month to pull the whole thing together. However, the theatre would be dark for the week leading up to the first night, with the Wednesday allocated to the tech rehearsal, the Thursday to the first dress rehearsal, and the Friday to the full dress rehearsal. Gary was still considering whether to have a small invited audience for the full dress rehearsal to help focus everyone's minds.

Unfortunately, in the meantime, there was *Marat/Sade* and *A Resounding Tinkle* to get through, but at least those had been in the repertory for some time and required no more retooling. There was also the staging of the four short finalist plays of the new writing competition to be considered. These would be staged on Friday the ninth and Saturday the tenth. He realised this was a lot of extra work for four rather brief performances, but he was hoping it would bring in a different kind of audience. On the plus side, the theatre would be dark after the final performance of *A Resounding Tinkle* on Saturday, the third of May until the first of the two evenings of the new writing showcase. That would give cast and crew four days to tech and dress rehearse the four playlets. Fortunately, the only company member in both the playlets and *The Palace of Tears* was Becky, although her part in one of the playlets was minor.

Buoyed up by the success of the morning session on *Palace*, there was very little grumbling from the actors, and they headed off to their lunches in high spirits. One or two people, including John and Becky, headed up to Hank's, but the majority, including Steve and Gary, chose the Zebra. Larry, as befitted his standing as leading man in the company, invited himself to join Steve and Gary at their table, which Steve found irksome but Gary clearly felt was appropriate under the circumstances. Quite a lot of the conversation was devoted to anecdotes from Larry's days on the cast of *Colditz*, in which he played the part of a German officer. No doubt, the purpose of these reminiscences was to justify why he was better suited to the role of Stasi colonel rather than junior British spy.

Having wolfed down his portion of gala pie and drained his pint of IPA, Larry sloped off to the gents. When he was safely out of earshot, Gary said, 'That was his way of granting his imprimatur to the change of roles. I could see you squirming, but well done for going along with it.'

'I wasn't sure how many more David Macallum anecdotes I could take.'

When Larry came back from the gents, he paused by the table for a moment as if he were going to resume his seat, but then said, 'I've got to pick up a few things at the newsagent, but I'll be back for part two of the read-through at two. Just wanted to say, Steve, that the new material is really good and I appreciate the way you have responded to comments from the company. I really feel we have a hit on our hands here.'

With that he slipped out of the door in search of the nearest newsagent. Gary chuckled. 'Well, that was quite a lot more than an imprimatur, a full-on blessing I'd say.'

Steve felt that it still translated as *pretentious cunt*, but kept his thoughts to himself.

Once it seemed certain that Larry had really gone, Sally came over to their table and said, 'May I join you?'

Gary waved her into the seat that Larry had just vacated. 'I just wanted to say, without being disloyal to one's colleagues, that the play will work much better like this.'

Gary said, 'Thank you, Sal. I know that the original casting wasn't ideal, but I wasn't aware of the rejected material that Steve had in his locker which, I must say, fits Larry like a black leather glove.'

Sally laughed. 'Well, if the new scenes were rejected material, I think we'd better force Steve to reveal what else he has in his locker.'

Steve blushed. 'Thank you, Sally, but I can assure you that the cupboard is bare.'

'Don't believe him, Sal. He originally had a two-hander ready to put on the boards for the new writing festival. I would have cast you and probably Larry in that, even though it was another tits-out production, to use your terminology.'

'So, we're not going to do that one?'

'It didn't seem right to have a Steve Percival play in the new writing festival and a full-length play shortly thereafter. There might have been dark hints that Steve had the creative director wrapped around his little finger.'

Steve interjected, 'No one who actually knows how terrified I am of Gary would ever say that.'

Sally said, 'We're all terrified of him, love, even Larrikins. That's what makes him such a good director. But we're also all a little in awe of you, too. I think you're a lot tougher than you make out. I was so pleased when Becky told me that she'd had the guts to talk to you after the first read-through and put the case for the female side of the company.'

Steve was flattered by Sally's words, but wished she hadn't uttered them in front of Gary, who was looking at Steve out of the corner of his eye. 'I have to say I didn't realise that she was doing that. I was trying to say as little as possible. But she seemed very adept at worming all sorts of things out of me that might better have been kept secret.'

'Yes, she is a bit of an operator. I'm afraid the whole cast knows that you used to sit for a previous girlfriend as a life model and that you are now living with your former teacher.'

Steve put his hand to his forehead and groaned, 'Oh no.'

Sally patted his knee. 'Don't fret, love, we think all the more of you now. You're one of us. We've found our author, and speaking for myself, I'm delighted that you have a thing for older women.'

With that she rose from her chair and glided across to the knot of actors at the bar.

Gary burst out laughing. 'You can't trust actors, Steve. One day they love you, the next you're the devil. Still, it sounds like you did a bit of a number on me too. You seem to have thought that if you'd come to me and told me that Becky had sounded out the women and that no one wanted to do a bed scene with Larry, I would have sent you away with a flea in your ear. By focusing on John you found a better way of persuading me. Of course, it helped that you had the Stasi colonel scenes up your sleeve.'

Steve wasn't sure how genuine the laughter was. 'Are you annoyed with me?'

'No, I'm impressed. You made the right calls. The worry about the finances is clouding my judgement. We're doing the right thing. I'm very pleased to be working with you.'

'Thank you, Gary, I hope I can repay your trust in me.'

On his way home that evening, Steve dropped into the Elm Tree to reflect on the day. He ordered a pint and found a table near the piano that the tiny pub could hardly accommodate. The afternoon session of the read-through had gone even more swimmingly than the morning session. Everyone now seemed on board, to the extent that Gary said that they'd start to block things out on the stage the following Monday. In the meantime, since there were now going to be no further cast changes, he wanted everyone to get their parts by heart.

Steve was still somewhat irritated with Becky for having been so indiscreet, but maybe he was expecting too much. The world of the stage seemed to operate on opposite principles to those of the world of espionage, openness rather than secrecy, simulation rather than dissimulation. Of course, the polarities weren't exact, but so much the better, one might think. In some way that he didn't entirely understand, the indiscretions of Becky and Sally, far from having made Gary doubt Steve's judgement seemed only to have enhanced his standing with him.

So he had good reason to be grateful to Becky. In her forthrightness and readiness to act on her own initiative, she reminded him of Jude. How strange then, a moment later, to see Jude standing in front of him.

'Jude!'

'Yes, Jude, your publisher.'

'Well, I suppose you are. Can I get you a drink?'

'You most certainly can.'

A few minutes later, with a glass of white wine and a fresh pint of bitter on the table between them, Steve said, 'How are you? Are you back in Cambridge?'

'Well, unless you think you're seeing a ghost, then that must be the case.'

'I realise your corporeal being is here in front of me at this precise moment. What I meant was, are you now back living in Cambridge?'

'I am and have been for some time. Whereas you seem to have been absent.'

'Ah, well, I was abroad for the whole of March.'

'Grace too?'

'She was with me for a couple of weeks.'

'Somewhere nice?'

'Nice wouldn't be quite the way of putting it. Interesting, certainly. We were in Berlin. My mother was working out there. She was knocked over and was in a coma for several weeks before dying from her injuries. We had to arrange her cremation and sort her things out.'

Jude's carefully arranged pose of mock outrage shattered into a thousand tiny pieces. 'Oh, Steve, I'm so sorry. Please forgive me.'

'You weren't to know. Actually at the very moment you materialised in front of me, I was thinking of you.'

'Good thoughts, I hope.'

'Yes, good thoughts, as the rescuer and, as you point out, the publisher of my poem. I was speculating on why I always seem to be so determined to try and hide the radical doubt that informs my work.'

'Phew, that's more like the Steve I know. Were you being serious about your mother?'

'I was. I'd rather not go into details. It has been terrible. I don't know what I would have done without Grace.'

'She strikes me as a good sort.'

'That and more.'

'Presumably that has put the kibosh on the writing?'

'Quite the opposite.'

'A sequel to *Event/Horizon*?'

'No, a play – well, two plays actually. I submitted one to the Festival Theatre's new writing competition, but they decided they liked the play I didn't submit better. We've just been casting it and had a read-through of the final draft today. I came in here because I needed to recharge my batteries. It's weird when you see your creations embodied in real human beings, and even weirder when an actor tells you he or she understands your characters better than you do yourself.'

'Six characters in search of an author?'

'Yeah, Pirandello knew what he was about.'

'Can I see your play?'

'Tickets will be going on sale soon.'

'What's it called?'

'*Palace of Tears*.'

'Nice title. Not a comedy, I presume.'

'It has its lighter moments.'

'Can you summarise it?'

'According to some, it's an excuse for female nudity on the stage, but I see it as a study of betrayal and devotion.'

'Of course.'

'But enough of me. What about you? The last time I saw you, you were up for an interview with the sardonic Peter Newman. How did it go?'

'I got the job. I'm the editorial director of Vanguard Books, which is now a wholly owned subsidiary of Inflexion Books.'

'Congratulations. Based in Cambridge?'

'Yes, the office is on Hills Road, quite close to the Great Northern. But I have to go down to London pretty regularly.'

'To report to Peter?'

'Yes.'

'What's he like to work for?'

'A tough boss, but fair. So far, he's just let me get on with it. That might change, I suppose. We'll see.'

'He has an eye for the ladies.'

'So I understand, but he's been perfectly decent with me. Even introduced me to Ginny recently.'

Steve felt a stab in his heart. 'Ah, Ginny. How was she?'

'Very pregnant.'

'Oh, yes.'

'You knew?'

(Should he have said that?) 'I'd heard.'

'They're getting married.' (Another stab.)

'So that the child is not born out of wedlock?'

'Perhaps. It is not something they discussed with me. But I did mention that you and I had been lovers briefly.'

(Ouch!) 'What did she say?'

'She was full of praise for you and asked me to send her love if I were to bump into you. You seem to have got under her skin.' (Another stab.)

'Presumably, Peter wasn't in earshot when she was saying all this?'

'No, he was working the room. She's an amazing woman, Steve.'

'I know.'

'You were lucky to have had a relationship with her.'

'I'm not so sure about that. Perhaps if I'd just enjoyed the moment as she told me to, I'd feel I was lucky. But I was always fretting that the moments were slipping away and that we were doomed – as a couple that is.'

'You're a fatalist.'

'I don't think so.'

'Will you tell Grace that you met me?'

'Maybe.' Steve stood up. 'Believe me, Jude, I'd like to stay and talk longer, but I need to get home. How do I get in touch with you?'

She opened her bag and took out a card, scribbling something on the back of it. 'I have a business card. I've put my home address and telephone number on the back.'

Steve took the card and turned it over. 'Magrath Avenue. Is the Rex still going?'

'No, thank goodness.'

'Oh, that's a pity. I remember seeing Nic Roeg's *Performance* there.'

As Steve turned to go, Jude said, 'Have you still got my novel?'

'Yes, but I'm afraid I haven't looked at it again since you gave it to me.'

'That's fine, but remember, it's the only copy. If you really aren't going to edit it, please let me have it back.'

Steve nodded and stepped out onto the street.

## Saturday, 19 April 1975

'Thank you, Grace, for coming in to see me at such short notice. It's nice to see you again after all these years.'

Grace shifted uneasily in her chair. 'I had rather been expecting to hear from you. I realised when I revealed details of my past to Mavis, and then when I went out to West Berlin to support Steve, that it might come to your attention.'

Sheena pursed her lips. 'Quite so.'

'What can I do for you?'

'You anticipate my purposes.'

'I did not think you wanted to reminisce about the inglorious past. You are far too busy for that.'

'You have lost none of your acumen. I have been wondering since you reappeared on the scene what to do about you. Now I find that Professor Müller, through the good offices of Dr Doyle, one of your Cambridge colleagues, has been made an extraordinary fellow of St Radegund's College. I also gather that, at somewhat late notice, you have been invited by Professor Müller to make a contribution to a forthcoming colloquium in Edinburgh.'

'News travels fast.'

'It will not have escaped you that we do not entirely trust Professor Müller.'

'Yes, that seemed fairly obvious to me.'

'I wonder if you shared that thought with Steve?'

'No, I didn't. He was having enough difficulty processing the turn of events.'

'I am not surprised. But did he share with you the unfortunate part I played in the operation?'

'Yes, he did. I am sorry for your loss.'

'Thank you, Grace. That is very sensitive of you on both counts.'

'Mavis did confide in me that she was in love, and I could see that she was very much looking forward to this new phase of her life. I think it was very brave of both of you and I am only sorry that the relationship has been cut short.'

'I have not yet come to terms with it myself. Of course, I regret the professional errors I made. But I have been cleared of misconduct and perhaps I have also struck a blow for same-sex relationships.'

'You have indeed.'

'Well, to return to Professor Müller: the fact that he is an admirer of your work and that he is moving to Cambridge immediately suggested possibilities.'

'It is gratifying to have one's work noticed.'

'But it is not only your work that he has noticed.'

'It is also the lot of the female academic to have to put up with unwanted attentions from a certain kind of male colleague.'

'What a world we live in. But there may be times when what is unwanted can also be beneficial.'

'I presume you mean you would like me to encourage those attentions?'

'In a nutshell. It is, after all, an area in which you have some experience.'

'I was much younger then.'

'Admittedly, but the stakes are higher now, and so are the rewards.'

'I am not sure that being anointed by Professor Müller is likely to improve my chances of getting a chair.'

'Oh, I don't know. On the other hand, were details of your activities in Berlin fifteen years ago to emerge, it might well jeopardise those same aspirations.'

'I can't believe you would stoop so low.'

'Then you have misjudged me.'

'But I am in a relationship with Steve, as you well know. We are planning to have a baby.'

'Yes, that is unfortunate. But I suppose his own attitude towards you might change were he to understand that you had worked as an informant for the Stasi, the very organisation that likely arranged his mother's murder.'

'That is an outrageous abuse of your position.'

'I really don't think it is. When you fell prey to a sweet-talking Stasi Romeo – Armin, was it? – all those years ago, you put yourself in an anomalous position. Matters were not pursued through the courts because you agreed to help us. We have not required anything of you for many years, but now it appears that you are well placed to keep an eye on Müller. It won't be for ever. We are under no illusions about the kind of man he is and we are keen to bring him down, but not before we've played out this hand of cards. We have to work with what we've got, and what we've got is you.'

'I can't believe that Müller is worth all this effort.'

'We understand that his masters wish him to establish a network of DDR well-wishers in the British academy. We would like to know who these people are.'

'Surely there are easier ways?'

'We are where we are. I am sorry that the relationship with Steve must suffer collateral damage. But, to be honest, I think it best for both of you. Steve may have told you that I have a quasi-parental role in relation to him and, unlike his mother, I consider him to be too young to take on the responsibility of being a father to your child.'

Grace's first impulse was to storm out of the room and challenge Sheena to do her damnedest. But in the same moment, she also realised that unless she was prepared to go all in on her profession-al ambitions and at the same time risk Steve finding out what had really happened in Berlin in 1961, it was pointless to call Sheena's bluff. Biting her lower lip and cursing under her breath, she said, 'Okay, Sheena, you win.'

Sheena nodded imperceptibly. 'Let's not think of it as winning or losing. Let's think of it more as a resumption of an earlier profes-sional relationship. In due course, I hope to be able to show how obliged the department is to you.'

'Well, then, speaking as colleagues, there is one problem I foresee.'

Sheena cocked her head. 'Which is?'

'Steve has got a play in rehearsal at the Festival Theatre in Cambridge. It deals obliquely with recent events in Berlin.'

'It will have to be stopped.'

'I think that approach is a bit heavy-handed and will only turn the attempt to ban it into a *cause célèbre*. I know the director, and that is exactly the kind of thing he loves.'

'Have you read the play?'

'I have.'

'Please outline it for me.'

Grace did so, to Sheena's mounting consternation. 'What in heaven's name does Steve think he's playing at?'

'He's a writer. He's trying to process what he's been through. His first draft involved a lesbian love affair between two British intelligence officers that brings a carefully planned operation to grief.'

Grace knew she was somewhat distorting the facts. 'The director wanted to spice up that strand of the play, but Steve felt uncomfortable about it and removed all those details from the play.'

'I'm glad to hear it.'

'He redrafted it as the rekindling of an old love affair between a British female intelligence officer and an East German professor who is close to the leadership. The British officer persuades him to pass secrets to the West, and when he comes under suspicion, arranges to get him out. In this she succeeds but loses her own life in what may be an accident, but is more likely an assassination. The young male courier and the female cut-out on the East Berlin side fall in love in the course of their work. But the play ends with the young East Berliner being arrested by the Stasi.'

'That does not make me feel much better. The play cannot go ahead. What if Müller gets wind of it?'

'What harm would that do? From what I gather, that is actually what you told Steve, which is also what the Stasi want us to believe.'

Sheena saw the validity of Grace's point. 'Okay, but if there are any changes to the plot that might embarrass us, I want to know.'

'Of course. I have one small request. I'd rather not tell Steve that things are over between us until his play has finished. It only runs for a week and should be over by the twenty-fifth of May.'

'I'm prepared to accept that, but I would like you to be developing things with Müller before that.'

'With luck, there will be an opportunity to get the ball rolling on the weekend of the colloquium in Edinburgh.'

'Good. Well, I think that is all highly satisfactory. It's good to have you back on the team.'

On her way back to Cambridge on the train, Grace turned her mind to how she was going to manage the uncoupling from Steve. Sheena had made it clear that she would be constrained in terms of what she could tell Steve. It would not do for him to suspect that she would be developing a relationship with Müller. Sheena had suggested that Grace might give him to understand that she had changed her mind about wanting to have a child. She had even said that women like Sheena and Grace really had no business having children. Grace had been on the point of saying that she was not a lesbian wedded to her job. But even as she framed the thought she realised that, the matter of her sexuality aside, there was an element of truth in what Sheena said.

Indeed, her commitment to the plan to have a child with Steve had already been waning. Increasingly, what had seemed a welcome change of circumstance at the start of her relationship with Steve, namely the frequent coupling with a virile younger man, was beginning to pall now that their lovemaking had perforce become less spontaneous, focused as it was on activity during the fertile periods of her cycle. It had indeed become something of a chore, even for Steve, she suspected.

Then there was the effect of Mavis's death on the arrangement with Steve. Grace had been aware from the start that the age difference between her and Steve had lent an element of maternal surrogacy to their relationship. While Mavis remained alive, that tension had been slight. But now, with the loss of his mother, Steve seemed to be cleaving to Grace in a way that he hadn't before. Grace had no desire to be both lover and mother to him. She had only ever wanted him as a lover. She recognised now that this impulse had perhaps been a subliminal move in the complicated game of emotional chess that she had been playing with Peter, in which, in effect, she had been submitting to the roulette of unprotected sex with Steve to determine what happened next. Sheena's intervention had merely crystallised that moment. There was no reason, though, why she shouldn't try to make their final weeks together as pleasant as possible, while now hoping that, in the meantime, she did not become pregnant.

## Monday, 21 April 1975

STEVE WOKE LATER THAN usual. It was the first day of rehearsals proper for *Palace of Tears*. He was excited but apprehensive in equal measure. In the end the read-throughs and the motivational workshop with the actors had gone well enough. But he was now more aware of the rifts and petty rivalries in the company and therefore the potential for capsize. No doubt Gary was a very experienced director and knew how to keep a tight rein on an unruly company of actors. At the same time, he was also aware that Gary's mind was occupied with financial matters. But what terrified him most was the thought that his banal lines of dialogue might resist the efforts of even the most determined actor to breathe life into them. He stood under the shower for so long, trying to work out the likelihood of a disaster, that Grace felt compelled to come into the bathroom to make sure he was alright.

Later over breakfast, she said, 'Steve, you're in safe hands with Gary. Try to enjoy it.'

'You know what I'm like. I need to imagine the worst outcome. I'm not superstitious, but if I were, I'd understand it as an attempt to avert the evil eye.'

'Okay, but you've done that now. Let me assure you the Furies are off looking for other victims.'

'How could you possibly know that?'

'How could I possibly tell you?'

Steve laughed. Sometimes Grace could be as enigmatic as Ginny. But curiously this seemed to be the balm that his soul needed.

'Thank you, Grace. As ever, you are right. It's high time I stopped being so self-obsessed.'

'You're not self-obsessed. You just have a well-developed sense of anxiety. Consider the positives. We've had a lovely weekend together with no unexpected intrusions.'

'Yes, it was wonderful. If only it were always like that.'

'You'd soon get fed up with my insatiable appetite for cuddles.'

Grace looked up at the kitchen clock, and said, '*Oh my ears and whiskers, how late it's getting!* It's alright for you thespians, not starting until ten-thirty. We in academia have a much harder time of it.'

Steve laughed. 'I'm sure you do, but I don't really see you as the White Rabbit. That's much more my territory.'

An hour later, Steve let himself into the Festival. He had expected the place to be buzzing, but there were no actors there yet. He went through to the auditorium to find Butch overseeing the stage crew who were getting things ready for the first rehearsal.

Butch came over and put his arm around Steve. 'Cheer up, petal. You look as though you're going to the dentist rather than about to see your play realised on the stage by a crack company of actors.'

'That's how I feel, Butch. I can't help thinking they'll all realise I'm a fraud.'

'Not a fraud, petal. We're all in the business of creating an illusion to your blueprint and you're the imagineer. You've got to trust the crew and the company. But best of all, you've got Gaz, the finest skipper on the high seas of illusion. Suspend judgement until the first drink after the curtain on the first night and tell me then how you're feeling.'

'Butch, you're such a great mate. I'm really looking forward to that drink. I think I'll need more than one.'

'Of course. We'll have a huge party.'

'A party?'

'You better believe it. We can't bring a new play into the world without wetting its head.'

'Where?'

'Here, on the stage. If nothing else, it's one way of getting your friends to come and see the show.'

'How many people can I invite?'

'How many friends have you got?'

'Who do I have to clear it with?'

'Who do you think? Uncle Butch, of course.'

Just then, a group of actors, including Sally, appeared at the back of the auditorium, talking at the tops of their voices and taking off their coats. Sally came down to the front and greeted Steve and

Butch, then said, 'Butch, love, could you make sure there's plenty of water in the wings? My throat's a bit dry.'

'Already set up, Sal. A range of herbal teas and some lozenges if it gets really bad.'

'Thanks, Butch. You think of everything.'

'That's my job, Sal.'

The rest of the cast of *Palace* straggled in and draped themselves over the red plush seats in the stalls, joshing each other with light-hearted banter.

Suddenly, Gary appeared and strode to the front of the auditorium. 'Morning Butch, morning Steve.'

Butch said, 'Morning, guv. We've set the stage for bedroom, East Berlin.'

'So I see. Thank you.'

Gary then stepped up onto the stage, clapped his hands three times and said, 'Right, everyone, thank you for being on time. This is getting to be a habit. Let's hope it's one we can maintain. But down to work now. Beginners for Act One, please. The rest of you, keep the chat down.'

Gary then moved to a point in the centre of the stalls, three rows back from the front, where a board had been set up as a kind of rudimentary desk. 'Steve, would you mind sitting with me?'

Steve went over and took the seat to Gary's right. He got his own copy of the script out of his bag and turned to the first page.

Steve watched with fascination as Sally and David proceeded to embody, in the opening scene, which he had only imagined – the relationship between Gertrude and Siegfried. He was captivated by Sally's performance, but was less taken with David's approach. It wasn't the acting as such; both were accomplished actors and delivered the lines with assurance. He couldn't put his finger on what was troubling him about David's performance, but they were soon moving on to the scene between Tristan and Freya, and he put his disquiet about David's interpretation to one side. The interaction between John and Becky crackled with electricity from the very start. Although Becky had never met Inge, she seemed to have *got* her perfectly. How had she been able to do that?

There was time for one more short scene before lunch, which was a scene between Larry as the Stasi colonel and two of his subordinates discussing their suspicions about Siegfried. Steve had found this a difficult scene to write. It was an expository section, showing the complexities of Siegfried's situation and the risks he was facing. Almost inevitably, Larry was playing the part of the colonel in full-on caricature mode, almost as if he were on autopilot from his *Colditz* days. But as Steve read over Larry's lines, he realised that the fault was in the writing. Larry was acting that way because that was how the part was written.

Later in his tiny office over a couple of bottles of beer and a plateful of sandwiches that Butch had ordered in, Gary said to Steve, 'I thought we could use the lunch break to review the morning's performances, out of earshot of the actors. What were your general feelings?'

'On the whole, it went very well. But I am a novice at this.'

'Okay, tell me what you thought worked.'

Steve praised the performances of Sally, Becky and David but something in his voice told a different story. Gary munched thoughtfully on a ham sandwich. 'So, does that mean you think swapping Larry and John was not the right thing to do after all?'

There was no point in beating about the bush. 'It's the writing. The Stasi colonel's lines are generic. There's no sense of a real personality behind the uniform.'

'I agree, Steve. Larry needs something a bit more nuanced to work with. I know he is in a position of power over Siegfried, but maybe if we were to imply that they've known each other as friends or drinking partners, it might add some depth. I know there's quite a lot of developmental material to get through in this scene, but we do need to try and particularise some of it.'

'I could work on it this evening.'

'That would be great. Otherwise I think we got off to a good start.'

The afternoon session threw up a number of similar issues, which meant that by the time the actors had finished for the day, Steve had acquired a fair bit of nipping and tucking to do overnight. But this was the kind of work he enjoyed. It was not as if he was having to create something *ex nihilo*; it was more a case of burnishing a facet here or refining a curlicue there. It helped that it was one of Grace's evenings for dining at High Table. So Steve made himself a simple supper of cheese on toast with a large glass of red wine and got straight down to work at the kitchen table. Even with the extra typing involved, he had soon completed the agreed rewrites.

At a loose end now, he decided to write to Angie. He was conscious that she was still unaware of Mavis's death. He fetched his notepad, unscrewed his fountain pen, carefully inscribing the Glisson Road address, date and an affectionate salutation at the head of the page and then paused. This was not a straightforward letter to write. How much to tell Angie of the events surrounding Mavis's death? Fifteen minutes later, he was no further forward. He got up and paced around the room. No, this was not the time for a detailed account. Perhaps there never would be such a time. The fact of his mother's death was shocking enough.

He picked up his pen again, wrote a simple paragraph outlining the bare facts and was searching for some way to sign off that was not too self-pitying when it occurred to him that neither Angie nor Rob were aware of his play. This might be a way to temper the solemnity of the main point of his note. After giving a brief account of the play's action, he asked rhetorically whether they might be able to make the first night. After all, he thought to himself, Butch had said that he was welcome to invite his friends to the first-night show and party. In which case, he might as well write similar letters to his immediate circle of friends.

An hour later, he'd assembled a small pile of letters for posting the next morning. In addition to Angie and Rob, he had also written to Al, and Harry and Jackie. He had made it clear to this particular group that they would not be able to offer them accommodation. He had briefly considered having the discussion with Grace, but had equally quickly decided that not even he had any desire to entertain guests on what was likely to be a nervy couple of days. He had even written to Dr Doyle. Doyle had, after all, met Mavis, even if only on Steve's graduation day and had always been encouraging about Steve's extracurricular activities. If he did decide to come to the first night, he might well be amused by the play's portrait of an East German specialist on the German Romantics caught up in the toils of rival intelligence agencies. Steve did wonder for a moment whether Doyle might recognise the portrait of Müller, but dismissed the thought as being improbable.

He had written a slightly different letter to those people who had not known or been aware of Mavis. This included Angie's friend Declan at St John's, Tom Borrowdale at Solstice bookshop, Jed Morgan in France, and Garth and Kelly at the Tenison Road house, to whom he made it clear that if they did come, clothing was not optional. He would have liked to write to Jon too, but had no address for him. It occurred to him that he could do worse than pin a message up in the Loco. Steve doubted that Jon had totally forsaken his longtime drinking haunt, despite living on the other side of town now.

More controversially, he had also written to Ginny who, when they had been living together, had shown absolutely no interest in meeting Mavis or introducing Steve to her father. Even so, he had spoken enough about his mother in their time together for her to be a significant figure for Ginny. On the other hand, Ginny would undoubtedly be fascinated by the idea of Steve having a play performed by a cast of professional actors. In fact, Steve thought she might be quite proud of him. But would he be brave enough to admit to Grace that he had written to her? Probably not. In any case, what was the likelihood of Ginny actually deciding to attend the play, not least because she must now be a considerable way into her pregnancy? Not high, he imagined.

But what if she did? And what if she were accompanied by Peter? Steve wasn't sure. He laid this last letter to one side and was mulling over whether to send it or not, when he heard a key in the lock. Still undecided, he quickly slipped it inside his notebook. A few moments later Grace walked into the room.

Steve leapt up and embraced her. 'How was your evening?'

'A dreadful bore. Nothing worth recounting. More to the point, how was *your* day?'

'Not too bad. Can I get you a glass of wine?'

Grace sat down and kicked off her shoes. 'No, I had more than enough at dinner. A cup of tea would be nice, though.'

Steve attended to making the tea. As he did so, Grace flipped through the pile of envelopes. 'Catching up with your correspondence?'

'I've been inviting people to the first night.'

'Who's Jed Morgan?'

'The great guitar player.'

'Will he come over from France to see your play?'

'I doubt it, but I thought I might as well ask him. Butch said I could get comps for my friends and invite them to the party. But then I realised that I didn't really have that many friends, so I was widening the net.'

'Oh, come on Steve. You've got more friends than this.'

'Well, I hadn't finished the task yet. I started off writing to people who knew Mavis to tell them about her death. I thought I might as well say something to those people about the play. Then I moved on to the people who only needed to know about the play.'

'So you were leaving Jude and Ginny for last. Did I return too soon?'

The unmistakably sardonic note with which these words were delivered immediately put Steve on his guard. Grace had been short with him several times since her return from her meeting in London. He had tried to get her to talk about what was on her mind, but she had simply closed him down, not even telling him what the meeting had been about. Or perhaps she had simply overindulged in High Table port. Steve was glad now that he hadn't mentioned his recent encounter with Jude the previous Friday and also glad that he had presence of mind to conceal the letter to Ginny.

Steve put the mugs of tea on the table. 'Grace, I presume you're teasing me, but the situation with those two is complicated to say the least. It would be uncomfortable having either of them at the first night, not least because, in Ginny's case, it would also imply Peter.'

'You don't have to protect me from big, bad Peter, Steve. I've had plenty of practice at that.'

Steve wasn't quite sure what to say. He watched Grace as she leafed through the rest of the envelopes, terrified that she would notice the letter to Ginny which was protruding slightly from his notebook. But at that moment, Grace turned up the letter to Dr Doyle. 'Richard Doyle? You're inviting him?'

'Yes, why not?'

'Just because you haven't been in touch with him since graduation day last year.'

'You don't know that for a fact.'

'I do. I was sitting next to him at High Table at St Rad's this evening.'

Steve felt a stab of guilt. 'You didn't tell me you were going to St Rad's.'

'I don't think I'm obliged to clear my timetable with you. Anyway, he was saying that he was sorry that you hadn't been in touch.'

'You know how it's been. He met Mavis last summer. They hit it off. I thought I ought to tell him.'

Grace bit her bottom lip. 'Steve, I'm afraid I've already told him. He sends his condolences.'

Steve felt a spasm of anger sweep through him. It was for him to pass on such news. He choked quietly, afraid of what he might now say if he didn't control himself.

Grace saw the emotion pass across his face and realised that she had angered him. 'I'm so sorry. I had no idea that you were going to get in touch with him. I feel terrible.'

Steve walked over to the sink and poured the dregs of his tea down the drain. 'I think I'll go up to bed.'

He picked up the pile of letters, his notebook and typescript. 'I'll take the typewriter up tomorrow morning.'

He didn't stop to kiss Grace. His thoughts were a mess of grief and resentment. Not many minutes later he was in bed.

When Grace came up, he was already buried under the covers, his face turned away from her. 'Steve, what is this? What's going on?'

He made no response or none that she could decode. She got undressed quickly, slipped her nightdress on and went next door to the bathroom. A few minutes later she returned, switched out the lights and got into bed beside him. Eventually, he allowed himself to be turned over, burying his face in her breast, huge sobs racking his body. It was clear to her now that, in trying to come to terms with the task that had been visited upon her by Sheena, she had already closed her heart to Steve. He had been almost absurdly stoical since their return from Berlin, but how could he not have sensed the change in her attitude towards him? Her insensitivity over the matter of informing Doyle of Mavis's death had clearly overwhelmed Steve's fragile composure. Shamed by her own callousness but also bitter at the turn of events, she cradled him for the next half hour and, when she was sure he was asleep, went next door to the spare room and allowed herself to weep too.

On reflection, she had been surprised at how calm he had been during those terrible days in Berlin and then when they had got back. But she saw now that this was only because he hadn't yet processed the grief. Instead he had thrown himself into the writing and production of *Palace of Tears*. But the play itself was just a cipher for those events in Berlin. If she'd been more sensitive, she would have realised that all sorts of things were woven into the emotional wound he had suffered as a consequence of Mavis's death. She should have trodden more carefully. Worryingly, his fragile state of mind did rather beg the question of how she was going to bring their relationship to an end without too much upset.

So it was as well that Grace had not mentioned that the other person who had been present at dinner that evening had been Dieter Müller. She now realised that Sheena must have already known that Müller was going to be present, which also suggested that she, or perhaps Collingwood on her behalf, was in close contact with Dr Doyle. That would explain why she had been hauled in at such short notice over the weekend. So even though she had had her card already marked on Müller's behalf by Sheena, there was no mistaking how charmingly complimentary he had been. It had certainly surprised one or two people around the table that Grace was already an acquaintance of this giant of European letters. When, later in the evening, it had become clear that she had also been personally invited by Müller to address the colloquium that he had organised in Edinburgh, there was a growing sense of Grace as a rising figure in her field.

# Tuesday, 22 April 1975

GRACE WOKE EARLY THE next morning with a slightly muzzy head from lack of sleep, but also angry with herself and clear about what needed to be done. Perhaps a spontaneous offer of sex on her part rather than the rather programmatic coupling they seemed to have settled on recently would go some way to making amends. She went downstairs, made two mugs of tea, and then went back upstairs and put the mugs of tea gently down on the bedside table. She walked around to her side of the bed, pulling her nightdress over her head as she went and slipped in beside Steve.

He was still fast asleep, hair tousled, a beatific look on his face. On closer inspection she could see from the movement of his eyes under their lids that he was in dream-sleep. She reached down and was not surprised to find a full erection. So much the better.

When, sometime later, Steve had got his breath back, he rolled over and took a sip of his tea. 'Well, what was that all about?'

'A wordless apology?'

'There's nothing to apologise for. I don't know what came over me. I should be the one apologising.'

'We don't have time for this now. I have a nine o'clock lecture. I just didn't want either of us to go through the day nursing recrim- inations. If you really feel you have something to say that won't keep until this evening, you'd better try and tell me while I'm in the shower.'

'No, I've got nothing that needs saying now, but I might just come and watch you shower anyway.'

'Okay, watching only, though. No touching.'

Later, while having his own shower after Grace had left for work, Steve returned to the events of the previous evening. Grace had not hidden from him that she would be dining at High Table that evening. But she had not mentioned that it was St Rad's she was dining at, rather than her own college. No doubt, it was not in her gift to invite him to a dinner at another college and Steve was in any case far too busy at the moment. But when Grace had first proposed becoming pregnant by him, she had been adamant that they should be open about it. They were to let their families and friends know and they were to appear in public as a couple. She would invite him to High Table to meet her colleagues. Family and friends had duly been notified, but invitations to High Table had failed to materialise. The fact that she had spoken to Doyle about him and passed on the news of the death of his mother had suddenly brought what now seemed like a deliberate omission sharply into focus. Was she tiring, or indeed despairing, of him?

Despite their best efforts in the sack (and out of it), Grace was still showing no signs of conceiving. Not that Steve begrudged the effort required of him. He had already lost count of their couplings, but he was pretty sure that it exceeded by a comfortable margin what he and Ginny had managed. He thought it might even exceed the number he and Angie had achieved despite their having been together for a considerably longer period.

It was odd how perspectives changed. This time last year, Ginny had seemed to be the *femme fatale*, Grace the strait-laced matron, and Angie the beautiful girl. But he could honestly say that sex with Grace, after a somewhat conventional start, had been much more experimental, if one could put it that way, than sex with Ginny had ever been. Grace had perhaps come to the conclusion that anything likely to increase Steve's ardour, any amount of hanky-panky, was also more likely to result in a fertilised egg. Steve doubted there was much physiological evidence for that. But he was more than happy to submit to her experiments. Or perhaps it was that they simply trusted each other more now.

He ought to have realised long ago that it wasn't one's body that Ginny messed with; it was one's mind. Meanwhile, Angie remained the inaccessible maiden. He realised this typology was not entirely apt, given that he and Angie had actually had a decorous but loving sexual relationship. But those days already seemed remote, almost mythological. So it was the divergent polarities between Ginny and Grace that had unsettled him the previous night. All these weeks later he was still feeling guilty about his encounter with Ginny in the Great Eastern Hotel, not so much that he had slept with her, but that she had burdened him with the knowledge that she and Peter were expecting a child.

It was that piece of information that would devastate Grace. That was the real reason he had hidden the letter to Ginny. Yet Grace had unerringly inferred its existence. She hadn't explicitly called him out on the matter, but that was how it had felt. He had then overreacted, protesting too much, and ended up tumbling into the bottomless pit of his grief.

He stepped out of the shower and dried himself. As he dressed, he came to the conclusion that it could do no good to be in touch with Ginny again. It would only lead to further heartbreak. He would tear up the letter he had written to her. The others could go, even the one to Dr Doyle. Now he must put such matters out of his mind and ready himself for the second day of rehearsals.

## Friday, 16 May 1975

STEVE AND GRACE DID not once during the next three weeks revisit the discussion that had derailed her account of the conversation at High Table with Richard Doyle. By some form of telepathy, they managed to avoid the subject and returned to the normal companionable tenor of life together.

Steve was utterly absorbed by the rehearsal process for *Palace*. Each evening he would spend a couple of hours up in his work room or preferably at the kitchen table fettling the play's dialogue. He had come to admire the actors, especially their powers of memorisation and improvisation. But Gary seemed to feel that the dramatic nub of the play was still not quite in focus and constantly urged Steve to be bold in his approach to rewrites.

As he reluctantly responded to Gary's prompting, he became aware of how small changes to the text could result in very different aspects of the play emerging, something that the actors were quick to pick up on. The process was very much like slowly turning the cylinder of a kaleidoscope. The component pieces remained the same, but formed themselves into different patterns with each rotation. So too with the play. With small changes to the text of a scene and new instructions from Gary on how best to incorporate those changes, gradually Siegfried's role was humanised and Gertrude was shown as a more equivocal figure. Her manipulation of Tristan and Freya had something much darker about it.

When Steve had started writing *Palace* he had simply wanted to contrast the drabness of East Berlin with the bright lights of West Berlin. It had been Richard Croft, the designer, and Tony Buttermere, the lighting designer, who had come up with the idea of using lighting to point up this contrast. Gary had been enthusiastic about this approach and had urged Steve to incorporate the imagery of light into his rewrites, something which Steve had been happy to do. Gradually, instead of being just an index of economic progress, the relative luminosity of the two halves of the city was now presented as a measure of social morality.

But, having persuaded Steve to frame the narrative in this way, Gary went on to suggest that a good guys versus bad guys scenario was simplistic and that there should be some *bleed* as he put it between the two systems. In the early drafts, Gertrude had been presented as a heroic figure fighting the good fight against the Soviet threat to the Western liberal democracies. But Gary detected a dissonance between the values that Gertrude stood for and the methods she used to defend those values. He wanted this dissonance to be made more apparent.

Initially, Steve was resistant to this reading, but didn't understand why. It took him some time to realise that, in the private world of his imagination, Gertrude had started off as a placeholder for the figure of his mother in her role as a British intelligence officer. Even though that character had evolved in unexpected directions, the elided codename still signified Mavis to him, which meant that, at some level, he was attributing a degree of moral equivocation to his mother. Only by severing the link back to his mother would he be able to let Gertrude develop into a fully realised character, not merely a cipher for a real person.

Having got Steve to this point, Gary went back to Tony and Richard, saying he wanted to reflect the *bleed* with the lighting and sound. Yes, the play should start with the East being dark and dingy, but in the second half, the darkness should also gradually infect the West. Steve was not entirely comfortable with this reading either. It seemed a little forced. But he had to admit that it made the play altogether more satisfyingly complex. One thing was certain: he could never have achieved something as nuanced on his own.

Grace was busy too. End of year exams were under way and the proofs of her book on existentialism and the existentialists had come back. She was also in demand on the academic circuit. Steve had been delighted when she told him she had been invited to deliver the keynote lecture at a conference at Edinburgh University. Unexpectedly, this had resulted in her ranting rather operatically for a few minutes at the short notice and extra work involved. It would mean her being away for a few nights. It was so damn inconvenient, not to mention that it was right in the middle of the rehearsals for *Palace*.

Steve laughed. 'You're not one of the understudies, so there's no need to worry. In fact it's a perfect time to go. If it were scheduled for the weekend of the first night, that would be a different matter.'

'Well, as long as you don't mind.'

'Grace, it's your job. I can hardly object. In fact, I don't object. I've got so much on that I probably won't even notice your absence.'

'You know how to make a girl feel loved.'

'I'm sorry, that was not well expressed. On top of Gary and his constant demands for rewrites, I've also got a load of correspondence to attend to.'

Because the batch of letters he had sown had yielded varying kinds of fruit. He had, almost by return, received separate letters from Angie and Rob. They were delighted at his news and they would most certainly attend the first night of *Palace of Tears*. It was not a problem that they could not stay at Glisson Road. Somewhat surprisingly, they had been invited to stay at Jeremiah Flynn's. Steve had forgotten about Rob's top notch networking skills. Al had also found somewhere to stay. With Jon and Tamsin, it seemed. Not quite as surprising as Angie and Rob's billet, but unexpected all the same, since Steve himself still didn't have Jon's new address.

Steve wrote back to Angie and Rob, telling them how pleased he was that they were coming. He also thought they might be interested in Grace's keynote at the Edinburgh colloquium on contemporary European thought. The title of her paper was '*Le regard* and *le rapport de face à face*: Beyond Essentialism in Sartre and Levinas'. If that was their cup of tea, they might want to pop along.

Sadly, Harry and Jackie were unable to attend. Nor could Declan make the first night, but he promised to try and get to one of the later performances and hoped to be able to catch Steve for a drink after the show. However, Tom said he'd definitely be there. He also said that he was in possession of some first-class acid and if Steve were to drop by Solstice, he'd let him have a couple of tabs. Steve had been shocked that Tom was so incautious as to include such information in a letter, but he thought he might well avail himself of the offer once the Festival season was over.

Of course, there was no reply from Garth. But that in itself meant nothing. Garth was not one for social niceties. A few days after all the other replies, and in complete contrast in terms of expectations, Steve received a letter from France. Jed might indeed be able to attend. He was supporting Stéphane Grappelli on a UK tour of obscure pubs with jazz clubs. No gig was booked for that particular evening as yet. He'd see if he could make it. Even if he couldn't, perhaps he and Steve could hook up. Steve was absurdly grateful to Jed, even though he did sign off by asking Steve to remember him to Ginny. That only left Jon. Steve resolved to drop into the Loco on his way home in the hope of crossing paths with the errant rock god.

Meanwhile the stage crew had been building the set, simple as it was and, more importantly, rigging the lighting. By the Wednesday before the first night, everything was ready for the technical rehearsal. The actors had blocked out all their moves on the stage, but they now had to be mapped onto lighting, sound and property cues. It was going to be a long and stressful day, and no one was looking forward to it. It would be everyone's first chance to get some impression of how things would look in performance.

Once again he and Gary took their places at the front of the stalls, this time joined by Butch. Each cue point was taken in turn, with lighting, sound and props set and actors on their marks, at which point they would speak the first few lines of that cue point. Crew and cast would then move forward to the next cue point and repeat the procedure with any lighting or prop changes and any actors involved on new marks. It reminded Steve of the stop-motion technique for making animated films, everything done in painstaking increments. It was a tedious process and it took many hours to get through the entire play.

He was also aware for the first time of differences of opinion between Gary and Butch. It was in Gary's nature to always demand more or to want to suddenly make a change. Obliging though he was, Butch would put his foot down at some of Gary's more radical demands. He only had a small crew and they were going to have to work late after the tech rehearsal to effect the changes already suggested. It was only fair to give them a couple of hours off between the rehearsal and the evening performance. At one point when he and Gary had locked horns over the positioning of one of the Stasi surveillance platforms, Butch had even invoked Equity rules. This had set Gary off on a five-minute rant. Butch suggested a short break and he and Gary went off to the cubbyhole to resolve their differences. They didn't ask Steve to join them.

But there were also positive moments to the process. Steve was able to see for the first time what a powerful influence the lighting effects had in Gary's interpretation of his text. For the first half of the play, up to the point where Gary had decided to have the interval, there was a strong contrast between the lighting for the

East Berlin scenes and the lighting for the West Berlin scenes, a foggy yellow effect for the East, brighter with the impression of flashing neon for the West. But in the second half, the one seemed to bleed into the other, as Gary had demanded of the lighting technicians. Steve was also delighted by the subtle sound effects that Richard Croft and Tony Buttermere had come up with, noisy, spluttering two-stroke traffic and rattling trams for the East; international airline announcements and the sound of American radio broadcasts for the West. Nothing so intrusive as to make it difficult to hear the actors' lines, just two very different city soundscapes. But the key sound effect was the noise of underground trains arriving at and leaving the Friedrichstraße underground station overlaid with the sound of sobbing and weeping which, in the final scene where Tristan and Inge take leave of each other, rises to a crescendo.

By the time the company had got through to the end to Gary's satisfaction, everyone was exhausted. Gary announced that the following day's session would be a first dress rehearsal, so they would be starting earlier to give the actors plenty of time to do makeup and get used to the costumes. To compensate for the early start, they would top and tail the scenes, moving from cue to cue as quickly as possible. The full dress rehearsal would be on Friday. Steve was aware of quite a lot of grumbling as the actors filed out, but Gary seemed oblivious to their grumbles. He was obviously used to it.

In fact, the first dress rehearsal went remarkably smoothly. The stage crew were absolutely on top of the cue changes and Butch was adamant that he was not allowing any further lighting or prop changes. The actors seemed to be excited by the chance to dress up, even though none of the costumes was particularly elaborate, with the exception of the Stasi uniforms. Gary had permitted the two women involved in the bed scenes to wear leotards because of the stop and start nature of that day's rehearsal. But the leotards would not be permitted for the full dress rehearsal. In contrast to the previous day, the session ended on a high, with little of the previous day's grumbling.

Unfortunately, things did not go so smoothly for the full dress rehearsal. Nerves were very evident. Gary had clear ideas about how long the play as a whole should take, and he said he would be very annoyed if there were too many pauses in the tempo of the performance. Steve thought this could only add to the pressure of the occasion, but he did appreciate that, as with playing a piece of music, you could not be said to know the piece until you were able to play it through without stopping to correct a mistake.

Inevitably, Sally fluffed her lines in the opening scene, mainly because this was the point at which she was undressed. Gary expostulated from the stalls, and Sally fled from the stage, the flimsy wrap pressed to her torso. Gary called a halt to the rehearsal and went down to Sally's dressing room to placate her. While he was absent, Butch took the opportunity for a brief conference with the deputy stage manager who was running the prompt book and together they moved the mark for the chair closer to the bed. This was the chair over which the wrap to preserve Sally's modesty was draped. He did not mention the adjustment to Gary when he returned.

Rather cruelly, Steve thought, Gary insisted on starting the rehearsal again from the very beginning. Steve, who knew the script backwards, realised that even on this second attempt Sally got the lines wrong, but this time at least she didn't falter, and Steve decided not to draw the error to Gary's attention. In any case, he was more interested in the movement involved in the scene and how Sally handled the awkward few seconds between getting out of the bed with Tristan and putting her wrap on. Butch's slight modification had made all the difference. Sally's fluff, however, was far from the only hiccup in the performance or the only pause. By the end of the rehearsal, Gary had shouted at all of the leads and brought nearly everyone to tears.

But not everything was a disaster. Becky was much more confident with her clothes off, indeed almost brazen. Consequently, the love scene between her and John really fizzed. It certainly helped that they were both fine physical specimens. Steve's heart went out to both actors. Even Gary seemed pleased with the scene. Unfortunately, Becky and John seemed to have let the successful negoti- ation of the bed scene go their heads and they both managed to screw up the final scene in which they said farewell to each other, possibly for ever, at the Palace of Tears station. It looked very much as if John, perhaps believing them home and dry, had corpsed Becky and her tears had morphed into giggles. Gary gave them both a severe ticking off. Steve thought that Gary was going to insist on them doing the scene again, but Butch whispered some- thing in Gary's ear, and he declared the rehearsal over.

Everyone was desperate for a drink. Becky invited Steve to join them. He couldn't think of anything nicer. But he noted that the invitation was not extended to Gary and Butch, who had in any case once again sequestered themselves in the cubbyhole. Steve realised not for the first time that his own position was anomalous. He was not quite a member of the company management team, but nor was he a member of the cast. Perhaps that's what it was to be a writer: neither one of the guys nor one of the bosses – in fact an outcast. With considerable regret, he turned the invitation down. He didn't want to be put in the awkward position where he became party to the grievances of the cast about the way Gary had conducted the rehearsal. Nor did he want to enter the day of the first public performance of his play with a hangover. He opted to go home and spend the evening with Grace.

## Saturday, 17 May 1975

EARLIER IN THE WEEK, Butch had suggested to Steve that it would be a nice gesture before the first performance to present each of the actors with a card and a small gift. The trouble was he hadn't provided any ideas as to what would constitute a small gift. Steve, reluctant to differentiate the gifts along gender lines by giving the women scent or chocolate and the men booze, decided to give everyone wine. He knew this said something bad about him, but surely anyone would welcome a decent claret? He'd got a local wine merchant to deliver a case of 12 bottles of Margaux the previous day. He was a little shocked at how much the case had cost, but at least that meant he had four bottles over for himself. So, while Gary and Butch were ensconced in the cubbyhole, Steve wrote cards and wrapped bottles of wine in tissue paper.

He thought it ill became a quasi-professional writer to inscribe the same message in every card, especially since everyone was getting the same gift. Consequently, the writing of cards took up much more time than he had anticipated, exacerbated by the fact that he tried to work in a line or phrase from each actor's part. It wasn't too bad for the leads because there was a lot of dialogue to choose from. But the guys who took the border guard roles and the surveillance team roles had relatively sparse lines of dialogue. He also knew that some of the actors liked to come in early to help them get into the right mental space. So he was relieved when he had finally put a wrapped bottle and a card propped against it at each seat in the tiny dressing rooms before the first actor put in an appearance.

Gary had scheduled a full company meeting for five o'clock, all cast, crew, and front of house. He'd asked Steve to say a few words. Steve could hardly decline, but he hadn't the slightest idea what

371

you might say on such an occasion. Furthermore, now that he'd despatched the practicalities of gift giving, he was starting to notice that he had butterflies in his stomach. Perhaps a breath of fresh air would help. He'd take a turn around Midsummer Common. He put on his coat and slipped out into the afternoon world.

He arrived back with ten minutes to spare. Butch came across to him. 'Where've you been, petal? We were starting to get worried.'

'I just needed to clear my head.'

'You'll be fine. It's over to the actors and crew now. Just focus on that first glass of wine afterwards.'

'Did you sort out the cues?'

'Yeah, it'll be fine. We've got some interesting people in tonight.'

'Don't tell me, Butch. It'll just make me even more nervous.'

Soon everyone was gathered at the front of the stalls. Gary and Butch climbed up onto the apron of the stage and waved to Steve to come and join them. Gary's speech was a mixture of notes, reminders, and exhortatory comments. He looked very tired. Somewhat selfishly, Steve hoped that the cause was financial rather than artistic, though he wouldn't have blamed Gary if he had come to the conclusion that his decision to back Steve's play had been a mistake. When Gary had finished, the company applauded him politely. Then Butch stepped forward and told a series of jokes, several of them quite lewd. Steve was dimly aware that Butch was warming the company up for him. But Steve's mind was a complete blank. Once the guffaws had died down, Steve stepped forward. In the absence of anything cogent to say, he thought he'd just try and thank as many people as possible.

'Ladies and gentlemen of the company, crew and front of house, you all know that I am the least experienced person in this gathering. I just want to thank you for the support you have all given me. *Palace of Tears* is so much better than it was when we did the first read-through three or four weeks ago. I am particularly grateful to Sally, Becky and Larry for their contributions. Each of them has brought their characters to life. I would also like to thank David for his huge professionalism and decency. I would like to thank John for his inextinguishable good humour and for seeing facets in Tristan's character that I had never suspected were there.

'And this is not to forget Bill, Reg and Harry who, though they may have fewer lines, are probably on stage longer than the actors just mentioned and will probably be fitter than they have ever been after climbing up and down to those platforms at the side of the stage several times a night. I would also like to thank Richard and

Tony. I can truly say that, until the stage was dressed and lit, I thought we had something worthy but lifeless. Now the way the flats and lights differentiate West Berlin from East Berlin with minimal change of stage props is little short of magical. Thank you both, and to your assistants, Colin and Graham. And thank you to Denise and her ushers and assistants in the box office. The foyer and the auditorium look wonderful.

'This beautiful old theatre has come to life again, thanks to the technical skills and the sheer hard graft from Butch and his crew, Adam, Toby and Jeff. Where would any of us be without them? And Butch is the sweetest guy, a reassuring shoulder to cry on, a man who can make or fix anything, a man who, as far as I can see, never sleeps.

'And finally, huge thanks to the person who has made everything, literally everything, possible, the boss, Gary Lewis. I still cannot believe that Gary has taken my horrible little play and turned it into something deep, complex and exciting. Before any of you saw it, he made decisive interventions that improved it beyond all measure. He didn't tell me *what* to write; he told me *how* to write. We all know that he has done everything in the world of the theatre – the National, the RSC, Broadway; he has directed the greats, and launched countless writing careers. He has also raised the money to bring back to life, even if only briefly, this beautiful old theatre. We all owe a huge debt to Gary, but the debt I owe him is beyond quantification. This has been a very special few weeks of my life. I know you are all going to do a brilliant job and I look forward to celebrating with you afterwards.'

Steve wasn't sure what he'd said, but everyone was cheering and Gary and Butch were patting him on the back. He'd spent all his emotional energy in that one speech. Thank God that he didn't have to act or do anything technical now. He was absolutely empty.

Gary let the cheers go on for a few more moments and then waved his hands up and down to indicate that people should calm down. When the hubbub had subsided, he said, 'Thank you, Steve, for that gracious and eloquent speech. Let's all now focus our thoughts and do the best job we can. Let's do this!'

With that the meeting broke up and the actors went off to the green room or their dressing rooms, the crew sloped off to the prop room for a brew-up, no doubt. Gary asked Butch to join him in his cubbyhole. Before they disappeared inside, he asked Steve what his plans were, which implied that once again he was not required in the compact meeting room.

Steve said, 'I don't know. I hadn't let my thoughts get to this point in the day.'

Gary said, 'A lot of playwrights like to go to a nearby bar before curtain-up on first night. In fact some of them don't come back until the final curtain.'

Steve said, 'I completely get that, but I'd like to watch from one of the boxes or from the back of the auditorium if every seat is taken.'

Butch said, 'The stage-right box is free. I sometimes pop in there to see how things look from the front.'

'Okay, I'll do that, but I'll go and get a pint in the Zebra until closer to curtain up time.'

Butch laughed. 'Good idea. Wish I could join you. But pace yourself. It's going to be a long evening.'

The show was scheduled to start at seven-thirty. Steve had agreed to meet Grace and Matt in the foyer at seven. But when he got back after his pint in the Zebra, he was shocked to see Grace standing with Peter and Ginny, Peter and Grace both looking awkward and Ginny looking triumphant, and very pregnant. Ginny, alert as ever, had already spotted Steve in the entrance to the foyer and waved him over.

'Steve, congratulations. We are probably the last people you expected to see.'

He glanced over at Grace. She did not meet his eye, but there was a stony look on her face. He took a deep breath. This could be a very awkward conversation. 'Ginny, you're pregnant. You look amazing.'

'How observant of you! And you look as though you are about to have a play performed in public for the very first time. Another form of birth, one might think.'

'Yes, and I'm terrified.' He caught Peter's eye. 'Hello, Peter. Congratulations, to both of you.'

Peter narrowed his own gaze. 'Hi, Steve. It would seem that congratulations are in order for you too. And condolences. Grace was just telling us about your mother. I am so sorry for your loss.'

Ginny echoed the sentiment. 'Yes, Steve, you poor love. Thank goodness you've got Grace.'

Steve winced briefly. 'Yes, Grace has been fantastic.'

Grace had not been enjoying the five minutes before Steve joined them. She had been dismayed to see Ginny and Peter in the lobby, Ginny seated demurely on a gilt chair and Peter standing guard over her. It was only when Ginny stood up at Grace's approach that Grace realised she was pregnant. A torrent of emotions had swept through her: anger, disbelief, sorrow. But most of all she was furious with Steve. He must have set this up, even though he had promised her that he was not intending to invite Ginny. Matt, sensing the awkwardness of the encounter, had abandoned her to go and find Gary. Having been silent since Steve's arrival, Grace now intervened. 'Peter says that your friend, Jude, is doing a very good job running Vanguard Books. I hope you invited her as well.'

What was Grace getting at? He glared at her. 'No, I didn't invite her. I feel rather bad about that. But it's been so busy.'

Ginny, keen as ever to stir things up, said, 'Oh, she's coming alright. It was she who told us about your play. She saw an ad in the *Cambridge Evening News* and your name was mentioned, Steve.'

Steve relaxed slightly. 'That's very sweet of her. Even as the author, I was limited to how many comps I could have. So I'm sorry you had to buy your own tickets. But please do join us after the show for a few celebratory drinks.'

Peter said, 'Are you feeling nervous?'

Typical of Peter, always sniffing out a weakness. 'Yeah, I was, mainly about addressing the company and crew earlier on, but not now. I'm just a member of the audience, hobnobbing with old friends.'

Ginny laughed her musical laugh. 'Well played, Steve.'

God, she looked beautiful, even pregnant – particularly being pregnant. He could scarcely imagine the thoughts that must be going through Grace's mind.

The conversation faltered once again, Grace tapping her glass of wine neurotically with a fingernail. All potential lines of conversation seemed equally dangerous. But at that moment Jon, all black leather and white silk scarf, with the shapely, low-cut Tamsin on his arm, entered the foyer. Without missing a beat, he strode towards Steve, hailing him with, 'Maestro, this is a step up from *Krapp's Last Tape*.'

The bubble of icy resentment in which the two couples had become trapped suddenly burst in the presence of Jon's irrepressible joviality. Steve laughed. 'It certainly is, especially since we never managed to make it to Edinburgh.'

Ginny was beaming at Jon. He leaned forward and kissed her demurely on the cheek. 'Ginny, amazing, with child, I see. It suits you. Congratulations.' Then, nodding at Peter, he said, 'You must be the dad.'

Peter, who had been trying to get the measure of this cocksure rocker, now spluttered quietly into his wine. Ginny, smirking like a Siamese cat, said, 'Jon, this is Peter, my husband. Peter, Jon'

This last statement seemed to take Grace by surprise. 'You're married?'

Peter, usually so confident, now became bashful. 'Yes, we thought it best to regularise matters. It was a very private affair.'

Grace seemed to be about to say something, but thought better of it.

Jon, still grinning broadly, said, 'Let me introduce my old lady, Tamsin. So Tam, this is Ginny, who you've heard about. And this is Steve, the crazy poet, and now a playwright. This is Peter, Ginny's husband, as we've just discovered. And this is Grace, I take it, who is now with Steve.'

Grace relaxed a little. 'Thank you, Jon, for putting everyone in the picture. Steve speaks highly of you.'

Jon raised his glass. 'Yeah. Me and Steve are like brothers. Haven't known each other all that long, but joined at the hip, because we both are.'

Steve's heart went out to Jon. Thank God he'd come. But the only universe in which they could be brothers was the one in which Ginny was their mother, the worrying implication of which was that Peter must be of the brotherhood as well. Steve glanced across at Peter. He looked as if he might be sizing up to punch Jon. If he did, he'd be making a big mistake. Even though Peter was a pretty sizeable guy himself, Jon's rippling physique was all too apparent beneath his unzipped leather jacket.

The intensity of Ginny's smirks had brightened by several hundred watts. She leaned across to Tamsin. 'What do you do, Tamsin?'

Some incomprehensible squelching noises emanated from Tamsin's mouth. Jon looked at her proudly. 'She's a psychic. Incredible powers.'

Peter stared at Tamsin. 'Is that a job?'

But as quick as a flash, Ginny said, 'It's a calling, darling.'

'Right,' said Jon, approvingly.

But Peter had just taken in Tamsin's improbable bosom and in that moment concluded that it was entirely immaterial what she did. All she had to do was be. He was rapidly revising his view of Jon.

Grace sensed the rebalancing of forces between the two older men and smiled to herself. She could see why Steve liked Jon. She was sorry she hadn't met him sooner.

Peter said, 'What do you do, Jon?'

'Axe for hire, man.'

Peter wrinkled his brow. 'A lumberjack?'

Jon tried again. 'Axe as in guitar.'

Steve could see Jon's clarification had not aided comprehension. Acting as translator, he said, 'Jon is a brilliant electric guitarist. Plays with some of the biggest bands.'

Jon nodded sagely. 'Yeah, regular stand-in for Rusty Blades in Alien Hand Syndrome.'

Peter said, 'Thank you, Steve. I am not familiar with the argot.'

Grace didn't know how much more she could take of this. She was beginning to think she'd indeed been kidnapped by Little Green Men and was being subjected to some mind-numbing experiment.

Fortunately (or maybe not – it remained to be seen, as far as Grace was concerned) Angie and Rob appeared on the scene at that moment and, spotting Steve and Grace, came over to join the group. Steve made the introductions. Ginny and Peter, for very different reasons, immediately zeroed in on Angie, Peter because of her transcendent beauty, Ginny because she was keen to see how the woman she had displaced in Steve's life nearly a year previously was prospering. But first she was obliged to accept another round of congratulations on her pregnancy. Not that she really minded. She could see that every additional compliment was like a dagger in Grace's heart.

Angie still seemed to be breathless. 'We never thought we were going to make it. The trains were total chaos.'

Peter, keen to exchange words with this beauty, asked, 'Where have you come from?'

It struck him as an ambiguous question. He would not have been surprised if she'd said Venus.

'Edinburgh,' Angie replied.

'Oh, how lovely. I grew up there from the age of ten.'

'It is a really lovely city. Where were you up to the age of ten?'

'Frankfurt, although I was born in Berlin.'

'Ah, very different.'

'They were very different times.'

Ginny watched this exchange with wry amusement. Peter never missed an opportunity to impress himself on a pretty woman.

Meanwhile, Grace had turned to Rob and was saying, 'I'm sorry we couldn't put you up. As you can imagine the last few weeks have been somewhat stressful.'

Rob was the soul of tact. 'Of course. Quite understand. And I'm sorry we were unable to attend the conference you were addressing in Edinburgh recently. It sounded fascinating. Quite a panel of speakers. I hadn't realised that Müller was still alive and free to travel to the West. Rather like Lukács or Gramsci turning up.'

Grace was caught off guard for a moment. She had forgotten that Rob and Angie were Edinburgh residents. Thank goodness, they had not been able to attend the conference. Regaining her composure, she said, 'Müller's not actually that old, but Lukács is definitely dead.'

'I wish I'd gone now.'

'It was a rather dry subject, but an honour to give the keynote. However, enough of that. Where are you staying in Cambridge? It starts to get busy at this time of year.'

'Jeremiah Flynn invited us to stay with him. He's agreed to write the foreword to my new book. We're going to work on it tomorrow before we head back.'

Grace was impressed. 'My goodness, Jem doesn't often do that kind of thing. That is an honour. Who's publishing the book?'

'Grassmarket Books. I'm being edited by Fiona Stewart. She's brilliant, but I don't suppose Flynn will let her change so much as a comma in his foreword. Never mind, we'll cross that bridge when we come to it.'

At the mention of Grassmarket Books and the name of Fiona Stewart Peter suddenly switched his attention from Angie to Rob. 'Grassmarket is a great little publisher and I have a lot of respect for Fiona. She's going places. I'm not so enamoured of the publishing director, Hamish McPherson, though.'

Rob actually knew who Peter was and his position as the boss of Inflexion, but said lightly, 'It sounds as if you're in publishing?'

Peter took a business card out of his wallet. 'I am.'

But at that moment, the bell went for members of the audience to take their seats. He handed his card to Rob and said, 'Perhaps I could get five minutes of your time after the performance or at the interval?'

Rob said he would be delighted. Steve explained to the group that it had been thought better if he didn't sit in the auditorium. This was not quite the case, but no one seemed surprised. Matt reappeared and prepared to escort Grace to her seat. He seemed a little surprised that the mood amongst Steve's immediate supporters now seemed warm and friendly, despite the tangle of relationships.

Steve watched his guests walk through to the stalls. As he did so, he realised with something of a shock that Al hadn't arrived. That was disappointing, but very typical of Al. He also now realised that Jude wasn't there either. That was less surprising in that, despite Grace's suspicions and Ginny's assurances that she would be there, he hadn't formally invited her. Now that he was running through the list of no-shows, there were others he could add: Garth and Kelly, Jed Morgan, Tom Borrowdale. None totally unexpected, but disappointing all the same. He made his way to the staircase that led up to the gallery and the boxes. He had expected to feel nervous and jittery but in fact he just felt sad.

Steve sat in the box that Butch had kept free for him. He peered discreetly over the balustrade. He was pleased to see that it was nearly a full house. There were a few empty seats, but it was not so many that it suggested a lack of support, and people were still coming in from the foyer. Of course, quite a few of the seats that were occupied were comps, so the box-office take would not have been all Gary might have hoped for, but momentum had to be generated somehow.

It was odd sitting up here on his own. He felt detached from the performance. No one had said that he couldn't be backstage, but he felt that he might unsettle people or he might accidentally overhear something disobliging about his script. He'd rejected sitting in the stalls for the same reason. But really, how likely was it that the person right behind him would pronounce the play rubbish? Even if someone did, so what? No one apart from his immediate friends knew him by sight.

He scanned the stalls and spotted Matt, Gary and Grace in the third row of the centre stalls. In fact, the seat to Grace's right was still empty. Grace appeared to be dabbing her eyes with a handkerchief as if she might be crying, and Gary was patting her on the shoulder. Was she telling him about the unexpected presence of Ginny and Peter, and Ginny's advanced state of pregnancy? Or was it simply that she hadn't realised that Steve wouldn't be sitting with her? Maybe that seat had originally been allocated to him and now she felt neglected. Perhaps he should go and join her. The house lights were still on, and one or two people were still taking their seats. If he went down now, he could, without too much disturbance, get into the seat beside Grace before the show started. But as he turned the idea over in his mind, the house lights started to go down. He had left it too late. Perhaps he could join her at the interval.

The first half of the show went by in a kind of blur. The performances were excellent. The nude scenes, which had been such a disaster at the dress rehearsals, worked perfectly. Both Sally and Becky were incredibly sexy. He thought he was in love with both of them, which was how it should be. But his text seemed burdened with a debilitating awareness of its own sass, unable to settle in one register. The plot seemed at once contrived and inconclusive. Neither fault was of the kind that could be fixed by notes to actors or judicious rewrites. He was losing all confidence in the production. He wished that he'd sat with Grace. She would have reassured him. Or maybe not.

Despite his fears, the applause at the interval was generous, even enthusiastic. He told himself that this was only because the audience was packed with friends and family of members of the company and crew. They were cheering their own on. If he'd had a more robust sense of self, he would have accepted the applause in the way that one should accept a compliment, with a simple acknowledgement and without any embarrassing show of false modesty. Now that the interval had arrived, it was his chance to join Grace. But at that moment there was a tap on the door of the box and an usherette appeared. 'Mr Percival, there's a gentleman downstairs asking to see you. I said I'd have to check.'

Amused at being addressed so formally by a member of the front of house staff, but also slightly worried, he said, 'Does the gentleman have a name?'

'He didn't give a name, but he said I was to say *Fare forward, don't look back*.'

Steve couldn't resist a quiet chuckle. It was Al. 'It's a friend. Show him up.'

'And Denise asked whether I could get you some refreshment.'

'Yes, please. A couple of glasses of white wine. What's your name?'

'Suzy.'

'Thank you, Suzy. Please call me Steve.'

Suzy hesitated at the entrance to the box. 'If you don't mind me saying, it's an awfully good play. Very sexy and exciting. All the different levels. I'm not sure who the villain is. Can't wait for the second act.'

'That's very lovely of you to say so, Suzy. It means a lot to me. But if there is a villain, I don't know who it is either.'

'I wish we could do something like this for A-Level drama.'

'Where are you at school?'

'The Perse.'

'I don't imagine your teachers would approve of the sex scenes.'

'No, probably not. Worse luck.'

'Just stick at it. You'll soon be off to university.'

Suzy withdrew and Steve burst out laughing. Wisdom from the mouths of babes, and Suzy was certainly a babe.

A few minutes later, Al put his head round the door. 'Mind if I join you, guv?'

'Al, I thought you'd stood me up.'

'As if. Bloody trains.'

The two friends embraced.

Al was serious for a moment. 'Sorry about your ma, Steve. Just not fair. She was a good old girl.'

'Yeah, it's crap.'

'Sounds pretty weird, the shenanigans in Berlin. Getting a hint of it from the play. Top job, mate. Didn't know you had it in you.'

'Yeah, I need to talk to you about Berlin.'

'Why didn't you contact me when you got back?'

'It's been crazy getting the play to this point. Never worked so hard.'

'The Freya chick is pretty tasty, isn't she, especially with her kit off?'

'I can't tell you the knots you have to tie yourself in to get a bit of nudity on the stage these days.'

'But you found a way.'

There was a knock at the door. It was Suzy again, with a bottle of white wine in a cooler and a couple of glasses. 'Denise said to bring a bottle.'

She put the tray down on the little table.

Steve said, 'Suzy, please thank Denise from me.'

'Yes, Mr Percival.'

'Who?'

'I mean Steve.'

'That's better. Thanks, Suzy.'

'See you later.'

Steve wondered what she meant by this. 'Later?'

'I'm working at the party.'

Relieved, and a little disappointed for a moment, that it didn't mean something else, Steve said. 'Great. See you then.'

Suzy left the box and Al burst out laughing. 'A little bit of celebrity and they're like moths to a flame, ready to drop 'em for Mr Percival.'

'Al, she's a schoolgirl.'

'But I bet she's legal.'

'I've got all three wives in tow tonight. You don't think I'm going to try anything like that, do you? You should have been in the foyer before the start of the show. It was like the shoot-out at the OK Corral.'

'Well, you could at least get her phone number.'

'True.'

'Or I could get it for you.'

'Hands off, Al.'

'So you don't rule it out?'

'Nothing ruled out, nothing ruled in.'

At that moment, the bell for the second part rang. Al poured the drinks and the two friends settled down to watch the rest of the performance.

Whether because of the effect of the wine that Suzy had brought them or the proximity of Alan, Steve enjoyed the second half much more than he had the opening scenes. Becky was revealed as the stand-out actor, partly because of the enhancements to the role of Freya, but mainly because she seemed to believe in the character. The farewell scene between her and Tristan was touching and extremely sad and Freya's arrest in the final scene and the realisation that she and Tristan would never meet again was an affecting bitter-sweet finale. At the curtain call, Becky got the loudest cheers. Even Steve found himself applauding enthusiastically, with Al patting him on the back, saying 'Nice one, mate.'

But suddenly, the cast were raising their outstretched hands to the stage-right box, and from somewhere in the stalls came the cry 'Author, author.'

Steve shrank back, but Al said, 'Stand up, you twit. You're obliged to acknowledge your public.'

Rather shyly, Steve stood to receive the ovation. After a few moments, he gestured back at the cast and applauded, which set off another cheer which didn't sound as if it was going to subside any time soon. Becky and Sally in the centre of the stage gestured for Steve to come onstage and join them. Once again, it needed a shove in the back from Al for Steve to move into action. Less than a minute later he was taking his place on the stage between Sally and Becky. The applause was now accompanied by stamping. Steve could hardly believe this was happening. After a third set of bows, the actors started to congratulate each other, sharing hugs and kisses, an interaction in which Steve was fully included.

Sally crushed him to her magnificent chest, which to Steve's mind seemed to have received its own round of applause when she had taken her individual bow as one of the principals. As he luxuriated briefly in the opulence of her curves, she whispered in his ear, 'Thank you for the card and gift. I hope you'll come and share a glass with me later on.' A moment later, the vistas that this invitation had opened up were shattered by John wrenching him from Sally's embrace and transferring him to his own more muscular caress. 'Don't let that old slag lead you up the garden path,' and then, after a beat, 'Only joking. But if you'd ever thought of swinging the other way or were even a teeny bit bi, I'm your man.'

Steve laughed and kissed John on the cheek. 'I'll bear that in mind. You were brilliant. You really inhabited the character.'

'It was easy. I made a close study of you, just not as close as I'd liked to have done.'

'John, I am *not* Tristan.'

'Course you're not, love.'

'If you knew the chaos my life is in.'

'I know, I know. Butch told me down the Scaramouche the other night. But congratulations anyway. I hope it all works out.'

Steve wasn't exactly sure what John was implying. It was one thing to say that one's own life was in chaos; quite another if others were saying it about you. He would have to have a word with Butch later, if possible.

But these speculations were brushed aside by Becky demanding her ten seconds with Steve. 'It was the best part I've ever played,' she said, clearly still elated.

'You were the star,' he assured her, whereupon she kissed him hard on the lips and slipped her tongue into his mouth as he yielded.

Steve was conscious that all these interactions were taking place in front of a couple of hundred people. He wondered how long the whole process was going to take. But gradually the noise in the auditorium was beginning to abate and some people were making for the exits. The actors too were starting to make their way to the dressing rooms. Steve noticed that Gary, Matt and Grace had moved to the bottom of the short flight of stairs that only a few minutes previously he had bounded up. He now walked down to join them.

Grace gathered him in her arms. 'You're probably already fed up with kisses and hugs, but I'm afraid you're going to have to submit to a few more.'

Steve said, 'Submission is my default mode.'

'Enough of this modesty, Percival. Own it, enjoy it. It was a triumph.'

They held each other close for a few moments. Steve gazed into Grace's hazel eyes, her auburn hair drifting across his face. God, she was so beautiful. He kissed her tenderly and said, 'Thank you for everything. I would never have done it without you.'

Grace seemed rather uncomfortable with this accolade and said briskly, 'I don't believe that for one moment. I am just happy to have been with you through this period.'

Steve released himself from her embrace and turned to Gary, who said, 'Congratulations, Steve, I think we pulled it off.'

Steve was at first disconcerted that Gary did not attempt a hug, but their interactions in the weeks they had been working together had been from the start almost formal and far from tactile. But this was no time to be niggardly with his very real feelings of gratitude. 'I can't express how much I owe you. You are a theatrical genius. Everything worked perfectly.'

Gary bowed his head imperceptibly in acknowledgment of the tribute. 'There's always room for improvement in any production, but that was a very good start. Let's hope the critics think so too.'

'Did any make it tonight?'

'Not as many as I'd hoped, but the local chap's here and a couple from the nationals. That doesn't necessarily mean we'll get noticed, but it's encouraging. There was also a chap here from the BBC. So we'll see.'

Matt intervened here. 'Great stuff, Steve. Quite a debut. Welcome to the fraternity.'

'When I have as many credits to my name as you do, Matt, I might consider myself a member.'

As they'd been talking, front of house staff and backstage crew had been transforming the stage and the front of the stalls into a party venue. Usherettes were checking that those members of the public who remained in the auditorium had invitations to the post-performance party, gently guiding those without towards the exits. Trestle tables were being brought in and spread with white tablecloths. Soon, cool jazz was emanating from the PA system and the house lighting was lowered, with coloured pools of light washing the trestle tables, which were now being loaded with glasses and bottles of wine and beer. The lighting guys had also rigged up one of the lights to produce a cloud effect on the cyclorama at the back of the stage. Surely there was no better place to have a party than on the stage of one of the oldest theatres in the country, thought Steve. As he surveyed the scene, he suddenly caught sight of Jude, standing back shyly to one side of the stage. He went over to her.

'Jude, thank you so much for coming.'

'It was fantastic. I feel completely overwhelmed, even more than I was by the poem.'

'A team of crack professionals can transform even the most unpromising material.'

'Just stop the modesty thing, Steve. Accept the congratulations.'

'Grace has just told me much the same. I'm sorry, it's so engrained.'

'It's a defence mechanism, I know, but why you feel the need to downplay your talent is another matter.'

'You're right. No more modesty, at least for tonight. I'm sorry I didn't formally invite you. How did you get into the party?'

'Peter arranged everything. I think he made some kind of donation to the Festival.'

For a moment, Steve even entertained warm feelings for Peter. 'Good for him.'

In the spirit of reconciliation that now seemed to be abroad, Steve said, 'Let me introduce you to Grace.'

'Oh, no, Steve, she looks far too grand and beautiful.'

'Don't be silly.'

Steve grabbed Jude's hand and gently coaxed her across to where Grace was standing.

'Grace, this is Jude. I thought it was time you two met.'

For a second Grace's eyes went dead, but then a friendly smile spread across her face.

'Jude, I've been wanting to meet you for a long time. Your letterpress edition of *Event/Horizon* is a beautiful thing. We have you to thank for rescuing the poem.'

'I'm glad to have been of service.' Jude almost had to stop herself from saying *ma'am*.

'I believe you are also an important person in my ex-husband's company.'

'I wouldn't say important, but I'm grateful to have been entrusted with the Vanguard list.'

Slightly narrowing her eyes, Grace said, 'Steve said that he hadn't invited you.'

'He didn't, but I'll forgive him. Peter made a considerable donation to the Festival Trust and was given tickets for tonight. He asked me as his guest.'

Grace now felt mean at having persistently disbelieved Steve. She would try and make amends later. 'Gosh, imminent fatherhood must be mellowing Peter.'

Matt materialised and tugged Steve's sleeve. 'Steve, I'd like you to meet a very good friend of mine. This is Fred Willets. He is a producer at the BBC. He's the person who gave me my break in screenwriting.'

Steve and Fred shook hands. Fred said, 'Congratulations, Steve, that was a great debut. Gary has a good eye for talent. I think *Palace of Tears* would adapt well for our *Play for Today* strand. Can you let me have a copy of the script and your contact details?'

'I'd be delighted to.'

Fred gave him his card. 'I can't promise, of course. But once I've got your script, we will send you a letter describing what's involved and what the process is. Do you have an agent?'

Steve laughed. 'No, unless Matt is.'

Fred said, 'No, of course not. Probably better that way at this stage. I am sure you will be celebrating deep into the night. As you should. I'm afraid I can't stay longer, but I look forward to meeting you again soon. I take it you don't mind coming up to London?'

'Not at all. It's my home town.'

They shook hands and Fred made his way to the exit.

Meanwhile, elsewhere in the auditorium, Steve's little band of supporters had gathered near one of the drinks tables and were catching up with each other. Jon and Al were, for the benefit of Tamsin, reminiscing about some of the gigs they'd played together, and all three were laughing uproariously. There wasn't much to choose between Jon and Al when it came to the lewd and inappropriate, but this was just what Tamsin loved. Al had told Steve earlier up in the box that he was staying the night with Jon and Tamsin. Steve imagined that session might go on quite late; he wished he could be part of it. A little away from this boisterous group, someone had found Ginny a chair and she and Angie were chatting quietly. After the encounter with Grace, Jude had drifted over to join the conversation Peter was having with Rob. No doubt the earnest discussion they were having was publishing-related. It would be typical of Rob to have impressed Peter and typical of Peter to steal Rob from Grassmarket Books or to acquire that imprint in the way that other men acquire fine malts. But Steve couldn't help noticing that while the two men postured, Jude was jotting down something in her notebook.

Steve felt emotionally drained. He wanted to go home. The trouble was it wouldn't be a good look to leave his own party early. But was it his party? Actually, he thought not. This was about the company and the theatre. He was just the contributor of the text for what was actually some kind of primitive ritual. He leaned wearily against the angle between the stage and the stairs, feeling desolate.

At that moment, Suzy, the little usherette, now playing the part of a waitress, came by with a bottle of white wine, replenishing glasses.

'Can I top you up, Steve?'

'I'm not sure where I left my glass.'

'I'll get you a fresh one. I'll be right back.'

A few moments later, she reappeared with a clean glass and filled it for him. 'Thanks, Suze.'

'Aren't you meant to be mingling?'

'I think I've mingled with everyone and I'm exhausted. I want to go to bed.'

'So do I, with you.'

Steve groaned. 'That's very lovely of you, Suzy, but absolutely out of the question. You're too young.'

'No, I'm not. I'm eighteen and I'm sexually experienced. I bet you're only twenty-two or three.'

For a moment, Steve was lost for words. He waved his hand at his friends. 'You see these women? I'm either in or have had a relationship with all of them, well actually not the woman over there with the guy in black leather, and the whole thing is a terrible mess.'

Why was he telling her this?

Suzy didn't seem surprised. 'Did you have a relationship with Freya?'

'If you mean the real person on whom the character is based, let me assure you, I am not Tristan.'

'You seem very Tristan-like.'

'Surely you mean Tristan is very like me.'

With a look of triumph on her face, Suzy said, 'Checkmate, I think, Mr Percival.'

Realising that he had just torpedoed the very flimsy coracle of denial he had been piloting for several weeks now, he said, 'No, you're right. Some aspects of Tristan are based on my experiences. I did have a brief relationship with a young woman in East Berlin and I am still worrying about her.'

'Did she really go to prison? I thought she was more likely to be a Stasi agent?'

Suzy didn't miss much. She was clearly a smart cookie. 'Who knows? In the world of spies, no one, or at least very few people, know what the score is, what's true and what's not.'

'Were you involved in all that?'

'To a very limited extent.'

'Should you be telling me this?'

'Of course not. Which means you can't believe a word I say.'

'So sleeping with you is not out of the question?'

'Apart from that. You can believe me on that particular score.'

'Does it really matter? Shouldn't you just do what you want?'

'Often what you think you want is not what you really want. Unless you want to ruin your life.'

'Is that what you did?'

'Yes.'

'So this,' she spread her hand to take in the whole party, 'is ruination?'

'For some reason I think it is.'

'Let me comfort you.'

'You have already. But you must get on with your job now. Or there will be trouble.'

Suzy looked around. 'Or what? Your wives will tear you to pieces.'

'Something like that. Are you working next week?'

'Yes, Friday and Saturday.'

'Okay, we can talk then. Only talk, mind. Now scoot.'

'Thanks, Steve.'

She tootled off, cool as a cucumber, to resume dishing out white wine.

Grace had been observing this overlong conversation to fill up a glass with wine. But she wasn't dismayed. A girl like that was what he needed: fresh, fearless, and closer to him in age. He was out of his league with Angie and Ginny and, sadly, with her too.

Some of the actors were now dancing on stage. Sally, all beads and silk scarves, shimmying for all she was worth, spotted Steve leaning against the apron of the stage and beckoned him to join them. Steve shook his head, but Sally had already drunk more than was good for her. She sashayed her way to the top of the steps and leaned forward in supplication, stretching her arms out and displaying to Steve a good deal of cleavage as she did so. Slowly, almost mechanically, Steve mounted the stairs and stepped onto the magical world of the stage. With her arms and hips and breasts, Sally wove an invisible silken net around him and drew him towards her. Someone turned up the music.

Steve closed his eyes and started to turn slowly, catching the pulse of the music and starting to ride it. Soon he had lift-off and freed his arms. Sally was now clapping and strutting like a flamenco dancer, circling Steve, twitching her skirt to reveal a shapely leg. More people were moving onto the stage, reducing the space for movement. The beat was irresistible. Sally was spinning Steve around, making him dizzy, until he was in danger of falling over, at which point she caught him in her arms and drew him to her. It was clear that at this point Sally could do whatever she wanted with him. Grace watched in fascination. How would this end? Presumably Sally would carry him off to her den and dismantle him.

But at that moment a new phalanx of dancers, spearheaded by Becky in a very short skirt and a tight top, had entered the motley and gradually drew Steve away from Sally and her beads and silks. This was a different kind of dancing, abrupt, athletic, pelvic. Steve was in a different world now. Becky leaned forward and unbuttoned Steve's shirt revealing his slim but strong chest. He too was strutting now, grounding himself. Grace admired the spontaneous choreography. If Becky ended up being the winner of this contest, she'd probably have Steve right there on stage with everyone gathered around. She supposed this was Steve's initiation ceremony, his rite of passage. The actors were admitting him to their guild or mystery. He was one of them now. She didn't need to see how this ended, and in view of what Sheena was requiring her to do, it was just as well.

She went over to the cloakroom to get her coat. As she was putting it on, the little waitress, who had been talking to Steve, came by with a tray of drinks. Grace touched her on the arm. 'Could you tell Steve I've gone home?'

The girl looked startled, as though she'd been found out. 'Yes, Mrs Percival.'

As Grace strode towards the door, she said over her shoulder, 'Dr Mitchell, actually.'

By the time Steve got back to Glisson Road, Grace had been asleep for more than an hour. His footsteps on the stairs had wakened her, but when he came into the bedroom she pretended to be asleep. It was to his credit that he did not try to wake her or attempt any kind of intimacy. No doubt he had already had his fill of female attention. She wondered who he had ended up with: Sally or Becky? Or maybe even the little waitress? Probably not the latter after Grace's rather heavy-handed intervention as she was leaving. No, given Steve's penchant for older women, she imagined Sally had been the victrix.

But in truth, she rather wished that he had made the effort to rouse her when he got home. She could have done with some comfort from the newly crowned master of the revels. After all, having promised Sheena that she would bring things to an end after the last night of Steve's play, there were not going to be that many more opportunities for them to make love. But Steve was a sensitive man and could not have been unaware of her already sullen mood. Whether he was aware of the vortex of negative emotions into which the sight of a very pregnant Ginny had plunged her was another matter. Whatever the case, by the end of the evening her envy of Ginny had been supplemented by anger at having been outmanoeuvred by Peter, jealousy of Jude, and above all resentment at Sheena's reappearance in her life. Everything had turned to ashes.

In the perverse way of the human heart, she now blamed Steve for all this. If she had never taken up with Steve, she would never have re-appeared on Sheena Ferguson's radar. But, in point of fact, her vulnerability in that regard was purely a consequence of her own past indiscretions. The intersection of events was certainly unfortunate, but it was none of Steve's doing.

The worst of it was that she was already grieving for a relationship that was not yet over. Now that it was too late, she saw that her recruiting of Steve to be the father of her baby had been an unnecessarily elaborate attempt to redeem the dismal years with Peter. It would have been more honest to have admitted to herself that what she had wanted was to rediscover the joy of sex. That was certainly what she had got with Steve. Had she become pregnant as a consequence, she would simply have had to deal with it. Procreation ought surely to be the result of a loving relationship, not an end in itself. The direct pursuit of happiness was more likely to end in the kind of tears she was now weeping. Nor would this be the end of the weeping. She shuddered to think what sex with Müller would be like. Sheena had said that it wouldn't be forever and that her aim was to bring Müller down. But however little time it took, it would be too long in terms of her chances of conceiving.

What was really troubling her, however, was the memory of the conversation she had had with Gary the previous evening, in which she had crudely traduced Steve. She had hinted to Gary that Steve had used force against her, but her vagueness had resulted in Gary assuming that Steve had hit her, or worse, and had triggered in him a strong antipathy towards Steve. Even as the words had left her lips, she knew that this was not the right way to deal with the situation. But she hadn't had the courage to withdraw the slander while there was still time. If it was a way of eliciting some sympathy from her oldest friend, it was a cruel, and more importantly, an unjust one. Her mother's long held view of her as impulsive and spiteful was perhaps not so far from the truth.

She sensed now, as she lay remorsefully in the pale light of dawn with Steve sleeping peacefully beside her, that she had probably sabotaged the run of Steve's play. It was no good her consoling herself that, without her intervention on the play's behalf with Sheena, it would never have gone on in the first place. She had in effect strangled it at birth. Not only would she be losing Steve at the end of the week, but when her lie became apparent, she would also probably be losing the trust of her oldest friend. The tears poured down her cheeks.

She slipped out of bed and tiptoed to the bathroom where she washed her face and dried the tears from her eyes. Well, she would try and make what remained of her relationship with Steve as pleasant as possible, regardless of whom he had fucked the previous night. She went downstairs and made some coffee and brought it back up to the bedroom. Steve stirred as she put the mug on the bedside table. He groaned and sat up rubbing his eyes. 'I'm sorry I was home so late.'

Grace put as much brightness into her voice as possible. 'If you can't paint the town red on the first night of your first play, when can you?'

'Thanks, Grace, for being so understanding.'

Grace climbed in on her side of the bed. 'I'm sorry for having left so early.'

'I don't blame you. I know you didn't believe it when I said that I didn't invite Peter and Ginny, but I do understand how galling it must have been for you to have had them there.'

'I'm sorry I doubted you. I was behaving like the brat my mother believes me to be.'

'You didn't. It was a difficult encounter for both of us.'

'Thank goodness for the actors. They at least seemed to have been ready to celebrate your achievement.'

'They were great. I suppose you think I succumbed to the attentions of one or other of them, but I can promise you that I didn't. I can't say I wasn't tempted, though.'

'It's honest of you to admit it and very restrained of you not to have indulged yourself. I would have tried not to blame you.'

'You know what I'm like, but if I was going to celebrate in that way with anybody, it was going to be with you. That's why I'm sorry I got back so late.'

Flinching at the patent untruth of it, she said, 'You should have woken me. I would have happily made up for the groupies.'

Steve laughed. 'There's no comparison between what we have when we make love and a quick shag in a dressing room.'

Disguising as best she could the anguish she really felt, she said, 'You've just talked yourself into a long morning in bed.'

When Steve arrived at the theatre the next afternoon, Gary was already giving the actors his notes. Steve was slightly shocked that Gary hadn't asked him to participate.

At the end of the session, when the actors had gone off to the green room, Steve said to Gary, 'Sorry I was late. I didn't realise you were starting earlier than usual.'

'There was a lot to get through, so I'd asked for a longer session. In fact, I think it'd be better if you didn't join us.'

Steve didn't know what to say. It felt like a snub. Gary seemed oblivious to the effect his remark was having on Steve. 'Did you see the review in the *Cambridge Evening News*?'

Steve had forgotten to pick up a copy, not expecting a review so soon. 'No.'

'It's not very generous. I'm afraid it's a bit insulting. Phrases like *apprentice work*, *facile*, and *pretentiously enigmatic* spattered around. I really don't think it's you he's getting at.'

'Who's he getting at then?'

'Me. His name is Cyril Sweeney and he and I have crossed swords in the past. I think it's a case of old scores to settle. Unfair really to unload like that on a new playwright. I'd advise you not to read it.'

As far as Steve was concerned, Gary's claim to be the target of the stinker didn't hold much water. The phrases he'd singled out as most wounding could only really be laid at the door of the writer. Steve supposed that he ought to be grateful to Gary, but he also felt that Gary's attitude towards him had already altered since the first night. Gary could see the look of disappointment on Steve's face.

'The world of the theatre can be vicious and petty, I'm afraid, Steve. Don't let it get to you. It certainly won't affect Fred Willets' attitude. The BBC makes up its own mind. Besides, we might get some better reviews in the nationals. The trouble is there won't be enough time for them to generate better sales at the box office, whereas that one snide review will have a highly negative effect. Like sailors, actors are very superstitious. So I'd like to set up a *cordon sanitaire* between you and them. That's why I think it better if you don't attend the pre-show meetings.'

Steve didn't quite buy into the logic that Gary was deploying, but how could he object? He nodded glumly. 'Do you mind if I watch the performances from the wings?'

'That's Butch's domain, but I think you might get the same answer. The box is available to you for the whole of the run. You can invite whoever you want to join you. I'm sorry, I've got to rush. I've got quite a few calls to make. Maybe catch you after the show for a drink.'

With that he departed for his little office, leaving Steve feeling absolutely gutted.

Despite Gary's warning, Steve was determined to read the whole review. He stepped out onto the street and walked up to the *Cambridge Evening News* offices a little further up the street. He picked up a copy of the late edition and turned to the review. It only took him a few seconds to read it. Yes, Gary had zeroed in on the most wounding phrases, but to Steve's mind the review was reasonably balanced. The critic had found good things to say about the production. He had been complimentary about the cast, especially Becky, thought the nude scenes had been handled with tact, and the set design had managed to cleverly differentiate the two Berlins. He also conceded that the current status of Berlin was a topic that was crying out for serious theatrical treatment, but the playwright's facile approach had not done justice to the complexities of the situation. Opportunities had been missed and the audience had instead been presented with a series of mysteries that were pretentiously enigmatic. No doubt this was an apprentice piece, but make no mistake the playwright had real talent as was evident from his snappy dialogue. He would definitely write better plays in the future. It was just a pity that this one had not been workshopped more thoroughly. It promised more than it delivered.

Well, it was certainly not a rave review, and it was mean-spirited in view of the resources available to the Festival, but it was hardly swingeing. Apprentice piece was an easy shot given that it was a first play by a new playwright. Facile was one of those words that had two very different meanings. The obvious sense here was that it ignored the true complexities of the issue. Well, yes, one had to simplify the issue to dramatise it. Hollywood did it all the time. And yes, it was enigmatic for a similar reason. But for some people enigmas were always pretentious to the extent that the phrase pretentiously enigmatic was essentially a tautology.

Steve had not thought of Gary as a glass half empty person. That was Steve's usual stance. But in this case, and not just because he was the author, he was inclined to take the glass half full view. If he'd had time to prepare properly and been allowed to speak to the company, that's what he would have said. With luck the cast had taken comfort from the little praise that had been directed at them. And perhaps Gary would, in due course, come to a more positive view of matters. No doubt the stress of keeping the Festival going financially was getting to him and making it difficult for him to keep things in perspective.

But Steve did feel, as a consequence of Gary's reaction, that he'd been cut adrift. It was as if his pass had been taken away or he'd been sent to Coventry. He thought of searching out Butch and getting his take on things. But he knew that Butch, kind as he was, saw himself as Gary's *consigliere* and Steve did not want to put him in a difficult position. He probably ought to have expected some sort of comedown or anticlimax after the euphoria of Saturday night. Hopefully, the actors would ignore the one carping notice and put in another slick performance.

But that was not the case. The second performance was a shambles, worse than the dress rehearsal. Steve couldn't quite put his finger on the problem. He got the feeling that Gary had given the cast so many notes that they had not had the time to incorporate them properly. There were a number of missed cues and Becky who had been so brilliant on Saturday actually fluffed her lines at one point. Even worse, Larry had reverted to his caricature German officer from *Colditz*. There were also noticeably fewer people in the audience. In a way, that was only to be expected, but the mood of despair, the sense of catastrophe did seem to be contagious.

Things did pick up over the next few days. There were a couple of good reviews in *Varsity* and *Stop Press* and from the Tuesday there were noticeably more undergraduates in the audience. The performances became smoother too. The last two performances had full houses and were well received. Steve was hopeful that he might now be readmitted to the fraternity, the curse, as it were, having been cancelled, but the cold shoulder was still very much in evidence, at least from Gary and Butch.

## Sunday, 25 May 1975

STEVE SAT OPPOSITE GRACE at the kitchen table and stared at her in disbelief. He was completely mystified by what she was saying. After the end-of-run party the previous night, they had made love and fallen asleep in each other's arms. So this sudden change of tone next morning was hard to comprehend.

The bleak mood at last night's party couldn't have been more different from the bacchanalian exuberance of the first-night party a week earlier. The guest list had been restricted to the company, most of whom seemed anxious and exhausted. The only outsiders had been Grace and Matt. There had also been a notable absence of largesse, attendees having been asked to each bring a bottle. In itself this was not surprising. The week's takings for *Palace* had been disappointing, despite the uptick in sales for the last two performances. A sense of financial crisis permeated everything.

But there were also compensations. Steve had mentioned to Grace in the course of the week that he seemed to be getting the cold shoulder from Gary and Butch. She had put it down to the brewing financial crisis at the theatre and had urged him not to take it personally. He had contemplated giving the end-of-run party a miss, but Grace had advised against it and said she would stand by him, which she had indeed done. In contrast to the earlier party, she had been exaggeratedly attentive to him.

Steve's first thought was that this was actually her way of warning off Sally and Becky. But, in fact, over the course of the evening, Grace went out of her way to establish cordial relations with both women. She and Becky got on particularly well, having discovered that they both came from Somerset. It was only later that Steve noted that, by contrast, Grace's interactions with Gary were surprisingly brief. It seemed remarkably petty if Gary was extending his disapproval of Steve to Grace, his oldest friend.

It was remarkable how quickly Steve's star had waned. It was as if he had been handed the black spot. Butch had hardly exchanged a single word with him throughout the week. Only kindly, sensitive Matt, presumably uncomfortable with the idea of Steve being ostracised, had attempted any kind of pleasantry.

Steve cleared his throat and leaned across the table to take her hand, but she withdrew it. Still trying to come to terms with the finality of her decision, he said, 'But this is completely out of the blue. We had a lovely evening. Neither of us was particularly drunk. We made love. You didn't seem reluctant.'

It was true. Realising what she was planning to do, she'd thought it would be good to have him inside her one more time, to feel him release himself in that way he had of shuddering and then subsiding. She'd thought he'd appreciate it too. She knew this was self-serving, of course. To have appreciated it in that way, he would also have had to have known that it was the last time.

'I know. It's not that you've displeased me. It's just that this is not right for either of us. You did nothing wrong last night. I was very proud of you. Certain members of the company were clearly delighted to have been involved in the premiere of your play, even if others weren't so gracious. But now that it's finished its run, it's a good moment to terminate our arrangement.'

'Do you mean that you have been planning to do this for some time?'

'Not planning, but the realisation had been sinking in.'

'Since when?'

'I can't remember, Steve.'

'You must have some idea. When we were in Berlin?'

'I can't give you a precise time.'

'Was it because I haven't been paying you enough attention?'

'No. There's no point trying to identify a moment.'

'It's because Ginny's pregnant and I've not been able to give you a baby, isn't it? It must be.'

'The fact that I'm not pregnant is not your fault.'

'So it's just in the last week, then. That, of course, makes complete sense.'

'I don't know why you say that.'

'Because after the first night I was frozen out at the Festival.'

'Frozen out?'

'No one spoke to me. Not even Butch. I wasn't allowed to address the company for the rest of the week. The final night party was like a wake.'

'Everyone must have been exhausted. Gary is a bit of a slavedriver.'

'Gary is not as big a man as I thought he was. He blamed me for the bad reviews.'

'Perhaps the financial pressure was getting to him.'

'A better person would have taken the hit and shrugged it off.'

Grace felt terrible. She should never have spoken to Gary in the terms that she did at the first night.

'I should have let you know the way my thoughts were going, but I could see how hurt you were by your mother's death and how hurt you would be when I told you that we were finished. Nor did I want to undermine the production. So I had to try and choose a moment with the least likelihood of collateral damage. It hasn't been easy to do.'

'But you still haven't given me a reason. There has to be a reason.'

That was true. She couldn't give him the real reason. But it would be beyond cruel not to give him something to hang onto.

'I wanted your seed, not you. Forgive me for putting it like that. But it had got to the point where you wanted *me*, not just plentiful sex and a place to live. That was shaping up to be a disaster.'

'And this isn't?'

'Perhaps it's damage limitation.'

'But what about the baby?'

'That's finished too. I realised that the other night when I saw Ginny. I don't want to be valued for my biological function; I want to be valued for my mind.'

'Isn't that part of your biology?'

'I suppose it is if you're a materialist.'

'So you wake up this morning, note that you've started your period and say right Percival has had his chances, now I'm kicking him into touch.'

'No, not that, but it does mean that it's possible for us to have a clean break with no unexpected surprises a few weeks down the line.'

'So, no time for reflection or second thoughts.'

'I'm afraid not. I would like you to move out of Glisson Road as soon as possible. Fortunately, you are the owner of a very nice flat in London.'

'I don't want to live in London. I want to stay in Cambridge.'

'Well, I'm sure you will be able to arrange something.'

'And that's it?'

'That's it. I'm going up to my room now to work. I realise that we are going to have to spend some days in this house together, but let's attempt to be civil to each other until you have made other arrangements. You can start by moving your things out of my bedroom.'

With that, Grace stood up. He searched her face. There seemed to be no sign of anger or sadness in it. Her voice had been steady throughout the conversation. It was as if the Grace that he had known for the last three years and intimately for the last few months had been packed up and put back in her box. In front of him was an imperious being, brooking no dissent and utterly sure of what she was doing. She turned and left the room without another word.

Steve was dumbfounded. He hadn't seen this coming. The, admittedly qualified, pleasure at the staging of his play and the energy and commitment the cast and crew had put into it now shivered into a million tiny pieces. Even the fact that Fred Willets, the BBC producer who had somehow shown up at the first night and asked for a copy of the script now meant nothing. He couldn't deny that there was a logic to Grace's case, but why hadn't she shared her doubts with him earlier? He had been trying to adhere to the conditions which she had set for the relationship. But clearly, he had overstepped the line and gone so far beyond the agreed parameters that she no longer wanted a child or at least no longer wanted him to be its father. But he also sensed something else had happened or some other factor was in play, but as to what it was he didn't have the faintest idea.

He felt that he hadn't given a good account of himself in the conversation that she had just terminated. She had taken advantage of him and he had been too shocked to challenge her. But now he felt a seam of anger opening deep in his belly. He had been subjected to a vicious attack. His impulse was to rush upstairs and shake whatever nonsense had got into her head out of it. But that would never do. It was too easy to lose control. No, he had to get out of the house. He'd rather be seen as a coward than a bully. All that new Steve stuff was nonsense.

It was raining and the pubs didn't open for another couple of hours. But so what? The rain would disguise his tears. He put his jacket on and opened the front door. For a moment, he stood there hoping to hear the door of her room opening and Grace calling him. But the house remained silent. He stepped onto the path and let the tears flow down his cheeks.

Half an hour or so later, he had reached the footbridge on Jesus Green. He was soaking, and there was still more than an hour to go until the pubs opened. He sheltered for a while on one of the benches at the back of the public conveniences, but the wind was driving the rain under the shallow overhang. At least when he was walking, he was warm. One thing was certain: he didn't want to go back to Glisson Road yet, not just because it would feel like a defeat, but because he still hadn't worked out what he was going to do. It then occurred to him that he wasn't far from Magrath Avenue. Perhaps Jude was in and would let him shelter there for a while. This was not really the best thing he could do, but he needed to get out of the rain and he needed to talk to someone.

Ten minutes later he was knocking on Jude's door. He had no idea whether she lived on her own or shared with others. If she was in and answered the door, he would assess the situation then. A few moments later, Jude opened the door. She was in her dressing gown.

'Steve? What are you doing here?'

'I was out for a walk and I didn't realise that it was raining so hard. I wondered if I could hang out with you until the pubs open. But only if it's not inconvenient. I'm sure your boyfriend wouldn't want me dripping on the carpet.'

'I haven't got a boyfriend. I'm just a little concerned to have you turning up here at eleven o'clock on a Sunday morning looking like a drowned rat. Have you been out all night?'

'No, I'm sorry I disturbed you. It was a stupid idea.'

He turned to go.

'No, no. Come in. You'll have to excuse the mess. You know what I'm like.'

She pushed the door wider open and let him step in. He stood on the doormat, water streaming off him. 'Steve, what's happened?'

'She's thrown me out.'

'Oh, Steve, what have you been doing now?'

'Honestly, nothing.'

'Get that coat off. I'll hang it over the bath.'

While she was doing that, Steve took his shoes off and squelched into the little front room, which was not much bigger than the one in the Ainsworth Street house. He stood there in the middle of the room, aware that he would soak the sofa or armchair if he sat on them. It would be better if he could sit on a wooden chair in the kitchen. Jude returned. 'You're soaked through. You're going to have to take those things off.'

'I shouldn't.'

'Don't be stupid. That's not an invitation to join me in my bed. I'll get you a dry t-shirt and a couple of bath towels which you can wrap around you. I'm afraid I don't have any men's underwear. I'll leave you to decide how you're going to handle that.'

She returned with the towels and the t-shirt. A few minutes later, Steve had stripped off his sodden clothes, put the t-shirt on, wrapped one of the towels around his waist and put the other over his shoulders. Jude took his wet clothes to join his jacket and then called through to ask whether he wanted tea or coffee.

When she returned with the coffees, she said, 'Well, at least you look slightly more human now.'

'Thanks, Jude. I'm sorry to do this to you.'

'I suppose it's my fate to be around whenever you hit rock bottom. Everything was looking so good for you at the first night of *Palace of Tears*. It was fascinating to see you in context, to meet your gang. I'm sorry Ginny and Peter were there. I let it slip, but I didn't expect them to come. But you know what Ginny's like.'

'Despite what you said in the foyer on the first night, Grace was sure that I was the one who'd invited Ginny.'

'Is that why she's chucked you out?'

'Probably.'

'I'm so sorry. I wasn't trying to mess things up for you.'

'I know. It's just that she had no idea that Ginny was pregnant.'

'Oh, no.'

'The bone of contention, well, one of the bones of contention between Grace and Peter, was that Grace wanted a child and Peter didn't. Then the first time that Grace sees him after their divorce has gone through, it turns out that Ginny is extremely pregnant. A bit of a slap in the face, really.'

'But why blame you?'

'Because I was meant to be providing her with a child. I was her sperm donor. But after five months of trying, she's still not pregnant.'

'That's not necessarily your fault.'

'No, but it's adding insult to injury.'

'Kind of, but I'm sure you were up for frequent sex.'

'I did my best.'

'I can imagine you did. So I still don't get it. Peter and Ginny had a head start on you. Another few sessions in the Glisson Road boudoir and you would have hit the cervical bull's-eye.'

'That's what I thought too.'

'So what happened?'

'I don't know. Everything was fine, through the weeks of rehearsals and then during the run of the play. Things were a bit downbeat at last night's end-of-run party, but I put that down to the *Palace* production being wrapped up. We even made love last night. Then she goes to the loo this morning, sees that her period has started and says, *That's it, sunshine. Sling yer hook.*'

'Blimey, that all sounds a bit crazy.'

'Yes.'

'But I have to say, Steve, the whole thing seems crazy. What draws you to these women? I had quite a long talk with that Angie at the first-night party. She's so ethereal and brainy. She doesn't seem like your type.'

'I don't have a type.'

'I beg to differ. But leaving that aside, what are we going to do with you now?'

'I've got a flat in London, but I need some time to sort things out here in Cambridge.'

'So you thought you'd come and appeal to good ol' Jude?'

'No, I had no idea what I was going to do. I just needed to get out of the house.'

'What does Grace expect you to do?'

'I have no idea.'

'So you'd like to come and stay with me?'

'Just until I've found somewhere else. Jon and Tamsin might put me up. I could try Tenison Road again.'

'I don't know, Steve. It doesn't make me feel very good. It's rather taking me for granted.'

'I'd sleep on the sofa, pay you rent, stay out of your way, cook your supper.'

'For how long?'

'A couple of weeks.'

'What happens then?'

'I'd move down to London. Or find a place here in Cambridge. I've got some money. The executor of my mother's will has given me some cash until the probate on her will is sorted out.'

'I really don't know.'

'We could work things out again, Jude.'

'But isn't some enigmatic, powerful woman going to come along and scoop you up? Then that'll be the end of Jude, for a second time.'

'No, I don't think so. They've had their fun. I'm yours, if you want me.'

'Steady on, Rover. I think this is where you go wrong. Let's just take this one step at a time. If you really want to be with *me* and you're not just taking shelter from the storm, then I'm afraid I can't let you stay here. In view of everything that's happened, you're going to have to earn the right to be with me.'

'How do I do that?'

'I can't tell you. In any case, I don't know.'

An hour later, having dried out somewhat but failed to convince Jude that he would be a model tenant and would crash on a mattress in her box room, Steve stepped back out onto Magrath Avenue. There was nothing for it; he would have to try Jon and Tamsin. Fortunately, it had now stopped raining and a watery sun was blinking through the clouds. He was disappointed that Jude had not succumbed to his pleas, but he knew she was right and he loved her all the more for it. He had also been heartened by the kiss she had given him.

It didn't take him long to get to the address in Ferry Path that Jon had given him at the first-night party. He wasn't hopeful of finding Jon in, because it was already past Sunday lunchtime pub opening time, but his hesitant tap on the front door of the little house was answered almost immediately.

'Steve, good to see you. Come in.'

Steve stepped into the hallway and took off his jacket. Delicious aromas were coming from the kitchen at the back of the house. Jon, noticing perhaps the twitching of Steve's nostrils, said, 'Tamsin's doing the full Sunday roast number. She's a genius in the kitchen and in the bedroom, as a matter of fact. You'd be welcome to join us. For lunch, that is. Not in the bedroom. But, I suppose, not even that's out of the question.'

Steve laughed. 'I'd love to stay for lunch. The bedroom can wait for a more suitable occasion.'

Over the lunch, which really was delicious, Steve explained his predicament. He didn't go into full details, thinking he'd save that for a *tête-à-tête* over a pint with Jon in due course. Jon had no hesitation in saying that Steve was welcome to stay as long as he liked. However, Steve could tell from the look on her face that Tamsin was not so enthusiastic. In an attempt to set her mind at rest, he said, 'I promise it will only be for two weeks, and I will pay you rent up front.'

He named a figure that was considerably in excess of going rates for lodgings and he was pleased to see Tamsin's demeanour soften. Jon in the meantime was, as ever, into practicalities. 'I've still got the VW. When will you have pulled your stuff together?'

'There's not much. I could be ready tomorrow afternoon.'

With luck, Grace would be out. She often was in the afternoons. If he announced his plans when he got back to Glisson Road, she would probably make herself scarce in any case.

Jon clapped his hands together and raised both thumbs. 'You're on. I'm looking forward to some axe time together and we could get back to *Krapp's Last Tape*.'

'I haven't played for ages and I'm finished with *Krapp*.'

Jon was having none of Steve's excuses. 'It's like riding a bike, man. You never totally forget. Sometimes, by the magic of inaction, you're even better after a lay-off.'

Steve laughed again. It was so nice hanging out with Jon. It would be good to share his optimistic take on life for a couple of weeks.

In the late afternoon, Steve walked back to Glisson Road considerably heartened. That was not to say that he was any the less confused or upset, but at least he now had somewhere welcoming to lay his head for the next couple of weeks. He still had to get through the rest of the evening and night with Grace. He wasn't at all sure that he would be able to maintain his composure, but it would at least give him an opportunity to try to convince her again that she was overreacting.

When he got home, however, she was not there. Clearly, she had decided on a strategic absence. He found a note on the kitchen table. She had gone to friends and wouldn't be back until late. He should go ahead and fix his own supper. She had made up the bed in his study and moved his things that had been in her bedroom there. She would be going out at nine the following morning and would be out for the best part of the day. If he had anything to say to her, they could talk over breakfast. The note was signed with a capital G, no kisses, no endearment.

After Tamsin's magnificent lunch, Steve had no need of any supper. He drew a bath and soaked in it for a long time. Afterwards, he went downstairs to the sitting room in his dressing gown and helped himself to a couple of small glasses of malt. For old times' sake, he listened to some Miles Davis and then one of Grace's treasured Serge Gainsbourg LPs. Before long, he found himself crying again and decided it was time for bed.

## Friday, 13 June 1975

GARY LOOKED AT GRACE over his wineglass. 'Well, this is nice. It's not often I get you to myself.'

'I hope Matt didn't mind.'

'Not in the slightest. It might have been a different matter if the invitation had been from a hunky young man.'

Grace laughed nervously. 'Well, it's about a certain young man that I wanted to talk.'

'Steve hasn't been pestering you, I hope.'

'No, I've heard nothing from him since we parted company.'

'Glad to hear it. I'm just sorry I put so much effort into his bloody play.'

'Gary, you and I both know that *Palace of Tears* was an exceptional piece of work from a young writer.'

'It doesn't matter how good a piece of work it was. It's unacceptable to strike a woman.'

'He didn't hit me.'

'But you told me he did.'

'Well, I didn't actually say he'd hit me. You're extrapolating that from Peter's behaviour. But I did imply that he had used force.'

'Grace, are you saying that I froze him out on the basis of something that wasn't the case?'

'Yes, and I feel terrible about it.'

'Really, I don't know what to say…'

'I can't tell you everything, but let me try to explain. You remember after we graduated that I went off to Berlin to start research on my thesis. It was just before the Wall went up.'

'I remember. You got involved in the student escape committees.'

'I did, but I also betrayed them.'

'To whom?'

'To the Stasi. I was in love… I thought I was in love with a young Communist, and somehow he convinced me that what the DDR was trying to achieve was honourable. I realise now that he was what has become known as a Romeo, an agent tasked with persuading silly girls to do bad things.'

'So you were part of an escape committee, but you were letting the Stasi know when your committee was running an operation.'

'Yes, several people were arrested as a consequence and spent time in prison. Fortunately, my activities didn't last long because I myself was arrested or more accurately detained.'

'By whom?'

'By the British security apparatus in Berlin.'

'But you weren't charged or sanctioned?'

'No, I was spared that for agreeing to betray my only recently acquired comrades.'

'You were a double agent.'

'Yes, and I went on being so when I went to Paris, reporting on what MI6 considered student subversives.'

'What about when you came back to Cambridge?'

'Then it was more about spotting people who might eventually work for SIS.'

'A recruitment scout?'

'Yes.'

'You're still doing that?'

'No, I stopped some years ago.'

'Okay, but I don't see why all that led you to tell me that Steve hit you.'

'Unfortunately, my visit to Berlin to support Steve when his mother was dying put me back on SIS's radar, indeed on the radar of the person who had interrogated me in 1961…'

'And?'

'And they've reactivated me.'

'Couldn't you just have refused?'

'In which case, the sordid details of my past would have found their way into the public domain…'

'…buggering up your chances of further preferment in the academic world.'

'Exactly.'

'But why lie about Steve hitting you? You could have done whatever the spooks wanted you to do and had your baby with Steve.'

'What they want me to do precludes that.'

'They wanted you to ditch Steve?'

She nodded, sniffing disconsolately. 'The sight of a pregnant Ginny at the first night of *Palace* enraged me so much that I just lashed out. Peter had been denying me a child for longer than I care to think about and then five minutes after taking up with Ginny he puts her up the duff.'

Gary took her hand. 'Why didn't you tell me about the bind you were in? You could have trusted me and we could have worked something out.'

Tears were pouring from her eyes. Gary unrolled a napkin from the table and handed it to her. As she dabbed her eyes, she said, 'When the situation was put to me, I realised that I wanted to be a professor more than I wanted a relationship with Steve. And then when I saw Ginny, I questioned my own desire to be a mother. But I didn't have the heart or the guts to discuss things with Steve. Inevitably, I found myself withdrawing from him. Both you and Matt noticed the chill that had entered our relationship at the first night of the play and I just made up that nonsense about Steve hurting me.'

'But why then?'

'I was asked to go in and see the director a couple of weeks after we got back from Berlin. I should never have gone to Berlin. Steve didn't really want me there. I rather got in the way of what he was being asked to do.'

'All that stuff with Inge?'

'Yes, and I reacted like a spoilt brat. You would have thought that I was the callow one.'

'But why the rush? Surely they could have given you some time to sort things out in your life.'

'I can't go into those details, but I was given a deadline which was the end of the first week of rehearsals of *Palace*.'

'I think we should get in touch with Steve and beg his forgiveness.'

'No, it's too late.'

'So why tell me all this?'

'I don't mind you thinking ill of me. I have behaved atrociously. In fact, when I look back over my life, I can see that really I'm not a very nice person. It's something my mother always said.'

'Nonsense. June can be a vicious old hag. Don't accept her view of you.'

'You're probably right, but the reason I wanted to make this confession is that I don't want you to go on thinking badly of Steve. He has behaved impeccably throughout.'

'Apart from sleeping with whatever girl crosses his path.'

'It's not like that. I exaggerated the whole thing. I suppose I felt insecure.'

'So what do you want me to do?'

'Not hate me too much and find some way of patching things up with Steve and encouraging him with his writing. He blossomed under your tutelage. There are not many people he submits to, but you are one.'

'Whatever I do, I doubt if he'll ever trust me again. I should have had it out with him when you told me, and it would have become apparent then that you were lying. This doesn't make me feel good, Grace. This changes our relationship.'

'I know. Let's finish now.'

Ginny directed a full beam smile at Jude. 'Thank you for coming to see me. I hope it hasn't inconvenienced you.'

Jude, hands crossed demurely in front of her, said, 'It's a pleasure, Virginia.'

Indicating with one hand that Jude should sit in the armchair on the other side of the fireplace, Ginny said, 'Jude, please. I consider us to be friends, even if I am the boss's wife.'

Jude greeted this ice-breaker with a simple 'Thank you.'

'Speaking of the boss, I understand that he has promoted you, which is why you are now working from the head office.'

'Yes, I'm grateful for the confidence Mr Newman has in me.'

'I hope Peter – let us call him by his name – has not behaved as if there were a quid pro quo involved.'

'I'm not sure what you mean.'

'Peter has a habit of acting inappropriately with the young women who work for him.'

'I can assure you he has been perfectly proper.'

'So far. The trouble tends to surface on business trips or late nights at the bar of the Frankfurter Hof during *Buchmesse* week.'

'Thank you for the warning.'

'To be quite honest, I wouldn't hold it against you if you succumbed. Not that you should take that as permission to move in on him. I just want to express, woman to woman, some solidarity.'

'I appreciate that and I can assure you that I have no interest of that sort in your husband. I just consider him to be a publisher of genius.'

'Indeed he is. And, if I'm not being too intrusive, your hopes lie elsewhere.'

'Again, I'm not sure what you mean. If you mean do I one day hope to find a suitable partner, then, yes, you are right.'

'Because you are not in a relationship right now.'

'No, I'm not.'

'Is that a matter of regret?'

'To an extent, but we can't always have what we want when we want it.'

'How true! And oddly enough I think we want the same person.'

Jude stiffened. 'Mrs Newman, I think I have made it clear that I have no interest of that kind in your husband.'

'You did say that and I believe you. No, I was referring to Steve Percival.'

Jude choked softly before saying carefully, 'I believe you were in a relationship with Steve. I would not describe what I had with Steve as a relationship.'

'Grace Mitchell snatched him before you were able to get to that stage.'

'I wouldn't put it like that either.'

'No, of course not. I am sorry, you are at a disadvantage in this conversation. Believe me, I wish you well. I would be delighted if you were to establish a relationship with Steve. Nothing would please me more. Nothing other than if I were able to be in a relationship with him myself.'

'So you feel you made a mistake in leaving him.'

'No, it was not a mistake, but it did mean the end of a different kind of life.'

'You do know that Grace has thrown Steve out?'

'Yes, it has come to my ears.'

'Everyone is mystified.'

'Ah, well, there is more to Ms Mitchell than most people imagine. Is Steve hurt?'

'Very.'

'You haven't swooped in to pick him up?'

'I don't want to have him on those terms.'

'My admiration for your stance increases by the minute.'

'Ginny, I'm not seeking to impress you.'

'I have no doubt, but please do not see me as the enemy. I would be delighted if you and Steve were able to find a way to be together. If I could give him to you I would.'

'One can't dispose of people like that.'

'Well, as you can see, I am not a fairy godmother. Not unless fairy godmothers can be pregnant.'

Jude laughed. 'When is the baby due?'

'Very soon. The real reason I have asked you around here today is in fact to do with the baby.'

Closing her eyes for a moment or two as if gathering herself, Ginny cradled her swollen belly in her hands. 'Steve is the father of this baby. If you take on Steve, you will also be taking on that fact.'

Jude was silent for a moment. 'Steve does not know this?'

'No.'

'But Peter does, I take it.'

'That is very perceptive of you. So now I have given you power over me, over all of us. Use it wisely.'

'Why? Why are you doing this?'

'Because I love Steve and I think you are the best person for him.'

'Ginny, this feels very weird.'

'I know. Just trust me. In the same way that I have just trusted you. I mean you no harm.'

They sat in silence for some moments, until Ginny stood up, went over to Jude and kissed her on both cheeks. Jude sobbed and said, 'What am I supposed to do?'

Ginny walked to the door of the room. Turning, she said, 'I honestly don't know what you should do. You'll work it out. I need to go and lie down. Please let yourself out.'

# Saturday, 14 June 1975

STEVE FOUND AN EMPTY compartment and settled into the window seat facing the front of the train. Soon he heard the whistle of the platform assistant and the slamming of carriage doors as the last few stragglers climbed onto the train. The train started to move forward and Steve unfolded his newspaper. He was thus engrossed when the door of the compartment slid open and a female voice said, 'Steve, I thought it was you.'

Steve looked up. It was Becky standing in the doorway of the compartment. 'Can I join you?'

Steve waved her in and she sat down opposite him. She looked hot and flustered. 'I saw you when I was queuing to get my ticket, but by the time I got onto the platform, I wasn't sure which carriage you were in.'

Steve smiled at her. 'Becky, there's no need to explain. It's good to see you. I thought you went back to London some time ago.'

'I did. But I've been up for a meeting with Gary. He wants to cast me in a new production.'

'At the Festival?'

'The Festival's gone dark again. No, at the RSC in Stratford.'

'Congratulations. When did the Festival close?'

'A couple of weeks ago. They ran out of money. I'm surprised you didn't know.'

'It's complicated, but things didn't end well. Gary seemed to give me the cold shoulder.'

'I wondered why you weren't at the end-of-season party.'

'I wasn't invited.'

'Why? What did you do?'

'I don't really know. I think that my sperm wasn't up to snuff.'

'What?'

'I'd rather not go into it, Becky, if you don't mind.'

'Of course. What are you going down to London for?'

'I'm moving back there. I seem to have been banished from Cambridge.'

'Surely not. You seemed to be the essence of Cambridge, at least to me.'

'Part of me would like to belong here. From the outside, it looks as if it's the last bastion of gentlemanly, and increasingly, gentlewo-manly – if that's a word – conduct, in which the exchange of ideas is conducted at a very elevated pitch. But it's not. When you're on the inside, you find that it's a hotbed of vicious competitiveness about not very much at all.'

Becky got out of bed and reached for the robe that Steve had lent her. It was not lost on him that this was another take on the scene he had written for her, which was in turn based on the scrambled sex he had with Inge in East Berlin. Becky, as befitted a rising starlet, was fragrant and delicious, and blessed with an almost perfect body. She noticed the way that Steve was watching her. 'What are you thinking?'

'I'm thinking how beautiful you are.'

'You're so sweet.'

'Is it too cold to leave the robe off?'

'No, why?'

'I just want to watch you move about without any clothes on.'

'I would have thought you'd got enough of seeing my tits and bum during the run of your play.'

'I don't think I could ever get enough of your tits and bum.'

Becky let the robe drop to the floor. 'You'll have to warm me up when I get back with the coffees.'

'It will be my pleasure.'

Becky opened the door of the bedroom and squeaked as the cold air from the passageway hit her. Over her shoulder she said, 'I'll be expecting an extra special seeing-to for having to brave the arctic conditions out here. My nips are already like chapel hat-pegs.'

Steve laughed. 'Make sure they're still like that when you get back.'

In her absence his thoughts went back to another pair of nipples that had enthralled him. He wondered how Inge was. He conjured up an image of her in his mind. In terms of looks, she came nowhere near Becky's artful pulchritude. She had been undernour-ished, her ribs showing through beneath her scrawny breasts. Her

413

hair had been lank and badly cut, unlike Becky's tousled barnet. Without scent or deodorant, her bodily odours had been all too evident. Her teeth had been yellowish and crooked unlike Becky's pearly smile. And yet. And yet. Sex with Inge had been ecstatic. No doubt the fear he had felt that day had added piquancy to the occasion. Whereas the energetic and prolonged bout of sex that he and Becky had just interrupted for a cup of coffee had been bland and prosaic.

Not that Becky was an incompetent lover. Her repertoire was extensive. Nor was she shy in advancing her own demands. Yet the fumbled, failed attempt by Inge to fellate Steve for the Stasi cameras had been sexier than all the tricks that Becky clearly had in her locker. It certainly wasn't anything to do with her personality. Becky was bright, easy-going, confident, and beautiful.

So why did he feel that this new encounter was already withering before they had even concluded their first amatory manoeuvres? Because he didn't love her? Because he loved Inge? But that was absurd. He had spent a few miserable hours with Inge, for the most part, when they weren't playing for the Stasi microphones, conducted in whispers. He really knew very little about her and what he did know was probably untrue. Even if she wasn't already in prison, she was at the very least inaccessible. But there it was. He was being served with Michelin-starred perfection on a plate, but he hankered after warmed-up leftovers in a greasy spoon.

Becky returned and put the mugs of coffee on the bedside table. Tweaking her nipples to return them to the state that the cold air had previously rendered them, she said, 'Which way up would you like me, sir?'

# Monday, 16 June 1975

'THANK YOU FOR COMING in to see me, Steve.'

Sheena looked at him over the tops of her glasses. On this second meeting, she was sitting behind her desk and had indicated that he should take one of the chairs in front of the desk. No cosy chat in the easy chairs around the coffee table this time, it would seem.

Steve tried to affect a light tone. 'It was convenient, really. I was sorting out a few things at the flat.'

'Because you are no longer resident in Glisson Road?'

Steve was caught off guard. 'Er, yes.'

'The idyll with Dr Mitchell has come to an end?'

Steve blinked and looked at his shoes. How did Sheena know this? It was not common knowledge yet. Or was she just guessing? 'Yes, that does seem to be the case.'

'How are you feeling about that?'

'Quite upset, actually.'

'But you found temporary refuge with a certain Mr Jonathan Chapman and his girlfriend?'

'Yes. Have you been having me watched?'

'No, most of this is from Dr Mitchell herself.'

'You've been talking to Grace?'

'Well, it was in her report.'

'She reports to you?'

'As and when.'

Steve suddenly felt as if the stage scenery was moving around him.

'She is concerned about you.'

'Well, she has a strange way of showing it.'

415

'She is constrained as to what she can say. So her explanations perhaps did not quite add up.'

'You can say that again.'

'Whereas I have a certain amount of discretion in such matters. I wonder whether you have caught up with the reaction to Dr Mitchell's paper that she gave at a colloquium at Edinburgh University.'

'She said it was well received.'

'Yes, it was. But what you do not know perhaps is that one of the other people to give a paper at the conference was Professor Müller.'

Steve shook his head, alarmed at the direction the discussion was taking.

'Well, Professor Müller was instrumental in arranging for Dr Mitchell to give the keynote speech. He had previously met her at your former college. They were both guests of Dr Doyle, your former director of studies. A mutual rapport was established if I could put it like that, which was cemented when she was in Edinburgh.'

Steve was about to intervene, but Sheena held up her hand. 'I know this must be distasteful to you, but please hear me out. It also transpires that Dr Doyle has managed to tempt Professor Müller away from Edinburgh and he is to be appointed to an honorary fellowship at St Radegund's College. He will be taking up his post, which has no teaching responsibilities, over the long vacation. Dr Mitchell is looking forward to collaborating with Professor Müller on a landmark overview of post-Enlightenment European thought.'

'But Grace can't stand Müller.'

'That's not quite the case, Steve. She is prepared to tolerate him.'

'Why would she do that?'

'Well, if we're being brutally honest about it, it will be beneficial to her career. But the main reason is she works for us.'

'But I thought that finished years ago.'

'Some things never really finish. Let us say that she has been on a lengthy furlough and now we have reactivated her. Her job is to keep an eye on Professor Müller.'

'But he was our agent.'

'It might well have seemed so, but there is more than a scintilla of doubt in that regard.'

'So my mother died for nothing.'

'Not at all. She was fully aware of the equivocal nature of Müller's position.'

'Do you mean that we have all been engaged in bringing to Cambridge a person who may still be working for the Stasi?'

'That is indeed the case. You seem to have a lively appreciation of these matters. There is a little more to it than that, of course. There always is.'

Sheena looked at him searchingly, as if inviting him to pursue this line of reasoning. For a moment, he wasn't sure what else there was to say. Then the penny dropped. 'But the Stasi don't know that we know they're still controlling him.'

'Exactly. Which is the only reason we allowed your play to be performed. I was in favour of closing it down, but Collingwood thought that putting pressure on Mr Lewis to cancel the production would only have drawn more attention to it. As it was, had Müller or his masters acquired a report of the play, they would have seen that it was a reflection of what we would like them to think was official thinking here.'

'But it wasn't. We made Inge, or Freya as we called her, the victim of the dramatic situation.'

'Which was a very good move on your part, especially since she really is a Stasi officer.'

Steve was taken off guard again. Could that possibly be true? But of course in the hall of mirrors, to use Gary's term, that he had been caught up in, it was all too likely to be true. What a naïve fool he was. 'But she was just a girl.'

'Many of us are or were just girls, Steve. That does not diminish our importance or how dangerous we can be.'

Sheena gave him a little more time to process this information and then said, 'Before we leave the matter of your play, let me make it clear that we will not permit it to be performed again and certainly not on the BBC. We have been in touch with them and they are shelving their interest in it.'

'You can't censor a play.'

'We're not censoring it as such, but the broadcasters in particular do accept our view on these matters.'

'But you just said that the way events were portrayed in the play is exactly what you want the Stasi to think we think.'

'If it goes on television, they might think that we're trying a little too hard. They will know by now exactly who you are and will not be surprised you have managed to get the play staged in Cambridge. But to the totalitarian mind, getting something on television requires official involvement. However Collingwood tells me your play was well received and he is sure you will write many more.'

Sheena poured Collingwood a tumbler of whisky. 'Water?'

Collingwood nodded. Sheena put the two tumblers on the coffee table and regained her seat. 'Do you think I was too hard on him, Jeremy?'

Collingwood shook his head. 'Not from what I heard on the audio link. No, it was important that he didn't feel there was a way back. Also that he shouldn't feel guilty about Inge.'

'Quite, he's hurting enough already without having to deal with the fact that the poor girl is going to have to spend the next few years in a Stasi prison. Why on earth did he leave the ten D-Mark note in her room? Tucking it into an architectural guide in English wasn't going to defeat the Stasi sweepers.'

'Because he's kind, because he's naïve, because he'd fallen for her.'

'Hook, line and sinker it seems.'

'I think she fell for him too.'

'What makes you think that?'

'It came out during her interrogation according to my contact.'

'But putting the receipt from the bar where they met into his wallet was an act of complete stupidity.'

'I think you're being a bit unfair, ma'am. If it's anyone's fault, it's mine. I should have remembered he'd had no tradecraft training. I really ought to have given him a crash course, but there was so little time.'

'Some people have a natural aptitude for these things. I am not sure our young friend is in that category.'

'But let us look on the bright side, ma'am. It has helped convince the Stasi that we are not onto Müller.'

'Yes, I suppose so. I'm just sorry for the girl.'

'Well, he need never know.'

'Do you think he'll get over the setbacks?'

'Oh, I think he has the natural resilience of youth.'

'I'm glad to hear you say so, Jeremy. I didn't really relish roughing him up just now. I felt particularly bad about stymying his prospects with the BBC. I will try to make it up to him, but not until the current hand of cards has been played out.'

'If it's any consolation, I gather he is finding solace in the arms of a young actress, one of those who is prepared to bare her all for art.'

'Oh, jolly good. Is she one for the long haul?'

'I don't think so, ma'am. She is already taking up an engagement with the RSC in Stratford.'

'So Steve will have to seek solace elsewhere.'

'I don't think he'll be without company. He is a young man with a central London apartment and some money in the bank.'

'I wonder if Mavis ever had any idea what a dark horse her little boy was.'

Collingwood shrugged. 'You have the advantage of me there.'

'And poor Grace Mitchell. She must hate the day she first set eyes on me, when I was her interrogator. Then all these years later, I turn up again and force her into the arms of that slimy excuse for an intellectual and deny her the baby she was intent on producing with Steve.'

'Perhaps Professor Müller might oblige.'

'And pigs might fly.'

'I believe the biological urge is quite strong and beggars can't be choosers.'

'Silly girl! Such an incredible brain, but so misguided.'

'I think her transgression has to be seen in the context of the revolutionary enthusiasm of the times.'

'Jeremy, are you feeling sorry for her?'

'I am a little, ma'am. In the few dealings I had with her, I found her very proper. She was clearly fond of Steve. I have also read her poetry and I have to say that it is in the first rank.'

'I didn't realise that you kept abreast of the poetry scene.'

'I keep it quiet, but I did have aspirations in that area myself.'

'Well, well. Is there any alumnus of your university who isn't a *poète manqué*?'

'It does rather seem like that at times.'

'Are my ward's poetic productions in the first rank too?'

'It's very hard to say. He is reputed to have written a book-length poem called *Event/Horizon*, but very few people have read it. It exists only in an exquisite but extremely limited letterpress edition, courtesy of a young up and coming publisher. There's a rather good poet who was a friend of Steve's when they were undergraduates and he has occasionally given readings from his own copy of the special edition. The reaction of those who have been vouchsafed this epiphany is not uniformly positive, but as is the way of these things, the more recondite the matter, the greater the enthusiasm in some quarters.'

'Steve is oblivious to all this?'

'I think he is. Or at least he has – had – his sights set on other goals.'

'This play? *Palace of Tears?*'

'Yes.'

'You liked it?'

'I did. It was nothing like the reality of what you and I actually do. Or for that matter, our friends in the Stasi. But it did show rather effectively what it's like to live in a city that is so ideologically riven and in which that rivalry is mapped onto the very geography of the city. As if south London and north London were entirely different polities.'

'Well, they are to a great extent.'

Collingwood laughed. 'The old jokes are the best ones, ma'am.'

'Indeed, Jeremy, and don't you forget it. Did Steve realise that you'd been to the first night of his play?'

'No, I kept a low profile. Then he rather got swept up in the first-night high jinks.'

'And you did not?'

'Sadly, I was not invited. But I was able to observe a number of the members of his milieu, some of whom were familiar from when we were vetting him.'

'Anyone we might be interested in?'

'Yes, perhaps there was.'

'Well, I look forward to your report in due course.'

As Collingwood got up to go, he said, 'Are we still thinking of having him join the firm more formally?'

Sheena examined her fingernails. 'I'm not sure. Let's see how he deals with the information we've given him and the new situation we've put him in.'

www.ingramcontent.com/pod-product-compliance
Lightning Source LLC
Chambersburg PA
CBHW022240020726
47496CB00004B/1000